THE JAYPEE INFRA INSOLVENCY SAGA

SUMANT BATRA is India's leading insolvency lawyer and among the top thirty globally, as rated by *Global Restructuring Review*. He has worked as senior international consultant to the IMF, World Bank Group, OECD and other development institutions. His book *Corporate Insolvency: Law and Practice* is considered the most authoritative work on the subject. He has contributed essays in numerous anthologies on insolvency.

A champion of cultural initiatives, Sumant is the founder and architect of a number of innovative projects to promote Indian heritage and literature, including the popular Kumaon Literary Festival. He is the author of *The Indians*, a bestselling coffee-table book that includes a foreword by Cherie Blair, an acclaimed work of historical fiction, *Anarkali*, and co-author of *An Actor's Actor: The Authorized Biography of Sanjeev Kumar*.

Advance Praise For The Book

'This book is an outstanding exposition of the bumpy ride and unprecedented judicial journey that the famous case of Jaypee Infratech Ltd went through, culminating in the creation of marvellous legal principles leading to the amendment in the IBC, which only the Indian Supreme Court is capable of doing. The judgment in Jaypee Infratech Ltd will always be remembered as laying down extraordinary jurisprudential norms in the field of insolvency law. The way in which it addressed the rights for homebuyers who had invested their hard-earned money in residential projects launched by Jaypee, along with creditors and lenders, is unparalleled. Articulating this journey with finesse and clarity, in an illuminating manner, was possible only at the deft hands of Sumant Batra who is not only an expert in insolvency law but was deeply involved in the case as well. He meets the expectations of the readers brilliantly. Sumant Batra is a multitalented person who not only sits on a very high pedestal in the field of insolvency law as a leading practitioner and jurist, but has also excelled in the field of art and literature. In his inimitable style, he has given a literary flavour in his narrative to this important judgment. This book is an outstanding amalgam of law and literature and proves that when law is explained by those who imbibe literary qualities, it can also become an interesting read, and the general perception that law is a dry subject, vanishes.' – **Justice Arjan K. Sikri, Former Judge, Supreme Court of India; International Judge, Singapore International Commercial Court**

'This is a remarkable book. Sumant Batra is a noted insolvency lawyer, who has been instrumental in the setting up of the Insolvency Law Academy. He is also the author of a book on corporate insolvency that has become a bit like a manual. But this remarkable book is quite different from a dense and esoteric volume, heavy with legalese and jargon. We know that Sumant is capable of authoring popular books. His biography of Sanjeev Kumar is an example. Jaypee Infratech Limited was a famous name in real estate and infrastructure, before insolvency rendered it infamous. Caught up in this web of ill-fame were the dreams of some 20,000 homebuyers, who had invested in Jaypee's residential projects. Corporate insolvency isn't rare, though the IBC (Insolvency and Bankruptcy Code) is of recent vintage. In this case, what was uncommon was the plight of homebuyers. Everyone empathized, much more than with financial institutions. Involved in the process as a participating lawyer, Sumant Batra gives us a timeline and a blow-by-blow account. Meant as a compliment, it is as if Sumant buried his lawyer's hat and donned that of a reporter. It is not common to find legal matters written about in this fashion. The book is a lesson in beautiful writing.' – **Dr Bibek Debroy, Chairman, Economic Advisory Council to the Prime Minister**

'The insolvency resolution of the corporate debtor JIL is a chronicle of complications ... it carries with it vexed and strikingly intricate issues.' – **Extract from *Jaypee Kensington Boulevard Apartments v. NBCC India Ltd & Ors.* (2022) SCC. 401, authored by Justice Dinesh Maheshwari on behalf of the three-member bench**

'In 2017, Jaypee Infratech Limited, a real estate and infrastructure giant, was declared insolvent, triggering a seven-year legal and financial battle that captivated the nation. With nearly 20,000 homebuyers and multiple financial institutions caught in the crossfire, the case became a litmus test for India's newly minted Insolvency and Bankruptcy Code. It prompted rapid evolutions of the Code and regulations, including recognizing homebuyers as financial creditors, introducing class voting, and allowing simultaneous voting of rival resolution plans.

'At the heart of this saga was Anuj Jain, the insolvency professional who deftly navigated the sinking ship through turbulent waters. Often standing alone, Jain fiercely defended stakeholders' rights, even facing arrest in the line of duty. His relentless efforts culminated in the recovery of thousands of crores lost in avoidance transactions, fighting all the way to the Supreme Court.

'Sumant Batra, a globally renowned insolvency lawyer, brings this saga to life in a narrative that reads more like a novel than a legal account. The Jaypee Infra Insolvency Saga offers not just a detailed chronicle of corporate restructuring but also a gripping tale of hope, perseverance, and the transformative power of law, against the backdrop of India's evolving legal landscape.' - **Dr M.S. Sahoo, former chairperson, Insolvency and Bankruptcy Board of India**

'In 2016, India implemented a comprehensive insolvency reform that, in addition to the adoption of an innovative creditor-in-control insolvency process, led to the creation of a new infrastructure to support the insolvency system. As in many other jurisdictions, insolvency law still faces many challenges in India. Yet, the new regime has represented a significant improvement of the legal and institutional environment to deal with financial distress. Moreover, the development of the insolvency ecosystem in India has been achieved in a remarkably short period of time. That journey, however, has not been easy. As clearly evidenced by *The Jaypee Infra Insolvency Saga*, lawyers and insolvency professionals were exposed to new principles and institutions; debtors and creditors had to navigate a new, complex procedure; judges had to interpret new rules; the legislature had to step in when some flaws were identified; and those challenges needed to be handled in a high-pressure environment with multiple stakeholders involved. Therefore, Sumant Batra's fascinating book not only deals with one of the most important cases in the recent history of insolvency law in India but more generally with the role and the challenges of insolvency law and how they have been handled in India. A must-read!' - **Aurelio Gurrea-Martínez, Associate Professor of Law and Head of the Singapore Global Restructuring Initiative, Singapore Management University**

'*The Jaypee Infra Insolvency Saga* eloquently articulates the successes, key learnings, major challenges and the many innovations made in one of the most complex insolvency cases of the country. The complicated case provided the stakeholders opportunity to experiment with a young and evolving law and in the process, make history. I cannot express my gratitude and thank Sumant enough for his support in navigating this trying case spanning nearly seven years.

'The story of Jaypee Infra's insolvency is no less than a Bollywood thriller with its ups and downs, highs and lows, successes and disappointments, ending with the famous proverb "All's well that ends well". There is no better person than Sumant to archive this important case in the early stages of IBC, given his unwavering commitment for a robust insolvency system, repertoire of experience, and his passion for storytelling. Notably, Sumant has not allowed his personal biases and opinions to come in the way of objective storytelling from the perspective of its diverse set of stakeholders.' - **Anuj Jain, Partner, KPMG India, Former Interim Resolution Professional of Jaypee Infratech Limited**

'Leading insolvency lawyer and scholar Sumant Batra has delivered yet another odyssey; indeed a saga of epic proportions. *The Jaypee Infra Insolvency Saga* is a clarion call to honour the elemental forces that shape our memories, our histories, and our world, told through a recounting of one of the largest Indian insolvencies.

'*Jaypee* explodes into a roaring journey through the complex intricacies and unpredictability of insolvency and through that, Batra weaves together a dazzling feat of storytelling, taking full advantage of his ringside seat as a lead lawyer, and to make us feel as if we are sitting alongside.

'Deploying his deep practical experience in the law and his capacity to make the complex disarmingly simple, Batra weaves cinematic anecdotes and literary insights into the fabric of this rich and illuminating text, delivering us an unforgettable work which raises big ideas of the power and effectiveness of the Indian corporate bankruptcy system, and the importance of courts and their role in shaping outcomes. He underscores a reality often forgotten: bankruptcy impacts people – homebuyers, farmers, bankers, judges, lawyers and many more.

'From its bravura opening through to its final pages, this is a fast-paced rendition of real events which, in his final assessment, leads Batra to observe that even in the darkest of clouds, there is a silver lining. Here it is twofold: both the story, and Batra's telling of it draws me in; but it is his grit and substance that held me to the last page.' – **Scott Atkins, former president, INSOL International**

THE JAYPEE INFRA INSOLVENCY SAGA

SUMANT BATRA

Om Books International

First published in 2024 by

Om Books International

Corporate & Editorial Office
A-12, Sector 64, Noida 201 301
Uttar Pradesh, India
Phone: +91 120 477 4100
Email: editorial@ombooks.com
Website: www.ombooksinternational.com

Sales Office
107, Ansari Road, Darya Ganj,
New Delhi 110 002, India
Phone: +91 11 4000 9000
Email: sales@ombooks.com
Website: www.ombooks.com

ISBN: 978-93-6395-441-0

Printed in India

10 9 8 7 6 5 4 3 2 1

Dedicated to the thousands of homebuyers of Jaypee Infratech Limited, who fought a relentless seven-year-long battle for their homes

Disclaimer

The author was the legal advisor and counsel of the interim resolution professional of Jaypee Infratech Limited and represented him in courts and insolvency proceedings. The data, statistics and other material in the book have been extracted from the various exhaustive judgments and orders passed by the NCLT, the NCLAT and the Supreme Court.

The contents of the book respect the client–attorney privilege and no confidential information or material to which the author was privy as counsel or as a participant in the meetings of committee of creditors, or other strategic meetings, has been used in the book.

Care has been taken to not take names of persons and institutions that do not otherwise appear in court orders or any other literature available in public domain. If any part of this book hurts the sentiments or feelings of any person or institution, I assure it is entirely unintended.

Contents

Part II
The Outcomes

Frequently Used Acronyms

CIRP Regulations: IBBI (Insolvency Resolution Process for Corporate Persons) Regulations, 2016

CoC: Committee of Creditors

G.O.: Government of Uttar Pradesh Order dated 29 August 2014

IBBI: The Insolvency and Bankruptcy Board of India

IBC: Insolvency and Bankruptcy Code, 2016

ILC: Insolvency Law Committee

IMC: Implementation and Monitoring Committee of JIL

IRP: Interim Resolution Professional

JAL: Jaiprakash Associates Limited

JIL: Jaypee Infratech Limited

ITAT: Income Tax Appellate Tribunal

KMP: Key Management Personnel

MCA: Ministry of Corporate Affairs, Government of India

NCLT: National Company Law Tribunal

NCLAT: National Company Law Appellate Tribunal

NOIDA: New Okhla Industrial Development Authority

NPA: Non-Performing Asset

RP: Resolution Professional

UP Act: Uttar Pradesh Industrial Area Development Act, 1976

YEIDA: The Yamuna Expressway Industrial Development Authority

Preface

On 9 August 2017, Jaypee Infratech Limited (JIL), a gigantic Indian real estate and infrastructure enterprise, was declared insolvent by the National Company Law Tribunal (NCLT), the bankruptcy tribunal under the Insolvency and Bankruptcy Code, 2016 (IBC). The IBC had just been given a seal of approval in the Parliament and operationalized only a few months before. The IBC did not grant any effective role or participation to homebuyers in the insolvency process. So when the news of JIL's bankruptcy broke, it caused uproar amongst thousands of its customers. Over 20,000 homebuyers who had invested a whopping sum of nearly Rs 13,000 crore (US$ 1,566 million) in the company's residential projects went up in arms. Many of them had invested their life's savings in the project. Although not opposed to JIL's resolution, any procedure without meaningful involvement of the homebuyers in the decision making was unacceptable to them.

JIL is no ordinary enterprise. Under its wings runs a gigantic project of national importance. Nearly fifteen years earlier, the Uttar Pradesh government announced plans to develop the region alongside the Yamuna River, from Noida (the suburbs of New Delhi) to Agra. The state government set up the Taj Expressway and Industrial Development Authority, a statutory body for anchoring the development. Prime land, spreading over 10,995 acres, was acquired from farmers to build a 165-kilometre toll road – to be called the Taj Expressway – from Noida to Agra. Land alongside the expressway was to be developed for residential, commercial, industrial and institutional use. The large-scale industrial and commercial activity that the project was expected to generate was to provide impetus to the state's economic growth and create jobs. Through it was also envisioned development of an otherwise industrially backward region of Uttar Pradesh. There was no parallel to such a large-scale project anywhere, and it was awarded to JIL's holding company, Jaiprakash Associates Limited (JAL) and subsequently to JIL while JAL served as the master contractor. The Taj Expressway Authority was later renamed by the state government as the Yamuna Expressway Industrial Development Authority (YEIDA), and the Taj Expressway as the Yamuna Expressway.

Although the expressway was operationalized in August 2012, the other projects either could not start, or were stalled for one reason or the other, or not used optimally. The residential projects launched by them went into trouble because of the financial crunch faced by JIL and JAL. The company offered a humungous 29,098 units spread over 250 towers in multiple projects in the market. It collected a staggering amount of advance from homebuyers but failed to deliver the units on time. JIL also borrowed thousands of crores of rupees from more than a dozen public and private sector banks and financial institutions but defaulted in repayment of the debt. JIL owed a sum of nearly Rs 9,738 crore (US$ 11,179 million) to banks and financial institutions. Some banks declared JIL as a non-performing account. The company had also raised funds by offering returns on fixed deposits under an investment scheme. An amount of Rs 38.42 crore (US$ 4.63 million) was overdue for payment to thousands of depositors who had submitted their claims in the insolvency process.

On a separate front, thousands of farmers had been protesting for years against acquisition of their lands for the project. To pacify them, the state government decided to pay them an additional compensation of Rs 1,689 crore (US$ 204 million). The YEIDA demanded this sum from JIL, which it refused to pay, denying its liability to pay additional compensation. This led to the government of Uttar Pradesh and JIL getting embroiled in litigation.

In 2017, the Income Tax Department demanded from JIL payment of tax for Rs 33,000 crore (US$ 3,976 million). The tax assessment and ensuing demand of an enormous sum threatened the very viability of JIL. It brought JIL another litigation. Although the irrational demand was stayed by the Income Tax Appellate Tribunal (ITAT), it continued to hang over JIL like the Sword of Damocles.

JAL, the contractor of the project, was also staring at insolvency. It was at this stage that the RBI decided to send JIL to insolvency. The stakes were high and financial exposure, colossal. JIL's stakeholders were large in number and of varying interests. It was a giant ship set sailing in rough waters. If it were to sink, its descent was to cause not just a slight turbulence but an economic impact of a tsunami.

Insolvency of a company involving such diverse set of creditors and stakeholders was new in India. As expected, the commencement of JIL's insolvency sparked a spate of protests from homebuyers. Lack of adequate knowledge about the IBC and unhelpful media coverage compounded the problem. They dragged the government to the Supreme Court, demanding a level playing field for homebuyers alongside banks and financial institutions. Their value and number as stakeholders were just as important as financial institutions, they claimed. The government gave in, recognizing that any outcome without the homebuyers partaking in the process would have little credibility. The IBC was amended to give homebuyers a status similar to the banks in the IBC processes. As a result of the revision, homebuyers got both a seat on the decision-making table and a decisive vote.

The process effectively started only after homebuyers were placated. But there were other prickly issues too. The IBC was a new law; its efficacy was yet to be tested. The start of JIL's insolvency process was in a way a leap of faith. No one had assessed or could foresee how the process would unfold. The law was new; there were no blueprints to guide the case; everything was to be innovated and experimented. The starting of JIL's insolvency was like pushing a ship to sail into choppy waters and that too without a rudder. To top this up, JIL's case was complex and loaded with tricky situations. In the words of Justice Dinesh Maheshwari, Supreme Court judge (since retired), who authored the key decisions on several matters arising from the company's insolvency, JIL's process was 'a chronicle of complications' vexed with strikingly intricate issues.

JIL's insolvency process actuated contentious litigation from many stakeholders, elicited hawk-eye media spotlight, and prompted keen scrutiny. Its insolvency process was conducted under full public glare. It had to navigate its way through one challenge after the other. The risks were enormous; the reputations of the decision-makers and their counsellors were at stake. It was expected to be a rough journey. All hands were on deck. Pressure on those at the helm of the process can only be imagined.

Midway through the process, the sensational arrest of the IRP, Anuj Jain, who was leading the case, by the Uttar Pradesh Police sent shockwaves through the insolvency industry. Not only was the manner of arrest arbitrary, the justification provided for it was ridiculous and invited outrage from the Supreme Court. While directing his immediate release, the Court called for an explanation by the Uttar Pradesh Police for this high-handed action. Anuj Jain was brought back by the author from the prison's doorstep. JIL's insolvency process became as convoluted as it could get. It was enough to inspire a Bollywood drama.

The turbulent insolvency proceedings finally ended on 7 March 2023. After overcoming countless hurdles, the resolution plan submitted by the Suraksha Group for reviving JIL received approval from the NCLT. This provided the much-sought and long-awaited respite to the thousands of homebuyers and, unexpectedly, to the farmers. By approving Suraksha's plan, the NCLT pushed an elephant through a needle hole. Sadly, litigation continued even after the approval of the plan. Ironically, of all the parties, the state government (YEIDA) and the Central government (Income Tax Department) latched onto the elephant's tail, trying hard to stop it from passing through. They took the matter in appeal to the National Company Law Appellate Tribunal (NCLAT). This delayed the implementation of the plan and prolonged the wait for homebuyers to get their homes.

The matter was finally resolved by the NCLAT in May 2024. Although, when the book was being written the matter had reached the Supreme Court, Suraksha decided to implement the resolution plan without waiting for the outcome of the Supreme Court's decision, bringing much-awaited respite to the homebuyers. How the Supreme Court decision in appeals might impact the implementation of resolution plan remains to be seen. As a matter of legal propriety and out of respect for the Supreme Court, the author is refraining from commenting on the matters pending before the Supreme Court. Whether a second edition of this book becomes necessary will depend on the outcome of the matters pending before the Supreme Court.

JIL's insolvency process has been one rollercoaster ride. The Supreme Court exercised its plenary powers under Article 142 of the Constitution of India three times to extend the process timelines and ensure complete justice in the case. Yet, for a variety of reasons, the insolvency resolution proved elusive for a long time.

Although long drawn out, the process was remarkable in many ways and historic in the outcomes it has produced. Wading through unstoppable spells of litigation, it advanced and became a catalyst for shaping insolvency policy, development of the IBC jurisprudence, and establishing many best practices of law. Some of the rulings established the bedrock of the IBC principles. Many pre-eminent decisions of the Supreme Court scripting the IBC jurisprudence have come out of the JIL's insolvency process. Significant changes made in the IBC and its regulations in the initial years were prompted by the outcomes and experiences of JIL's volatile insolvency. The incredible outcomes from the process and the resolution plan of Suraksha maximized the takeaways for JIL's stakeholders, the central objective of the IBC.

This book is the tale of an extraordinary insolvency process of this real estate and infrastructure enterprise. The first part of the book narrates the circumstances leading to the filing of insolvency petition, the seven-year journey of the insolvency process, the approval of Suraksha's resolution plan, its challenge before the NCLT and higher courts and the final nod for its implementation by the NCLAT. The second part reflects on the outcomes, and reviews and analyses the process in retrospect. In conclusion, the book documents the astounding journey of this riveting insolvency case.

This book is not penned to boast about the author's role in the insolvency process and its outcomes, nor is it about adding a feather in his cap. It is also not about the huge outcomes from JIL's insolvency process and the numbers it will add to the IBBI's statistics. The journey of JIL's insolvency process and its outcomes – maximizing the value of the company and balancing the interest of disparate stakeholders – is a story of the triumph of IBC.

The book is also about the resolute fight that the thousands of homebuyers put up to get their homes, a way to chronicle their resilience in times of utter helplessness and their undying hope that someday they will get the keys to their homes. It is also about the predicament of millions of other homebuyers in India and beyond, who put their hard-earned money to buy homes but are let down by developers and regulators, and many times by policymakers.

With JIL's insolvency saga having finally come to an end with the upholding of Suraksha's resolution by NCLAT, this is a story waiting to be told – a story of endless hope.

PART I

A Long Struggle for Homes

1
The Dirty Dozen

A man may well bring a horse to the water, but he cannot make him drink without his will.

– John Heywood, *A Dialogue of Proverbs*

On 4 May 2017, in an unprecedented move, the Union government amended the Banking Regulation Act, 1949 by promulgating an Ordinance,[1] which authorized the Reserve Bank of India (RBI) to issue directions to the banks for initiating proceedings under the IBC for timely resolution of distress in defaulter companies. An Ordinance enables the government to take an urgent legislative action when the Parliament is not in session. It is issued by the President of India on the recommendation of the Union cabinet, which has the same effect as a law passed by the Parliament.

Although the Insolvency and Bankruptcy Code 2016 (IBC) had become operational for the insolvency resolution process for companies and limited liability partnerships from 1 December 2016, financial institutions had not shown much enthusiasm

1 The Banking Regulation (Amendment) Ordinance, 2017

around the new law. Most were sceptical of the IBC because their experience with previous insolvency reforms had not been encouraging. They were still reeling from the erstwhile insolvency regime. Some were of the opinion that the IBC should be tried out first with smaller cases to prepare it to test its ability to handle large stressed assets in the course of time. But the government was determined to roll out the IBC with full vigour.

An independent advisory committee of the RBI shortlisted companies whose fund- and non-fund-based outstanding amount was greater than Rs 5,000 crore (US$ 600 million) as on 31 March 2016. The committee identified twelve companies, whose defaulted loans constituted about 25 per cent of the then gross non-performing assets (NPAs) of the banking system, for being referred to the NCLT, the new bankruptcy tribunal set up under the IBC. These twelve NPAs were Bhushan Steel Limited, Bhushan Power and Steel Limited, Essar Steel Limited, Electrosteel Limited and Monnet Ispat and Energy Limited (from steel sector); Alok Industries Limited (from textiles sector); Jaypee Infratech Limited (from real estate sector); Amtek Auto Limited (from automotive sector); Lanco Infratech Limited, Jyoti Structure Limited, and Era Infra Limited (from construction and infrastructure sector); and ABG Shipyard Limited (from shipbuilding sector). These accounts roughly translated to Rs 2.5 lakh crore (US$ 30 billion) of banks' NPAs. The RBI requested the NCLT to accord priority to these cases.[2]

Following the RBI's directions, insolvency petitions were filed by the lenders of these twelve defaulting companies with the NCLT. The twelve defaulters have since then become infamous as the 'Dirty Dozen', named so by the media, drawing from the title of the 1967 American war film.

---

2 'RBI identifies Accounts for Reference by Banks under the Insolvency and Bankruptcy Code (IBC)', Reserve Bank of India, 13 June 2017. Last seen on 15 May 2024 at: https://rbi.org.in/scripts/BS_PressReleaseDisplay.aspx?prid=40743

This extraordinary step was taken by the government in the wake of the frightening levels of stress that had been built in the Indian banking sector over the course of a few years. The NPAs had assumed an alarming proportion of the loans made by the banks, severely impacting the availability of much-needed credit to inject investment in the economy. It wouldn't be an exaggeration to say that public sector banks in particular were on the verge of a crisis due to their high NPAs.[3] Their NPAs constituted over 90 per cent of the total bad loans of the industry. In absolute terms, the NPAs continued to mount over the 1990s, except for the year 1995. On 31 March 2002, the total of gross NPAs in public sector banks was Rs 564.73 billion, that is, 11.1 per cent of gross advances and 4.9 per cent of total assets.

Thereafter, the gross NPAs showed a decreasing trend and by the end of March 2007, reached the amount of Rs 389.68 billion. But the trend reversed after 2008. The NPAs soared the most between the years 2009 and 2012, as the gross NPAs increased from Rs 449.57 billion in 2009 to Rs 1124.89 billion in 2011–2012 and further to Rs 1,644.62 billion in 2012–2013. For the year 2013–14, the gross NPAs of public sector banks increased almost four times from March 2010 (Rs 599.26 billion) to March 2014 (Rs 2,272.64 billion).[4] In its Financial Stability Report (December 2013), the RBI identified five sectors

3 The banking system in India consists of commercial banks and cooperative banks, of which commercial banks account for more than 90 per cent of the banking system's assets. Based on the ownership pattern, commercial banks can be grouped into three types: (i) state-owned or public sector banks, that is, the State Bank of India and its subsidiaries and the nationalized banks; (ii) private banks under Indian ownership; and (iii) foreign banks operating in India.

4 'Non-Performing Assets and Public Sector Banks in India', Lok Sabha Secretariat, Reference Note No. 11/RN/Ref./November/2014. Last seen on 21 May 2024 at https://loksabhadocs.nic.in/Refinput/New_Reference_Notes/English/Non-Performing.pdf

– infrastructure, iron and steel, textiles, aviation, and mining – as stressed sectors.

Many factors were responsible for the incidence of the NPAs in banks:[5] Diversion of funds for expansion/modernization/ setting up new projects/helping promoting sister concerns; time/ cost overruns while implementing projects; external factors like raw-material shortage, raw-material/input price escalation, power shortage, industrial recession, excess capacity, natural calamities like floods, accidents, etc.; business failures like product failing to capture market, inefficient management, strike / strained labour relations, wrong technology, technical problems, product obsolescence, etc.; failure, non-payment / overdues in other countries, recession in other countries, externalization problems, adverse exchange rate, etc.; government policies like excise, import duty changes, deregulation, pollution control orders, etc.; wilful default, siphoning of funds, fraud, misappropriation, promoters/ management disputes, etc. Besides the above, factors such as deficiencies on the part of the banks, viz., deficiencies in credit appraisal, monitoring and follow-up; delay in release of limits; delay in settlement of payments/subsidies by government bodies, etc., were also attributed for the incidence of NPAs.[6]

NPAs have a vicious effect on the sustainability and growth of the banking system. If not managed properly, they can lead to bank failure. An important business implication of NPAs is that it leads to credit risk management assuming priority over other aspects of the bank's functioning. The bank's whole machinery is thus preoccupied with recovery procedures rather than concentrating on expanding business. A bank with a high level of NPAs would be forced to incur carrying costs on non-income-yielding assets.

---

5 Ibid.

6 Lok Sabha (14th), Estimates Committee (2004–05), Sixth Report, presented on 25 April 2005, pp. 11–12, 23–24, New Delhi, Lok Sabha Secretariat, April 2005

The enactment of the IBC, and the RBI's crackdown on the bad loans situation[7] were amongst many steps taken to address the NPA issue with urgency. Later, the RBI released another list of twenty-eight companies which owed roughly Rs 2 lakh crore (US$ 24 billion) to banks. The dues of these forty companies[8] (twelve from the first list and twenty-eight from the second) put together accounted for 40–45 per cent of bad loans in the banking system.

The RBI's action to initiate insolvency process in respect of the large defaulters prompted many fence sitters to start using the IBC for resolution of their stressed assets. The action also reaffirmed the government's faith in the new law and its commitment to resolve the NPA crisis. Since then, a number of large cases have been sent into insolvency under the IBC.

Insolvency resolution of one out of the infamous dirty dozen, namely, Jaypee Infratech Limited, will go down in the history of the IBC as the most extraordinary case to have undergone insolvency under the new insolvency regime.

---

7 Sumant Batra, *Corporate Insolvency: Law and Practice* (2017), Chapter 1, Part 1

8 'Insolvency and Bankruptcy Code: Whose Loss, Whose Gain? A Critical Analysis of Performance of Two Years of IBC', Centre for Financial Accountability, May 2019

2

The JIL of JAL

Size, we are told, is not a crime. But size may, at least, become noxious by reason of the means through which it was attained or the uses to which it is put.

– Louis Brandeis, *Other People's Money: And How the Bankers Use It*, 1913, Andrew Ross Sorkin, *Too Big to Fail: Inside the Battle to Save Wall Street*

JIL is part of the Jaypee Group founded by Jaiprakash Gaur, a government-servant-turned-entrepreneur. Jaiprakash was born in a small village named Chitta in Bulandshahar district of Uttar Pradesh. After completing his early education at various schools in small towns of the state, Gaur joined the Thomason College of Engineering in 1948, now the Indian Institute of Technology, Roorkee, and acquired a diploma in civil engineering in 1950. In the same year, Gaur joined the irrigation department of the Government of Uttar Pradesh and worked there for seven years. He quit the job in 1959 to start his entrepreneurial journey with a small capital of Rs 10,000 (US$ 120).

In 1979, he founded Jaiprakash Associates Limited (JAL), a civil engineering and construction company. With his keen business acumen, Gaur transformed his business into Jaypee Group, which soon expanded into diverse businesses of hydel power projects, construction, infrastructure, cement and fertilizer manufacturing, healthcare and hospitality, among others. Jaiprakash won many accolades and awards including Druk Khorlo, one of the highest civilian honours of Bhutan. He remained the chairman of the group until his retirement in 2010. His sons, Manoj and Sameer, took over the reins after he stepped back.

Sometime in 2003, JAL ventured into real estate development, which changed its fortunes. Following an open bidding process, it was awarded the giant Yamuna Expressway Project by YEIDA. The project was to be executed on an immense scale, envisaging development of 6,175 acres of land along the Yamuna, from Noida to Agra – a development of 25 million square metres was estimated.

YEIDA and JAL entered a concession agreement in February 2003 to document the key terms of the project and their respective obligations. The land was to be transferred to JAL on a long lease of ninety years; only the toll road was to revert to YEIDA after thirty-six years. As sale consideration for the land was allotted, it was decided that JAL would pay the actual cost of acquisition of land plus a lease rent of Rs 100 (US$ 1.2) per hectare per year. The land was to be developed by JAL at its own cost as per the Master Plans approved by YEIDA. External development of the project area, such as sewage, power and water supply, etc., was the responsibility of YEIDA, but their costs were to be borne by JAL as per established norms. Within the project area, the onus of these services was on JAL.

II

Although the Yamuna Expressway Project was conceived in 2001 and the work was awarded to JAL in 2003, the work could not start with the project getting stuck in litigation. The 10,995 acres of land (6,175 acres for development and 4,820 acres for right of way) required for development of road and real estate projects were located across the districts of Gautam Buddh Nagar (Noida), Bulandshahar, Aligarh, Mahamaya Nagar (Hathras), Mathura, and Agra in Uttar Pradesh. The project included five land parcels (of approximately 1,200 acres each) meant for development in Noida, Mirzapur, Jagganpur (district Gautam Buddh Nagar), Tappal (district Aligarh), and Agra (district Agra).

Over 20,000 farmers owned small or large parcels of this land. The state government's decision to acquire this enormous land created unrest among the farmers. As a result, two successive commissions of enquiries were set up. While the report of the first commission was quashed by the Allahabad High Court, the second commission of enquiry could not proceed at all as the members resigned. Eventually, an enquiry commission was appointed by the state government under the chairmanship of Justice Siddheshwar Narain, a retired judge. Justice Narain completed the enquiry and submitted his report in October 2006. The Yamuna Expressway Project was cleared in the enquiry with a recommendation that the project may be undertaken through a special-purpose vehicle. This led to the incorporation of JIL by JAL. In the meantime, a public interest litigation came to be filed by way of a writ petition before the Allahabad High Court, which was later dismissed.

Against this backdrop, the government decided to invoke the urgency clause under the Land Acquisition Act, 1894. The clause authorizes the government to acquire land for public purpose by following a summary procedure in prescribed circumstances. The process of the acquisition of farmers' land commenced in September 2007. In the first phase, land for the expressway was acquired, and subsequently the remaining land for development. This started another round of litigation with farmers, which would also cast its shadow on JIL's insolvency process as the case progressed.

The acquisition of land was challenged by farmers in the Allahabad High Court. The High Court upheld (2009) the use of urgency clause and the matter went on appeal to the Supreme Court. In *Nand Kishore*[1] (2010), the Supreme Court upheld the High Court's decision. The court stated that invocation of the clause by the government was justified as the land had been acquired for a public purpose and that the expressway and development of land alongside it was of national importance. The court noted that the state gains advantages from the construction of an expressway and so does the general public. A corridor for fast-moving traffic would curtail travelling time as also speed up the transport of goods. These were some factors, the court noted, that made the project beneficial for the public. The creation of the industrial, commercial, residential, amusement, and other zones would be complementary to the creation of the expressway, it held. It would give impetus to the industrial development of the state, creating more jobs and helping the economy, and thereby the general public. The implementation of the project would also create five developed centres within Uttar Pradesh for the use of its citizens. In conclusion, the project would offer planned development of an otherwise industrially backward area, the court held. The Supreme Court decision in *Nand Kishore* finally paved the way for the implementation of the Yamuna Expressway Project.

III

Following the recommendation of the Justice Narain Commission, YEIDA directed JAL to undertake the project through a special-purpose vehicle so that the land and development made on it would be ring-fenced and not get mixed up with JAL's other

1 *Nand Kishore Gupta & Ors. v. State of UP*, (2010) 10 SCC 282

projects and businesses. Thus came into existence, Jaypee Infratech Limited, the JIL of JAL, in April 2007. JIL was incorporated only for the development of the project and the concession agreement was assigned to it. The land for the project was also assigned to JIL with the approval of YEIDA.

Although JIL was set up as a separate legal entity, in reality, it functioned as an alter ego of JAL. JIL appointed JAL as the principal sales agent and master contractor for the development of the entire project. JAL was to carry out construction on a cost-plus basis and get paid 15 per cent of the actual cost of construction as fees. JAL was also entitled to charge indirect costs and overheads. JIL granted a huge amount to JAL as mobilization advance against construction. JIL also transferred to JAL economic interest for developing some parcels of land in Noida. JAL remained responsible for the day-to-day management of JIL. The employees of JAL continued to perform JIL's functions.

IV

A project of such an immense scale naturally required colossal finance. JIL mobilized funds from many sources. It borrowed money from fourteen public and private sector banks: IDBI Bank Limited, India Infrastructure Finance Company Limited, Life Insurance Corporation of India, Corporation Bank, State Bank of Patiala (which later merged into State Bank of India), Syndicate Bank, Bank of Maharashtra, ICICI Bank Limited, IFCI Limited, Union Bank of India, State Bank of Hyderabad (which also merged into State Bank of India), Jammu & Kashmir Bank Limited, and Axis Bank Limited. Some money was also borrowed from the SREI Equipment Finance Limited, a non-banking finance company. To secure the repayment of loans, JIL mortgaged 1,903 acres of land to the banks. The borrowing was further secured by creating a lien on toll collection from the Yamuna Expressway.

Corporate guarantees of JAL and personal guarantees of promoter shareholder were also provided to secure JIL's debt.

Besides making substantial equity investment in JIL, JAL facilitated borrowing by JIL from lenders by providing its guarantee for repayment and pledging its equity holding in JIL with the lenders. JAL also assured JIL's lenders of the availability of adequate liquidity to meet JIL's costs of the project. A promoter support agreement was executed by JAL to meet the debt service coverage ratio obligation of JIL to its lenders. Bank guarantees were also given by JAL to meet the debt service account of JIL.

A sum of over Rs 13,000 crore (US$ 1,566 million) was collected from homebuyers of JIL as advance for sale of flats and plots. JAL also received substantial advance and interest-free maintenance deposit from homebuyers in lieu of sale of units. Money was raised through public offer as JIL was converted into a public company and listed on the stock exchanges. Just before commencement of JIL's insolvency, JAL held approximately 71.64 per cent of its equity shareholding. Rest of the equity was held by the public and others. The Jaypee Group also floated a scheme inviting investors to make interest-bearing public deposits with JIL. Hundreds of crores were deposited by investors spread across the country. The details of these amounts are mentioned in many orders of the NCLT and the Supreme Court.

V

The Yamuna Expressway was the first of its kind to be developed in the country. Due to increasing number of people visiting Agra and Mathura, the national highway connecting Delhi to Mathura and Agra was facing incessant traffic snarls, especially in the urban areas, making the journey strenuous and killing the joy of road trips. The 165-kilometre toll road was designed to minimize travel time from Delhi to Agra and facilitate faster and uninterrupted movement of passengers and freight traffic. The Yamuna Expressway starts from Greater Noida and ends at Agra along the left bank of the Yamuna. The first forty kilometres of toll road are located in the district of Gautam Buddh Nagar, passing Noida, Dhankaur, Mirzapur and Jewar (the site where the new Noida international airport is under development), followed by twenty kilometres in Aligarh and passing Tappal. The next ninety kilometres fall in the district of Mathura and passes Nohjhil, Mat, Raya and Baldev, followed by approximately fifteen kilometres in Agra, ending near Etmadpur, a village in the district of Agra.

The aim was also to connect the main existing and proposed townships and commercial centres on the eastern side of the Yamuna while relieving traffic congestion on National Highway-44 (which runs through the cities of Faridabad, Ballabhgarh and Palwal) and the Old Grand Trunk Road (National Highway-34). Besides, the development of land along the expressway for residential, commercial, industrial and other use, high-end facilities such as rest areas with parking, shelters and toilets, fuel stations, coffee shops, restaurants, motels were proposed.

The construction of the Yamuna Expressway was completed by JIL on 7 August 2012, and it was opened for the public. The toll collection commenced from 16 August (midnight of 15 August) 2012. As envisaged, the toll road dramatically reduced the travel time between the historic cities of Delhi and Agra, making a lasting impact on villagers, tourists, traders and working professionals. The area also hosts the Noida International Airport at Jewar, which is being developed as the largest airport in India. The Yamuna Expressway is the lifeline of F1 Track (Buddh International Circuit), a sports city, an international cricket stadium and a proposed plan for India's largest film city. With upcoming developments and monumental projects like the aerotropolis and the Olympic city, this region is moving ahead to becoming a key economic and commercial hub. YEIDA is developing a semiconductor park on 700 acres of land and bringing in employment opportunities for local and international firms. The region has become attractive for builders and developers. Many reputed builders are developing residential as well as commercial projects along the Yamuna Expressway.

It featured in the list of world's top 100 innovative infrastructure projects prepared by Klynveld Peat Marwick Goerdeler (KPMG).[2] It is the country's lengthiest access-controlled concrete expressway. In a first for military aviation in India, on 21 May 2015, the Indian Air Force successfully landed a French Dassault Mirage 2000 on the Yamuna Expressway, near village Raya in Mathura.

VI

JIL also ventured into healthcare as part of the project and set up a subsidiary, Jaypee Healthcare Limited. Jaypee Hospital in Sector 128, Noida, is its flagship hospital constructed across a sprawling 25-acre campus. This hospital has been planned and designed as a multi-speciality facility. It has commissioned more than 500 beds in the first phase of its intended 1200-bedded tertiary care multi-multispeciality complex. At the time the book was being written, Jaypee Healthcare Limited had also been admitted into insolvency under the IBC.

Another major project of the group, although not part of JIL, was the Buddh International Circuit, the first circuit to bring international motorsport to India, bursting onto the scene as the host of the Formula One Indian Grand Prix in 2011. Originally known during planning and development as the Jaypee Group Circuit or the Jaypee International Circuit, after the circuit's owners, it was later renamed in recognition of the area where the racetrack is situated. Stated to have been designed by Hermann

---

2 See website of JSW Steel. Last seen on 15 May 2024 at https://www.jswsteel.in/yamuna-expressway

Tilke, the track has been largely well-received by the drivers and was set to firmly establish India on the international motorsport calendar. Sadly, the Grand Prix was later suspended and ultimately dropped from the calendar altogether. Some alleged that JIL diverted advances taken from homebuyers for construction of the expressway and other projects of Jaypee Group.

VII

JIL failed to capitalize on the successful completion of one of the pre-eminent expressways of the country and also faltered on the remaining commitments of the project. Most consequential was its failure to deliver the housing projects, eventually pushing it into insolvency.

The development of housing projects was started mainly in Noida as gated communities. JIL launched twelve projects, namely, Aman, Garden Isles, Kasa Isles, Kensington Boulevard, Kensington Park Apartments, Kensington Park Heights, Klassic, Kosmos, Krescent Homes, Kube, Orchards and Pebble Court, consisting of 250 towers and 29,098 units. Nearly 88 per cent of inventory was sold by the end of year 2010 with over Rs 13,000 crore (US$ 1,566 million) collected from homebuyers as advance for sale of flats and plots. Handover of homes was promised starting 2011 but JIL was unable to deliver. The timelines kept dragging.

VIII

The problem was compounded by the global recession triggered by the fall of Lehman Brothers (2008). Until then the Indian real estate market was booming, property prices were soaring, and developers were launching ambitious projects. High on the boom, many developers diverted funds of one project to the other. The crisis had a cascading impact on the real estate sector. Liquidity dried up and potential homebuyers became wary, resulting in a slowdown in property sales. This was aggravated by other factors, including the RBI restricting Indian banks from financing real estate companies, and a construction ban imposed by the National Green Tribunal (NGT) in October 2013 till it was lifted in August 2015. The developers struggled to complete construction and service their debts. Assets of many real estate sector enterprises started defaulting in repayment to their lenders and customers.

According to the Indian Banks' Association, 4.12 lakh (0.4 million) stressed dwelling units involving Rs 4.08 lakh crore (US$ 49 billion) were impacted in these stalled real estate projects. About 2.40 lakh (0.24 million) stressed dwelling units of these are situated in the National Capital Region of Delhi.[3] JIL is one of them. Homebuyers accuse JIL and JAL of having diverted advances taken from homebuyers for construction of other projects.

IX

From time to time, RBI issues prudential norms on income recognition, asset classification and provisioning pertaining to advances by banks. If the payment of interest or principal by a borrower remains overdue for a period more than ninety days, the loan account of that borrower is classified as NPA. JIL started defaulting in repayment of debt to its lenders. On 30 September 2015, its account was classified as NPA by the Life Insurance

---

3 'Report of the Committee to Examine the Issues Related to Legacy Stalled Real Estate Projects', Amitabh Kant Report, July 2023. Last seen on 14 May 2024 at https://mohua.gov.in/upload/whatsnew/64e31f9e36e0creport.pdf

Corporation of India. A few other lenders too declared JIL as NPA on 31 March 2016. Default in payment of interest or principal, and classification of an account as NPA triggers a number of consequences. A lender can invoke rights under many laws to recover money or push the defaulter into insolvency.

With the delay in the completion of flats, homebuyers started losing patience. As JIL's financial stress worsened, pressure from homebuyers rocketed, and the company's troubles spiralled. Hundreds of homebuyers filed cases in different forums in Delhi, Allahabad and other places, seeking cancellation, refund, penalty, compensation or other reliefs.

In May 2016, the IBC was enacted. After it was operationalized in December 2016, the RBI decided to send JIL into insolvency, alongside the other infamous eleven, a decision that was to start a new chapter in the history of the IBC. A few days later, a similar decision was taken in respect of JAL.

3
Do Beegha Zameen

Cultivators of the earth are the most valuable citizens. They are the most vigorous, the most independent, the most virtuous, and they are tied to their country and wedded to its liberty and interests by the most lasting bonds.

- Thomas Jefferson

India's agriculture sector is the backbone of its economy. It supports the livelihood of 70 per cent of the population, roughly 93.09 million agricultural households – 82 per cent of which are sustained by less than two hectares of land.[1] Yet even this land is precious to them even if it barely helps them make ends meet.

The government regularly acquires land from the general public for development of projects in larger public interest. The Land Acquisition Act, 1894, has served as the basis for all acquisition of land for public purposes by the government.

1 See website of Food and Agriculture Organisation of United Nations in India. Last seen on 14 June 2024 at https://www.fao.org/india/fao-in-india/india-at-a-glance/en/

Initially, due to a lack of clear definition of 'public purpose', there had been considerable difference of opinion in various judgments of the Supreme Court, which resulted in granting very broad discretionary powers to the state in terms of deciding the contours of 'public purpose' in particular circumstances. In many large-scale projects, however, the compensation and rehabilitation packages were determined through negotiations between the authorities and landowners, outside of the acquisition process under the Land Acquisition Act, 1894. The adequacy and fairness of the compensation awarded has remained a matter of debate for years.

Acquisitions, in particular from farmers, result in stiff opposition not just because the compensation proves to be inadequate but also because giving up land is a deeply emotional issue for a farmer, particularly one with a small landholding. It's only natural then that they take to protests to assert their resistance against the acquisition of the lands dear to their life and livelihood. Film-maker Bimal Roy's celebrated film *Do Bigha Zamin* (1953) aptly captures the plight of a small peasant who does everything within his means to save his land from being taken away to justify 'development' from enterprises and the state. The film sketches the intangible sorrow of farmer who is made to part with land which means more than a mother to him.

History is replete with instances of such protests in different parts of the country. In 2007, violent protests broke out in a hundred villages near Nandigram in the East Medinipur district of West Bengal when the government attempted to acquire 10,000 acres of land for a special economic zone. West Bengal saw similar protests by farmers in Singur in 2008. The protests started in 2002 when Tata Motors acquired over 900 acres of land for its Nano car project, and the situation worsened over the next six years. In June 2011, about 2,000 villagers in Odisha began protests against the South Korean company POSCO as it laid down its plan of acquiring 4,000 acres of land for a steel plant. Similar violent protests broke out in Uttar Pradesh after the government announced acquisition of hundreds of acres of land for the Yamuna Expressway Project.

II

Approximately 11,000 acres of land located between Noida and Agra was acquired from 20,000 farmers for the development of the Yamuna Expressway Project by YEIDA. Although the project was conceived in 2001, its commencement was delayed for eight long years. In the aftermath of the announcement, there was public outcry by the farmers against the project which threatened to take away their parcels of land. The Uttar Pradesh government appointed a commission of enquiry to examine the justification for the land acquisition. A public interest litigation was also filed in the Allahabad High Court. The project was cleared in the enquiry and the public interest litigation also ended in favour of the government. However, it took eight years for the processes to get completed, and to accelerate the start of project, the government decided to invoke the urgency clause under the Land Acquisition Act, 1894, to acquire the land. The urgency clause allows acquisition of land for public purpose by following a summary acquisition process, which started another round of litigation by farmers.

III

The acquisition of land using the urgency clause was challenged by farmers in the Allahabad High Court. The High Court upheld the use of the urgency clause for the acquisition of land (2009). The matter was then appealed to the Supreme Court. In *Nand Kishore*[2] (2010), the Supreme Court upheld the High Court decision. It noted that going through the ordinary procedure for acquisition of land would have taken years, given the time it would have taken to dispose of the objections received against acquisition, while land was urgently required for public purpose. This interval of time would have propelled encroachment on the land, which would have increased the trouble. The acquisition process would have taken years, given the enormity of the project, involving 20,000 farmers. The cost would have only soared up further.

The Supreme Court held that invocation of the urgency clause was justified since the project was a work of immense public importance. Both the state and general public would gain from the construction of the expressway. With its complementary industrial, residential, and other projects it would also give an impetus to the industrial development of the state, creating more jobs and helping the economy, thereby helping the general public.

IV

In 2011, in an unrelated challenge (*Gajraj Singh*) to a different plan of acquisition of land by NOIDA and Greater Noida authority, a full bench of the Allahabad High Court ordered payment of additional compensation to the farmers from whom land was acquired. The High Court held that there was no urgency for acquisition of land parcels in that case, dispensing with the enquiry contemplated by S. 5A of the Land Acquisition Act, 1894, and holding that it was not justified. The *Gajraj Singh* decision was upheld by the Supreme Court in *Savitri Devi.*

2 *Nand Kishore Gupta & Ors. v. State of UP*, (2010) 10 SCC 282

In the light of the *Gajraj Singh* judgment of Allahabad High Court, farmers whose land was acquired by YEIDA for many projects under their jurisdiction, including the Yamuna Expressway Project, also demanded additional compensation. This was despite the fact that invocation of the urgency clause for acquisition of land for the Yamuna Expressway Project had been upheld by the Supreme Court in *Nand Kishore*. The farmers' protests began and many of them refused to give access to the acquired land. The protests snowballed into a confrontation with the state government, threatening to escalate into a law and order situation. On account of the farmers' agitation, vast stretches of lands could not be developed by YEIDA and JIL.

In April 2013, the CEO of YEIDA addressed a letter to the state government, requesting a solution. On the same day, the state government instructed the commissioner of Meerut division, to meet various groups of farmers and submit a report. The commissioner held a meeting with various groups of farmers and the district magistrates of concerned areas and submitted a report to the state government recommending that a high-level committee be set up to find a solution.

In August 2014, the government set up the Chaudhary Committee to examine the demands of the farmers. It recommended payment of additional compensation of 64.7 per cent of acquisition cost to farmers as 'no litigation incentive' to be paid on priority basis. On 29 August 2014, the Uttar Pradesh government issued an order (G.O.) directing YEIDA to ensure payment of additional compensation to the landowners on the condition that they withdraw the petitions that challenged the acquisition proceedings and undertake not to pursue any litigation or create hindrance in the development work. It was clarified in the G.O. that the state government would not bear the burden of the additional amount, which was to be paid to those whom YEIDA had leased the land. YEIDA in turn demanded the additional compensation from JIL for onward payment to the farmers. This was one of the major issues that preceded JIL's insolvency process which commenced in 2017.

V

This demand was challenged by JIL before the Allahabad High Court by way of a writ petition. The petition was later withdrawn to seek recourse to arbitration, as the concession agreement entered into between YEIDA and JIL for the Yamuna Expressway Project (See Chapter 1) provided that any dispute between the parties shall be resolved by arbitration.

4

The Leap of Faith

Faith is taking the first step even when you don't see the whole staircase.

~ Martin Luther King Jr.

Nudged by the RBI, the lead member of the consortium of banks that financed JIL, the IDBI Bank, filed a petition for commencement of JIL's insolvency under the IBC before the Allahabad bench of the NCLT. A financial creditor[1] can file a petition against the debtor if there has been a default in payment of debt of Rs 1 crore (US$ 120,000) or more. Simply put, a financial creditor is one who has lent money to the debtor against interest or similar return on the amount borrowed.

Later, the president of the NCLT, using powers granted under the IBC, transferred JIL's proceedings from the Allahabad bench to the principal bench of the NCLT at Delhi. The NCLT, a tribunal set up under the Companies Act, 2013, to settle company law disputes, is designated as the adjudicating authority under the

1 The IBC, Ss. 5(7) and 5(8)

IBC and given many powers. Chief of them is to admit a corporate debtor into insolvency and to approve or reject the resolution plan for a debtor, as provided by the committee of creditors (CoC). If the resolution plan is rejected, the NCLT may pass an order for liquidation of the debtor, following which the debtor is dissolved. The debtor should be a corporate person, not an individual. The IBC refers to such debtor as a corporate debtor.

The NCLT also has the power to extend the insolvency process period to seek cooperation from the debtor's personnel and to rule on applications so as to avoid questionable transactions filed by the resolution professional (RP), or against the rejection of claims by the liquidator, as explained later in this chapter. Further, the NCLT has jurisdiction to entertain or dispose of any application or proceeding by or against the debtor; any claim made by or against the debtor; or any question of priorities or any question of law or facts arising out of or in relation to the insolvency resolution or liquidation proceedings of debtor falling under the IBC.

In its petition, the IDBI Bank claimed that JIL had defaulted in repayment of debt and owed Rs 526.11 crore (US$ 63.4 million) to it as on 15 June 2017. JIL opposed the petition on many grounds but later withdrew the objections. The petition was admitted by the NCLT on 9 August 2017. This put into motion the insolvency process of one of the largest real estate and infrastructure companies in India.

It also catalysed, inter alia, many policy responses, in quick succession, to address the difficulties experienced in JIL's case and for effective implementation of the IBC. An order of moratorium was also passed by the NCLT prohibiting any legal action against JIL by any creditor. Such restraining order is passed under S.14 of the IBC. The reason behind such prohibition is that after its start, an insolvency proceeding takes the form of collective creditors' action. The assets of the corporate debtor must be protected from individual enforcement actions by creditors, which can destroy the going-concern value of an otherwise economically viable business. The aim is to provide a standstill period in which a revival of the distressed enterprise can be attempted and the value of its assets maximized for the benefit of all the creditors.

Anuj Jain, an insolvency professional licensed by the Insolvency and Bankruptcy Board of India (IBBI), with more than twenty years of finance experience and associated with KPMG, was appointed as the Interim Resolution Professional (IRP) of JIL. He was selected by IDBI Bank after a competitive process to pick the most suitable person to handle what was going to be an intricate insolvency proceeding.

The process of insolvency is often turbulent and distressing for the company and its stakeholders. It is the proficiency of the insolvency professional that can allow troubled businesses to stay afloat and, where this is not possible, enable vulnerable creditors to maximize their returns through liquidation. His work affects the lives, prospects and livelihood of both creditors and debtors and often involves dealing with many competing interests.

He must be able to balance the interests of all stakeholders, and such stakeholders should have confidence in the insolvency regime and its practitioners. Besides legal obligations, an insolvency professional has ethical and moral obligations to creditors, employees and other stakeholders. Integrity and experience of the insolvency professional is central to the functioning of the insolvency system. An insolvency professional must possess not only qualities such as resourcefulness and business acumen, but also a good sense of judgement and fairness when balancing the interests of stakeholders inter se or against other interests and statutory objectives. He also needs written and interpersonal skills to deal with creditors, anxious directors, concerned employees and a range of other stakeholders in the business. He must have a fair degree of appreciation of cultural, social and other factors surrounding an insolvency proceeding.

Insolvency is not just another profession but an institution onto itself.[2]

Entrusting Anuj Jain with the insolvency process of a complex case like that of JIL was a testimony to the faith banks had in his abilities. Later, he was also to earn the confidence of the homebuyers, another large stakeholder. His abilities and skills were put to trial throughout the seven-year-long insolvency process of JIL.

II

The admission of JIL into the insolvency process was like pushing a gigantic ship to sail into rough waters. The IBC had become only partly operational since 1 December 2016. It introduced many new concepts and principles alien to the Indian market which had no precedents to guide or fall back upon. The law made a paradigm shift from the debtor-in-possession regime under the Sick Industrial Companies (Special Provisions) Act, 1985 (since repealed), to a 'creditor in control' system.

The IBC provides for four processes for insolvency resolution of corporate persons, namely, corporate insolvency resolution process, fast-track resolution process, liquidation process and voluntary liquidation process. These processes came into force in 2016 and 2017 and are listed under Part II of the IBC. It also provides for the insolvency resolution process and bankruptcy process of personal guarantors to corporate debtors which came into force in 2019.

Broadly put, the scheme of corporate insolvency resolution process under the IBC provides that when an order of commencement of insolvency of a corporate debtor is passed by the NCLT, its management is transferred to an independent

---

2 'Report of IBBI Working Group on Graduate Insolvency Programme', December 2018. Last seen on 14 May 2024 at https://ibbi.gov.in/uploads/resources/report-low.pdf

insolvency professional appointed to serve as an IRP. The powers of the board of directors of the corporate debtor are suspended and vested with the IRP. The affairs and assets of the corporate debtor are also placed under control of the IRP. In a single stroke of the NCLT's order of admission, the right of the founder-shareholder to be in the saddle is taken away.

The IRP invites claims from the corporate debtor's creditors by making a public announcement. He verifies and collates the claims received and constitutes a CoC comprising unrelated financial creditors of the corporate debtor who have lent money to the corporate debtor against time value for money or provided guarantee. The voting share is assigned to the member of the CoC based on the amount of its claim as verified by the IRP. In the CoC, no priority is accorded amongst financial creditors on account of being secured, unsecured or for providing a guarantee. An alternative provision in the IBC provides that the CoC be formed with operational creditors when corporate debtor has no financial creditor or when all its financial creditors are related parties. Simply stated, operational creditors are trade creditors or those from whom the corporate debtor has availed services (including employees) but has not paid them. The central and state governments and statutory bodies also fall under the category of operational creditors if any dues are owed to them by the corporate debtor.

The CoC is responsible for taking many key decisions during the insolvency process. Amongst the first decision that is required to be taken when it meets is to either confirm the IRP as the RP or replace him with another independent insolvency professional. It is the duty of both the IRP (during her term) and the RP to run the corporate debtor as a going concern and conduct its insolvency process. The RP invites resolution plans from eligible and credible resolution applicants (investors) for resolution of insolvency of the corporate debtor on the terms approved by the CoC. The resolution plans found compliant of the provisions of the IBC are placed by the RP before the CoC for consideration.

If the CoC approves a resolution plan within the stipulated time with 66 per cent majority in value of total debt, the RP moves the NCLT to seek its approval. The NCLT approves the plan, binding it on all concerned, if the resolution plan is found to be in conformity with the IBC and the prescribed regulations. If the CoC does not approve any resolution plan placed before it, it can resolve to liquidate the corporate debtor. If the NCLT finds the plan approved by the CoC as non-compliant of the provisions of the IBC, the NCLT may pass an order of liquidation of the corporate debtor. In other words, the CoC decides the fate of the corporate debtor by approving a plan for its resolution or opting for liquidation. If the NCLT passes an order of liquidation, an insolvency professional is appointed as liquidator to conduct the liquidation process. Generally, an order of liquidation is passed by the NCLT after ensuring that adequate effort has been made for resolution of the corporate debtor.

The processes under the IBC are time bound. The insolvency process is required to be completed within a period of 180 days, with two extensions of up to ninety and sixty days permissible from the NCLT, if requested by the RP at the behest of the CoC. Liquidation of the corporate debtor has to be completed within one year.

III

The decision to push the 'dirty dozen' into insolvency at the same time, during the early days of the IBC, was fraught with risk. The IBC's effectiveness was yet to be tested. Not only the law was new, even the institutions under it were newly set up. Most members of the NCLT had little to no familiarity of insolvency laws. The IBBI was also like a start-up with no repository of knowledge of insolvency regulatory functions. Not all insolvency professionals licensed by the IBBI had past experience of handling cases in formal insolvency processes. Those from large firms like Ernst & Young, KPMG, Deloitte, Grant Thornton, Alvarez and Marsal, and PricewaterhouseCoopers (PwC) had their main learning from advising on informal restructurings but had the advantage of being able to draw know-how from their counterparts located in other countries. To hope that the insolvency processes, particularly for the large twelve cases, would be completed within 270 days was unrealistic.

But clearly, the government was confident that the legal and institutional infrastructure needed to deal with the cases was ready, and any gaps spotted in implementation could be filled later. The RBI also appeared convinced of the IBC's potential and its ability to deliver. The IBC was a law that was put, within months of its implementation, to its biggest test.

IV

The insolvency process of all twelve cases was not only complex but was also mired in litigation. But it is JIL which turned out to be the most difficult of all, and garnered the most attention.

With no precedents to guide the insolvency process of a high-profile real estate enterprise involving thousands of stressed homebuyers and other stakeholders, the risks for IRP Anuj Jain were high. There was no room for trial and error. His reputation was at stake. He needed experienced advisors. After all, a danger foreseen is half avoided.

The IBC allows the IRP to appoint professionals to advise and assist her in discharging duties. On his appointment as IRP, Anuj Jain appointed Kesar Dass, a leading law firm, with the author leading the legal team, as his legal advisor. The playing field was set. For the next seven years Anuj Jain and the author would have to negotiate their way through one hurdle after the other in this unprecedented case.

5

The First Forty-eight Hours

All great beginnings start in the dark, when the moon greets you to a new day at midnight.

~ Shannon L. Alder

In the words of Aurelio Gurrea-Martinez,[1] insolvency systems can be pro-debtor and pro-creditor, anti-debtor and anti-creditor, or somewhere in the middle. The IBC is a creditor-in-control law, friendly to a particular set of creditors of a corporate debtor. It provides for placement of the insolvent company under the control of its financial creditors. The management of the debtor is placed under the RP's control from the time insolvency commences. The powers of the board of directors of the debtor is suspended and vested in the RP. Amongst his many other functions, the RP has to ensure the going-concern nature of the insolvent debtor during the resolution process; take control of the debtor's assets and prepare a list, while ensuring assets are preserved; verify the claims

1 Aurelio Gurrea-Martinez is Head, Singapore Global Restructuring Initiative, Yong Pung How School of Law, Singapore Management University

received from creditors and put together a list of liabilities, prepare an information memorandum containing all the vital information about debtor, which later provides a baseline to the CoC and the prospective resolution applicants for their decision making.

A successful insolvency resolution under the IBC hinges on the RP's ability to fulfil these multiple tasks simultaneously. Cooperation from former directors and management personnel is critical for the RP to achieve this. In fact, cooperation is needed from the very start for the RP to be able to stabilize the debtor's business. Also needed is the whereabouts of assets and access to quality information. The claims received can only be verified if relevant material is made available and support is provided by management personnel in verifying them. As such cooperation is critical for efficiency of the process and its successful outcome.

To elicit cooperation from the debtor, both the IRP and the debtor have to understand that the IBC is friendly to financial creditors, but it is not anti-debtor. Amongst the main objectives of the IBC is to revive the debtor and in the process maximize the value of assets for the benefit of creditors and other stakeholders. The founder, shareholders or the erstwhile management of debtor is/are permitted to participate in the insolvency process unless disqualified under S.29A, an ineligibility provision later introduced in the IBC to provide criteria for disqualification for submitting resolution plan in insolvency process.

The objective of the ineligibility criteria is to preclude persons, who by their misconduct have contributed to the defaults of the corporate debtor from submitting resolution plan. It prevents such persons from regaining control on the corporate debtor at the cost of the creditors during the resolution and the liquidation stages. The provision disqualifies a company whose account is classified as NPA from submitting a resolution plan if more than one year has lapsed from the date of such classification. Related parties of such person are also disqualified. The provision, however, does not impose a blanket bar on the promoter or the erstwhile management of debtor to participate in the insolvency process. The directors are given opportunity to participate in the CoC meetings albeit without voting right, even if they fall under the disqualification criteria. However, the IBC is not debtor-friendly. It is also, arguably, not friendly to creditors other than financial creditors.

The IBC imposes an obligation on former employees, promoters, and anyone who previously held management positions, including ex-directors, to assist the RP in managing the affairs of the corporate debtor during the insolvency proceedings.[2] Ensuring cooperation from the debtors' management and promoters is one of the pressing goals of the RP. It is the duty of both the RP and the directors to create an environment that enables cooperation. If cooperation is not forthcoming, the IBC empowers the RP to seek intervention from the NCLT, which can compel the non-cooperating party to fall in line.[3]

Soon after Anuj Jain was appointed as the IRP by the NCLT, his first task was to visit JIL's office and take control of its management and assets. He called JIL's managing director Manoj Gaur, a man of humble demeanour, to inform him of the visit. Gaur assured his full support and cooperation. In due course, the IRP and debtor's management earned each other's respect, and the management extended cooperation to the IRP even as both pursued cases against each other for seven long years.

II

A clear and upfront communication from IRP helped in breaking the ice and paving the way for a congenial dialogue with stakeholders, particularly homebuyers.

---

2 The IBC, S. 19(1)
3 The IBC, S. 19(2)

A press release was issued by the IRP to inform the public at large of the start of insolvency process of JIL, of the IRP taking over JIL's management, and about the steps that they would follow. The press release was published on a full page of a national daily, which agreed to publish it free of charge if the release was exclusively reserved for that newspaper.

The press release read as below:

> A Corporate Insolvency Resolution Process (CIRP) has been initiated in respect of Jaypee Infratech Limited (the Company) by an order dated 9 August 2017 passed by the Hon'ble National Company Law Tribunal, Allahabad under the Insolvency and Bankruptcy Code, 2016 (IBC). A copy of NCLT order can be found on the Company's website.
>
> By the same order, the Hon'ble NCLT has appointed me as the Insolvency Resolution Professional (IRP). In accordance with the provisions of the IBC, on commencement of the CIRP, the powers of the Board of Directors of the Company stand suspended and shall be exercised by me. The management of the affairs of the Company also vests with me.
>
> The CIRP is not a proceeding for liquidation. It is a process to find a resolution for the current situation. I am conscious of the interest of key stakeholders including flat owners. As IRP, it is my duty to endeavour to protect and preserve the value of the property of the Company and manage its operations as a going concern including continuation of ongoing construction. The promoters and management of the Company are under legal obligation to extend all assistance and cooperation to me.
>
> Over the next few days I will collect the necessary information to prepare an information memorandum of the Company. I will prepare a list of creditors of the Company and their claims. For this purpose, a Public

Announcement has already been made in two newspapers on 12 August 2017 inviting claims from creditors including the flat owners of the Company.

The claim is required to be filed in the requisite format as prescribed by IBC and the regulations framed thereunder. The requisite format of all the above forms will be placed on the website of the Company on Monday, 14 August 2017 and can be downloaded from there.

The last date for submitting the clams is 24 August 2017.The information in respect of claims received, the name of creditors, the amounts claimed and admitted will be included by me in the information memorandum. Thereafter, I will invite interested parties to submit a plan for revival of the Company. The plan for resolution of the Company will be submitted for approval before the Hon'ble NCLT. The entire process is time bound and to be completed in 180 days with a provision of extension of maximum period of 90 days, with the approval of Hon'ble NCLT.

I will continue to update the status of the CIRP regularly on the Company website and communicate with all stakeholders from time to time.

For Jaypee Infratech Limited
Anuj Jain
Interim Resolution Professional

On the afternoon of 12 August 2017, Anuj Jain and the author, with their team members left for JIL's office in Noida. Although the NCLT had passed the order of admission on 9 August 2017, a copy of NCLT's order appointing Anuj Jain as the IRP was not available until 10 August 2017. News of the commencement of JIL's insolvency had spread like wildfire.

While the IRP and the author were on their way to JIL's office, they were apprised by a senior executive of JIL that a large number of homebuyers were gathered in front of the main entrance to JIL's office complex. Some local politicians had also joined the agitated homebuyers to earn some brownie points. Naturally, the media had also arrived. The security guards and staff struggled to calm everyone. All of them wanted to meet Anuj Jain.

JIL's management had informed the local authorities and requested for adequate police deployment outside the office to avert the situation from spiralling into a law and order problem. The gentleman cautioned that the situation was tense and that the IRP and his team should consider deferring the visit till the agitation of homebuyers had subsided.

The IRP and his team thanked the gentleman for his counsel but after some deliberation decided to not cancel their visit. The situation demanded that the IRP meet the homebuyers sooner than later. Seeing their persistence, the IRP and his counsel were requested by the debtor's representative to keep their arrival discreet. It would allow the IRP to gauge the situation and decide his next steps, he recommended. That was a fair suggestion. The IRP, the author and their teams took off their jackets and ties so as to not invite attention, and unobserved, entered JIL's office.

III

Inside the premises, the IRP and his team gathered with JIL's key management personnel (KMP) and representative of the IDBI Bank to assess the situation.The homebuyers were angrier at the government. While banks were considered as JIL's lenders and classified as financial creditor in the IBC, homebuyers had been left out despite having higher financial exposure in JIL than the banks. Moreover, as members of the CoC, banks would get the seat behind the wheel, while the homebuyers would remain bystanders in a case whose outcome was going to heavily affect them. They were livid at not being delivered the promised flats, and the lack of a level playing field under the IBC compounded their ire. Furious homebuyers were demanding answers to their questions. It was clear that the IRP needed to communicate with homebuyers to save the matter from getting out of hand.

In course of his duties, the RP is required to communicate with multiple stakeholders. It plays a pivotal role in gaining support of the stakeholders and impacts the outcome of the insolvency resolution process. It is equally vital to keep the communications clear, precise, polite and relevant so it can calm anxious stakeholders, mobilize support, and also help the RP earn cooperation of otherwise reluctant stakeholders. It was thus, not just necessary but critical that Anuj Jain communicate with the hundreds of homebuyers and address their doubts meaningfully.

Encircled by JIL's security guards, Anuj Jain went to meet the homebuyers. They were agitated but cordial. After hearing them, it was clear that the main cause for their anxiety was their lack of clarity about the features of the IBC due to which they were not able to comprehend JIL's outcome from the insolvency process. They were worried because of the uncertainty generated by the fear of not understanding the intricacies of a process that could impact their future, and potentially put it at risk.

The IRP briefly explained to them the objectives and scheme of the IBC in simple words. He clarified that this was not a process to liquidate JIL but to revive it quickly so that the construction of projects could resume at the earliest. He assured them that the IRP is an officer of the NCLT, and that he had come to take over JIL's management and would be in charge of affairs going forward. He emphasized that the IBC required him to be neutral and act independently and that even though they as homebuyers were not part of JIL's CoC, as an independent officebearer he would keep their interests foremost in all his actions and decisions.

Affected by the homebuyers' barrage of questions about the process and next steps, the IRP and the author decided to post a comprehensive list of frequently asked questions (FAQs) on

JIL's website the very next morning to address the homebuyers' doubts. This helped calm the homebuyers. It was already known that a smooth and orderly conduct of the insolvency process was unthinkable without homebuyers being kept adequately informed of key developments. It was crucial to maintain transparency and regularly provide them updates on the process.

To address these concerns, a whole night was devoted in drawing a comprehensive communication plan. A list of all conceivable FAQs that could potentially be weighing on the minds of homebuyers and other stakeholders was drafted. Twenty-three FAQs were uploaded on JIL's website on the morning of 13 August 2017. An email and phone number was posted on website so that homebuyers could direct their queries or call to clarify their doubts to a dedicated source. A meeting room was set up in the office of JIL and the IRP's office with staff that would meet and resolve queries of walk-in customers, individually as well as in groups.

The start of JIL's insolvency triggered all kinds of speculations and rumours. Some misguiding media reports appeared over the next few days suggesting that homebuyers would be refunded the advance booking amount paid by them albeit with a 'haircut'. This led to a spate of emails and calls from homebuyers seeking clarification. With such a large number of stakeholders, some degree of supposition, guesswork and opinions is expected. But the IRP had to issue another press release on 18 August 2017 to put the rumours to rest and nip them in the bud. The proactive approach by the IRP helped in settling the gossips and allowed the IRP to control the narrative.

On 18 August 2017, three additional FAQs were updated and another three on 22 August 2017. The press releases and FAQs, frequently updated, aided in calming down thousands of homebuyers of JIL living in different parts of the country, and around the world.

Recognizing the importance and need for a continued and supportive communication with the homebuyers, a training session was organized for JIL's customer relationship team so that they could suitably handle the queries received from homebuyers. A team comprising two to three members was deployed to reply to the queries received on a dedicated email account. Letters were sent by the IRP to the chief executives of YEIDA and NOIDA, informing them to henceforth communicate with the IRP, and advising them not to take any coercive steps against JIL. The district magistrate and senior police officer of the area were also contacted in the same capacity.

All the lenders of JIL and other statutory authorities were informed of the commencement of the insolvency process of JIL and the moratorium order passed by the NCLT. It was important to ensure that the creditors and authorities did not start reacting by taking enforcement or coercive actions against JIL after reading reports appearing in the newspapers. These were the early days of the IBC and the moratorium imposed under its S.14 needed to be appreciated.

This communication strategy was maintained throughout the process and significantly helped in gaining the homebuyers' cooperation. It also contributed in the successful culmination of JIL's insolvency process with the sanction of Suraksha's resolution plan by the NCLT.

Later, the IRP upgraded the technology for more efficient communication and sharing of information with homebuyers. The communication through WhatsApp groups, website portal, and other models facilitated active engagement of the homebuyers with insolvency process. After the homebuyers became members of the CoC, notice for meetings, agenda notes and minutes of meetings of the CoC were shared with them using this technology solution developed especially for JIL, allowing for a two-way communication and transmission of information, and enabling voting by the homebuyers on the agendas put to vote in the CoC meetings. Today, such strategies valuing communication may have become a normal practice, but when devised for JIL, it was considered a novel step and applauded by the insolvency industry.

IV

Having calmed homebuyers and rolling out the communication plan, the IRP started the process of taking control of JIL's management and affairs. A formal communication had already been made to JIL's KMP, advising them to report to the IRP and not the promoters or JIL's managing director. JIL's directors were informed of the suspension of powers of JIL's board of directors as one of the outcomes of the commencement of insolvency. The IRP took control of all key areas of JIL's business. A steering committee comprising senior members of the IRP, KMP and JIL's consultants was formed for making key strategic decisions.

It was made clear to the KMPs that all key decisions were to be made only with the prior approval of the IRP. The banks with which JIL maintained its accounts were also forthwith apprised of the commencement of insolvency process, and advised not to make any transaction unless authorized by the IRP. The personnel authorized by JIL to operate bank accounts were substituted with the IRP's team. A revised delegation of authority was instituted requiring approval of the IRP in addition to existing approvals, for incurring expense or making payments.

In consultation with the author, the IRP decided to continue registering sublease deeds in favour of homebuyers during the insolvency process. They were of the clear view that restriction on the debtor under moratorium from transferring fixed assets did not apply to subleasing flats as the units put to sale were considered inventory and not fixed assets of the corporate debtor. In any case, stopping registration of sublease had the potential of creating havoc. The delegation of authority for issuing letters of offers of possession was revised. Senior government officials in the concerned ministry, and the IBBI, were apprised of the decision taken to continue to execute and register sublease. A public statement was also made by the IRP in this regard. Much later, as discussed in later chapters, the IBBI clarified that registering properties for cases in which the allottee had paid their dues could continue during the corporate insolvency resolution process.

Most of this was accomplished within the first twenty-four hours.

The meetings with the management of JIL continued through the night. JIL's promoters and KMP extended their cooperation even as they planned their next steps to put in their resolution plan in the insolvency process. S. 29A of the IBC, disqualifying the promoters from taking back the debtor company through the corporate insolvency process, had not been brought into the law until three months later. Apparently, hoping to earn back homebuyers and creditors' trust, they did not want to be seen as being uncooperative with the IRP in performance of his statutory duties.

V

While the IRP's team engaged with JIL's KMP to understand the status of housing projects and other aspects of business, the author and his team focused on the IBC compliances required to be made by the IRP.

One of the earliest compliances required of the IRP was to take out a public announcement in newspapers within three days from his appointment to invite claims from JIL's creditors. The form of public announcement, procedure and deadline for submission of claims, and their verification by the IRP are provided in the CIRP Regulations.

The NCLT's order was passed on 9 August 2017. The public announcement was required to be made by 12 August 2017;

creditors were to submit claims within fifteen days, i.e., 24 August 2017, and the IRP was to verify the claims within seven days and constitute a CoC within two days. The first meeting of the CoC had to be held within seven days thereafter.[4]

Although the order was passed by the NCLT on 9 August 2017, a copy of the order was not available until the evening of 10 August 2017. The author advised the IRP that public announcement should only be made after a copy of the NCLT Order was received by the IRP. Making the public announcement was not proper unless the copy of the order was received and read by the IRP.

Another difficulty that arose from non-availability of the copy of order on the same day when the order of commencement of insolvency was passed was the confusion over counting 180 days provided for completion of the resolution process. While the IBC requires 180 days to be counted from the date of order, which date also serves as the cut-off date for creditors to file claims, if the various steps to be actioned following the start of the process get delayed because of the copy of the order not being made available on the same date, it can impact the timelines provided under the IBC for completing the various steps and the process. This difficulty was later addressed by an amendment made in the definition of the 'insolvency commencement date' in the IBC by adding a proviso which has the effect of making the date of appointment of interim insolvency professional as the date of commencement of insolvency if the appointment is made on a date later than the admission of petition.

It has also been clarified by the NCLT in many cases that if a copy of order of admission passed by the NCLT is made available on a later date, the NCLT can exclude the time between the passing of the order of admission and availability of copy of order so that time for compliances corresponds to the date of availability of copy of order.

---

4 The CIRP Regulations, R. 6 to R. 14, and R. 17

As thousands of creditors were expected to submit claims, the IRP and his lawyers braced themselves for the humongous task of verification of the enormous number of claims in mere seven days. As they prepared for this, they encountered a peculiar problem around midnight which almost caught them off guard.

A unique issue was identified by the author and his team while drafting the public announcement. They discovered that no form had been prescribed in the CIRP Regulations (as applicable at that time) for the homebuyers to submit their claims. The CIRP Regulations provided Form B for submission of claims by operational creditors and Form C by financial creditors. But no form had been provided for a homebuyer, as creditors of JIL, to submit claim. The homebuyers' claim was for advance paid towards delivery of a housing unit in the future. As per decisions of the NCLT and the National Company Law Appellate Tribunal (NCLAT) to which appeals from the NCLT order are made, prevailing at that time, a homebuyer was neither an operational creditor nor a financial creditor.

In *Nikhil Mehta v. AMR Infrastructure*,[5] the NCLT held that a homebuyer is not a financial creditor as there is no consideration for the time value of money involved as required for a creditor to qualify as a financial creditor, and that these are simple sale transactions. However, the NCLAT took an opposing view holding that the amounts invested by the homebuyer was not a mere sale transactions, but would indeed come under the ambit of financial debts under the IBC in cases where an allottee was assured returns on the investment in a real estate project's unit.[6]

The absence of the form meant homebuyers of JIL would be left clueless and confused about the form they should submit their

5 *Nikhil Mehta and Sons v. AMR Infrastructure Ltd*, C.P. No. (ISB) – 03 (PB)/2017 decided on 23 January 2017

6 *Nikhil Mehta and Sons v. AMR Infrastructure Ltd*, Company Appeal (AT) (Insolvency) No. 07 of 2017 decided on 21 July 2017

claim in. This would have augmented the resentment of nearly 20,000 homebuyers already feeling left out of the scheme of the IBC. It had the potential of sparking another wave of protests by the homebuyers and cause disruption to the insolvency process as it was progressing. If not addressed appropriately and without any delay, this unintended anomaly in the CIRP Regulations could have also created a major embarrassment for the IBBI. Thus began the efforts by the IRP and his lawyers to manage the first amongst many difficulties that were to follow in JIL's insolvency process.

VI

On 13 August 2017, at 7 in the morning the author and the IRP brought the anomaly to the attention of Dr M.S. Sahoo, the then chairperson of the IBBI. Recognizing the problem and realizing it demanded urgent attention, Dr Sahoo assured swift action. He requested for a brief note on the issue so that he could escalate the matter to the IBBI's governing board. True to the assurance provided, the IBBI promptly amended the CIRP Regulations on 16 August 2017 and inserted R.9A in the CIRP Regulations. Form F was added in the CIRP Regulations to provide for creditors other than operational and financial creditors to submit claim. A press release was made by the IBBI on 16 August 2017 for information of the general public.[7] This speedy intervention by the IBBI averted a major crisis and paved the way for homebuyers to submit their claims before the expiry of the last date for submission of claims mentioned in the public announcement.

Later on, the IBC was amended by the government to make the homebuyer a financial creditor of corporate debtor. This

7 The IBBI Press Release dated 16 August 2017. Last seen on 14 May 2024 at https://ibbi.gov.in/FormforSubmissionofClaims.pdf

changed the dynamics of insolvency of real estate companies and notably of JIL's.

VII

The first forty-eight hours of JIL's insolvency process were very testing of the IRP's communication skills, his capabilities to respond to crisis, his temperament to deal with difficulties, and his leadership abilities. It required much innovation and, to an extent, calculated risk taking and considered experimenting by the IRP as the IBC was a new legislation and there were no established precedents for the IRP to fall back upon. The IRP had to stay firm and assertive all within the ambit of the IBC but not become authoritative. He took charge of the affairs without assuming the status of a big boss. It was this foundational approach adopted by Anuj Jain that helped him steer through many crises.

6
A Staggering Debt

If you owe your bank a hundred pounds, you have a problem. But if you owe a million, it has.

~ John Maynard Keynes

A robust process involving the submission and consideration of claims is the epicentre of an insolvency process. In fact, there is no issue more important to the individual creditor than the establishment of its claim in an insolvency or liquidation proceeding. Admission or rejection of a claim crystallizes the liability of the corporate debtor towards the creditor and the security interest, if any, held by the creditor in the debtor's assets. It is necessary for determining the eventual distribution in a resolution plan or liquidation. It also settles if the creditor can vote in the proceedings as also the value of the vote. If claim made by a financial creditor is admitted, it gets a seat and vote in the CoC. An operational creditor gets neither of the two unless such debt constitutes 10 per cent or more of the total aggregate debt of the corporate debtor in which case such creditor gets a seat in the CoC but without a vote.

The process of receipt and collation of claims plays a pivotal role in ascertaining the overall financial position, helps determine the liabilities and value of a corporate debtor, provides a participatory opportunity to the creditors, and prevents extinguishing claims without due consideration. It also assists the CoC and the prospective resolution applicant in ascribing fair value to the corporate debtor.

The IBC and CIRP Regulations provide a comprehensive framework for submission, verification and admission of claims, and the consequences of failure of submission or verification of a claim. A creditor wishing to be a part of the insolvency procedure of a corporate debtor is required to submit a claim. Any creditor including the government and statutory bodies can also file claim under the IBC.

The IBC incorporates a broad definition of claims, including determinable and indeterminable rights, which are not limited to mere monetary obligations of the corporate debtor. It is a right to payment and right to remedy. The right to payment underlines the claim. If there is no right to receive payment, no claim exists, whether or not such right is reduced to judgment, fixed, disputed, undisputed, legal, equitable, secured or unsecured.[8] As a general principle, claim can only be submitted in respect of debt incurred prior to insolvency commencement date. At the time when JIL was put into insolvency, the meaning and scope of claim was yet to receive clarity, as was the meaning of creditor.

A staggering 47,891 claims were received in the first few weeks of the public announcements made by JIL's IRP in the newspapers on 12 August 2017 and 14 August 2017, inviting claims from JIL's creditors. Out of these, 12,640 claims were received by post or delivered in person in Anuj Jain's office in Gurgaon; another 1,934 claims were received in JIL's office in Noida; and 33,317 claims were received by email. In many cases, the same claim was

8 The IBC, S. 3(6)

submitted through multiple modes resulting in duplication. All were accompanied by voluminous documents as proof of claim. The claims received were primarily from homebuyers, fixed deposit holders, banks, statutory authorities like the YEIDA and Income Tax Department, and other creditors or persons claiming to be creditors. The claims received also included those submitted by many creditors of JAL since the market perceived JIL and JAL as two sides of the same coin.

It was impossible to complete verification of such a large number of claims in the prescribed time of seven days. It was estimated that the reconciliation process of claims would take at least three to four months to complete. Obviously, while drafting the CIRP Regulations in 2016, IBBI had not made specific provisions to deal with insolvency resolution process of companies which may have a very large number of creditors because of the nature of its business. The IRP decided to prioritize verification of claims of financial creditors so that the CoC could be constituted in time, and insolvency process could progress. The IRP kept the IBBI informed of this practical challenge so that he was not accused of breaching the timeline.

II

What constitutes verification of claim lacked clarity in the early days of the IBC's implementation. In *Swiss Ribbons*,[9] the Supreme Court held that the RP has the duty to receive and collate all the claims submitted by creditor – she does not have quasi-judicial power but only administrative power. Even when she exercises discretion in verifying claims, it is only in an administrative capacity. This means that she cannot decide to reject the submitted claims.

---

9 *Swiss Ribbons Pvt. Ltd v. Union of India*, 2019 (4) SCC 17

Relying on *Swiss Ribbons*, the NCLAT has held that since the RP does not have any quasi-judicial power, she would not have the jurisdiction to decide or adjudicate upon the claim submitted by a creditor. R.14 of the CIRP Regulations grants the RP power to 'make the best estimate' of the claim if the amount claimed by a creditor is imprecise due to contingencies. It can be stated that the RP has the jurisdiction to estimate the value of a disputed claim, which could be reviewed by the NCLT; but in practice, the existence of such jurisdiction has been consistently denied by the courts. The IBC grants the NCLT the power to entertain claims made by or against the corporate debtor. However, there are limitations to the NCLT's powers and jurisdiction on the kinds of disputes it can adjudicate.

Given the magnitude of claims, the IRP constituted two separate teams for verification of claims. The team in charge of verifying claims of banks and financial institutions reconciled the balances with the contractual terms, especially with respect to security, interest and penal interest, if any. A participative approach was followed in a series of meetings with banks to reconcile and come to an agreement regarding the claim amounts, thereby minimizing the risk of litigation in the future.

The second team handled the more complex task of the verification of claims of homebuyers and retail fixed deposit holders. It was humanly not possible for a couple of members to verify all claims and there were no technological solutions available in the market. The IRP decided to train customer care representatives of JIL, along with data entry operators, to convert all the claim information into unique electronic records. Separately, the information and technology team of JIL together with external specialists hired by the IRP wrote special programmes and codes to extract detailed financial information for 20,000-plus homebuyers from the database. Thereafter, the claim data was matched with information extracted from the database. The cases of differences were identified and narrowed down often in discussion with the homebuyer. In some cases, the claim verification exercise helped in identifying genuine mistakes in posting payments to correct account. As per JIL's KMP, such a massive reconciliation exercise had never been undertaken in the past.

The homebuyers' claim verification exercise took a team of eighteen to twenty dedicated people over three to four months to complete. The updated claim list was displayed on the website of JIL as proof of claim admission as it was not possible to communicate individually to nearly 20,000 homebuyers.

After verification of the total claims aggregating to Rs 33,876 crore (US$ 4,071 million) received by the IRP and his team, the claims of Rs 23,083 crore (US$ 2,781 million) were admitted by him. The claims were also received from 860 out of 7,451 fixed deposit holders. These deposits were raised by JIL for a fixed period but were required to be repaid in full as the scheme inviting deposits was found to be faulty. There was a liability of about Rs 130 crore (US$ 15.66 million) in JIL's books towards fixed deposit holders but their complete details like their addresses, contact numbers, even full names, were not available. Given the cash crunch, JIL had not been able to repay the deposit holders. The Allahabad bench of NCLT, acting in jurisdiction under the Companies Act, 2013, was monitoring the repayment.

As per the IBC, a fixed deposit holder is a financial creditor. After verification, the IRP admitted fixed deposit holders' claims aggregating to Rs 29 crore (US$ 3.49 million). This number kept fluctuating as more claims kept coming in. Some fixed deposit holders were facing hardships. They desperately needed their money back to meet medical expense, or to meet other costs like wedding of a child, etc. Their money was returned during the process with the consent of the CoC.

The team was inundated with a mammoth number of claims that were received from homebuyers. Their verification process was going to take a long time, and their number only kept increasing. The homebuyers were not then treated as financial creditors under the IBC. However, on verification of records, the IRP found that as on insolvency commencement date, JIL had collected Rs 13,569 crore (US$ 1,635 million) from homebuyers as advance payments towards sale of flats. The outstanding advance included Rs 74 crore (US$ 8.92 million) to be refunded to customers towards cancelled units. In fact, the homebuyers kept filing claims even after Suraksha's resolution plan was approved by the NCLT in March 2023.

Based on legal advice, the IRP decided not to reject any claim for the reason that it was submitted in an incorrect form or after the cut-off date or without complete information. He was also informed by the author that the cut-off date in the CIRP Regulations is directory, not mandatory, and that it will not be proper to disregard any claim for lack of complete information. It was decided to prefer substance over form. The IRP issued a press release on 18 August 2017 to announce his decision:

> A corporate insolvency resolution process (CIRP) has been initiated in respect of Jaypee Infratech Limited (the Company) by an order dated 9 August 2017 passed by the Hon'ble National Company Law Tribunal (NCLT), Allahabad under the Insolvency and Bankruptcy Code, 2016 (IBC). A copy of NCLT order can be found on the Company's website.
>
> By the same order, the Hon'ble NCLT has appointed me as the insolvency Resolution Professional (IRP). In accordance with the provisions of the IBC, on commencement of the CIRP, the powers of the Board of Directors of the Company stand suspended and shall be exercised by me. The management of the affairs of the Company also vests with me.
>
> There are speculative news articles appearing in various media reports which are attributed to the IRP, Jaypee Infratech Ltd. and their representatives suggesting

refund can be made to certain categories of flat buyers/ projects.

The IRP has made no statement of commitment to any authorities or media representative suggesting that refund can be made to certain categories of flat buyers/projects. The flat buyers and other stakeholders are therefore advised not to rely on any media report including any statement attributed to me. They are further advised to file claim by 24th August 2017 in terms of public announcement. Clarifications and answers to Frequently Asked Questions (FAQs) are available on the website of the company (http://jaypeeinfratech.com). By FAQs, it has already been clarified that that no claim will be disqualified by IRP due to filing of incorrect Form or incomplete information. Any information in support of claim can be provided even after the deadline of 24 August 2017 has passed but before a Resolution Plan is filed with Committee of Creditors (CoC).

The IRP needs approval of the CoC before undertaking any significant decision.

I will continue to update the status of CIRP regularly on the Company website and communicate with stakeholders from time to time.

For Jaypee Infratech Limited

Anuj Jain

Interim Resolution Professional

The position taken by the IRP in the press release of 18 August 2017 was frowned upon by some, including a few members of the CoC, as being inconsistent with the CIRP Regulations. But the IRP acted on the advice received from the author that no claim can be rejected based on the mere technicality of having been filed in an incorrect form. The duty of the IRP under the IBC is to verify the claims received from the financial records of JIL. Even the timeline provided in public announcement and the CIRP Regulations are directory. It would be improper to reject a claim received on a reasonable date, before the deadline for submission of resolution plan by the prospective resolution applicants expires. Such deadline is necessary so that the prospective resolution applicant has the time and opportunity to consider the claim and provide a treatment in the plan. This stance taken by the IRP was, however, hailed by the homebuyers.

IBBI (Insolvency Resolution Process for Corporate Persons) (Third Amendment) Regulations 2018

A few months later, the IBBI amended the CIRP Regulations to provide that claims which are not submitted within the deadline stipulated in the public announcement may be filed by the creditor within ninety days from date of commencement of insolvency.[10]

A few years later, the understanding of the IRP and the author on the intent of the IBC in this respect was affirmed by the Supreme Court in an unrelated case. In *Rainbow Papers Limited*,[11] and later, in *Prabhjit Singh Soni*,[12] the Court held that the claim has to be verified by the RP on the basis of financial records; it cannot be disregarded merely because it has been filed in a wrong form. Despite that, unfortunately, confusion persists on this issue despite the intent of the law being clear. The issue is riddled by a few other conflicting decisions – some holding that

---

10 The CIRP Regulations, R. 12(1); IBBI (Insolvency Resolution Process for Corporate Persons) (Third Amendment) Regulations 2018, w.e.f. 3 July 2018

11 *State Tax Officer (1) v. Rainbow Papers Ltd.*, 2022 SCC OnLine SC 1162

12 *Greater Noida Industrial Development Authority v. Prabhjit Singh Soni & Anr.*, 2024 SCC OnLine SC 122

homebuyers can submit their claims until the time the CoC has approved the resolution plan, others stating that if the software maintained by the corporate debtor shows a homebuyer as an allottee, the resolution plan must deal with such allottee. No claim can be ruled out for consideration by the RP or resolution applicant merely for the reason that no formal submission of such claim was made. As long as the debt of that person reflects in the account books or other records of the debtor, the RP is obliged to take it into consideration and, to the extent it is undisputed, include it in the list of creditors and claims. If it is not certain, an appropriate disclosure should be made in the information memorandum provided to prospective resolution applicants so that they include, in the treatment, the purpose to the various claims submitted or otherwise. In fact, at the tail end of the JIL's insolvency process, this very issue surfaced with respect to a significant claim that had not been submitted – but more on that later.

This and the many soft law approaches adopted by the IRP and the author in the first forty-eight hours of JIL's insolvency are classic examples of how best practices can fill the lacunae that come forth when laws are implemented. Best practices serve as the most useful soft law method to address social, economic, and legal challenges by providing exemplary models for future action. They are the activities that have been shown, over time, to be the most effective and valuable. Many best practices followed by the IRP in JIL's case helped in chartering the course of insolvency process despite the grey areas encountered in the IBC in its nascent days; some were even incorporated in the IBC or the CIRP Regulations, as discussed later in the book, or endorsed jurisprudentially.

Banks and financial institutions submitted a claim of Rs 9,907.70 crore (US$ 1,194 million), out of which an amount of Rs 9,895 crore (US$ 1,192 million) was admitted after verification (See Table 1). This number later underwent minor changes.

Table 1: Details of Claims by Financial Creditors

Claims filed by financials creditors		Claims filed INR Crore	Claims admitted INR Crore
IDBI Bank Limited	Common loan agreement	4,334.10	4,334.10
India Infrastructure Finance Company Limited	Common loan agreement	1,034.50	1,034.50
Life Insurance Corporation of India	Common loan agreement	757.1	757.1
Corporation Bank	Common loan agreement	704.2	704.2
State Bank of Patiala **	Common loan agreement	429.2	429.2
Syndicate bank	Common loan agreement	390.1	390.1
Bank of Maharashtra	Common loan agreement	403.2	398
ICICI Bank Limited	Common loan agreement	304.1	304.1
Union Bank of India	Common loan agreement	338.5	334.8
State Bank of Hyderabad **	Common loan agreement	326.8	326.8
IFCI Limited	Common loan agreement	280.4	280.4
The Jammu & Kashmir Bank Limited	Common loan agreement	244.3	244.3
Axis Bank Limited	Non-Convertible debentures	218	218
Yes Bank Limited	Corporate Guarantee	112.4	112.4
SREI Equipment Finance Limited	Equipment Finance	30.8	27
Total		**9,907.70**	**9,895.00**

Claims of Rs 6,111 crore (US$ 736 million) were received from operational creditors. The Income Tax Department also filed a claim for Rs 3,334.3 crore (US$ 402 million). Only a part of these claims was admitted by the IRP after verification.

III

Satisfying creditors in respect of their claims is amongst the most challenging tasks of the RP, and perhaps the most testing of his skills as a lawyer. The IBC gives jurisdiction to the NCLT to adjudicate upon decisions of the IRP and the RP concerning the admission of claims, if brought before it. Many creditors, whose claims are not admitted by the RP or admitted only partly, challenge the decision before the NCLT. Some of this litigation goes to the NCLAT and from there to the Supreme Court, delaying the closure of insolvency process.

In this case, claims from the homebuyers kept coming in, and the IRP Anuj Jain's decision in respect of some was also challenged before the NCLT, but none of it obstructed or delayed the process. Their claims were considered with empathy by the IRP. The CoC did not show any rigidity in considering the legitimate claims of homebuyers even if filed after time. Everyone recognized that unlike commercial players like banks, homebuyers' claims had to be approached differently. JIL was a unique case where homebuyers' claims were both increasing and decreasing. The overall claim amount increased as new claims were filed each month but reduced as a result of successful settlement of claim on completion and registration of the promised housing unit.

IV

Long and costly litigation with a few creditors and the promoters of JIL delayed the conclusion of JIL's insolvency. Some of it requires a very brief mention here, although they are discussed in detail later in the book.

Yamuna Expressway Industrial Development Authority

In response to the public announcement, YEIDA submitted a claim of Rs 6,111 crore (US$ 736 million) against JIL mainly for additional farmers' compensation and as external development charges. After verification, the IRP admitted part of the claim of Rs 461 crore (US$ 55.54 million) towards external development charges and pending civil works on the toll road. The claim for the remaining external development charges was rejected as it was found by the IRP to be not payable by JIL. The claim of Rs 1,689 crore (US$ 203 million) made by YEIDA towards additional farmers' compensation was not admitted as the dispute over its payment was sub judice – subject matter of an arbitration – which was later decided in favour of JIL.

Arbitration proceedings with YEIDA were initiated and completed during the insolvency process when JIL was under the control of the IRP. The arbitral tribunal (with a majority of 2:1) held that payment of additional farmers' compensation was not the liability of JIL. An appeal against the award made by the arbitral tribunal was pending. YEIDA did not challenge the decision of the IRP in any manner. The final outcome of the dispute over claim towards additional farmer compensation is discussed in Chapter 22.

Income Tax Dues

The tax department submitted an aggregate claim of Rs 3,334.3 crore (US$ 402 million) based on tax demands for two financial years. The IRP did not admit the claim as the tax demand for the year 2010–11 had already been set aside by the ITAT and appeal against the demand for 2012–13 was pending before the ITAT. The decision was not challenged by the tax department before the NCLT. However, this issue was to later resurface as an interesting turn threatening the very revival of JIL as discussed in detail in Chapter 22.

Claims by the Axis Bank Limited and the ICICI Bank Limited[13]

The rejection by the IRP of claims submitted by the ICICI Bank and Axis Bank also led to prolonged litigation. These banks were the lenders of JAL. JIL had mortgaged some of its land parcels with

13 *Jaypee Kensington Boulevard Apartments Welfare Association v. NBCC (India) Ltd*, (2022) 1 SCC 401

the banks to secure the debt availed by JAL. They submitted claims with the IRP claiming to be a financial creditor of JIL on the basis of the mortgage created by JIL to secure the debt availed by JAL. Admission of their claim would have given both the banks a seat and vote in the CoC of JIL, thus adding to their bargaining power and payment from the resolution plan approved by the CoC.

After considering legal advice, the IRP rejected the claim of the banks on the ground that a mortgage of JIL's assets to the banks to secure JAL's debt does not make them a financial creditor of JIL. The two banks challenged the rejection of their claim before the NCLT. Agreeing with the IRP's stand, the NCLT dismissed both the applications in May 2018. The NCLT order was eventually upheld by the Supreme Court in *Anuj Jain*,[14] which decided a number of other important questions of law arising from the rejection of the claim of these banks by the IRP. While this issue did not cause any delay in the resolution, it did add to the cost of the process.

YES Bank

The YES Bank submitted a claim of Rs 112.4 crore (US$ 13.54 million) on the basis of its invocation of a corporate guarantee provided by JIL to secure the debt availed by its subsidiary, Jaypee Healthcare Limited, from the YES Bank. The corporate guarantee was invoked after the moratorium had set in. Although the IRP accepted the claim provisionally, he later rejected it based on the author's advice that invocation of guarantee by YES Bank after moratorium had set is not a lawful invocation; although a claim based on uninvoked guarantee is admissible, being a future liability, if the principal borrower, whose debt is secured by guarantee, has defaulted.

---

14 *Anuj Jain (RP) v. Axis Bank Limited & Ors,* (2022) 8 SCC 401

Housing Finance Companies

Many housing finance companies provided loans to homebuyers of JIL. Some of these companies submitted their claims for debt arising from these loans. The IRP did not entertain these claims as the loans were not availed by JIL, nor was the repayment of the debt JIL's liability. Although this issue did not escalate in JIL's case, the interest of housing finance companies continues to stay alive in many insolvency cases of real estate companies. Orders favourable to housing finance companies have been passed in some cases while in others the matter remains pending before the NCLAT at the time the book was written.

Jaiprakash Associates Limited

JAL also submitted a claim of Rs 261.80 crore (US$ 31.54 million) for various amounts including running bills of construction and repayments of amounts under bank guarantees furnished by JAL, which were invoked by JIL's lenders.

V

Anyone who considers themselves to be a creditor of a corporate debtor and believes they have a claim, have a right to submit a claim. If not admitted by the RP, such person also has the right to seek remedy provided in the IBC, which allows any aggrieved person to approach the NCLT. A person cannot be faulted for pursuing a lawful remedy even if it incurs cost or causes delay unless the litigation is frivolous or malicious.

The decision of the IRP in respect of claims submitted by the YEIDA, tax department, Axis Bank, ICICI Bank, JAL and others, had huge financial implications. The IRP's decision on the claims, and their treatment by NBCC and Suraksha in their resolution plans raised complex questions of law, which were required to be tested in court. Ironically, the litigation arising from the rejection of claims by the IRP or their treatment in resolution plans by NBCC and Suraksha led to settlement of many foundational principles of law in relation to the IBC and its various provisions by the Supreme Court. The importance of this jurisprudential contribution cannot be undermined.

7

An Impossible Meeting

If you had to identify, in one word, the reason why the human race has not achieved, and never will achieve, its full potential, that word would be 'meetings'.

~ Dave Barry

Soon after the commencement of the insolvency process, IRP Anuj Jain faced another uphill task; this time in respect of yet another important matter – convening the first meeting of the CoC. As stated earlier, the IBC prescribes that after the verification of claims received from creditors, the IRP must constitute a CoC comprising all the unrelated financial creditors of the corporate debtor. The first meeting of the CoC has to be convened within seven days from submission of a report of its constitution to the NCLT. The CoC of JIL constituted by the IRP comprised 824 members, fifteen of those being JIL's lending banks and 809 its fixed deposit holders.

Till then everybody was talking about how the insolvency proceeding against JIL had left homebuyers of its under-construction houses in the lurch. But they were not the only group of retail investors affected by the insolvency proceedings. There were also those who had invested in fixed deposits of JIL.

Companies are allowed to raise investments by inviting fixed deposits, subject to certain conditions, from the general public. Like fixed deposits in banks, they too offer a predetermined interest rate. However, their interest rates are usually 2–3 per cent higher than those of banks. Despite paying a higher interest rate, for companies it is still cheaper compared to raising money from financial institutions. And while companies do offer better interest than banks, deposits with them also come with higher risks. Although these depositors are financial creditors under the IBC, they are unsecured creditors. Thus, if the company is liquidated, they will get their money only after the claims of creditors, whose precedence is higher than theirs, are satisfied.

A few years earlier, JIL had come out with a scheme to raise funds by inviting people to make fixed deposits and offered interest on the deposit. A large number of people made deposits aggregating more than Rs 131 crore (US$ 15.78 million). These were unsecured deposits ranking below banks and financial institutions having a secured debt. After JIL went into financial trouble and couldn't repay the deposits or interest, many fixed deposit holders approached the courts. JIL was granted time till 5 September 2017 to return the money. The refund by JIL was being overseen by the NCLT in a separate proceeding against JIL and JAL. These proceedings were outside of the IBC.

At the time JIL's insolvency started, there were 7,451 persons holding fixed deposits whose money had yet to be refunded. In response to the public announcement, 860 fixed deposit holders submitted their claim within the deadline. More were expected to come forward in time as the depositors got to know of the insolvency process. Some fixed deposit holders had made claim of amounts as small as Rs 25,000 (US$ 300). The admitted claim of fixed deposit holders who submitted their claim before the cut-off date was Rs 29.3 crore (US$ 3.53 million). However, it was far less in amount at the time when the CoC was constituted by the IRP.

II

These 860 fixed deposit holders comprised 99.8 per cent of the CoC members in number, but ironically, their aggregate debt then admitted was only Rs 21 crore (US$ 2.53 million), less than 2 per cent in value of total debt of the other 98 per cent members of CoC – the fifteen banks and financial institutions which held a total debt of Rs 9,895 crore (US$ 1,192 million). This was subsequently revised to fourteen banks and financial institutions, admitting a claim of Rs 9,783 crore (US$ 1,179 million). As stated, the number of fixed deposit holders in the CoC was expected to go up in the future. As and when a claim received from a financial creditor was admitted, the IBC requires such creditor to be included in the CoC.

The CoC was constituted on 31 August 2017 and its first meeting convened on 8 September 2017.

III

The CIRP Regulations require every member of the CoC to be invited to the meeting, and notice of the meeting with its agenda is to be delivered ahead to them at their postal or email address, but in any event served by email. A member can attend the meeting in person or through an authorized representative, but such authorization is required to be provided to the IRP/RP in advance. The CIRP Regulations provided an option to the CoC members to participate through videoconferencing or other audio and video connection. The RP is required to make arrangement for uninterrupted and clear audio and video connection and ensure that participants attending virtually are able to hear and see, if applicable, other participants clearly. The RP is also required to safeguard the integrity of the meeting by ensuring security and identification procedures.[1]

The particulars of deposit holders available in JIL's records were scanty. It was impossible to serve notice of the CoC meeting and its agenda to hundreds of depositors living in different parts of the country, with most not having provided complete postal or email address. Serving them notice by email was nearly impossible. Besides, inviting such large number of depositors to the meeting posed many challenges. An auditorium or a stadium was needed to hold a meeting to accommodate the number. Identifying such large number of people and controlling them during the discussions would have been more challenging. Many critical decisions were required to be taken by the CoC. Holding an orderly meeting was critical for the outcomes that would lead to the progress of the case. Moreover, the deposit holders were mainly concerned with the refund of their money; deliberations around continuation of business, JIL's construction and resolution of insolvency would be of no interest to them.

The presence of such large number would have also required adequate security arrangements. On the other hand, their participation through audio or videoconferencing, assuming their email addresses were available, was not commercially justified. Videoconferencing applications such as Zoom, Microsoft Teams, Google Meet had not been developed in those days. The cost of hiring services of a vendor to organize audio or videoconference meetings would have been disproportionate to the small percentage of debt held by the large number of deposit holders. There was another practical problem. Most deposit holders wouldn't have had the Internet speed or bandwidth needed for the video calls. Many wouldn't even have had access to it at all.

1 The CIRP Regulations, R. 19 to R. 24

Moreover, folks from media were keenly interested in JIL's process. It would have been impossible to keep the discussion of the meeting confidential, as is intended under the IBC, with such a large number of participants attending virtually.

There was then no provision in the IBC to allow a large number of similar creditors to form a class of their own, like deposit holders, and authorize a person to represent them in the CoC.

After giving the matter a careful consideration, it was decided by the IRP, on the author's advice, to dispense with individual notice of meeting to deposit holders and seek their representation through an authorized representative. Even though there was no provision in the IBC to enable participation of a class of creditors and allowing them to vote in the CoC through a representative, there was also no provision prohibiting their participation through a representative. It was hoped that a representative would be appointed by the NCLT.

IV

On 30 August 2017, an application was filed in the NCLT to apprise it of the practical problems in serving notice of the CoC meeting to hundreds of fixed deposit holders. The NCLT was requested to exempt the IRP from serving notice to them and instead appoint a licensed insolvency professional to represent them in the CoC meeting. Examples of many jurisdictions which allow creditors in a class to nominate a representation to attend creditors' meetings on their behalf were provided to the NCLT. Appreciating the practical difficulties and procedural hardships in convening a meeting with hundreds of members of the CoC, the NCLT requested the Ministry of Corporate Affairs and the IBBI to submit their response to the issue raised by the IRP before a decision could be taken.

The IBBI's senior lawyer Swarupama Chaturvedi opposed IRP's request. She argued that provisions of the IBC give right to each individual financial creditor to be invited to the CoC meeting and attend it, that serving notice on each financial creditor was a requirement of law, and that there was no provision in the IBC to allow creditors like fixed deposit holders to attend meetings through a representative. The government was fully mindful of the limitations expressed by the IRP. However, understandably, in the NCLT, it had to officially defend the provisions of the IBC and the procedure laid in its regulations in respect of holding the CoC meetings.

Meanwhile, the NCLT judicial member H.P. Chaturvedi showed pragmatism and foresight. On 1 September 2017, the NCLT passed an order permitting the IRP to convene meeting of the CoC by dispensing the serving of notice on fixed deposit holders. The judicial member directed the Ministry of Corporate Affairs and the IBBI to nominate a senior officer each to attend the CoC meetings to safeguard the interest of fixed deposit holders. The IRP had requested for the appointment of an insolvency professional as representative of deposit holders and not government officials. With the IBBI being the regulator, directing it to represent a set of creditors in the CoC should have been avoided. Nevertheless, the solution to a major problem had been found.

But before the first CoC meeting could be held, the Supreme Court stayed JIL's insolvency proceedings. The first meeting of the CoC was eventually held on 19 September 2017 after the stay was lifted by the Supreme Court. The NCLT order allowed the CoC meetings to be held in an orderly manner with fixed deposit holders participating through an NCLT-appointed representative.

In the meantime, the NCLT directed the IRP to continue to make efforts to reach out to fixed deposit holders. There was no way the CIRP Regulations could be complied by the IRP in the absence of availability of postal and email addresses of fixed deposit holders. The IRP took out a notice in newspapers, calling upon deposit holders to furnish their addresses. However, only a few responses were received.

V

The problem faced by JIL's IRP on account of a large number of financial creditors was later taken up in the meeting of Insolvency Law Committee (ILC) held on 26 March 2018. The ILC is a standing committee constituted by the government to advise on issues arising under the IBC. In its report, the ILC noted that companies may have a large number of creditors to whom certain debts may be owed, for instance, debenture holders or fixed deposit holders. Such creditors being financial creditors are entitled to attend and vote at the meetings of the CoC as per the current provisions of the IBC.

In practice, the number of such creditors may be huge in case of large companies, and it may be inefficient, unmanageable, and expensive to hold meetings of the CoC with all such creditors present. Decision making in meetings with a large number of the CoC members poses significant logistical challenges. Notices must be issued to a huge number of persons and arrangement made for a venue which can accommodate them, which may be a challenge and drain resources of the corporate debtor. Moreover, too large a forum with many participants of varying interests could significantly jeopardize constructive discussion and decision-making ability of the CoC in such meetings.

Also, if the CoC comprises a large number of creditors, the likelihood of abstinence by individual financial creditors could be very high, leading to disruption in decision making. This, the ILC stated, defeats the very objective of creditor participation as envisaged under the IBC. The ILC recommended that it may be prudent to mandate a representative to act and vote on behalf of such classes of creditors that exceed a certain high number, as was done in JIL's case through the NCLT order.

Insolvency and Bankruptcy Code (Second Amendment), 2018

The meeting led to the second amendment in the IBC made by way of an Ordinance issued on 6 June 2018. While recognizing the homebuyer as a financial creditor, the government also introduced in the IBC a comprehensive framework for the formation of a class of creditors and their representation in the CoC meetings by an authorized representative – an insolvency professional selected by the class and appointed by the NCLT. Subsection 6A was inserted in S. 21 of the IBC for representation of financial creditors in a class, and S. 25A was introduced for appointment of an authorized representative to represent and vote for the class in the CoC. Duties and functions of the authorized representative were also prescribed.

The Insolvency and Bankruptcy Board of India (Insolvency Resolution Process for Corporate Persons) (Third Amendment) Regulations, 2018

The CIRP Regulations were also amended to provide that ten or more financial creditors shall comprise a class of creditors and require appointment of an authorized representative to represent in the CoC.[2] Where such a class is formed, the RP shall

2 The Insolvency and Bankruptcy Board of India (Insolvency Resolution Process for Corporate Persons) (Third Amendment) Regulations, 2018, No. IBBI/2018-19/GN/REG031 dated 3 July 2018; Insolvency and Bankruptcy Board of India (Insolvency Resolution Process for Corporate Persons) Second Amendment Regulations, 2023, w.e.f. 18 September 2023

offer to it a choice of three insolvency professionals to select as its authorized representative. The insolvency professional, who is the choice of the highest number of creditors in the class, will get appointed as the authorized representative of the creditors of the respective class. The authorized representative has to collect voting instructions from the respective class of creditors, attend the meetings of the CoC and cast vote on behalf of the said class in accordance with the instructions he receives from the creditors. The authorized representative is entitled to receive a fixed fee under the CIRP Regulations. The important duties of the authorized representative include:

- reviewing the contents of minutes prepared by the RP to ensure its correctness and completeness;
- assisting creditors in evaluating resolution plan;
- regularly updating the creditors in a class on the progress of the insolvency process;
- and assisting in modifications of the resolution plan on behalf of the class of creditors represented by her.

A procedure for replacement of the authorized representative has also been introduced.

This is yet another significant contribution of JIL's insolvency in the evolution of the IBC. The innovative solution of appointing an authorized representative of deposit holders to overcome the difficulty faced in holding JIL's CoC meeting was yet another example of how best practices can step in to plug the gap between the law on paper and the law in action. The role and duties of authorized representative are also provided in law. This not only facilitated the smooth conduct of insolvency process of JIL but also of other real estate companies undergoing insolvency process.

VI

Later, insolvency professional Anju Agarwal was appointed as authorized representative for fixed deposit holders. The number of fixed deposit holders in class increased with more claims received over the period of insolvency process. However, their voting share shrunk to 0.01 per cent after homebuyers were classified as financial creditors and joined the CoC.

8

Chitra Sharma Goes to Court

You don't know a woman until you've met her in court.

~ Norman Mailer

Exactly twenty-seven days after JIL's insolvency commenced, a bench of the Supreme Court comprising then Chief Justice Dipak Misra, Justice D.Y. Chandrachud (Chief Justice during the time the book was being written) and Justice A.M. Khanwilkar, by an order passed on 4 September 2017, stayed the NCLT's order directing commencement of JIL's insolvency proceedings. The stay order was passed on a petition by Chitra Sharma, a former airhostess and a homebuyer of JIL, questioning the constitutional validity of the provisions of the IBC. Many other homebuyers joined her, prominent among them Jaypee Aman Owners Welfare Association led by Colonel S.K. Nagarath.

The principal grievance expressed by homebuyers was that the IBC did not provide them any role or allow their participation in the insolvency process even though they were JIL's key stakeholders. While the banks had been classified as financial creditors of JIL, which made them eligible to become members of the CoC and make all decisions, homebuyers had been completely left out despite their investment being in no manner less significant than that of the financial institutions. The IBC was discriminatory, they contended. Homebuyers claimed the status of financial creditor and demanded a level playing field under the IBC.

The CoC plays a pivotal role in providing a creditor greater control over the amount and method of payment of its prepetition claim and greater control over the direction of the corporate debtor's business. Depending on the circumstances of the case, creditors who play an active role in insolvency can make a significant difference to affect best returns for them. The Supreme Court prima facie agreed with homebuyers and decided to examine the constitutional validity of the IBC. The 20,000 homebuyers who found it unacceptable to have been excluded from the CoC were jubilant.

II

The stay of the NCLT's order had many unintended consequences. It reverted the control of JIL to its promoters, who had lost the trust of both the homebuyers and lenders. It ended the moratorium under the IBC which meant any creditor could start or continue legal action against JIL. This exposed JIL's assets to multiple proceedings in different forums. The homebuyers were bearing the brunt of it as neither the insolvency process could progress nor the construction.

Acting swiftly, the IDBI Bank moved an application before the Supreme Court requesting lifting of the stay. The bank apprised the Court of the effects of staying the NCLT order. Although the homebuyers did not resist the lifting of the stay, they insisted that there should be a representative for the homebuyers on the CoC or that the Court appoint someone on the CoC to espouse their interests.

Taking note of the bank's submissions, on 11 September 2017, the Supreme Court modified its earlier order and directed IRP Anuj Jain to once again take over JIL's management. The NCLT's moratorium order of 9 August 2017 was restored. Shekhar Naphade, a senior lawyer, along with Shubhangi Tuli, advocate on record, were appointed to participate in the CoC meetings to espouse the cause of the homebuyers and protect their interests.

III

Seven days later, three peculiar directions were passed by the Supreme Court while lifting the stay. First, the Court directed the IRP, Anuj Jain, to formulate an interim resolution plan with necessary provisions to protect the interests of homebuyers and submit that in the Court within forty-five days. The interim resolution plan, the order stated, shall make all necessary provisions to protect the interests of the homebuyers. This directive was a departure from the scheme of the IBC.

A resolution plan is the tailpiece of the reorganization proceedings. It is a proposal that aims to sort the problems that result in insolvency of the corporate debtor, while dealing with the claims of its creditors, in accordance with the terms laid down in it which should be consistent with the insolvency law. Simply put, it is a rehabilitation plan for a corporate debtor.

In the scheme of the IBC, resolution plans are invited by the RP from the market; it is not the responsibility of the IRP or the RP to prepare the plan. A person or entity who steps forward to submit the resolution plan becomes a prospective resolution applicant. It is provided all the necessary information about the corporate debtor so that it may prepare and submit the resolution plan. The RP only manages the process of the plan. He examines the plan received to ensure that it meets the standards laid down in the relevant provisions of the IBC. If thus satisfied, the plan is presented to the CoC. If there is more than one plan received and they comply with the conditions laid down under the IBC, all such plans are presented to the CoC. The ultimate decision to approve or reject a plan lies with the CoC. A sanctioned resolution plan is a manifestation of the judgement made by the CoC that reorganization based on the agreed plan will provide a better maximization of value than if the debtor were to be liquidated.

The Supreme Court's direction put Anuj Jain in a state of quandary. But on a careful reading of the direction, the author and the IRP deduced that the direction was, in fact, consistent with the IBC since the interim plan suggested by the Court denoted the plan to keep JIL afloat as a going concern (meaning, continue construction of housing projects) and take other requisite steps as part of the insolvency resolution process. The Court initiated this step to protect the interests of thousands of homebuyers.

The IRP prepared and submitted to the Supreme Court an action plan to keep JIL as a going concern and the many other steps taken or to be taken as per the IBC. The interim plan also apprised the Court of the measures needed to accelerate construction where ongoing and resume where stalled. The following timelines were proposed for the resolution plan, keeping in mind the timeline of 180 days provided under the IBC (See Table 2):

Table 2: Timeline Proposed for the Resolution Plan

Steps	Description	Timeline
Step 1	Publish advertisement in leading business daily inviting expression of interest (EOI) for submission of resolution plan for JIL.	Day 0
Step 2	Last date for receipt of EOI from eligible resolution applicants.	Day 0 + 2 weeks
Step 3	Screening of EOIs and developing shortlist of eligible resolution applicants.	Day 0 + 3 weeks
Step 4	Discussion on shortlisted resolution applicants with COC.	Day 0 + 4 weeks
Step 5	Sharing of Information Memorandum with resolution applicants, subject to obtaining signed confidentiality undertaking.	Day 0 + 4 weeks
Step 6	Sharing of additional information, documents, site visits, meetings, clarifications, presentations, data room, etc.	Day 0 + 10 weeks
Step 7	Submission of resolution plans by resolution applicants.	Day 0 + 12 weeks

Steps	Description	Timeline
Step 8	Screening of resolution plans by RP and his team of advisors, final round of discussions with applicants, suggestions for improvement of plans and resubmission of revised plan to RP, if required.	Day 0 + 16 weeks
Step 9	Submission of all final plans to CoC and discussion with CoC on the resolution plans.	Day 0 + 17 weeks
Step 10	Resolution applicant to incorporate changes as suggested by CoC and resubmit the final plan for voting.	Day 0 + 19 weeks
Step 11	Final voting by CoC.	Day 0 + 20 weeks
Step 12	Submission of CoC-approved final resolution plan to NCLT for its approval.	Day 0 + 21 weeks
Step 13	Order of NCLT approving the final resolution plan.	[-]
Step 14	Implementation of the approved resolution plan.	Immediately on approval of final plan by NCLT

As regards the construction plan, the IRP informed the Supreme Court that JIL's erstwhile management had submitted a revised schedule of construction to Real Estate Regulatory Authority (RERA) in July 2017, just a month before insolvency process of JIL commenced. The schedule promised delivery of about 5,000 flats from October 2017 to March 2018.

To honour this commitment and scale up the ongoing construction activity to the desired level, about Rs 600 crore (US$ 72 million) were required. JIL did not have that kind of money. The amount collected from toll was not adequate to meet this cost. The IBC allowed an interim finance to be raised subject to approval of the CoC. The IRP informed the Court that he would explore the possibility. The Supreme Court took note of the action report, but no further direction was given to the IRP.

IV

The second direction issued by the Supreme Court ordered JAL to deposit Rs 2,000 crore (US$ 241 million) in Court. It put a restraint order on JAL to sell or transfer its assets in any manner, but if JAL required any assets or property to be sold for raising Rs 2,000 crore that could be done only after obtaining prior approval of the Court. It was further ordered that the directors and managing director of JIL and JAL, except the nominee directors of lending institutions, shall not leave the country without prior permission of the Court. The Court passed this direction taking note of the crucial background aspects and the fact that JIL was essentially an alter ego of JAL.

Thus, even while consciously noting that JAL was not a party to the insolvency proceedings, the Court directed that JAL shall deposit a sum of Rs 2,000 crore. Restraints were also put over the disposal of assets or property of JAL and over the movement of the directors and managing directors of JIL or JAL away from the country.[1] This was again an instance of the Supreme Court lifting the corporate veil and holding JAL, a separate listed company, responsible for the plight of homebuyers.

Later, JAL requested the Court to allow it to transfer the rights under the concession agreement in respect of the Yamuna Expressway to raise Rs 2,000 crore. JAL's request was opposed by the IRP, stating that the rights under the concession agreement belonged to JIL. JAL's request was turned down by the Court. JAL tried hard to wriggle out of the obligation to pay. The Court did not yield to JAL's requests; however, the time for depositing the amount was extended. Eventually, over the following months, JAL deposited, from time to time, an amount aggregating Rs 750 crore (US$ 90 million). The claim over this amount would end up becoming the subject of contentious litigation with JAL in the years to come.

V

In another set of directions, the Supreme Court mandated that it be found out which homebuyers wanted refund of the advance paid to JIL and which preferred the flats. Pawanshree Agarwal, a lawyer, was appointed as the amicus curiae, who was directed to open a web portal on which homebuyers could exercise their choice. JAL was ordered to provide all the details as required by the amicus curiae and also to meet the cost of this task. It turned out that 92 per cent homebuyers wanted flats and not refunds. The amicus curiae informed the Court that a sum of Rs 1,300 crore (US$ 157 million) was required if the remaining 8 per cent homebuyers were to be refunded only the principal amount of their investment.

---

1 As explained by the Supreme Court in *Jaypee Kensington* judgment

This exercise was alien to the IBC. While understandably, as explained by Justice Maheshwari in *Jaypee Kensington* later, this order was passed by the Supreme Court in the interest of homebuyers, it sent a confusing signal to the market about the fate of the IBC in general and of JIL's insolvency process in particular. The IBC required the operations of the insolvent debtor to be stabilized and the enterprise to continue as a going concern. For JIL it meant that the IRP would try to have the construction and delivery of flats continue till a resolution plan was approved by the NCLT. Ordinarily, the investor would decide on the resolution plan, which may or may not include an option for refund.

Another order passed by the Supreme Court which made matters more convoluted was the restraining order against collection of balance payments from homebuyers. The terms of allotment of flats provided for a construction-linked payment plan. As and when a threshold of construction was achieved, payment was demanded from flat owners. Homebuyers opposed such demand being made during the insolvency process. Taking note of homebuyers' objection, JIL was restrained from raising demands towards outstanding or future instalments in respect of those buyers who had chosen to get refund.

These directions, although a boost to homebuyers' morale, made it evident that the Supreme Court was going to micro-manage JIL's resolution process. Many investors who had started showing keen interest in taking over JIL through the IBC's process became doubtful about the fate of JIL's insolvency process. These directions had a deterring effect and the IRP had a tough time persuading the prospective resolution applicants to not lose faith and forgo their participation in the process.

VI

A few months later, on the IRP's request, the Court permitted him to submit the resolution plans received to the CoC for their consideration and approval. The Court gave the go-ahead subject to the condition that the plan approved not be implemented without the leave of the Supreme Court. Although the order paved for JIL's insolvency process to continue but not much progress could be made due to uncertainties based in homebuyers' lack of trust in the process, and the pendency of matter in the Supreme Court.

The promoters of JIL also continued to press upon the Court to give them an opportunity to complete the construction – they were in the best position to complete the task, they pleaded before the Court. The realty of the situation was that until the homebuyers were to feel consoled and granted effective, legal participation in the insolvency process, no progress in resolution plan process was going to be possible. The mood in the CoC was pessimistic.

During this period, the IRP focused on stabilizing the business and continuing the construction of flats using the proceeds generated from the toll on the Yamuna Expressway. He continued to perform his other functions and duties. The motto hereon was: hope for the best, prepare for the worst. The Supreme Court continued to monitor the progress of compliance of its directions until the case was closed, exactly a year later, on 9 August 2018.

During this period, the IRP took an exemplary step that was to create history. He filed an application in the NCLT to seek clawback of 858 acres of JIL's prime land which had been mortgaged by the erstwhile management to secure the debt of JAL. The filing of application and its outcome created a sensation in the market, as you will read further in later chapters.

VII

JAL suffered another jolt on 23 November 2017 when the government promulgated an Ordinance to insert S.29A in the IBC to provide a criteria for disqualification for submitting resolution plan in the insolvency process. The objective of this ineligibility criteria is to preclude persons who by their misconduct have contributed to the defaults of the corporate debtor from submitting resolution plan so that such persons do not regain control of the corporate debtor at the cost of the creditors during the resolution and the liquidation stage.

JIL's account had been classified as NPA by Life Insurance Corporation of India on 30 September 2015 and by some of its other lenders on 31 March 2016. As a result, JAL and its connected persons became ineligible to submit resolution plan for JIL.

9

The 758 Acres

Be sure you put your feet in the right place, then stand firm.

~ Abraham Lincoln

On 18 April 2018, Anuj Jain filed an application in the NCLT for cancellation of certain transactions carried out by JIL, JAL and several public and private sector banks. If allowed by the NCLT, the effect of the IRP's request would be retrieval of 858 acres of prime land mortgaged by JIL with these banks to secure the repayment of JAL's debt. While this would have given JIL its valuable asset back, banks would have lost substantial security taken by them to secure JAL's debt. The value of the land was estimated to be about Rs 5,000 crore (US$ 600 million) when mortgaged, which had gone up significantly by the time JIL's insolvency process commenced in 2017. It is far more today. As per the IBBI's newsletter[1] the estimated value of recovery in JIL is 83 per cent of total amount clawed back under the IBC at Rs 6,599 crore (US$ 795 million).

1 *The IBBI Newsletter*, January–March 2024. Last seen on 25 May 2024 at https://ibbi.gov.in/en/publication

The IRP's action sent shockwaves in the industry. This was the first case of avoidance of transactions at this scale under the IBC after its operationalization. No one had expected the IRP to take this extreme step. These were powerful banks, some of them also sitting in JIL's CoC, and held the influence to remove Anuj Jain as the IRP. Most such banks like the State Bank of India took the IRP's decision in stride, recognizing that he was only performing his duty. They decided to contest legally and not disrupt JIL's process or its CoC meetings. However, a few members, who had a small voting share in the CoC and were also lenders of JAL, turned hostile and made no effort whatsoever to hide their contempt for the IRP and the author, who they saw as the brain behind the IRP's move.

Eventually, the IRP's application succeeded, and the transactions were found illegal and set aside. JIL got back 758 out of 858 acres of land valued at thousands of crores. The final pursuit of application and its outcome will go down in IBC's history as one of the biggest gains made in any insolvency case during its insolvency process. This chapter recounts the story of Anuj Jain's courage and the disdainful conduct of a few members of the CoC, and what was perhaps the most contentious matter in the entire insolvency process of JIL.

II

It all started a few weeks after JIL's insolvency process commenced in August 2017. One of the main objectives of the IBC is to maximize the value of assets of the corporate debtor for the benefit of its stakeholders. The IBC casts a duty on the RP to preserve and protect the assets of the corporate debtor and take steps to claw back the property the erstwhile management and given up by indulging in questionable transactions. These dealings may also be challenged if the corporate debtor has given preference to a creditor over another. If the RP discovers any questionable transaction, she can make an application to the NCLT under appropriate provisions and seek necessary orders for their cancellation or compensation for any loss caused to their account to the corporate debtor or any of its creditor.

Under the IBC, these questionable transactions fall mainly under five broad heads: preferential, undervalued, extortionist, wrongful trading, and fraudulent trading or transaction. If the transaction took place during the year preceding the date of commencement of insolvency it is deemed a questionable transaction. If the transaction is made by corporate debtor with a related party, the period goes back to two years. In insolvency phraseology, this period is known as lookback period or relevant period/time, and these actions are referred to as clawback or avoidance actions.

Avoidance provisions are one of the key tools in an insolvency law to preserve the debtor's asset pool for the collective benefit of all stakeholders in the twilight period[2] and uphold the equality of the distribution of an insolvent debtor's assets among its creditors during the lookback period.

As stated, the IBC makes the RP duty-bound to file an application for avoidance of such transactions, if any.[3] As on date, the CIRP Regulations require the RP to form an opinion within seventy-five days of commencement of insolvency of the corporate debtor based on the criteria of questionable transactions during the

---

2 See 'Twilight Zone', Chapter 12, Part III, Sumant Batra, *Corporate Insolvency: Law and Practice* (2017)

3 The relevant parts of Section 25 read: 'Duties of resolution professional. – (1) It shall be the duty of the resolution professional to preserve and protect the assets of the corporate debtor, including the continued business operations of the corporate debtor.
(2) For the purposes of sub-section (1), the resolution professional shall undertake the following actions, namely:...
(j) ...file application for avoidance of transactions in accordance with Chapter III, if any;...'

lookback period. If of a prima facie opinion that any such transaction has been made, the RP is required to initiate an audit and determine definitely within 115 days from the insolvency commencement date if such transactions have been made. After such determination is made, she must apply to the NCLT for appropriate relief within 130 days from the insolvency commencement date. The RP is also duty bound to share a copy of the application made to the NCLT with the prospective resolution applicant so that it can consider and factor the impact of such transactions while submitting the resolution plan. The IBBI has also to be kept informed.[4] These regulations were introduced only on 27 March 2018 and did not exist at the time JIL's insolvency commenced.

III

It will be useful to explain briefly the main features concerning these questionable transactions for the benefit of readers not familiar with their characteristics.

Simply put, the IBC provides that a corporate debtor shall be deemed to have given a preference if two conditions are satisfied: there is a transfer of property (or an interest thereof) of the corporate debtor for the benefit of a creditor for or on account of an antecedent debt; and the transfer has the effect of putting such creditor in a more beneficial position than it would have been in the event of a distribution of assets being made in accordance with the priorities mentioned under S. 53 of the IBC. To know about these priorities, see Chapter 14. The IBC creates what is recognized in law as a legal fiction whereby preference is deemed to have been given if the stated requirements are satisfied. Preference should have been given during the lookback period prescribed under the IBC.

4 The CIRP Regulations, R. 35A

Even when the corporate debtor is deemed to have given preference during the lookback period, such deemed preference may not yet be an offending preference if it has been entered into during the ordinary course of business of the corporate debtor or transferee or results in acquisition of new value.[5] If found to be preferential, the NCLT has power to cancel the transaction and order the property or its value to be returned to the corporate debtor.[6]

A transaction can be considered as undervalued if the corporate debtor has given a gift to a person or has entered into a transaction with a person that involves the transfer of an asset for a consideration, the value of which is significantly less, and such transaction has not taken place in the ordinary course of business of the corporate debtor. The NCLT can appoint an independent expert to assess evidence relating to the value of the transactions.[7]

An extortionate credit transaction involves receipt of debt by the corporate debtor where the terms of such transaction requires exorbitant payments to be made by the corporate debtor. But, any debt extended by any person providing financial services under any law in force at the time is not to be regarded as extortionate credit transactions.[8]

There are two kinds of transactions under the IBC from which personal liabilities may arise for persons responsible for the business of the corporate debtor, including directors and officers: fraudulent, and wrongful transactions. This relates to transactions with intent

5 As per S. 43 of the IBC, 'new value' means money, or its worth in goods, services, or new credit, or a release by the transferee of property that was previously transferred to such transferee in a transaction that is neither void nor voidable by the liquidator or the RP under the IBC, including proceeds of such property, but does not include a financial debt or operational debt substituted for existing financial debt or operational debt.

6 The IBC, S. 43 and S. 44

7 The IBC, S. 45 to S. 48

8 The IBC, S. 50, S. 51

to defraud creditors of the corporate debtor or for any fraudulent purpose. Any person who is found to be responsible for transacting business for any fraudulent purpose or with intent to defraud creditors of the corporate debtor may be liable to pay compensation. Such persons include those that have knowledge of the fraud and its purpose, or of the intent behind the transaction to defraud the creditors, and yet decide to participate in such transaction or facilitate it. The fraud may have been committed on a creditor of the corporate debtor or on the corporate debtor itself.[9]

The CIRP Regulations allow the RP to seek expert legal opinion to assist in evaluating the transactions to find out if any of them need to be avoided. The final decision is of the RP.

IV

After taking over JIL's affairs, while reviewing the financial and other records, IRP Anuj Jain discovered that JIL had mortgaged 858 acres of unencumbered land, valued at about Rs 5,000 crore (US$ 600 million), to a number of public and private banks, in order to secure the debt of JAL. This transaction had been made during the lookback period. The security interest on valuable land parcels was created without any economic consideration. Notably, large parcels of land were given away at a time when JIL was itself reeling from financial stress. The company had failed to honour deadlines to deliver homes due to a crunch and default in repayment of debt to its own lenders. JIL's lenders had already classified JIL's account as NPA when the transaction was made.

Out of 858 acres, 167.229 acres of land were mortgaged on 29 December 2016 to secure term loans of Rs 21,081.5 crore (US$ 2,540 million) taken by JAL from a consortium of banks, and yet

9 The IBC, S. 66

another 167.9615 acres were mortgaged on the same day to secure term loans of Rs 21,081.5 crore (US$ 2,540 million) taken by JAL from a consortium of lenders. Again 158.1739 acres of land were mortgaged on 7 March 2017 to secure a term loan of Rs 1,200 crore (US$ 145 million) granted by a large private bank to JAL; and yet another 151.0063 acres were mortgaged on the same day to secure another term loan of Rs 1,200 crore (US$ 145 million) granted by the same private bank to JAL; 25.0040 acres were also mortgaged earlier on 24 May 2016 to secure from another private bank a loan of about Rs 1,800 crore (US$ 217 million); and 90 acres were mortgaged on 4 March 2016 to secure a loan of Rs 1,000 crore (US$ 121 million) taken by JAL from India's largest public sector bank. The details of transactions are recorded by the Supreme Court in its decision on these transactions.

Peculiarly, many banks to which land was mortgaged were also the lenders of JIL and members of its CoC.

At the time Anuj Jain was appointed as the IRP, there was only one provision in the IBC that cast a general duty on the RP to file an application for avoidance of transactions.[10] The timelines and other duties of the RP in respect of avoidance transactions were introduced in the CIRP Regulations on 27 March 2018 and another amendment made much later. The IRP sought counsel from the author whether such transactions fell under any of the avoidance transactions under the IBC. He needed firm, candid and clear advice. There couldn't be any room for error. There was no judicial precedence available on avoidance transactions under the IBC. The author studied in depth the transactions and jurisprudence on similar provisions under the erstwhile winding-up regime under the Indian companies law, and best practices in other jurisdictions.

In his written opinion provided to the IRP, the author stated that at the time these transactions were made JIL was itself in

10 The IBC, S. 25 (1)(j)

dire need of funds, faced severe liquidity crunch to complete the construction of projects, and was unable to fulfil its own obligations to deliver flats to homebuyers as well as honour the payment obligations to banks and fixed deposit holders due to financial distress. Without receiving any economic consideration for land worth thousands of crores, JIL mortgaged unencumbered land to secure the debt of a related party. This benefited the lenders of JAL over JIL's. The land could have instead been sold by JIL to raise funds to complete the construction of flats in a timely manner and discharge its own liabilities. The mortgages were created in a highly questionable manner and in complete disregard of the interests of JIL's own creditors and stakeholders. Giving away land by the erstwhile management in mortgage was in nature of asset stripping and amounted to preferring a related party's creditors over JIL's own creditors. Proper approval of JIL's shareholders was also not taken for the mortgage. The transactions creating mortgages were clearly preferential and undervalued.

This was a clear case of failure of JIL's directors to discharge their fiduciary duty. It is well recognized that in normal circumstances (when the company is financially stable), the primary duty of directors under the common law is to promote the success of the company with reference to the interests of its shareholders. However, when faced with the risk of insolvency, the directors must consider the interest of creditors in priority over that of shareholders. The justification for this shift in duty is that the directors have incentives to encourage the company to continue to trade when insolvent or financially distressed.

These incentives are varied and may relate to saving their position, avoiding reputational loss arising from business failure or maximizing value of their own shares (in private companies the directors are often also major shareholders). These incentives primarily arise due to the limited liability of the company under which shareholders enjoy all the benefits of high-risk activities but are not held responsible personally for their consequences, in this case, debts. Hence, there is an incentive for the directors to continue to trade to protect their own and the shareholders' interests, knowing that if the company is already on the verge of insolvency, the downside risk would fall wholly on the creditors while the upside benefit may get the company out of distress.

The directors have to keep their eyes open for the warning signs that appear, although there may not always be enough clarity on when a company is in the zone of insolvency or near insolvency or on the verge of insolvency. It is also true that the exact meaning of these terms remains elusive and it may be difficult for the directors to know when exactly their duties to creditors start under the common law.[11] It may vary from case to case. In JIL's case, its directors were aware of the financial stress the company was facing and of the defaults committed in repayment of debt.

Although Anuj Jain was equipped with the author's advice, it was he who had to take the final decision. It was his duty to officially determine if the transactions were questionable. He could rely on his lawyer's advice but it was he who had to make an assessment of the facts presented to him. Anuj Jain was mindful of the implication of his action. These were reputed and powerful banks. If he declared the transactions questionable, he would be making serious allegations. Thousands of crores were at stake besides the banks' reputation. They were going to fight hard. There were already enough irons in the fire; he had to be absolutely sure of the sustainability of his decision. He alone was going to be held responsible for his actions.

---

11 'UK: The Road to Insolvency, and Directors' Duties in the "Twilight Zone"', Roderic McLauchlan and Ros Chipperfeld, Barlow Lyde & Gilbert LLP. Last seen on 15 May 2024 at http://www.mondag com/x/76804/Directors+Officers/The+Road+To+Insolvency+And+Directors+DutiestInt

The more they discussed, the more the IRP and the author were convinced that this was a classic case of preferential and undervalued transactions, and the IRP had to act and file avoidance application. The rest was for the NCLT to judge.

V

As the next step, the IRP wrote to the banks and JAL asking why the land mortgaged to them by JIL should not be clawed back under the IBC's avoidance provisions. The banks vehemently defended the transactions, claiming they were made by JIL in the ordinary course of business and fell in the exception of preferential transaction provided in the IBC. It is a norm in the industry for a member of a corporate debtor to secure or guarantee the repayment of debt of another member, they argued in justification of their action.

Finding their replies unsatisfactory, the IRP informed the CoC of his intent to file an application in the NCLT to seek avoidance of these transactions. Although the IBC does not require the IRP or the RP to obtain approval of the CoC for filing avoidance application, the IRP considered it prudent to keep the CoC informed. The application was likely to be contested and could create substantial litigation cost. CoC approval would be required for payment of all costs incurred by the IRP. In this case, the IRP could have arguably taken a position that an approval was not required given that many members of the CoC, although in their capacity as lenders of JAL, were in a conflicting position as applications were being filed against their banks.

But, the author advised that if the members of the CoC were to disapprove payment of cost, the IRP could approach the NCLT to seek an appropriate direction; but he had to seek approval of cost by the CoC as that was the requirement of law. Their instincts also told the IRP and the author that it was unlikely that sensible members of the CoC would allow the cost to be disapproved as that would be poor optics. It should be mentioned again that most banks took note of the IRP's decision to file application but refrained from commenting on it. A few lenders of JAL, sitting in JIL's CoC, however, went up in arms. Some of them openly intimidated the IRP in the CoC meetings. It is to the credit of the IRP that he held his ground despite tremendous pressure. Credit also goes to the State Bank of India and IDBI Bank which played an important role in maintaining a semblance of order in the CoC meetings.

VI

While *Chitra Sharma* was still pending before the Supreme Court, the IRP went ahead and filed an application before the Allahabad bench of NCLT and sought cancellation of mortgage deeds. The homebuyers were elated. Anuj Jain had honoured his assurance to them that he would act independently and in the interest of JIL and its stakeholders. After all, they were amongst the main sufferers of such misdeeds by JIL's erstwhile management and would benefit from the clawback of land.

A battery of lawyers travelled to Allahabad to defend the actions of JAL and its bankers who sought to implead themselves as parties in the application. They argued that JAL was helping JIL in various ways; hence, creation of mortgages was merely reciprocal and such accommodation made by JIL could not be termed without consideration. It was argued that such transaction was permitted by law and made transparently. They defended the mortgages on the grounds that they had not been created on account of any antecedent debt liability owed by JIL but had been made in the ordinary course of business of JIL and the JAL's lenders. Transactions by JIL to create mortgage in favour of JAL's lenders was an act of reciprocity as JAL too had been extending help to JIL in its projects. Transaction being reciprocal could not be termed as without consideration or undervalued. They could also not be termed as actions carried out for a fraudulent purpose.

VII

On 16 May 2018, after extensive arguments over many hearings, the then judicial member of the NCLT's Allahabad bench, V.P. Singh, accepted the IRP's application and cancelled the transactions creating mortgages. The NCLT bench decided that the transactions questioned by the IRP were preferential, undervalued, and even a fraud on JIL's creditors and homebuyers. Endorsing the grounds of the IRP's application, the judgment noted that JIL mortgaged its unencumbered land to secure the debt of its related party (JAL) in the midst of an immense financial crunch, while defaulting with homebuyers and its own lenders and that too after it had been declared as NPA.

The NCLT held that this was done in utter disregard of fiduciary duties and duty of care to its own creditors. At the time, when mortgage of such valuable land was created, JIL was already in default to its lenders, and it was unlikely that they would have consented to mortgages to secure the debt of JAL if their consent was sought. Providing consent would have compromised not only the recovery of their dues but also the interests of thousands of homebuyers. The NCLT opined that even though the nominees of lenders attended JIL's board meeting in which the decision to mortgage the land was taken, it cannot be treated as their approval or no-objection. It was noted that the lenders invariably have covenants in loan agreement which require their specific prior written approval to be taken by the borrower to create interest in favour of any one of the encumbered or unencumbered assets of the borrower. This is done to maintain the adequate value of security interest or the assets from which a lender might have to eventually recover its dues in the event of default by the borrower.

When the directors of JIL were fully aware that they were in the twilight zone,[12] and insolvency was imminent, they ought to have exercised due care in minimizing the potential loss to the creditors. Instead, they entered into such transactions which, on the face of it, gave benefits to a related party, with the clear intent to defraud JIL's creditors, the NCLT held. The land in question could have been sold to generate cash which would have been sufficient to complete the construction of flats. The decision directly and adversely affected the homebuyers. It was further held that the transaction would not fall in the exception of ordinary course of business or financial affairs given in the IBC. While it is true that collateral security is a common practice in loan transactions, in this case, JIL was under liquidity crunch and such transaction cannot be treated as transfer in the ordinary course of business or termed as part of financial affairs.

Also, the mortgage of land was without any consideration, which itself made the transactions questionable. The NCLT concluded that the challenged transactions amounted to a transfer of interest in the property of JIL for the benefit of creditors of JAL and putting them (and JAL) in a beneficial position vis-à-vis JIL's creditors. The NCLT ordered the release and discharge of security interest created by JIL on 858 acres of land. It declared that the mortgaged properties would be vested back in JIL.

VIII

The NCLT's order was historic in more than one way. It was the first order on avoidance application involving transfer of property at this scale after the IBC's enactment. It was perhaps the first such order

12 For a discussion on Twilight Zone, please see, Chapter 12, Part III of Sumant Batra, *Corporate Insolvency: Law and Practice* (2017)

cancelling transactions involving large number of banks because they were preferential and undervalued. It was also the first formidable jurisprudence on avoidance transactions under the IBC which provided clarity on the relevant provisions. It was a well-reasoned order, which was later cemented by the Supreme Court upholding it. The order found a pride of place in the history of the IBC.

The NCLT's order sent the affected banks scurrying for cover. They rushed to top lawyers for counsel. Meanwhile, homebuyers celebrated. It was their victory. They had been crying hoarse that assets were taken out of the company which adversely impacted completion of construction of their flats. JIL could now have more unencumbered land to monetize if needed and to spend on construction.

IX

Months later, as happens in court cases, the situation was suddenly overturned. Now, it was the banks' chance to celebrate. The IBC provides that any person aggrieved by the NCLT's decision may appeal to the NCLAT. Aggrieved banks appealed against the NCLT's order before the NCLAT, which is located in New Delhi. A battery of lawyers appeared for JAL and banks to attack the NCLT order. The NCLAT stayed the NCLT's order cancelling the mortgages.

After hearing arguments over months, on 1 August 2019, a bench of the NCLAT, presided by its chairperson, Justice S.J. Mukhopadhaya, a former judge of the Supreme Court, upturned the order of the NCLT holding that although JIL had created interest over its property, such interest had not been created in favour of any creditor of JIL or a surety or a guarantor for or on account of an antecedent financial debt or operational debt or other liabilities owed by JIL. The NCLAT held that the mortgages were made in the ordinary course of business and were part of financial affairs of the transferees. The NCLAT further held that there was no evidence that the transactions were made to defraud the creditors of JIL or for any fraudulent purpose.

X

Any person aggrieved by the decision of the NCLAT may file an appeal to the Supreme Court of India under S. 62 of the IBC, provided the grievance is based on a question of law arising out of the order. As the NCLAT's order raised many important questions, it was challenged by the IRP and some homebuyers in the Supreme Court. Again, top lawyers were hired by the banks and JAL to defend the transactions.

After hearing the matter for days, the Supreme Court delivered its decision on 26 February 2020 in what has come to be known as the *Anuj Jain* judgment. In their judgment, authored by Justice Dinesh Maheshwari (since retired), the Supreme Court set aside the order of the NCLAT and restored the NCLT order with only one modification. Instead of the entire 858 acres of land, the Supreme Court found the transaction of mortgage of 758 acres as preferential and undervalued. The other 100 acres were mortgaged prior to the lookback period and so could not be questioned even though they were not made in the ordinary course of business, the Court held.

In their detailed judgment, the Supreme Court decided many important and contentious questions of law, which are summarized in Chapter 26. The *Anuj Jain* judgment now stands as the most authoritative jurisprudence on avoidance transactions. It will serve as a guide to not only the law on avoidance transactions in India but also in many other jurisdictions.

XI

As a result of the Supreme Court decision, prime real estate of 758 acres, valued at about Rs 5,000 crore (US$ 600 million)[13] today,

13 *The IBBI Newsletter*, January–March 2024. Last seen on 25 May 2024 at https://ibbi.gov.in/en/publication

was clawed back into JIL and became part of its assets. The fight to retrieve this land from the clutches of powerful banks was long and unpleasant. It created many tense moments in the CoC meetings due to the contemptuous attitude of a couple of members who were also JAL's lenders and had to give up their security interest. They tried hard to provoke the IRP in the CoC meetings, hoping he would do something unbefitting of his office and vitiate the cordial environment. This they hoped could provide them with an excuse to ask for his replacement. The homebuyers, who later joined the CoC, however supported the IRP. They also thwarted moves by those banks to instigate other banks to get Anuj Jain replaced with another insolvency professional as the IRP.

Other members of the CoC showed restraint, perhaps, recognizing that the IRP was only doing his duty. They were of the view that difference in understanding or interpretation of legal provisions was no reason to be at daggers drawn with one another in the CoC. The fight about preferential transactions was to be confined to court rooms. Anuj Jain and the author kept their composure, fighting hard in court but demonstrating complete objectivity in the CoC and in performing other functions. The IRP stayed polite but firm. After all, backed by solid legal advice, he was acting only in the interest of creditors and homebuyers. Hopefully, the example set by Anuj Jain will be emulated by other insolvency professionals.

The author was apparently blacklisted by two banks out of the many against whom orders for entering into preferential transaction were passed, for having advised IRP to file avoidance applications as even after four years, these banks have not used his services.

10

A Seat at the Table

Don't underestimate the power of a common man!

– *Chennai Express* (2013)

Finally, the government gave in to the demands of homebuyers. On 6 June 2018, an Ordinance was promulgated to amend the IBC to make homebuyers financial creditors. An *Explanation* was inserted in the definition of financial debt. The net effect of the *Explanation* is that any amount raised from an allottee under a real estate project shall be deemed to be an amount having the commercial effect of a borrowing, thus qualifying a homebuyer as financial creditor. A homebuyer could now also initiate an insolvency process under S.7 of the IBC and become member of the CoC. On 17 August 2018, the Parliament approved the Ordinance by passing the Insolvency and Bankruptcy Code (Second Amendment) Act, 2018, with effect from 6 June 2018.

II

The amendment made to the definition of financial debt was challenged by many parties, mainly real estate developers, before the Supreme Court. It was contended that the amendment flies in the face of what the IBC sought to achieve. It was contended by them that if the amendment was upheld, a single allottee will be able to knock at the doors of the NCLT and obtain an admission order. A perfectly good management with several projects on its hands could be removed at the instance of one allottee's admission order and either get replaced – in which case the massive funds infused by the developer himself would be set at naught – or worse still, lead to commercial death, if there are no resolution plans or all resolution plans are rejected by the CoC. A perfectly solvent company would then be liquidated, which would not be in the interest of anybody, least of all the bulk of allottees themselves. The homebuyers would want possession of the flats and apartments, not liquidation of the company, it was argued.

The developers also argued that homebuyers, being an amorphous and disparate lot, would speak in different voices in the CoC, concerned only with their own interest. Involving them in the negotiation process of the resolution plan would mean infracting the principles that needed to be followed in commercial consideration of resolution plans to pull the debtor out of distress. Given their number and diverse interests, coupled with no knowledge or commercial expertise of the corporate debtor, they should not and ought not to be allowed to participate in the CoC, they tried to reason with the Court.

The government defended the amendment stating that allottees were made financial creditors because, in substance, they were financing the project in which they would ultimately be given flats/apartments. At every stage in the building process, certain amounts have to be paid by allottees which are then supposed to be utilized in constructing the apartments/flats.

The Supreme Court approved the amendment in *Pioneer Urban Land & Infrastructure.*[1] In the judgment delivered by a bench of three judges – Justice R.F. Nariman, Justice Sanjiv Khanna and Justice Surya Kant – the Court held that parliamentary intent cannot be thwarted even if it operates a bit harshly on a small section of the public, if otherwise made in larger public interest. Experience of the real estate sector in this country has not been encouraging. Huge amounts are advanced by ordinary people to finance housing projects which are massively delayed on the part of the developer or, even worse, fall through. The developer of real estate projects is the supplier of the flat/apartment and is a debtor inasmuch as the homebuyer funds its own apartment by paying amounts in advance to the developer for construction of the building in which their apartment is to be found. An allottee disburses money in the form of advance payments made towards construction of the real estate project against consideration for the time value of money. This is because the money that is disbursed is no longer with the homebuyer, but is with the real estate developer who is legally obliged to give money's equivalent back to the homebuyer, having used it in the construction of the project and being at a discounted value so far as the homebuyer is concerned, the Court held.

A homebuyer pays less by way of instalments than she would if she were to pay for the ultimate price of the flat/apartment. The Supreme Court held that given that the homebuyer gives advance to the real estate developer and thereby finances the real estate project at hand makes them a financial creditor. If individual creditors like debenture holders and fixed deposit holders can be financial creditor, why can't homebuyers? It was further held that homebuyers' inclusion as financial creditor

1 *The IBBI Newsletter*, January–March 2024. Last seen on 25 May 2024 at https://ibbi.gov.in/en/publication

has to be read with effect from the date IBC was notified in 2016 and not from the date of amendment in 2018, as the amendment was only clarificatory in nature and did not add any new provision. Thus, the Court held that the IBC amendment was valid in law.

Consequential to changes made in the IBC, the homebuyers of JIL became its financial creditors and also members of its CoC. This was a unique case whereby, by virtue of the amendment, the customers of a company became its financial creditors.

However, even after six years, the debate around the merits of making homebuyers members of the CoC or competent to file insolvency petition continues. Many real estate cases have been dragged into insolvency, and their process drags on for longer. It becomes more complex if a substantial part of the project is complete and allottees of the unfinished part drag the entire company into insolvency. This elicits resistance from the allottees who have got the possession of their units or have no complaints against the developer. The NCLAT has been trying to find a way out of such cases by restricting the insolvency process to the unfinished projects. This is a smart but complicated solution as the IBC does not contain regulations to deal with limited insolvencies. The entire process is governed by judicial orders and parties have to keep approaching the NCLAT for clarifications. The government is considering making changes in the IBC to accommodate such cases.

III

In the light of the amendment made in IBC, the Supreme Court decided that there was no need to continue to hear the cases filed before it by Chitra Sharma and others. The IRP's lawyers maintained that homebuyers would now be part of the CoC and have substantial voting power so as to be able to effectively protect their interests. Therefore, the discipline of the IBC enacted to streamline the resolution of corporate insolvencies should be followed and JIL's insolvency process should continue as per the IBC. It was argued that the Court should not take upon itself the burden of supervising the intricacies of the resolution process outside the IBC, as it would put on the Court an insuperable burden of evaluating intricate matters of financial expertise on which the Parliament has legislated specific mechanisms.

Exactly a year from the date on which the NCLT had ordered commencement of JIL's insolvency process, on 9 August 2018, the Supreme Court disposed of the matter by its judgment in what has come to be called the *Chitra Sharma*[2] *case.* Agreeing emphatically with the pleas made by the IRP in favour of relegating the matter to the IBC process, the Court decided it would not be appropriate for it to assume the task of supervising the work of the CoC. It held that the Court must be particularly careful not to supplant the mechanisms which have been laid down in the IBC by mechanisms under judicial directions.

The Supreme Court relegated the insolvency process of JIL to the IBC. To do justice to the interests of all the concerned stakeholders of JIL, and to prevent it from going into liquidation, the Court directed that the initial period of 180 days be revived with effect from 9 August 2018 (extendable by ninety days, if required). It was further ordered that a new CoC be constituted in accordance with the amended provisions of the IBC to enforce the statutory status of the homebuyers as financial creditors.

The Court also made it clear that the IRP would have the option of inviting fresh bids for a wider field of choice provided to the CoC. Following S.29A, inserted in the IBC by an amendment made on 23 November 2017, the Court clarified that all bids

---

2 *Chitra Sharma & Ors v. Union of India and Ors,* (2018) 18 SCC 575

must follow the IBC provisions and only eligible bidders shall participate. It was also noted in the judgment that JAL had become ineligible under S.29A.

Recognizing homebuyers as financial creditors, the Supreme Court left the question open as to whether homebuyers are secured or unsecured creditor.

Another issue that arose before the Supreme Court while closing *Chitra Sharma* was how to deal with the large amount of Rs 750 crore (US$ 90 million) deposited in Court by JAL. Homebuyers who had earlier opted for refund requested the Court to distribute the amount to them pro rata while JAL requested that the same be refunded to it. The Court rejected the plea of both the homebuyers and JAL. It provided four main reasons for declining their requests.

First, during the pendency of the insolvency process, it would, as a matter of law, be impermissible for the Court to direct a preferential payment to be made to a particular class of financial creditors, whether secured or unsecured. Directing disbursement of the amount of Rs 750 crore to the homebuyers who sought refund would be manifestly improper and cause injustice to the other (secured) creditors. Moreover, once the Court took recourse to the IBC framework, it was necessary that its statutory provisions be followed to facilitate the conclusion of the resolution process.

Second, only 8 per cent homebuyers had expressed preference for refund while 92 per cent evidently preferred possession of the homes which they purchased. Many of these 92 per cent would also have obtained loans to secure a home. They would have a legitimate grievance if the corpus of Rs 750 crore (together with accrued interest) got distributed among the homebuyers who sought refund. The purpose of the process envisaged by the IBC for the evaluation and approval of a resolution plan was to form a composite approach to deal with the financial situation of the corporate debtor. Allowing a refund to one class of financial creditors wouldn't have been in the overall interest of a composite plan being formulated under the provisions of the IBC.

Third, the concerns of the secured creditors of JIL could not be ignored. One of the major reasons for the enactment of the IBC was to protect the interest of lenders. As such, the debt owed to the banks and financial institutions was secured by the assets of JIL. This debt originated in the public deposits of the banks and financial institutions, which are answerable to their stakeholders. Their interest could not be disregarded by preferring homebuyers over them in disbursing Rs 750 crore.

Fourth, the RBI had sought the Court's permission to initiate an insolvency resolution process in respect of JAL. The RBI initially referred twelve accounts to the IBC. Subsequently, it recommended another twenty-eight accounts which had been classified as NPAs on 30 June 2017. JAL was one of the twenty-eight. No viable resolution plan could be found for JAL, as a result of which it was also required to be referred to the IBC. Refunding Rs 750 crore to JAL at this stage was not proper.

Considering the above, the Supreme Court directed that the amount of Rs 750 crore shall together with the interest accrued thereon be transferred to the NCLT which shall abide by directions as may be issued by the NCLT. The sum of Rs 750 crore with the interest accrued was thereafter transferred to the registry of the Allahabad bench of the NCLT which kept the amount in an interest-earning fixed deposit.

The Court also acceded to the RBI's request to initiate JAL's insolvency process in order to address its financial distress. A point of note was that if JAL was undergoing insolvency or liquidation process at the time of the distribution of Rs 750 crore, the money it was entitled to receive would go to its RP or the liquidator as the case may be.

All earlier interim orders passed by the Supreme Court were lifted with *Chitra Sharma* case being disposed of on 9 August 2018.

IV

The decision of the Supreme Court in *Chitra Sharma* allowed the insolvency process of JIL to move forward. However, a different set of problems awaited the IRP. Although homebuyers gained the status of financial creditor and were eligible to become members of the CoC, the IBC lacked clarity on the evaluation of votes cast by the class of creditors. There were thousands of homebuyers but not all came forward to participate in meetings or vote on the agenda items put for polling. This became another stumbling block in the progress of JIL's insolvency process. A year was lost until the government once again amended the IBC in August 2019 to break the impasse and the Supreme Court exercised its plenary powers under Article 142 of the Constitution to give a new lease of life to JIL's insolvency resolution process. JIL's insolvency case continued to be the ground for both legislative changes and evolution of jurisprudence on the IBC.

V

The amendment was a moral victory for homebuyers who were fighting for justice. Homebuyers have generally been mistreated by developers. An audit conducted by the Comptroller and Auditor General of India made a scathing assessment of the situation in Noida alone. It found that in the period between 2005–06 and 2017–18, NOIDA allotted sixty-seven group housing plots measuring 7,103 lakh square metres to developers, which were subdivided into 113 plots by the allottees. The audit observed that 63 per cent of the total projects were incomplete or partially completed, which accounted for seventy-one out of the 113 projects.

Out of the 130,005 flats sanctioned, occupancy certificate was not issued for 44 per cent of flats due to which homebuyers who had invested hard-earned money in the purchase of flats were still deprived of its possession. Though the Uttar Pradesh Industrial Area Development Act, 1976 (UP Act), has prescribed penal measures for defaulters, NOIDA had failed to take action for huge dues against the builders even after lapse of the tenure for payment. Against allotment value of Rs 14,050.73 crore (US$ 1,693 million) between 2005–06 and 2017–18, dues of NOIDA pending receipt, as on 31 March 2020, spiralled to Rs 18,633.21 crore (US$ 2,245 million). This has also adversely affected the finances of NOIDA.[3]

The homebuyers' plight was depicted by Dibakar Banerjee in his 2006 satire, *Khosla Ka Ghosla*, which tells the story of a middle-class family whose patriarch invests his entire life's earnings in a plot of land to build his dream house, only to be let down by the broker. The film attained cult status over the years and is counted among one of the best satirical comedies of Indian cinema. The realism of Khosla's situation and the overarching issue of the movie struck a chord with many. Broker rackets are heard of all the time. But the tit-for-tat solution employed in the film's narrative is hardly plausible, even if commendable. Real-life cases, as you are witness to JIL's account, face tremendous complexities before reaching a resolution.

For homebuyers, getting a financial creditor status under the IBC was a step forward in what was going to be a long struggle for homes with no end in sight.

---

3 See The Comptroller and Auditor General of India Report, Last seen on 17 May 2024 at https://cag.gov.in/uploads/download_audit_report/2021/5.%20Executive%20Summary-061bc91242c09b8.00984926.pdf

11

An Impasse

It's not the voting that's democracy; it's the counting.

~ Tom Stoppard

In the 365 days between the start of the insolvency resolution process of JIL by the NCLT (9 August 2017) and the order of the Supreme Court in *Chitra Sharma* (9 August 2018) relegating the matter back to the NCLT, the chaos had subsided substantially, but trouble still loomed large over JIL's insolvency process.

After the Supreme Court order in *Chitra Sharma*, the IRP issued a public announcement inviting claims from creditors who had not submitted them earlier in August 2017. After verifying the claims received, the IRP reconstituted the CoC by including homebuyers as its members. JIL's homebuyers held 58.1 per cent voting share. As a result, voting share of banks in the CoC was reduced to 41.8 per cent and that of fixed deposit holders to 0.01 per cent.[1]

1 The voting share of homebuyers and fixed deposit holders kept fluctuating as the IRP kept receiving and accepting claims through the insolvency process, till the Supreme Court put a freeze on it on 24 March 2021 as part of its judgment in *Jaypee Kensington*

The amended CIRP Regulations require that ten or more creditors of a corporate debtor form a class to be represented in the CoC by an authorized representative. The representative is selected by members of the class by voting from amongst three insolvency professionals whose name is proposed by the IRP. Consequently, the IRP proposed names of three insolvency professionals each to homebuyers and fixed deposit holders and asked them to choose their representative.

The next step was to convene a meeting of the CoC with both homebuyers and fixed deposit holders represented in the meeting by their authorized representatives. Votes in the meeting by both the classes were also to be cast through the authorized representative.

II

Empowered by the IBC to take all significant decisions, the CoC exercises its power of decision making through the process of voting. The meetings are convened and chaired by the IRP or the RP. The notice of the meeting has to be shared with all the participants along with all relevant documents. The notice has to be in any case served by electronic means. Quorum of at least 33 per cent of the voting rights present either in person or by videoconferencing or other audio or visual means is required for conduct of the meeting. If this is not achieved, the meeting stands adjourned to the same time and place on the next day. The CoC has the power to modify the quorum requirement. The quorum requirement is to be maintained throughout the conduct of the meeting.

The IBC provides that the threshold for general decision making in the CoC should not be less than 51 per cent of the total votes. Instances involving significant decisions that impact the working of the IBC or the insolvency process require a higher threshold of 66 per cent, which was 75 per cent until the amendment of 6 June 2018. A still higher threshold of 90 per cent is required when the CoC decides to approve withdrawal of insolvency petition after its commencement. These are statutory requirements to which the CoC is bound.

The amount of detailing the CIRP Regulations provide regarding the voting procedure reflects its importance in the insolvency process. The solemnity of the decisions the CoC is required to make warrants the process be fair and of uncompromising integrity. Instructions regarding the process and manner of voting are communicated as part of the notice. The RP is also tasked with the responsibility of providing a secure system for voting through electronic means. The CIRP Regulations go to the extent of describing the requirements of a secured system of electronic voting in detail. Where the CoC includes an authorized representative for a class of creditors, the CIRP Regulations provide for the manner of voting by members in the class of creditors and the role of their authorized representative. The authorized representative participates and votes in the CoC meetings after taking views of the class of creditors.[2]

III

Through an electronic voting process which concluded on 28 August 2018, insolvency professionals Kuldeep Verma and Anju Agarwal were selected as the authorized representative of homebuyers and fixed deposit holders respectively. Their

---

2 See Sudhaker Shukla and Kokila Jayaram, 'Promoting common good amidst anti-common behaviour of stakeholders: Role of Committee of Creditors, the IBC, Ideas, Impressions and Implementation', 2022. Last seen on 14 May 2014 at https://ibbi.gov.in/uploads/resources/bcb6b096e766e07c164ad5f61ebe2b01.pdf

appointment was confirmed by the NCLT on 5 September 2018. Post-finalization, the first meeting of the reconstituted CoC was conducted on 12 September 2018. All of this followed a month after the *Chitra Sharma* judgment.

Another meeting of the CoC was convened on 17 October 2018. The agenda for the meeting included crucial items for discussion and decision: confirmation of IRP Anuj Jain as RP or appointment of another insolvency professional in his place; approval of terms on which expression of interest could be invited from persons wanting to submit resolution plan; finalizing the request for resolution plan – the process entailing submission and consideration of resolution plans by eligible prospective resolution applicants, and their consideration by the CoC including the criteria for evaluation of plans. Other important matters included approval of expenses incurred in running JIL as a going concern by the IRP, approval of appointment of experts and advisors to assist the IRP and the CoC, and approval of cost incurred on court cases and professionals hired by the IRP, and other important decisions to keep JIL afloat.

Despite having a significant overall voting share of 58.1 per cent based on admitted claims, only a fraction of homebuyers actually participated or voted in the CoC meeting. As a result, decision on many key agenda items could not be taken since the threshold required to pass resolutions could not be achieved. Most items were rejected on account of not having met the minimum voting threshold under the IBC while others were deferred. Only 17.18 per cent homebuyers were present. Since homebuyers held more than 25 per cent voting share (in fact, 58.1 per cent; in a way, they held the decisive vote) no resolution could be passed unless they voted in its favour.

In another meeting of the CoC held on 27 November 2018, barring one, all other voting items were held to be rejected by the CoC on account of not having met the required voting threshold. The problem was compounded by the IBC provision requiring an abstaining vote to be counted as a negative vote – a vote against the resolution. Therefore, the vote of abstaining homebuyers was counted as vote against the resolution. Due to lack of participation and voting by adequate number of homebuyers, vital decisions could not be taken in the CoC. This deadlock brought the insolvency process to a grinding halt.

IV

In the meantime, some banks in the CoC moved a resolution to replace Anuj Jain with another insolvency professional as IRP. The homebuyers sensed that this move was at the behest of banks which were lenders of JAL and were visibly infuriated by Anuj Jain's decision to file and pursue avoidance application for cancellation of mortgage of 858 acres of JIL's land.

The agenda for Anuj Jain's replacement could not go through as it could not garner majority of voting share. The homebuyers stood rock solid in support of Anuj Jain.

V

In many jurisdictions, votes of members in class who are present and voting in meetings only are counted; the decision taken by a majority of members present and voting is considered the decision of the entire class. For instance, in the USA, a plan requires 66 per cent or more voting share in value and 50 per cent or more in number for each class of creditors. Similar principles apply in Canada and the UK, with different thresholds. In Singapore, a higher threshold is set. The IBC, however, did not provide for such mechanism of voting or counting of homebuyers' vote. Its provision then in force provided that the authorized representative must vote based on instructions received from the creditors in the class he represents. If a creditor does not give instructions, the authorized representative must not vote on its behalf.[3]

It was not possible for the authorized representative to vote for homebuyers who had not given them instructions. This issue was brought to the attention of the IBBI by the IRP, who continued to keep the regulator informed and updated about the key developments in the case.

VI

On 25 October 2018,[4] the IRP published a public notice inviting expressions of interest from the prospective resolution applicants. The last date for submission was 9 November 2018. Five parties submitted letters expressing interest: Suraksha Realty Limited with Lakshdeep Investments and Finance Private Limited; NBCC (India) Limited; Kotak Investment Advisors Limited; Cube Highways & Infrastructure Pte Ltd.; and L&T Infrastructure Development Projects Limited.

VII

To resolve the deadlock caused by voting in the CoC, some homebuyers and the IDBI Bank approached the NCLT and requested it to decide how the IBC provisions related to counting of votes should be interpreted to provide them a progressive meaning. The confusion persisted because of two conflicting views of the courts. While the NCLT had held in *Nikhil Mehta* that provisions of voting threshold have to be read as directory, and in the CoC, comprising of only the homebuyers, decision

3 The IBC, S. 25(1)
4 CIRP Regulations, R. 36A

can be taken by simple majority, in another unrelated decision, the NCLAT had held the provisions relating to voting and their counting as mandatory.

Homebuyers suggested to the NCLT that only the votes cast by homebuyers should be counted and not those that were not polled. The banks, however, opposed the homebuyers' proposition. They maintained that the view of a handful homebuyers cannot be deemed as also being the view of thousands of homebuyers who did not vote at all.

On 13 December 2018, the NCLT gave a split decision, perhaps another first in the IBC. The judicial member of the NCLT held that where homebuyers comprise up to 50 per cent of voting share or more in the CoC, and when there is a deadlock in passing the resolutions, the highest number of voting share in favour of resolution has to be taken into consideration without looking at the threshold limit provided under the IBC. This rule should apply for decision making in all matters except in respect of petition withdrawal, approval of the resolution plan by the CoC, and decision to liquidate the corporate debtor so that insolvency process can continue. The judicial member suggested that this arrangement continue until the government brings an amendment to address the issue.

The technical member, however, had a differing opinion. His view was far progressive. To resolve the deadlock, he suggested homebuyers be recognized as a separate class for voting with en-block voting rights. The decision taken by the number of homebuyers who vote shall be deemed as the decision of the entire class of homebuyers, since their interests are common. Once homebuyers are given proportional representation in their class, it would also not be necessary to lower the threshold limits laid down under the IBC. Therefore, he concluded, the votes cast by the homebuyers in favour of or against the resolution shall be taken to represent the views of the class as a whole and their voting share shall be proportionately increased based on the total voting share.

No detriment will be caused to other lenders in the process, as their total voting share is determined in terms of their total investment and does not impinge on voting share of other lenders. On the contrary, if their voting share is reduced due to absentees, it would be unfair and detrimental to homebuyers. He also proceeded to suggest another methodology of calculating votes. In sum, he decided that a lasting solution to the problem of voting impasse can only be found by treating homebuyers as a class and their voting pattern considered with reference to total voting share to reflect the will of the class.

VIII

By now it was clear that JIL's insolvency process was not going to be a smooth ride. Because the two NCLT members had delivered a split verdict, the matter had to be referred to the NCLT president, who is required in such circumstances to appoint a third member.[5] The decision of the third member, and of the member whose view the third member aligns with, is considered as the decision of the NCLT. On 13 December 2018, the Allahabad bench of the NLCT requested the NCLT president to appoint a third member to hear the matter. The NCLT president appointed the third member to hear the case on 19 March 2019.

The third NCLT member requested the IBBI to provide its views on the matter as interpretation of the IBC provisions on the contentious issue was likely to have significant implications on many pending and future cases under the IBC. The IBBI stuck to the provisions of the IBC. Eventually, an order was passed by the third NCLT member on 24 May 2019. In his order, the NCLT member stated that the legislature has given preference

5 The Companies Act, 2013, S. 419(5)

to individual vote and not the class or the majority vote. The legislature was conscious that a financial creditor should be given a choice to abstain from voting. He also did not agree with the principle of attendance and voting. The threshold of votes needed for passing resolution was mandatory in nature and couldn't be understood as directory. He opined that the class-wise voting of financial creditors is not permissible in law; voting share of financial creditors who had abstained or who voted against the resolution could not be taken as the will and vote of the entire class in the CoC. In sum, the NCLT member largely agreed with the IBBI's view.

IX

The order of the third member was challenged by one of the associations of homebuyers before the NCLAT. In the meantime, the stalemate in the CoC persisted. As a result, Anuj Jain continued to remain IRP during the entire process which ended on 7 March 2023. He is probably the longest-serving IRP under the IBC, which promoted another amendment in the IBC.

Insolvency and Bankruptcy Code (Second Amendment Act), 2018

On 6 June 2018, subsection (5) of S. 16 of the IBC was amended to provide that the term of interim insolvency professional will continue till the RP is appointed.

With regards to the impasse, the government once again stepped in to provide a solution by making appropriate changes in law. It recognized the critical nature of decision making within the CoC, especially when there is a lack of majority due to many homebuyers abstaining from voting.

Insolvency and Bankruptcy Code (Amendment Act), 2019

On 16 August 2019, the IBC was amended by the Insolvency and Bankruptcy Code (Amendment Act), 2019, to provide that the authorized representative shall cast his vote on behalf of all the financial creditors he represents in accordance with the decision taken by a vote of more than 50 per cent of the voting share of the financial creditors he represents, who have cast their vote.[6] The net effect of the amendment is that the minority in the class of homebuyers and fixed deposit holders is bound by the decision of majority (51 per cent), as explained by the Supreme Court in *Jaypee Kensington*. Homebuyers who were advocating this view had the final say yet again.

It took another amendment in IBC for JIL's insolvency process to progress. The effect of the amendment was explained by Justice Dinesh Maheshwari in *Jaypee Kensington*. It was held that the language of subsection (3A) of S. 25A clearly provides that once a decision is taken, either to reject or to approve a particular plan, by a vote of more than 50 per cent of the voting share of the financial creditors within a class, the minority of those who vote, as also all others within that class, are bound by that decision. While divergence of the views may exist within the class, when coming to their vote in the CoC, it would be representative of a class.

For common good, the democratic principles of the determinative role of the opinion of the majority have been duly incorporated in the scheme of the IBC, particularly in the provisions relating to voting on the resolution plan and the binding nature of the vote of the authorized representative on the entire class of the financial creditor/s she represents. To put it in more clear terms, qua the homebuyers, the judgment holds, and the operation of

6 The IBC, subsection (3A) of S. 25A

the amended provision is that their authorized representative is required to vote on the resolution plan in accordance with the decision taken by a vote of more than 50 per cent of the voting share of the homebuyers. This 50 per cent will be counted with reference to the voting share of such homebuyers who choose to cast their vote for arriving at the particular decision. Once this process is carried out and the authorized representative has been handed down a particular decision by the requisite majority of voting share, he shall vote accordingly, and his vote shall bind all homebuyers as the single class that he represents.

This was the first instance of 'cram down' on minority within a class who either dissented or chose to abstain. This is different from a dissenting vote in the IBC where dissenting creditors for the approval of a plan are assured minimum liquidation value as a safeguard, whereas minority within a class are forced to take what the majority is getting with no special rights or safeguards.

X

All this time, while the logjam in the CoC stalled the process, another major crisis was brewing. Counting from 9 August 2018, the date of the *Chitra Sharma*, the total period of 270 days provided in the IBC for completion of insolvency process was ending on 6 May 2019. The resolution plans received by the IRP were still under examination while simultaneous commercial negotiations were taking place between the resolution applicants, banks, and homebuyers. Eventually, IDBI Bank was compelled to approach the NCLT to find a solution. After the NCLT's decision, the matter landed before the NCLAT for ruling. The next chapter explains how the time period of the corporate insolvency resolution process got extended.

12

The Clock Is Ticking

Remember that time is money.

~ Benjamin Franklin

Time is of essence in any insolvency proceeding. At the time, the IBC provided that the insolvency resolution process should be completed within 180 days from the date of admission of the corporate debtor into insolvency. The RP could seek extension of this period by ninety days from the NCLT, if instructed to do so by a resolution passed in the CoC by a vote of 66 per cent of the voting shares. However, this is only a one-time extension. Thus, 270 days was the maximum time available for completion of the process. The consequences of not completing the resolution process in 270 days were harsh – the corporate debtor had to be sent into liquidation.[1]

On request of the CoC, the NCLT had already granted an extension of ninety days by an order passed on 28 January 2019.

---

1 The IBC, S. 33

There may arise instances where despite the best efforts of the IRP and the CoC, the completion of insolvency process may not happen within the prescribed time. It would be illogical to send a corporate debtor into liquidation even if it is viable just because 270 days have ended before a resolution could be found. For instance, a resolution plan may have been agreed by the CoC or instructed to put for vote on day 269, but the voting result may be known only on day 271, and based on the technicality of the rule, the prescribed time for the process has passed. A resolution plan thus cannot be allowed to fall through in such cases merely because 270 days have lapsed. It is correct that the IBC timelines are sacrosanct, but they are still directory and not mandatory, as eventually held by the Supreme Court.[2]

In his book, *Corporate Insolvency, Law and Practice* (2017), the author expressed that the total time period of 270 days provided under the IBC may prove to be highly inadequate given the complexities and multiple stakeholders involved in a resolution process. This timeframe could only be effective if the provisions of law and framework of regulations are clear and provide fair treatment to parties; institutions involved in the process have the necessary capacity and infrastructure; and the best practices that operate around the legislation complement and support implementation of the timeframe. Otherwise, the parties will challenge actions and decisions taken during the process before higher courts, leading to compromises being made to the set timeframe.

This is high risk in India in particular because the insolvency profession is at a nascent stage and the institutions under the IBC are also relatively new. The law itself has some grey areas that need to be dealt with. In particular, the effectiveness of the policy shift from debtor-in-possession law in the Sick Industrial Companies

---

2 *Committee of Creditors of Essar Steel India Limited v. Satish Kumar Gupta*, 2019 SCC OnLine SC 1478

Act (SICA) to a creditor-in-control regime under the IBC is yet to be tested. The author had further reasoned that, in fact, reading the language of S. 33 of the IBC makes it clear that the intention of the legislature is to provide the NCLT powers to extend time beyond 270 days in cases where it is satisfied that the objective of the IBC will be served by such extension and that grave injustice may be caused to a party without the extension.

The author advocated that the NCLT's evaluation in considering requests for extension beyond 180 or 270 days should be based in good faith and assessment of the irretrievable loss being caused to the party affected by grant of such extension. If the NCLT is satisfied that the person seeking extension is doing so for bona fide reasons, it will normally not refuse request for extension. The only exception to that rule might be where a party opposing such extension is able to satisfy the NCLT that granting extension will result in irretrievable loss and injury to it. It would be fair to expect from the NCLT that extension orders are passed by it only in deserving cases. Extension beyond 270 days by the NCLT should be in rare cases. Liberal grant of extensions beyond 270 days, however, might defeat the sanctity of time period and its objective, the author cautioned. It was inevitable that the courts will treat the time period as directory although the endeavour should be to observe the timeframe strictly.

II

The NCLAT found an innovative way to allow more time for deserving cases. In *Quinn Logistics*,[3] the NCLAT held that some time can be excluded while counting 270 days, without having to breach the outer timeline provided in the IBC. In cases where

3 *Quinn Logistics India Pvt. Ltd v. Mack Soft Tech Pvt. Ltd*, 2017 SCC OnLine NCLAT 474

the insolvency process was stayed by the NCLT, or was delayed on account of litigation or other reasons, the period for which the progress of insolvency process was impacted could be excluded; no need for extending the time arises in such cases, it held.

In this trendsetting judgment, the NCLAT held that if a request is made by the RP or the CoC or any aggrieved person for justified reasons, it is up to the NCLT or the NCLAT to exclude a certain period for the purpose of counting the total period of 270 days as long as the facts and circumstances justify that exclusion.

The NCLAT decided that after exclusion of the period, extra time allowed cannot exceed 270 days. Unfortunately, gradually, the rule of exceptions propounded by the NCLAT in *Quinn Logistics* has become the norm. Now, the NCLT extends the timelines almost mechanically if requested. Endless exclusion of time is justified on the grounds of preventing the consequences of a chopper falling, as stated by Justice Rohinton Fali Nariman in *Arcelor Mittal.*[4] In his eloquent style, Justice Nariman said, *'We cannot forget that the consequence of the chopper falling is corporate death … We must not forget that the corporate debtor consists of several employees and workmen whose daily bread is dependent on the outcome of the corporate insolvency resolution process. A reasonable and balanced construction of this statute would therefore lead to the result that … the period of time taken in litigation ought to be excluded.'*

In *Swiss Ribbons*, Justice Nariman wrote that the IBC is a beneficial litigation for revival of enterprises, and that liquidation is the last resort. The NCLT often relies on this decision of the Supreme Court to justify extension in timelines. Of course, exclusion or extension of timelines can be justified based on facts and circumstances of a given case. It is also fair to allow a reasonable opportunity for revival of a troubled enterprise if the commercial expert, that is the CoC, is of the opinion that

4 *Arcelor Mittal India Pvt Ltd v. Satish Kumar Gupta & Ors*, (2019) 2 SCC 1

revival is possible. But to say that liquidation is the last resort is, in the author's humble opinion, a misreading of the IBC and the fundamental principles on which any insolvency law, including the IBC, rests.

One of main objectives of the IBC is the maximization of value of assets. The IBC makes the CoC responsible to exercise its commercial judgement to achieve this objective. The law unequivocally empowers the CoC to achieve maximization of assets by approving a resolution plan for revival of the corporate debtor under S. 30(4) of the IBC, or through the process of liquidation. Consistent with best global practice and economic principles of insolvency law, S. 33 gives the CoC unfettered power to decide to liquidate a corporate debtor at any stage of the insolvency process if it reaches a commercial decision that revival is not possible, a provision whose import was overlooked by Justice Nariman in his judgment.

The Supreme Court, while recognizing the supremacy of commercial wisdom of the CoC, took away that very commercial power from the CoC by overlooking the fact that maximization of assets is also possible through liquidation. As a result, even for companies which have no assets, employees, or prospects of revival, effort must be made for revival. The can is kicked again and again down the lane to complete 270 days or more before liquidation is finally ordered. By then, any value that remained in the insolvent company is depleted. It becomes bankrupt – literally and not just by definition in the IBC. This has become one of the main obstacles in early conclusion of insolvency cases and in maximizing the value of assets.

III

Coming back to JIL, out of the five expressions of interest received, only Suraksha and NBCC submitted their plans and entered a negotiation stage with the CoC; the other prospective resolution applicants either did not submit any plan or sent across a proposal that did not qualify as one. While NBCC is a premier government enterprise, Suraksha is part of the Suraksha Group, promoted by Sudhir Valia (co-founder of Sun Pharmaceutical Industries Limited), with experience of acquiring and resolving stressed companies. The resolution plans of both NBCC and Suraksha were under reckoning, but undisputedly, NBCC was way ahead in the race. The homebuyers perceived the plan put in by a government company as far more reassuring. Having burnt their fingers with private sector developers, JIL and JAL, they were sceptical of putting their faith in another private party.

Most banks also seemed comfortable backing the NBCC's plan. The resolution plans of NBCC and Suraksha contained many complex commercial and legal provisions. It required a lot of back and forth between the CoC, IRP, and both NBCC and Suraksha and their respective advisors. The banks needed adequate time to negotiate the terms with NBCC and obtain approvals from their competent authorities before they could green signal the plan for voting. Homebuyers were also negotiating hard with NBCC, but they were also desperate for a closure before completion of the IBC-prescribed cycle of 270 days.

As stated, there was little clarity in those days if the timeline of the process could be extended. Even as per *Quinn Logistics*, it was the NCLT's discretion to allow it or not.

IV

IDBI Bank requested the IRP to approach the NCLT and request for the exclusion of the time lost due to voting impasse in the CoC because of homebuyers not voting in adequate numbers. Also, the applications seeking clarification on the manner of counting the votes were still pending before the NCLT. Most banks suggested that while time could not be extended, request for exclusion could be made by the IRP. The IBC requires the CoC resolution be approved by 66 per cent majority for making an application for extension, but arguably, no such resolution was needed if it was being sought by the IRP on account of legitimate hurdles faced in timely completion of the process.

In the CoC meeting held on 26 April 2019, both resolution plans were discussed. However, the NBCC resolution plan was found by the IRP to be non-compliant of the IBC thus leaving only the Suraksha plan for consideration by the CoC. The CoC decided to put the Suraksha plan to vote. It was rejected by the CoC as only 23.47 per cent voted in its favour whilst others either rejected or abstained.

On 6 May 2019, day 270 of JIL's insolvency process, the NCLT directed the IBBI and the representatives of allottees to respond in writing to the IRP's request if any period could be excluded from JIL's insolvency process. While adjourning the matter for a later date, the NCLT provided an opportunity to the CoC to vote on the NBCC resolution plan, subject to the outcome of final orders on the application for exclusion for time made by the IRP.

V

In the pre-scheduled meeting of the CoC, on 9 May 2019, the banks expressed relief on having been granted time to consider the NBCC plan. Homebuyers pressed that the NBCC resolution plan be finalized and put to vote at the earliest. The NCLT had given them a small window to consider the plan; they did not want to miss it, they argued. The banks, however, insisted that NBCC plan was still not refined enough to put to vote and more time was needed to close outstanding terms with NBCC. The CoC meeting was rescheduled to 14 May 2019.

In that meeting too difference in opinion persisted. The banks wanted more time while homebuyers pressed upon the IRP to put the resolution plan of NBCC to vote. Homebuyers representative interpreted the NCLT order as a direction to the CoC to take the NBCC plan to its logical conclusion within the time specified; the banks insisted that there was no such direction. As the NCLT had provided a short window, and liquidation of JIL could not be risked, the IRP decided to put the NBCC plan to vote and requested banks and NBCC to finalize it before voting commenced on 20 May 2019. The banks did not agree with the IRP's decision. Later, the NBCC plan was also rejected by the CoC upon voting.

VI

The banks decided to approach the NCLT to seek clarification of its order of 6 May 2019. However, the Allahabad bench convened only twice a week in those days due to shortage of the NCLT members. As a result, it was not available to consider the banks' application before voting commenced. It decided to instead approach the NCLAT for clarification. IDBI Bank pleaded in its application filed on behalf of the banks that more time was needed to discuss the plan with NBCC to make it feasible and viable. By an order passed on 17 May 2019, the NCLAT annulled the ongoing voting and provided time to the CoC to negotiate the plan further with NBCC. The date for voting was extended to 31 May 2019 when the plan was rejected by the CoC. In a way, both plans were stillborn mainly due to a large section of the CoC, comprising homebuyers, abstaining from voting.

During the pendency of IDBI Bank's appeal, Adani Infra (India) Ltd filed an application and sought permission of the NCLAT to submit a resolution plan.

VII

Now, the NCLAT had two appeals before it: one being against the order passed by the third member of the NCLT on the method of calculation of votes cast by homebuyers in the CoC, and the other being the appeal from the NCLT order on extension of time.

The NCLAT decided on both the appeals on 30 July 2019. Noting that lack in clarity on counting of votes by homebuyers in a class of creditors created an extraordinary situation and resulted in a logjam, the NCLAT chairperson stated that it was a fit case to exclude certain days while calculating 270 days. The NCLAT observed that in fact 260 days could be excluded – from the date when the application was filed by IDBI Bank and the homebuyers for clarification (17 September 2018) to when the final decision on the applications was made by the third NCLT member (4 June 2019).

However, as JIL's insolvency process was pending since long, the NCLAT decided that it was inclined to exclude only ninety days and not the entire 260 days. It further ordered that the voting share of the allottees be counted in terms of the IBC as it existed on the date of voting or in accordance with the majority decision of the NCLT. This part of the NCLAT Order became redundant due to amendment made in the IBC two weeks later – on16 August 2019, the government amended the IBC to provide a mechanism for counting votes polled by members in a class of creditors, as discussed in the previous chapter.

The NCLAT directed the IRP to start the resolution plans process afresh; none of the resolution plans received earlier were to be considered, the NCLAT ordered. It permitted Adani Infra (India) Ltd to submit a plan, if eligible. Liberty was, however, denied to JAL in view of the observation and decision of the

Supreme Court in *Chitra Sharma*. Fresh resolution plans were to be submitted and considered within forty-five days; and in the remaining period of forty-five days, the NCLT was to consider the resolution plan placed before it for approval.

Homebuyers were furious with the order of extension by ninety days and the NCLAT's direction to start the process of invitation of resolution plans afresh and permitting new parties like Adani Infra (India) Ltd to come in at this stage. They decided to knock the Supreme Court's door for the second time with their grievances.

VIII

JAL and some homebuyers challenged the NCLAT's decision in the Supreme Court. This was JIL's second trip to the apex court. The main contention of JAL was that neither the NCLT nor the NCLAT had the power to extend the timeline of 270 days sans any express provision in the IBC for extension of time. They maintained that the insolvency process should be held to have come to an end, and since liquidation was not feasible, interest of homebuyers could be protected by allowing JAL to complete the construction of the projects.

Homebuyers, on the other hand, stated that an opportunity should have been granted to consider the NBCC plan only rather than inviting new resolution plans all over again. Moreover, they argued, only a short window should have been granted for this and not a duration of three months.

IX

While the matter was pending in the Supreme Court, the government amended the IBC on 16 August 2019 to provide for overall time limit for completing insolvency process.[5] A proviso was added to S. 12(3) of the IBC which states that the insolvency resolution process shall be completed within a period of 330 days from the insolvency commencement date. This period of 330 days includes the actual period of 180 days; one-time extension, if any, up to ninety days; and another extension of up to sixty days after 270 days. Any exclusion of time taken in legal proceedings has to be made from the total period of 330 days. It also mandated that an insolvency process which was pending and not completed within the period of 330 days as on the date of amendment, that is, 16 August 2019, shall be completed within a further period of ninety days, that is, by 14 November 2019. Thus, JIL's insolvency process became instrumental in yet another legislative change.

Later on, in *Essar Steel India Limited*, the Supreme Court struck down the term 'mandatorily' inserted in S. 12 while amending it, as being manifestly arbitrary under Article 14 of the Constitution of India and as being an unreasonable restriction on the litigant's right to carry on business under Article 19(1)(g) of the Constitution.

The effect of this declaration is that ordinarily the time taken in relation to insolvency must be completed within the outer limit of 330 days from the insolvency commencement date, including extensions and the time taken in legal proceedings. If, however, in the words of the Supreme Court, the delay or a large part thereof is attributable to the tardy process of the NCLT and/or the NCLAT itself, it may be open in such cases to extend time beyond 330 days, but that remains applicable for only exceptional cases; the general rule being that a period of 330 days is the outer limit for resolution of the stressed assets of the corporate debtor, beyond which it is to be driven into liquidation.

5 See Insolvency and Bankruptcy Code (Amendment Act), 2019; S. 12

X

The Supreme Court considered the appeals on 6 November 2019. After cogitating over the submissions made by the parties, Justice Dinesh Maheshwari in writing the decision for the Court in *Jaiprakash Associate* noted that the ultimate fallout of accepting the stand taken by JAL and homebuyers was that the NCLAT order would be set aside and the parties be relegated to a situation where the only option left would be to proceed with JIL's liquidation on the premise that no resolution plan was received or approved upon voting before the expiry of the prescribed period. The Court noted that there was complete unanimity between all the stakeholders that the liquidation of JIL must be eschewed as it would do more harm to the interests of the stakeholders, particularly the large number of homebuyers.

As both legal issues raised in appeals (method of counting of votes and power to extend time) had been resolved by amendments made in the IBC on 16 August 2019, the Court found it neither necessary nor appropriate to dilate the issues as urged before it. The Supreme Court noted that the project was implemented partially, and out of over 20,000 homebuyers, a substantial number were put in possession while the remaining work was either in progress or at an advanced stage of completion. Against this backdrop, the Court decided it would be in the interest of all concerned to accept a viable plan reflecting the recent legislative changes. It proceeded to again exercise the plenary powers under Article 142 of the Constitution of India to ensure substantial justice in the cause.

Drawing from *Chitra Sharma*, the Court rejected the suggestions given by a section of homebuyers that the entire process be kept outside the dispensation of the IBC and that the Supreme Court oversee it instead. The temptation of accepting the said submission was in conflict with the opinion expressed by the three-judge bench of the Supreme Court in *Chitra Sharma*, Justice Maheshwari noted.

The Court observed that an extraordinary situation had arisen in JIL's case because of the constant experimentation in the IBC which went about at different levels due to lack of clarity on matters crucial to the decision-making process of the CoC. Besides that, many other legislative changes made in the CIRP Regulations had expanded the scope of the resolution plan to include provisions for restructuring the corporate debtor by way of merger, amalgamation, and demerger. The power has been bestowed on the CoC to not only consider the feasibility and viability of the resolution plan but also the manner of distribution proposed, which may consider the order of priority amongst the creditors by amendment in S. 30 of the IBC.

In this peculiar and extraordinary situation, the Court decided it would be proper to permit the IRP to reissue the request for the resolution plan. The Court, however, did not agree with the NCLAT's order that resolution plans should be invited afresh from all eligible resolution applicants. Only the two bidders – NBCC and Suraksha, who had earlier submitted the plans – should be called upon to submit revised plans, which could be placed before the CoC. This was because the CIRP Regulations unambiguously postulate that with the approval of the CoC, a request for resolution plans can be reissued by the RP if the resolution plans received are not satisfactory, subject to the condition that the request is made to all prospective resolution applicants in the final list.

In JIL's case, only two bidders had participated and submitted their resolution plan which were placed before the CoC. It was made clear that the IRP shall not entertain any expression of interest or improved resolution plan individually or jointly or in concert with any other person. The Court reiterated that directions were being issued in the exceptional situation in the face of JIL's case and shall not be treated as a precedent. The Supreme Court restated that JAL was disallowed from submitting a plan as already decided in *Chitra Sharma*.

The Supreme Court directed that the insolvency resolution process shall be completed within a period of ninety days from the date of its decision. During the first forty-five days, the IRP will invite revised resolution plan only from Suraksha and NBCC, and if a plan is approved by the CoC, submit it to the NCLT. In the second phase commencing from 21 December 2019, the NCLT will pass appropriate orders within the remaining forty-five days. The Court also passed an extraordinary order stating that the pendency of any other application before the NCLT or the NCLAT shall be no impediment for the IRP in receiving and processing the revised resolution plan from the two bidders and taking them to its logical conclusion as per the provisions of the IBC.

Once again, the Supreme Court reaffirmed the supremacy of the IBC by not taking it upon itself to monitor the process or allowing any resolution applicant to come forward after the resolution plans were received. Pertinently, the Court's interpretation of the CIRP Regulations was to change the fate of Suraksha, which seemed otherwise out of the race.

13

The Cakewalk

A government big enough to give you everything you want is a government big enough to take from you everything you have.

– Gerald R. Ford

Following the Supreme Court's decision of 6 November 2019 in *Jaiprakash Associates*, the IRP invited NBCC and Suraksha to submit revised plans. The revised resolution plans received from both were placed for consideration in the CoC meeting held on 7 December 2019. The members of the CoC requested both the resolution applicants to improve their offers. Many negotiations went on with NBCC and Suraksha on the legal compliance of their plans. Both the resolution applicants agreed to submit addendum to their plans. Suraksha submitted an addendum on 7 December 2019 and NBCC on 8 December 2019. Everything happened seamlessly. It appeared that finally, after nearly two years, a semblance of order had come about in the insolvency process. But unfortunately, it proved to be the lull before the storm.

II

The attention of the entire CoC had been on the NBCC plan from the very start. Even in this round, after the Supreme Court's intervention, NBCC was the frontrunner. In its resolution plan, NBCC proposed that against the admitted claim of Rs 9,783 crore (US$ 1,179 million) of lender banks, ownership of 1,526 acres in various land parcels of JIL would be transferred to lenders. The NBCC plan estimated the value of 1,526 acres at Rs 5,001 crore (US$ 603 million). It proposed the formation of special purpose vehicles (SPV) where different assets of JIL, including some parcels of land and the Yamuna Expressway, would be hived off. Lenders would be transferred 100 per cent ownership of the Yamuna Expressway including the remaining concession rights. Expressway SPVs would raise fresh borrowings of Rs 2,200 crore (US$ 265 million) and pay it to JIL as part of the consideration for transfer of the expressway. Transfer of rights of the Yamuna Expressway was a term to be stipulated in the plan.

Against the admitted claim of the principal amount of Rs 9,588 crore (US$ 1,155 million) of homebuyers, the NBCC plan provided that they would get their completed units between nine and forty-two months from the date of transfer of JIL to NBCC as per schedule provided in the plan. NBCC would not pay penalty for past delays in units to be constructed and delivered. It would, however, pay delay penalty at Rs 5 per sq. ft. (US$ 0.06) per month only if there was delay in delivery for more than one year from the dates mentioned in the plan subject to force majeure event. Homebuyers who had not filed their claims would be treated the same as other homebuyers and would be provided units, subject to customary check for compliance of the customers. The entire admitted claim of the refund seekers of Rs 64 crore (US$ 7.71 million) would be settled by payment of an amount not exceeding Rs 62.40

crore (US$ 7.52 million) of which 20 per cent would be paid upfront and the remaining amount paid in equal parts over a period of four years, that is 20 per cent each year in the manner provided under the resolution plan. Fixed deposit holders had a claim of Rs 29 crore (US$ 3.30 million) which was proposed to be paid in full upfront within ninety days; liability of fixed deposit holders who did not file their respective claims would be relinquished, the NBCC plan provided.

The CoC was convinced that the NBCC plan was commercially reasonable. But the problem with it was that the NBCC had its eyes on the Rs 750 crore deposited by JAL in the Supreme Court and kept with the Allahabad bench of the NCLT. The NBCC's plan sought the transfer of Rs 750 crore (with interest) to JIL to be used exclusively for construction of houses. The NBCC retained the right to withdraw its resolution plan in case the sum along with interest accrued thereon was not made available to JIL.

The NBCC plan was also very demanding on YEIDA. The plan stated that liability for additional farmer compensation of Rs 1,689 crore claimed by YEIDA was not payable by JIL as there was an arbitration award by an arbitral tribunal holding that additional compensation was not JIL's liability. Hence, no provision was made in the plan to pay it. However, if this amount was found payable on account of the arbitration award being upturned by a higher court, YEIDA should collect this money directly from the end-users, i.e., homebuyers. The NBCC would have no responsibility in this regard, the plan stated.

It was unreasonable in that it sought a direction from the NCLT that YEIDA and other concerned authorities extend the concession period (thirty-six years) under the concession agreement with an additional period of ten years. Another fatal provision in the NBCC plan was in respect of additional floor area ratio (FAR). JIL had won an award by an arbitral tribunal on sanction of additional FAR, which had been challenged in court by YEIDA. The plan proposed that YEIDA withdraw the appeal filed challenging the award. It sought a direction that JIL get the right to use additional FAR as per the resolution plan.

The resolution plan provided for deemed approval of YEIDA for transfer of land and toll road to designated SPVs without incurring any costs such as stamp duty, transfer charges, etc., to JIL. It also said approval given by the NCLT to the resolution plan shall result in business transfer to be undertaken between JIL and Expressway SPVs, without requiring a separate approval from YEIDA. Most terms of the NBCC plan were in dissonance with the concession agreement. These provisions reeked of a sense of entitlement by a government company and would come back to haunt the NBCC. For now, the NBCC proposed to make payment of debt of dissenting financial creditors in the form of equity in the SPVs.

Assets of subsidiaries, holding and other companies in the group to which the corporate debtor belongs are distinct from its own assets, as every entity is considered a separate legal person. Jaiprakash Healthcare Limited (JHL) borrowed money for its own needs from many lenders, one of them being YES Bank. Its immovable properties were mortgaged by JHL to banks to secure repayment of its debt. JIL had provided a corporate guarantee to YES Bank to promise repayment of debt of JHL if default in repayment occurred. YES Bank invoked the corporate guarantee and submitted a claim with the IRP. As stated earlier, the IRP initially admitted the claim but subsequently rejected as the invocation was done after the moratorium had come into effect on 9 August 2017. YES Bank filed an application for initiation of insolvency process in respect of JHL which was pending at the time when the NBCC resolution plan was approved by the CoC. In its resolution plan, the NBCC had proposed a mechanism for sale of assets of JHL and satisfaction of dues of the creditors of JHL. This irked YES Bank which objected to any term in the plan intruding on its rights as a creditor of JHL.

In sum, the NBCC's resolution plan was very fragile and contained many legal flaws and commercially unacceptable terms.

III

To meet the various requirements of provisions contained in the IBC as also the CIRP Regulations, the resolution plan invariably becomes a vast document carrying business plan and financial proposal including treatment of creditors, equity commitment, projected steps, and expected reliefs and concessions. The IBC requires the RP to present only such resolution plan, compliant of its provisions, before the CoC for vote. Simply put, she must place before the CoC the plan along with a report confirming that the plan is in conformity with law. There are many challenges for the RP to provide such affirmation. Amongst many requirements, the IBC necessitates that the resolution plan must be compliant of all the laws in force in India. This is a very broad requirement to satisfy and for the RP to verify. It often becomes difficult for the RP to definitely certify a plan is compliant.[1]

Often, whether a resolution plan is compliant of a law or not may become debatable with the resolution applicant claiming that the plan meets the requirement of applicable laws but the RP maintaining a contrarian view. In such a situation, both solicit opinion from legal experts to form a view. As a measure of caution, the RP seeks an appropriate declaration in the plan by the resolution applicant that no law is violated in any proposal made in the plan. The RP cannot refuse to place the plans before the CoC even if in her opinion it is not compliant of law, but in her report, she must inform the CoC of her views and make other appropriate disclosures and disclaimers.

The plans submitted by NBCC and Suraksha contained many contentious clauses. The NBCC plan sought to make a number of structural changes in the concession agreement between JIL and YEIDA. There was also difference of opinion amongst a few members

1 The IBC, S. 30(2)(e)

of the CoC, homebuyers, the IRP, and both resolution applicants on the conformity of their plans with the IBC provisions. The IBC was a new law, and such differences were not entirely unexpected. The contentious terms were discussed extensively in the CoC meetings and recorded transparently. Both the resolution applicants were requested to provide a declaration and representations confirming that their plans were in compliance with law.

It was impossible for the IRP to sit in judgement of which plan was superior or preferred by each financial creditor, especially when interests of homebuyers, banks and financial institutions were not aligned – homebuyers wanted priority in construction of their homes whereas banks and financial institutions wanted recovery of money against their loan. Thus, again departing from established market practice, the IRP presented both the resolution plans before the CoC for voting as both were compliant of the IBC.

A major disagreement broke out between a member of the CoC and the IRP. ICICI Bank insisted that only one plan can be put to vote and not both. The bank pointed that R. 39 (3) of the CIRP Regulations provides that the CoC shall evaluate the resolution plans received strictly as per the evaluation matrix to identify the best resolution plan and may approve it. It was then suggested that a separate pre-vote be taken to decide which plan should be put for vote before the CoC. The IRP contended that his duty was to put all compliant plans before the CoC for vote as the IBC did not limit consideration to one plan only. The IBC remained silent on this while the author advised the IRP to stay firm on his decision.

IV

In the meeting of the CoC held on 7 December 2019, the matter was again raised for discussion by ICICI Bank. The author explained to the CoC members that the IBC and the CIRP Regulations clearly envisage that if there is more than one compliant resolution plan, the CoC should simultaneously consider and vote upon more than one resolution plan at the same time for selecting one of the available options. He stated that the IRP was obliged to place both the plans if they were found conforming to the conditions stipulated by the IBC. Thereafter, it was for the CoC to consider the plans and vote upon the same. Of course, the CoC can approve only one resolution plan.

The IRP further mentioned that in *Jaiprakash Associates*, the Supreme Court specifically provided that both Suraksha and NBCC would be invited to submit revised plans for consideration. In any case, a regulation cannot override the provision of statute. In law, words are the skin of language. The language is the body of expression for the intention and the object that a particular provision or the statute seeks to achieve. Therefore, it is necessary to ascertain the intention. This view held by the IRP and the author advanced the objective of the IBC.

The CoC lawyers made a bona fide point – what if both resolution plans receive more than 66 per cent votes? They expressed their concern that it could lead to a peculiar situation. It was suggested that to avoid such a situation, the CoC members should consider allowing only one of the two resolution plans to be put to vote. The authorized representative of the homebuyers stated that a majority of homebuyers wrote to him indicating NBCC as their preferred choice.

The *Jaiprakash Associates* judgment also directed placing both revised plan(s) before the CoC, and therefore, to avoid the scenario of liquidation or non-compliance of the Supreme Court direction, the representative suggested that both the resolution plans be put to vote. In the event both the plans receive more than 66 per cent votes, the successful resolution applicant will be decided based on the resolution plan that has received higher number of votes.

After deliberation, IDBI Bank agreed for simultaneous voting over the two plans. The suggestion was also accepted by almost all

CoC members except ICICI Bank and Axis Bank, whose voting share together was only about 2.3 per cent of the total. It was finally decided that both resolution plans would be put to vote simultaneously, and if both secured the minimum threshold of 66 per cent votes, the plan that got an overall higher vote will be considered as the preferred resolution plan. This decision, however, was later challenged before the NCLT.

V

The difficulty faced by the IRP in putting more than one resolution plan to vote came to the notice of the IBBI. Recognizing that this gap needed plugging, the IBBI decided to amend the CIRP Regulations. On 14 February 2020, the IBBI issued a discussion paper to invite comments from public, inter alia, on voting on two or more compliant resolution plans simultaneously. The discussion paper noted that the IBC requires the RP to present to the CoC for its approval resolution plans which conform to the conditions prescribed under the IBC and its regulations.[2]

The language of S. 30(2) of the IBC suggests that all resolution plans which meet the requirements prescribed in the IBC are to be placed before the CoC for its approval. Further, S. 30 (4) states that the CoC may approve a resolution plan by a vote of not less than 66 per cent of voting share of financial creditors. This further seems to indicate that all resolution plans submitted by successful resolution applicants which are compliant can be put to vote simultaneously. It appears that the language of R. 39(3) of the CIRP Regulations – which provides that the CoC shall evaluate the resolution plans received strictly as per the evaluation matrix to identify the best resolution plan and may approve it with

2 The IBC, sub-sections (1) and (2) of S. 30

such modifications as it deems fit – is inconsistent with the IBC provisions. While the IBC envisions that multiple resolution plans can be placed before the CoC for voting, based on the evaluation matrix, its regulations seem to restrict the choice to only the best resolution plan. The assessment of resolution plans based on the evaluation matrix may be subjective on certain parameters. Therefore, exclusion of otherwise compliant resolution plans, merely on the basis of application of evaluation matrix and without subjecting them to a vote, may not always yield the best resolution.

CIRP Regulations Amendments dated 7 August 2020

The difficulty encountered in JIL's case and the approach followed by the IRP became instrumental in yet another amendment to formally include simultaneous voting on two or more plans. The amended regulations provide that the CoC shall evaluate the resolution plans received as per evaluation matrix; record its deliberations on the feasibility and viability of each resolution plan; and vote on all such resolution plans simultaneously. Where only one resolution plan is put to vote, it shall be considered approved if it receives requisite votes. But where two or more resolution plans are put to vote simultaneously, the resolution plan which receives the highest votes, but not less than requisite votes, shall be considered as approved. If two or more resolution plans receive equal votes, but not less than requisite votes, the CoC shall approve any one of them, as per the tie-breaker formula announced before voting. But, if none of the resolution plans receive requisite votes, the CoC shall again vote on the resolution plan that received the highest votes, all subject to the timelines under the IBC.

Later, in *Jaypee Kensington*, the Supreme Court held that the amendment made by the IBBI to provide for simultaneous voting is clarificatory in nature and that the decision of the IRP taken on the basis of pre-amended regulations was, in any case, in accordance with law.

VI

Back to the plans – the ball was now in the CoC's court. It will be useful to mention at this stage that the IBC vests in the CoC the absolute authority to pick the best feasible resolution plan for a company's long-term survival. The CoC is entrusted with the responsibility of unlocking the valuable assets trapped in defaulter companies for their more productive use in the economy. The CoC also decides payments to be made to various stakeholders while being mindful of the priorities of payments mentioned in S. 53 of the IBC, security interest held by creditors, and if any inter se priorities exist amongst creditors.

The Supreme Court has held that commercial wisdom of the CoC is supreme and non-justiciable and the NCLT cannot sit in judgment over the commercial terms of resolution plan approved by the CoC. Its jurisdiction is circumscribed by S. 31 of the IBC which provides that the NCLT has only to test the legality of the resolution plan against the backdrop of the IBC provisions mentioned in S. 30(2) and the CIRP Regulations. Pertinent to mention that decisions taken by the CoC impact not only the life of the corporate debtor and consequently its stakeholders, but has wider ramifications for the country's economy. The CoC is expected to discharge this responsibility with great care.

The resolution plans were put to e-voting from 10 December 2019 to 16 December 2019. NBCC's resolution plan was approved by a vote of 97.36 per cent. The voting results were circulated by the IRP to the members of the CoC on 17 December 2019. On the instructions of the CoC, the IRP issued the letter of intent to

NBCC on the same day, which was duly accepted by the NBCC. Later, the IRP filed an application before the NCLT seeking approval of NBCC's resolution plan.

At this stage, given the significance of the case, the principal bench of the NCLT at New Delhi transferred the proceeding to itself, and the plan was confronted by tough objections from YEIDA and ICICI Bank.

14

Must Shylock Have His Pound of Flesh?

He hath disgraced me, and hindered me half a million; laughed at my losses, mocked at my gains, scorned my nation, thwarted my bargains, cooled my friends, heated mine enemies – and what's his reason?

~ *The Merchant of Venice* (Act 3, Scene 1)

Distribution of proceeds from the corporate debtor's estate is the penultimate and the most anticipated event. Parties expecting their claims to be paid eagerly wait for this moment. In fact, they may have had to wait for years and mostly not without struggle. But distribution of proceeds is not free from challenges and can often result in disappointment for many claimants as insolvency laws generally rank creditors by reference to their claims for the purposes of distribution of the proceeds of the estate in liquidation.

The priority rules are necessary to provide an equitable treatment to different types of creditors with diverse and competing interests. Most claims are based on a legal and contractual relationship the creditors had with the debtor prior to the insolvency. There are creditors, however, who have not entered such an arrangement with the debtor, such as taxing authorities. The rights of such creditors are governed by many different laws.

While many creditors will be similarly situated with respect to the kinds of claims they hold based on similar legal or contractual rights, others will have superior claims or hold superior rights. The ranking of creditors may be justified by the desirability of the insolvency system to recognize and respect the different bargains, preserve legitimate commercial expectations, foster predictability in commercial relationships, and promote equal treatment of similarly situated creditors.

The Report of the Working Group on Tracking Outcomes under the IBC, IBBI, 10 November 2021states:[1]

> Nobel laureate in Economic Sciences, Mr. Oliver D. Hart argues that a company enters into a series of incomplete contracts which allow every creditor foreclosure rights over the company's assets in lieu of credit. Every creditor feels comfortable on a standalone basis and the company meets commitment towards each creditor in a normal course and life goes on. However, when the company is stressed, it can honour claims of one or a few creditors fully, but not all creditors simultaneously. It is a situation where the claim of an individual creditor is consistent, but the claims of all creditors together is inconsistent with the assets of the company. If every creditor sticks to its pre-insolvency rights, neither resolution of stress is possible, nor can a creditor realise its dues.

However, it is not a simple task for countries to achieve these goals. Public interest and political and social compulsions outweigh the above

1 See the IBBI website for the Report; https://ibbi.gov.in/uploads/whatsnew/4b74947e21c8b01f95bdcb348635ece5.pdf

considerations in many jurisdictions. In addition to this, creditors must make way for priority payments, such as the remuneration of insolvency professionals and the expenses of the insolvency administration. Money may need to be set aside to pay essential suppliers to ensure the continuation of the business and its reorganization and to pay its workmen and labour. In many countries, priority is also provided for post-commencement finance. To the extent that these broader public interests compete with private interests, they may lead to a distortion of normal commercial incentives.

II

Establishing a clear and predictable ranking system for distribution can help to ensure that creditors are certain of their rights at the time of entering into commercial arrangements with the debtor and, in the case of secured credit, facilitate its provision.[2] Global standards on priorities in distribution are well established. The order of priorities is often also termed as 'waterfall' in insolvency parlance.

Under the IBC, S. 53 provides the priority rules. The dues of secured creditors and workmen dues for twenty-four months preceding the insolvency commencement date rank pari passu and must be paid in priority over all the other dues except the costs of resolution or liquidation, which take precedence over all other dues. A major change made in the IBC from the erstwhile insolvency regime was the abolition of priority of crown debt – state dues under the IBC rank below unsecured creditors in the list of priorities. In India, there were no priority rules until 2011 when the government established the Central Registry of Securitisation, Asset Reconstruction and Security Interest of India under the Securitisation and Reconstruction of Financial Assets and

2 The UNCITRAL Legislative Guide on Insolvency Law, UNCITRAL, p. 267

Enforcement of Security Interest Act, 2002 (SARFAESI Act), as a notice-based registry for security interest.[3]

III

In simple words, ranking of priorities under S. 53 of the IBC is as follows:

1. The insolvency resolution process costs and the liquidation costs paid in full.
2. Workmen's dues for the period of twenty-four months preceding the liquidation commencement date; and debts owed to a secured creditor (where he has relinquished security).
3. Wages and any unpaid dues owed to employees other than workmen for the period of twelve months preceding the liquidation commencement date.
4. Financial debts owed to unsecured creditors.
5. The debt of the following ranks equally:

   (a) Any amount due to the Central government and the state government including the amount to be received on account of the consolidated fund of India and the consolidated fund of a state, if any, in respect of the whole or any part of the period of two years preceding the liquidation commencement date.

   (b) Debts owed to a secured creditor for any amount unpaid following the enforcement of security interest.

3 A Working Group under the chairmanship of Mr M.R. Umarji, then Legal Advisor, the Indian Bank's Association, was set up to recommend measures for strengthening of secured transactions framework. The Working Group presented its report to the Ministry of Finance, Government of India. The report was written by the author for the Working Group. The report led to amendments in SARFAESI.

6. Any remaining debts and dues.
7. Preference shareholders, if any.
8. Equity shareholders or partners, whatever the case may be.

The workmen's dues, however, continue to rank pari passu with the dues of secured creditors as in the past. The decision to include payment of dues of workmen in priority to dues of other unsecured creditors is a political and social compulsion for India and is not uncommon in insolvency laws. Insolvency laws often attribute priority rights to certain (mainly unsecured) claims, which in consequence will be paid in priority to other unsecured and non-privileged (or less privileged) claims. These priority rights, which are often based upon social and sometimes political considerations, militate against the principle of pari passu distribution and generally operate to the detriment of ordinary unsecured creditors by reducing the value of the assets available for distribution to them. The provision of priority rights has the potential to foster unproductive debate on the assessment of which creditors should be afforded priority and why. It also has an impact on the risk premium and cost and availability of credit, which increases as the amount of funds available for distribution to other creditors decreases.

Some priorities are based on social concerns – such as social welfare legislation – that can be addressed more readily by law than by designing an insolvency law to achieve social objectives that are only indirectly related to questions of debt and insolvency. Providing a priority under the insolvency law may at best afford an incomplete and inadequate remedy for the social problem and, at the same time, render insolvency proceedings less effective.

Similarly, employee claims are afforded priority over dues of unsecured creditors under the IBC. In many countries, they rank equally with taxes and social security claims in a single class of priority claims and may be satisfied proportionately in the instance of insufficient funds. In others, no priority is provided for employee claims and they are ranked as ordinary, unsecured claims; although, in some cases, payment of certain obligations accrued over specified periods of time (for example, wages and remuneration arising in the three months before commencement of insolvency proceedings) may be guaranteed by the state through a wage guarantee fund or insurance scheme providing a separate source of funds to ensure the settlement of employee claims. The fund guaranteeing the payment of such claims may itself have a claim against the estate and may or may not have the same priority vis-à-vis the insolvency estate as the employee claims, depending upon policy considerations such as the use of public monies (as opposed to the assets of the insolvent debtor) for funding the provision of wage compensation. A usual practice would be for the fund to enjoy the same rights as the employee claims, at least in respect of a certain specified amount that may be denoted in terms of the amounts of wages or the number of weeks of pay.

Once the claims of all secured and priority creditors have been satisfied, the balance of the insolvency estate would generally be distributed pro rata to ordinary unsecured creditors. There may be subdivisions within the class, with some claims being treated as subordinate or with a priority as noted above. Owners and equity holders may have claims arising from loans extended to the debtor and from their equity or ownership interest in the debtor. Many insolvency laws distinguish between these different claims. In respect of the claims arising from equity interests, many insolvency laws adopt the general rule that the owners and equity holders of the business are not entitled to a distribution of the proceeds of assets until all other claims that are senior in priority have been fully repaid (including claims of interest accruing after commencement). As such, these parties will rarely receive any distribution in respect of their interest in the debtor. Distribution would generally be made in accordance with the ranking of shares specified in the company law and the corporate charter. Debt claims, such as those relating to loans, however, are not always subordinated. The priority of these dues under the IBC is no different.

IV

Distribution of proceeds in the resolution plan is a commercial prerogative of the CoC. The effect and interpretation of priority rules for distribution were unclear in the early days of the IBC. The government had to amend the IBC on 16 August 2019 to clarify certain aspects of distribution in the resolution plan.[4] Some of these have been explained by the Supreme Court in cases unrelated to JIL, but these were to have a direct bearing on distribution in JIL's case, which is addressed at relevant places in the book. But the direct decision of the Supreme Court came in *Jaypee Kensington* in respect of distribution proposed for the dissenting financial creditors in NBCC's resolution plan as discussed in the next chapter.

V

As stated, objections opposing approval of NBCC plan were filed primarily by YEIDA, ICICI Bank, and JAL, while YES Bank objected to terms of plan that concerned JHL. Their concerns are discussed here briefly:

ICICI Bank Limited

ICICI Bank objected to approval of resolution plan mainly on the ground that as a dissenting financial creditor it was entitled to

4 The Insolvency and Bankruptcy Code (Amendment) Act, 2019

receive payment of debt not less than the amount it would receive in the event of a liquidation under S. 53 in terms of money and not equity or land as proposed by the NBCC. While the assenting financial creditors were receiving an upfront payment of Rs 300 crore, the same benefit was not being extended to the dissenting financial creditors, it complained. NBCC on the other hand defended the proposal on the grounds that when the assenting financial creditors had accepted equity and land parcels, payment to the dissenting financial creditors in cash would cause prejudice to the rights of the assenting financial creditors. It also argued that the meaning of the word 'payment' includes payment in form of money or in kind.

The NCLT approved the NBCC resolution plan by an order passed on 3 March 2020. Agreeing with ICICI Bank, the NCLT held that payment to dissenting financial creditor must be made in cash. The NCLT also held that it is in its jurisdiction to interfere with the plan and modify it to correct an error to the extent it does not alter the basic structure of the plan. The NCLT then proceeded to modify the terms of the resolution plan to provide that NBCC pay the dissenting financial creditors their dues in twelve monthly instalments along with interest starting from six months from the date of order. In the event that the NBCC failed to repay as prescribed, dissenting financial creditors would be entitled to claim commercial interest over the admitted claim from the date of default, that is, from the first month of twelve monthly instalments. As the case would further play out, it would be realized how by modifying the resolution plan, the NCLT committed a grave error which was to cost the NBCC heavily.

YEIDA

YEIDA made it clear right at the start that it was not opposing the plan but only its construct inasmuch as it proposed changes in the concession agreement by providing for transfer of JIL's rights and obligations to SPVs without incorporating any necessary documentation involving YEIDA, JIL, and the SPVs. Its consent and necessary documentation could not be dispensed with as YEIDA had to keep exercising its rights over the SPVs concerned. It opposed the proposal's claim that the liability of additional farmers' compensation was not of JIL and the stipulation in the plan that in case of the arbitration award being overruled, YEIDA would collect the amount of additional compensation from the end-users of the project land. It also opposed provisions requiring YEIDA to withdraw its challenges to the arbitration awards in respect of additional FAR and additional farmers' compensation.

In its order approving the plan, the NCLT opined that YEIDA being a statutory authority, the CoC should not have approved the condition that the additional compensation would be collected from the end-users. The NCLT proceeded to modulate the terms of the resolution plan to read that YEIDA shall have the right to collect the acquisition cost through the SPVs concerned. With regards to the term in the NBCC plan that the additional compensation need not be paid in respect of the expressway since it would revert to YEIDA after thirty-six years, the NCLT found it appropriate to read down the resolution plan, leaving it open to the parties to have proper recourse over this issue in the competent forum when the occasion so arose. The NCLT observed that the concession agreement was based on the statute created by the state government and, therefore, any violation of its terms and conditions amounts to violation of the law in force.

YEIDA, however, made it clear that it is not opposed to the approval of the resolution plan, and as a government agency, it only wanted to ensure that the terms and conditions of concession agreement were observed.

Jaiprakash Associates Limited

Amongst many other objections, JAL opposed NBCC's proposal to stake claim over Rs 750 crore. It raised various other objections against many things in the plan, including its treatment of the guarantees extended by JAL and Manoj Gaur to secure JIL's debt. The NCLT rejected JAL's objections and allowed NBCC to use the amount of Rs 750 crore for construction of units for homebuyers. The reasoning given by the NCLT to support its order was that this money had to be utilized for the creditors of JIL and the obligation owed to them; in the case that the money is returned to JAL, it would be nothing but overreaching the wisdom of the Supreme Court and its directions. The money paid by JAL towards an obligation as per directions of the Supreme Court can no more be considered as the assets of JAL.

As to whether it has been stated in the information memorandum that this amount of Rs 750 crore is an asset of JIL or not, the NCLT stated that every case has to be seen in the context of its facts. If at all, for any reason, this is not shown as the asset of JIL in the information memorandum, can it be said that the Supreme Court transferring the deposit to the NCLT has no meaning? Any order that has been passed by the Supreme Court is binding on all courts and the NCLT. For there being no direction to return this money to JAL or to determine as to whether it has to be paid to JAL or not, it is not for the NCLT to draw any inference other than that this money is an asset of JIL. Since JAL is not under further obligation to complete construction of homes, there is no occasion to assume that if this money goes back to JAL, it would be utilized for the cause of the creditors of JIL.

YES Bank

During the pendency of the application before the NCLT, discussions started between the NBCC and YEIDA to find a way to address YES Bank's concerns. The NCLT was apprised on the development, and decided not to pass any order on YES Bank's application in view of the ongoing discussion, which appeared to be close to finding a solution.

Objections raised by YEIDA and ICICI Bank were argued for days before the NCLT. The process of approval of resolution plan took longer than forty-five days as granted by the Supreme Court. Hence, the IRP filed an application before the Supreme Court pointing out various difficulties and unavoidable circumstances which had caused the delay even though the proposal was submitted within the prescribed timeframe. While accepting the reasons stated by the IRP, the Supreme Court, by another order dated 3 February 2020, extended the time for approval of the resolution plan by four weeks.

The NCLT finally approved the NBCC's resolution plan on 3 March 2020 with some modifications. It was clear that the insolvency process of JIL was not going to end there. The NBCC and YEIDA were both going to assail the NCLT order in appeal. And so was the IRP.

VI

As stated, the IBC has vested the CoC with the power to decide distribution to be made to the creditors under the resolution plan approved by it, taking into consideration the relevant provisions of the IBC. In recent years, the IBC has faced criticism for having become lopsided in favour of financial creditors and ignoring the interest of operational creditors (referred to as trade creditors in many jurisdictions). An operational creditor is an individual to whom an operational debt is owed or to whom any such debt has been legally assigned or transferred. An operational debt is a claim for the provision of goods or services, including employment or a debt for the repayment of dues, arising under any law in force for the time being and payable to the Central government, any state government, or a local authority. An operational creditor can file a petition for insolvency against a corporate debtor and has a right to file its claim with the RP during the process. An operational creditor does not have the right to become a member of the CoC as it comprises financial creditors only. An operational creditor is invited to the CoC meeting only if its total dues are 10 per cent or more of the total aggregate debt of the corporate debtor. It can only attend the CoC meetings and participate in its deliberations, but does not have right to vote on agendas placed before the CoC.[5]

A resolution applicant is 'legally bound to pay the operational creditors amount of debt which is not less than the sum it would receive under S. 53 in the event of liquidation'[6] and 'make such payment before any payments are made to those financial creditors which have voted in favour of the plan'.[7] In the waterfall, operational creditors stand way behind in the queue. As a result, many operational creditors do not get paid anything. Because of the assertion of the NCLT, at least employees and workmen of corporate debtors are being voluntarily offered some payment by resolution applicants, if not in full, even if no amount is payable to them because of liquidation value of their debt being nil.

While this approach is consistent with the waterfall, nothing stops the resolution applicant or financial creditor from sparing a reasonable sum for operational creditors. Experience shows that most financial creditors prefer to keep amount proposed under plan for themselves. Thankfully, the NCLAT has held in the case of *Jet Airways*[8] that the provident fund and gratuity payable to employees and workmen has to be paid in full as it is their own

5 The IBC, S. 21

6 The IBC, S. 30(2)

7 The CIRP Regulations, R. 38

8 *Resolution Professional of Jet Airways (India) Ltd. & Ors.*, reported in (2022) SCC OnLine NCLAT 418

money held in trust with the corporate debtor, and does not constitute part of the corporate debtor's assets.

Although the IBC envisages and enshrines a fiduciary responsibility on the CoC to consider and safeguard the interests of all stakeholders including the operational creditors, a summary study of data of the recovery made by the stakeholders from the corporate insolvency resolution process shows that even though recovery of total claims averaged around 32 per cent, with a median of 24 per cent, median recovery for operational creditors has remained as low as 6 per cent. When considering the cases with some of the largest approved plan value (greater than Rs 2,500 crore, US$ 300 million), the average recovery of 34 per cent (with median of 29 per cent) to financial creditor does witness an uptick to average recovery of 46 per cent (with median of 42 per cent). But the median recovery for operational creditor falls further to a median of 5 per cent.[9] This has created resentment amongst operational creditors.

Operation creditors often may not possess the resources or sufficient economic stakes to hire their own advisors or fight for their dues. The priority of treatment of creditors is fundamental to bankruptcy liquidations but strict application of the principle in some cases creates the risk of undermining the reorganization. Thus, from its earliest days in the nineteenth century, the bankruptcy reorganization practice has recognized that certain creditors are 'more important' than others in the sense that, if such creditors are not paid, they could hurt the process of reorganization itself.[10]

9 'Hybrid Insolvency Resolution Process, A Creditor-led, Debtor-in-Possession Resolution Process for India, Insolvency Law Academy, July, 2024. Last seen on 13 August 2024 at: https://insolvencylawacademy.com/wp-content/uploads/2024/08/hybrid-insolveny-resolution-process-v3.pdf

10 'The Triumph of the Trade Creditor' in Chapter 11, 'Reorganizations', Brad B. Erens and Timothy W. Hoffmann, *Pratt's Journal of Bankruptcy Law*, January 2013. Available at https://www.

Although new to India, the need and benefit of paying certain unsecured creditors (including trade creditors and employees) in a case and not others have been a facet of the reorganization practice for a long time. In the US, trade creditors are treated as unsecured creditors. Unlike under the IBC, they have right to participate in a bankruptcy case through official committees of unsecured creditors, which represent the interests of all unsecured creditors. After the enactment of the US Bankruptcy Code, the concept of paying critical vendors has become increasingly common in insolvency cases filed under it, as, for a debtor trying to reorganize, the concept is quite logical. Parties increasingly began to recognize that a debtor's ability to obtain trade terms from key vendors is often critical to the survival and success of a struggling business. From this perspective, one may deem payment to critical vendor as money well spent. This may remain true even from the perspective of an official committee of unsecured creditors, which has the responsibility of representing the interests of the debtor's unsecured creditor body as a whole.

Once the concept of being able to pay critical vendors became relatively mainstream, the concept itself began to broaden.[11] One of the original concepts was that a debtor needed to pay certain vendors who were the 'sole source' of a key good or service.[12] If the payment were not made, such vendor, if it were sufficiently dependent on the debtor, might actually go out of business. Alternatively, the key vendor might instead simply refuse to do business with the debtor. In either case, the debtor would be without a vital product or service needed for its business.

If the operational creditor is a small or medium enterprise, it only aggravates the problem for such creditor. Indian micro,

---

jonesday.com/en/insights/2013/01/the-triumph-of-the-trade-creditor-in-chapter-11-reorganizations-ipratts-journal-of-bankruptcy-lawi

11 Ibid.

12 In CoServ, LLC, 273 B.R. 487, 498-501 (Bankr. N.D. Tex. 2002)

small and medium enterprises contribute more than 29 per cent to the country's gross domestic product (GDP). They are responsible for 50 per cent of country's total exports. They employ more than 11 crore (110 million) people.[13] The sector contributes significantly to the economic and social development of the country by fostering entrepreneurship and generating large employment opportunities at comparatively lower capital cost, next only to agriculture.

Micro, small and medium enterprises are complementary to large industries as ancillary units and this sector contributes significantly in the inclusive industrial development of the country. They form the foundation of the Indian economy.[14] Their distress can cause a cascading effect on economy. A fair and equitable treatment to operational creditors thus serves a larger economic cause of a country.

Indian policymakers are in a fix. While insolvency standards require operational creditors to stand far back in queue, many financial creditors sitting in the CoC have not shown enough maturity thus far to provide equitable treatment to operational creditors. For this reason, the demand for introducing pre-insolvency resolution process is rising in the country. In such

---

13 Annual Report 2022-2023, Ministry of MSME, Government of India. Last seen on 15 May 2024 at https://www.google.com/search?client=safari&rls=en&q=Annual+Report+20222023%2C+Ministry+of+MSME%2C+Government+of+India&ie=UTF-8&oe=UTF-8

14 As per the National Sample Survey (NSS) 73rd round, conducted by National Sample Survey Office, Ministry of Statistics & Programme Implementation during the period 2015–16, there were 633.88 lakh unincorporated non-agriculture MSMEs in the country engaged in different economic activities (196.65 lakh in Manufacturing, 0.03 lakh in Non-captive Electricity Generation and Transmission, 230.35 lakh in Trade and 206.85 lakh in Other Services) excluding those MSMEs registered under (a) Sections 2m(i) and 2m(ii) of the Factories Act, 1948, (b) Companies Act, 1956 and (c) construction activities falling under Section F of National Industrial Classification (NIC) 2008.

processes, operational creditors get better treatment when it comes to the payment of their dues.

This has converted the IBC into a law favourable to secured creditors. It can, however, also be stated that the IBC is anti-operational creditors. Operational creditors neither have a seat in the CoC (unless their aggregate debt is 10 per cent or more of the total debt of the corporate debtor) nor do they have a vote. Invariably, the value they receive for debt is insignificant because of how they are placed in the priority list for distribution under S. 53 of the IBC. In a way, the IBC is both anti-debtor and unfriendly to creditors other than the financial creditors. Some semblance of balance has been brought about by the Supreme Court in *Prabhjit Singh Soni* for operational creditors such as landowning authorities like YEIDA and NOIDA which have allotted or leased land to developers as discussed in later chapters of the book.

15

He Who Grasps All Will Lose All

Ah, but a man's reach should exceed his grasp,
Or what's a heaven for?

\- Robert Browning

As expected, appeals were filed before the NCLAT against the NCLT order approving the NBCC resolution plan. The NBCC was aggrieved by modifications made in its plan by the NCLT changing commercial terms of the plan instead of relegating the matter to the CoC to consider the resolution. Members of the CoC had the right to reconsider their views on the resolution plans and vote afresh after the NCLT held that payments to dissenting financial creditors have to be made in the form of money and not land or equity. JAL too challenged the order of the NCLT.

By an interim order passed on 22 April 2020, the NCLAT asked various parties to file their responses. Meanwhile, the NCLAT directed that affairs of JIL would be managed by an interim monitoring committee. It directed the IRP to constitute the committee comprising NBCC, the IRP, and three major institutional financial creditors (who were members of the CoC)

– IDBI Bank, Indian Infrastructure Finance Company Limited (IIFC), and Life Insurance Corporation (LIC) of India.

II

Some homebuyers approached the Supreme Court and requested that the matter be heard by the apex court to prevent any further delay. As contentious issues were involved, it could take long for the matter to be finally decided by the NCLAT, they urged. As the aggrieved party was likely to approach the Supreme Court for decisive decisions on these issues anyway, the Supreme Court might as well hear the matter earlier than later, they reasoned. Considering that the insolvency process of JIL had already dragged for long, the Supreme Court decided to transfer all the appeals to itself on 6 August 2020. The Court stayed the NCLAT's order forming the interim monitoring committee and directed the IRP to manage the affairs of JIL.

The Supreme Court order had the effect of putting the IRP, Anuj Jain, back in charge of JIL to oversee the corporate debtor as a going concern and protect the interest of JIL, all subject to the outcome of the appeals. Later, on the IRP's request, the Supreme Court passed an order restoring the moratorium under S.14 of the IBC. It's important to note that the IBC provides that order of moratorium shall be lifted on passing of the order of approval for the resolution plan by the NCLT. Since technically the NBCC plan had been approved, the moratorium stood vacated.

III

The Supreme Court heard the appeals over many days. Finally, the *Jaypee Kensington* judgment was pronounced on 24 March

2021. While providing clarity on the meaning of many IBC provisions, the judgment put to rest many contentious issues in JIL's case. The questions of law settled by the Supreme Court in *Jaypee Kensington* are discussed in Chapter 26. Their implications on JIL's case in general and NBCC's plan in particular are summarized as follows:

Modification of Concession Agreement

The Court held that the concession agreement executed between YEIDA and JIL is not a statutory contract but is one by a statutory authority, that is, YEIDA. Its terms can be modified through the resolution plan approved under the IBC. However, if the changes proposed have the effect of tinkering the basic structure of the agreement, approval of YEIDA would be required. The stipulations and assumptions made by NBCC in its resolution plan of transferring leased lands and parts of the Yamuna Expressway Project into SPVs were substantive changes in the agreement; these could not be deemed to have been approved by YEIDA because of the NCLT's approval of the NBCC plan.

Although creation of two special purpose vehicles – one for the expressway and another for the remaining land for commercial development – is not altogether prohibited in law, NBCC cannot suggest that creation of such entities could be done without necessary documentation involving YEIDA. Any alteration in the essentials of the concession agreement would require the consent of YEIDA, the Court decided. Such documentation is even otherwise necessary to avoid any ambiguity about rights and obligations and for YEIDA to properly monitor the functioning of SPVs, each of which would stand in the capacity of a concessionaire and would be carrying the rights and obligations as specified under the agreement.

Additional Farmers' Compensation

The Court also faulted NBCC for unilaterally deciding that in the event of the arbitration award being turned down by a higher court in the future, collection of additional farmers' compensation will be made by YEIDA directly from allottees. No such arrangement existed in the concession agreement according to the Supreme Court. The Court also held that as litigation was pending and JIL's liability of additional farmers' compensation was yet to be finally determined, contingency for payment of additional compensation to farmers should be made in the plan, and the CoC should consider its commercial implication on the plan.

Withdrawal of Litigation by YEIDA

The Court held that YEIDA is a statutory authority; NBCC cannot force it to withdraw the challenge to arbitration award that was made on the issue of FAR and additional farmers' compensation.

The Amount of Rs 750 Crore Belongs to JAL

The Supreme Court decided that the amount of Rs 750 crore belongs to JAL and NBCC cannot stake claim to this money. It should not have prepared the resolution plan by assuming that this amount was the property of JIL when it was not stated so in *Chitra Sharma*. The Court held that the overt reliance by NBCC on the contents of the information memorandum of JIL was also misplaced because the IRP never stated in it that the amount was part of JIL's assets. The Supreme Court, however, allowed JIL to recover its due amounts from JAL after a reconciliation exercise supervised by NCLT, as discussed in later chapters.

Payment to Dissenting Financial Creditors

The Court held that payment to the dissenting financial creditors to discharge obligation of payment of liquidation value should be in the form of a sum of money and not in kind. But, in case a dissenting financial creditor is a secured creditor and a valid security interest created in his favour exists, payment could also be made by allowing such dissenting financial creditor to enforce the security interest. However, such payment shall be to the extent of the value receivable, and in the order of priority available to it. A dissenting financial creditor may choose to accept any other method of discharge of payment obligation by resolution applicant, but such arrangement should be permissible by law, and it should be part of the plan.

Plan of Both Suraksha and NBCC Can Be Put to Vote

The Supreme Court endorsed the decision of the IRP of having put the plans of both Suraksha and NBCC before the CoC for voting.

Many other findings, observations and orders made in *Jaypee Kensington* played a part in the case in varying ways, as is discussed in the later chapters.

IV

The decision of the Supreme Court in *Jaypee Kensington* paved the way for JIL's resolution process to recommence for the third time, after the judgments in *Chitra Sharma* and *Jaiprakash Associates*. Having lifted the clouds of doubt, the Court exercised its plenary powers under Article 142 of the Constitution for the third time in the case to remand the process for approval of resolution plan back to the CoC. It directed the IRP to again invite modified or fresh resolution plans from the NBCC and Suraksha and complete the process within forty-five days. It was made clear that the IRP shall not entertain any expression of interest by any other person.

Another significant direction given by the Supreme Court was to freeze JIL's information memorandum, which effectively meant that the list of JIL's creditors, claims and liabilities could not be altered any further. It is pertinent to mention here that it is the duty of the IRP to continue updating the list of claims and, consequently, the CoC's composition, if it becomes necessary during the process. The claims from homebuyers were still coming in. Apparently, the objective of this direction was to provide certainty to both resolution applicants in preparing revised resolution plans so that no additions could spring new issues in the future.

The Court's order made it abundantly clear that both Suraksha and NBCC shall also take into account the facts and findings recorded in the judgment. The NCLT was directed to decide the plan approval application expeditiously. These directions, particularly for extension of time to complete JIL's insolvency process, the Court clarified, were issued in exceptional circumstances of JIL's case and shall not be treated as a precedent.

As Fennel Hudson said, 'Nature it seems has a way of returning things to how they should be.' NBCC was back before the CoC, having to compete with Suraksha once again.

In the background of the resolution plan process being pushed back to square one, another impediment arose as a sensational disruption in JIL's insolvency case. Anticipated by no one, it was the shocking arrest of the IRP, Anuj Jain.

16

A Dramatic Arrest

No oppression is so heavy or lasting as that which is inflicted by the perversion and exorbitance of legal authority.

~ Joseph Addison

The lowest point of JIL's insolvency process was the arrest of Anuj Jain by the Uttar Pradesh Police from his sister's house in Mumbai. The sensational manner of the arrest made the IRP look like a hardened criminal. The Supreme Court was appalled by the arbitrary action of the Uttar Pradesh Police and ordered his immediate release. Neither the police cooperated nor did the magistrate to release Anuj Jain. The author had to prevent the arrest and bring back Anuj Jain from the doorsteps of the jail.

The justification provided by the investigating officer (IO) for making the arrest was found unreasonable and unconvincing. The IO was reprimanded by the Supreme Court for arresting Anuj Jain and had to tender an apology to the Court. On the legal advice of Tushar Mehta, the Solicitor General of India, a closure report was filed by the IO, and the magistrate closed the case.

Although his arrest was prevented at the last minute, it sent shock waves in the industry. Insolvency professionals across the country wrote to the IBBI to take appropriate steps to protect insolvency professionals from such high-handed actions.

II

The effectiveness of the insolvency and bankruptcy system rests largely on the expertise, dedication, and ethical conduct of the professionals of the insolvency ecosystem. Regardless of the fact that the IBC regime is relatively new, there is a sense of accomplishment in it 'attaining systemic maturity and extraordinary outcomes'. It provides a code of conduct for insolvency professionals, who, as important stakeholders, are required to maintain an equilibrium between 'high degree of proficiency and ethical standards. She is expected to act in good faith in discharge of her duties, with utmost integrity, objectivity, independence, impartiality and make earnest efforts to maximize the value of assets of the corporate debtor. The professionals are expected to maintain the highest standards of professional competence and professional ethics while discharging their duties.'[1]

The duties of an insolvency professional may often involve undertaking tasks that entail serious risks. She may have to deal with antagonistic stakeholders, receive threats or face hostile litigation. The IBC protects actions of the insolvency professional taken in good faith. No suit, prosecution or other legal proceeding shall lie against an insolvency professional or liquidator for anything which is done or intended to be done in good faith under the IBC or the rules or regulations made thereunder.[2]

But what happened to IRP Anuj Jain could not have been prevented by any law. A police officer misusing power and acting at the behest of higher authorities who want to harass a law-abiding citizen, can only be stopped by a court.

1 The IBBI (Insolvency Professionals) Regulations, 2016

2 The IBC, S. 233

III

The Supreme Court had concluded hearing in *Jaypee Kensington* and reserved orders in the case. While the judgment was awaited, a first information report (FIR)[3] was registered on 24 February 2021 against IRP Anuj Jain and the interim monitoring committee (IMC) under Ss. 283 and 431 of the Indian Penal Code 1860, read with S. 7 of the Criminal Law Amendment Act 1932 (now replaced by the Bharatiya Nyaya Sanhita and Bharatiya Nagarik Suraksha Sanhita respectively).

These were serious charges.

S. 431 of the IPC provides that whoever commits mischief by doing any act which renders or which he knows is likely to render any public road, bridge, navigable river or navigable channel, natural or artificial, impassable or less safe for travelling or conveying property, shall be punished with imprisonment of either description for a term which may extend to five years, or with fine, or with both.

According to S. 283 of the IPC, if someone's actions or negligence with any property under their control cause danger, obstruction, or injury to any person in a public place or waterway, they can be punished with a fine of up to two hundred rupees.

S.7 of the Criminal Law Amendment Act deals with molesting a person to the prejudice of employment or business. It provides that whoever with intent to cause any person to abstain from doing or to do any act which such person has a right to do or to abstain from doing, obstructs or uses violence to or intimidates such person or any member of his family or person in his employ, or loiters at or near a place where such person or member or employed person resides or works or carries on business or happens

3 FIR No. 0098 dated 24 February 2021 in Police Station, Greater NOIDA Beta II

to be, or persistently follows him from place to place, or interferes with any property owned or used by him or deprives him of or hinders him in the use thereof, or loiters or does any similar act at or near the place where a person carries on business, in such a way and with intent that any person may thereby be deterred from entering or approaching or dealing at such place, shall be punished with imprisonment for a term which may extend to six months, or with fine which may extend to five hundred rupees, or with both.

The offences listed are as complex as the sections read. If proven, they could lead to imprisonment.

Apparently, the FIR was registered at the insistence of YEIDA, which had written to police authorities alleging that an accident had occurred on 23 February 2021 at Yamuna Expressway in which seven people died. The letter stated that the accident was caused due to the negligence of the IRP and the IMC in taking adequate road safety measures. The police registered the FIR on the same day the letter was written by YEIDA.

It is telling as the police in India is not known to be very prompt in registering FIRs. The reason was apparent; the accident was reported widely by the media and the state government was asking YEIDA for an explanation. To ward off pressure from media and the political establishment, YEIDA insensitively passed the buck across to the IRP. In the process, it did not even spare the IMC members who comprised, besides the IRP, senior officials of three leading banks of the country and NBCC.

The police officials arrived at the office premises of the IRP located at Gurugram in Haryana late in the night, much past the office hours. The police left a notice under S. 160 of the Code of Criminal Procedure, 1973, which called upon Anuj Jain to visit the police station at any point of time within three days from the receipt of the notice to get his statement recorded.

Anuj Jain learnt of the notice and registration of FIR the following morning. Obviously, he was alarmed and contacted the author for advice. The author moved the Supreme Court without any delay to seek quashing of the FIR on the grounds that the IRP was managing the affairs of JIL pursuant to the Supreme Court order dated 6 August 2020 and was thus serving as an officer of the Court; the IRP enjoys immunity under the IBC from any action taken in good faith; and, of course, the allegations made in the FIR were without any basis.

In his petition, Anuj Jain explained that there was no laxity or delay on his part in taking steps to provide for road safety measures; he was carrying out his professional duties to the best of his ability in managing the affairs of JIL in such trying times amidst so many complexities and challenges; targeting him by lodging an FIR against him was completely arbitrary and showed high-handedness on the part of the UP Police; he had taken all reasonable steps within his means to provide safety measures and had acted in good faith.

IV

A brief background about the safety measures at Yamuna Expressway may be useful here in understanding the premise of the FIR filed against the IRP. Over a decade earlier, in a matter unrelated to the Yamuna Expressway, the Supreme Court had constituted a committee to monitor road safety measures being undertaken by the Central and state governments and other concerned authorities.[4] After the Yamuna Expressway became operational in August 2012, the committee directed YEIDA and JIL to get road safety audit of the expressway conducted from a third party. In consultation with YEIDA, JIL appointed the Indian Institute of Technology, Delhi, to conduct the road safety audit. The Institute submitted its report in April 2019.

---

4 Writ Petition (Civil) No. 295 of 2012. Order dated 22.04.2012.

The audit report inter alia recommended installation of guardrails, that is, metal beam crash barrier (MBCB) (Thrie-beam type) on both sides of the median, including MBCB metallic markers all the way from Greater Noida to Agra, and replacing median kerbs with flush medians. It also recommended that the work to be carried may be vetted by experts appointed by YEIDA.

JIL commenced the work. However, the IIT-Delhi report raised some technical issues. YEIDA was requested to form an expert committee comprising the National Highway Authority of India (NHAI), State Public Works Department, engineers from Agra Lucknow Expressway Authority, and the Indian Institute of Technology, Roorkee, to check the technical feasibility of the recommendations made by the IIT-Delhi.

The work was in progress when JIL's insolvency process started on 9 August 2017. Although JIL was facing a liquidity crunch, keeping in mind the safety of users of the Yamuna Expressway, the IRP approved Rs 85.42 crore (US$ 10.39 million) for installation of MBCB on the Yamuna Expressway, in a phased manner, to be completed in the next three years. When the IMC took over JIL's management, in its meeting held on 11 June 2020, it was decided to invite bids for supply and installation of MBCB (Thrie-beam type). A committee was formed to consider the bids received and select the bidder.

V

Back in the Supreme Court, the problem was to get the application listed before the Court in a case where orders had been reserved. The registry of the Supreme Court does not accept filing of any application in a case reserved for orders. The matter had to be brought before the bench of Justice A.M. Khanwilkar who graciously permitted the IRP to file the application. The matter was expected to be listed by the registry in the next couple of days. It was decided that in the meantime Anuj Jain will appear before the concerned IO and provide him the information he needed. It seemed like the right course of action, except that no one anticipated the turn of events that was to take place the next day.

While the registry was taking steps to get the matter listed, Anuj Jain left for Mumbai to see through pre-scheduled meetings. It was an overnight trip that had been scheduled long ago. After his meetings got over, Anuj Jain went to his sister's house for dinner. To his utter shock, the IO reached the house and arrested him at 8 p.m. on 1 March 2021. The only way the police could have known his whereabouts was by tapping his phone or by following him illegally.

Not only was arresting Anuj Jain in this manner utterly outrageous, it was also illegal, because the three days given to him under the notice issued had not yet expired. Anuj Jain had already scheduled to meet the IO and a written communication to that effect had been sent by the author's colleagues. There was no justification for the arrest and the team that arrived in Mumbai to arrest him wasn't willing to listen to anything. Their orders were to arrest Anuj Jain and remand him to police custody so that the media could be informed that the police had acted promptly and arrested the accused in connection with the Yamuna Expressway accident.

Anuj Jain was brought to Delhi on a late-night flight. They arrived on the morning of 2 March 2021 and took Anuj Jain straight from the airport to the magistrate's court in Greater Noida to produce him before the concerned magistrate and seek his remand, which meant he would be sent to jail where the police could investigate him.

The author and his team had to prepare an application of bail and once again mention the matter before the bench of Justice A.M. Khanwilkar. He was furious to learn of the arrest and directed the registry to place the matter before the bench at once. An advance copy of the petition was directed to be served on the standing counsel of the Government of Uttar Pradesh in the Supreme Court.

The Supreme Court expressed deep anguish and shock at Anuj Jain's arrest in its order:

> We are appalled to see that the manner in which the Uttar Pradesh Police has handled this case emanating from F.I.R. No.0098/2021, registered at Police Station Beta-II in District Greater Noida, including to take the extreme step to arrest the Interim Resolution Professional, Mr. Anuj Jain, who was working in that capacity pursuant to the order passed by the Court and entrusted with the functioning of the Company in question.
>
> It is seen that the police official dealing with the case is not familiar with the provision of privilege of Interim Resolution Professional appointed by the Court, in terms of Section 233 of the Insolvency and Bankruptcy Code.
>
> Mr. R.K. Raizada, learned senior counsel appearing for the State of Uttar Pradesh, on instructions, submits that the Investigating Officer, Mr. Bijendra Singh, was of the view that the applicant may leave India at any time to avoid the prosecution and for securing his presence thought it necessary to arrest him from Mumbai.
>
> We will examine this aspect of the matter elaborately at appropriate time by treating this application as substantive writ petition filed by the applicant under Article 32 of the Constitution of India and to be numbered accordingly.
>
> In the meantime, we direct immediate release of the applicant, Anuj Jain, who is presently in custody of Police Station, Beta-II, District Greater Noida, Uttar Pradesh and had been produced today i.e. 02.03.2021 before the Court of Chief Judicial Magistrate, Gautam Buddh Nagar, Uttar Pradesh.

> We further direct the Investigating Officer not to take any coercive action against the applicant in connection with the subject F.I.R. until further orders.
>
> We also issue notice to the Investigating Officer, Bijender Singh, Sub-Inspector, as to why appropriate action is not taken against him for taking such drastic action against the applicant. He shall file his personal affidavit explaining the position within two weeks from today.
>
> List the writ petition after two weeks.
>
> Copy of this order be forwarded to the office of the concerned Judge and Police Station Beta-II, District Greater Noida, Uttar Pradesh through e-mail and the Registrar (Judl.) of this Court shall personally intimate the office of the concerned Judge on telephone to ensure immediate release of the applicant, Mr. Anuj Jain, without imposing any conditions.

Not only did the Supreme Court direct immediate release of Anuj Jain, it directed the registrar (judicial) of the Supreme Court to personally intimate the office of the concerned judge on telephone to ensure his immediate release, without imposing any conditions. The gravity of the matter is made evident by the fact that such orders are passed by the apex court only in very exceptional cases.

VI

Equipped with the directions of the Supreme Court, the author reached the magistrate's court at around 2 p.m. By then, he had ordered the remand of Anuj Jain. The magistrate was sitting in his chamber. A message was sent to him by the author through his staff to apprise him of the order passed by the Supreme Court. He insisted on seeing a copy of the order passed by the Supreme

Court. This was a strange request because as a member of the judicial institution he was supposed to be aware that a copy of the order can only be available after judges rise for the day and sign copies of orders passed during the day. The Supreme Court was still in session and the bench was likely to rise only at 4 p.m.

The author requested the magistrate to accept the author's statement at the Bar as he was present in the Supreme Court when the order was passed. Notwithstanding that, he prepared a written application recording the transcript of the proceedings that took place in the Supreme Court. The magistrate refused to entertain the application. He wanted to see a copy of the order, and he was entitled to do so. Meanwhile, the author's team was chasing the registrar of Supreme Court to get the copy of the order signed and uploaded and to send a copy to the district judge, as ordered by the Court and make the phone call.

The order of Anuj Jain's release was passed by the Supreme Court at noon. Everyone waited for the bench to rise and a copy of the order to be made available. Finally, a copy of the order was put up on the website at around 5 p.m. At the same time, outside the magistrate's court, Anuj Jain sat anxiously waiting in a police jeep.

A copy of the order was downloaded and sent to the magistrate inside his chamber. Much to everyone's horror, the magistrate insisted on a certified copy of the order. Everyone in legal and judicial circles knows that obtaining a certified copy from the registry takes a few days. This was now appearing to be very unusual conduct on the part of the magistrate. The magistrate was again requested to wait for a few minutes as a copy of the order was also expected to reach the magistrate through the office of the district judge who had been sent a copy of the order by the Supreme Court registry.

All this time, the magistrate showed complete disregard for the Supreme Court's order. He refused to sit in court to hear the matter or meet the author in his chamber. He communicated only through his staff.

The author rushed to the office of the district judge located in the same premises as the magistrate's office. His staff was very courteous and cooperative. As soon as the district judge's office received the copy of the order from the registrar, they reached out to the magistrate so that he could pass appropriate orders. By then it was 6 p.m. However, for reasons best known to him, the magistrate had left for his home. When the district judge learnt of this, he directed his staff to arrange to send the file to the magistrate's residence so that he could pass the formal order of release.

Anuj Jain was finally released at 8 p.m. from custody. It is unfortunate that such judicial officials and police officers are part of our justice system. Imagine, this was someone appointed by the Supreme Court being put through such an ordeal, someone who was part of the legal system. One shudders at the thought of what a layperson might have to go through under similar circumstances.

The author advised Anuj Jain to file an affidavit to apprise the Supreme Court of the magistrate's conduct so that the magistrate could be disciplined, but he did not want to prolong his agony any further. He had suffered enough, he said. The two days had been full of mental agony for him and his family.

From the time Anuj Jain was arrested till his release the following evening, neither Anuj Jain nor his family members slept a wink. These were the most anxious and horrible twenty hours of the JIL's insolvency process for the IRP.

VII

Sensing the mood of the Supreme Court, the investigating officer filed a report admitting his mistake. YEIDA also withdrew its letter. The investigating officer filed a report before the magistrate stating that no offence was made out against Anuj Jain and other members of the IMC; the magistrate ordered that no criminal case appeared to be made out against Anuj Jain and ordered closure of the case. The writ petition is still pending in the Supreme Court.

The efforts of the Supreme Court of India in protecting the liberty of citizens of the country deserve to be applauded. In this case, the role of Tushar Mehta, the Solicitor General of India, also needs to be acknowledged. He intervened and advised the higher authorities in the state government to take steps to close the case without any delay as no case was made against IRP Anuj Jain and the IMC.

Anuj Jain was released, and even as JIL's insolvency process has ended, and we may say all is well that ends well, the scars of this episode will always remain for Anuj Jain and his family to feel.

17
When the Going Gets Tough, the Tough Get Going

Patience is not the ability to wait but how you act while you are waiting!

~ Joyce Meyer

Modern insolvency laws require that the debtor company should be kept going during the insolvency process. In simple terms, it means that the business of the debtor should continue uninterrupted during the insolvency process. Keeping the debtor functional has a direct correlation with maximizing the value of the enterprise. The continued operation of the debtor's business after the commencement of the insolvency process and before a plan is prepared and approved is critical to reorganization proceedings.

Going concern is also a concept central to the IBC. The RP is entrusted with the responsibility of keeping the corporate debtor sailing. However, this task is not without challenges in a creditor-in-control insolvency system like that of the IBC. Some disruption in the business is bound to take place on account of change in management when the IRP, who might also be replaced with another insolvency professional and confirmed as the RP a few days later, takes over the affairs of the debtor. The transfer of affairs from the IRP to the RP in such cases may also cause disruption. Yet another transfer takes places when a resolution plan is approved and the successful resolution applicant takes charge from the IRP/RP or the liquidator sells the debtor's enterprise to a bidder as a going concern.

II

When Anuj Jain took over the functions of JIL on 9 August 2017, amongst his first few tasks was taking control of JIL's business and affairs with minimal disruption. Having got a grip on the management, he realized that to keep JIL afloat he would have to do more than just hold the fort for a successful resolution applicant or maintain the status quo. Homebuyers had reposed faith in the IRP. They had hopes that the construction could be accelerated.

Meanwhile, he had also to ensure uninterrupted operations of the Yamuna Expressway. It is a different matter that he never imagined he would have to hold the fort for nearly seven years. Of course, there were other challenges to meet which would have had a direct impact on the going concern status of JIL or in running JIL efficiently in the wake of multiple challenges and distractions. But then, as American educator and professor Randy Pausch said, 'We cannot change the cards we are dealt, just how we play the hand.' He had no choice but to do his best.

The Yamuna Expressway

Managing the expressway was no mean task. It is one of the longest toll roads in the country with heavy traffic. The expressway has six major bridges, including a rail overbridge, forty-one minor bridges, seventy vehicular underpasses, seventy-five cart-track underpasses, and 179 culverts. Barbed-wire fencing is provided along the expressway for unobstructed traffic flow. There are service roads with a total length of 65.51 km to provide access to local commuters. It has dual carriageway consisting of three 3.7-metre-wide lanes in each direction. The expressway also has a 0.7-m-wide paved shoulder and a provision on the median side to facilitate potential future expansion to four lanes in each direction. CCTV cameras are installed at ninety-six locations throughout the expressway; users' call point have been installed at every 5 km for safety and accident assistance; mobile radars are used to monitor and regulate the compliance of minimum and maximum speed limits. All these provisions had to be maintained constantly to ensure quality and standards of the infrastructure and safety of commuters.

There are five security vehicles, five ambulances, six patrol vehicles, six cranes and six firefighting vehicles spread throughout the expressway. These are required to be kept functional at all times.

The expressway has many toll plazas. Of these, the major ones are located near Jewar (38.84 km), Mathura (95.22 km) and near Agra (150.27 km). In addition, there are four exit and four entry ramp toll plazas along the expressway. JIL collects toll from the users of the Yamuna Expressway and earns a handsome amount every day. The revenue is collected from time to time, generally at an interval of three hours; after counting, cash is kept in a safe vault. The cashier hands over the daily collection to the banking cashier and the total collection is deposited into an escrow account maintained with the nominated bank.

At the time of the insolvency commencement date, nearly 98 per cent of toll was collected in cash. This was also a big security risk for JIL and its employees handling the large quantum of cash. During the insolvency process, YEIDA insisted on transitioning to a cashless model of toll collection. This required complete change in the toll collection system and processes. The exercise was completed under the supervision of the IRP in 2021, resulting in nearly 95 per cent of toll now being collected electronically.

Cranes, towing vehicles, and vehicle repairing facilities are available at each toll plaza. Hundreds of persons are employed for toll collection, maintenance of the expressway and for providing many other services. Amongst other, the staff includes doctors, nurses, firemen, and security personnel. A trauma centre is also maintained at each toll plaza with a minor operation theatre, trauma ward, crash cart, advanced ventilation system, etc. Each toll plaza has necessary first-aid medical facilities including ambulances. Doctors are also available at toll plazas. Nitrogen-filling facilities are also provided at each plaza. Solar light facilities are provided for pedestrian underpasses and vehicle underpasses.[5]

The operation and maintenance of the expressway meant maintenance of shoulders, toll plazas, median, tree plantation; undertaking major maintenance such as resurfacing of pavements, repairs to structures and refurbishment of tolling system and hardware and other equipment; undertaking routine maintenance, including prompt repairs, of potholes, cracks, joints, drains, lighting, and signage; carrying out periodic preventive maintenance of the expressway including the tolling system; highway patrolling; maintenance of electrical and communication system and Highway Traffic Management System (HTMS); and medical first aid. The IRP had to ensure that all of this happened seamlessly through his term.

During the insolvency process, the estimated amount of toll collected at the Yamuna Expressway was Rs 2,035 crore (US$

---

5 See Accelerating Infrastructure Investment Facility in India, Jaypee Infratech Limited, Environment and Social Due Diligence Report, November, 2015, prepared by India Infrastructure Finance Company Limited for the Asian Development Bank

245.18 million). Year-wise breakdown of toll income is presented in Table 3 below:[6]

Table 3: Year-wise Breakdown of Toll Collection from Yamuna Expressway

Year	Toll collected (Rs crore)	Toll collected (US Dollar million)
FY17–18 (8 months)	214	25.78
FY18–19	340	40.96
FY19–20	338	40.72
FY20–21	334	40.24
FY21–22	380	45.78
FY22–23	429	51.69

With the Yamuna Toll Expressway being an infrastructure project which operates 24/7, the IRP was required to undertake major capital expenditures and maintenance projects with multiple objectives of sustaining operations, improving safety, and enhancing value. Noteworthy projects undertaken during the insolvency process include installation of metal beam crash barrier across the entire length of the Expressway; resurfacing work on bituminous road surfaces at various places; resurfacing on structures and approaches with micro-surfacing; implementation of Fastag on all toll plazas in a phased manner; construction of new ramps at a few places for easy access; providing and making of precast reinforced cement concrete (RCC) jersey barrier; installation and commissioning of speed cameras; providing and fixing barbed wire for protection at various places; restoration and replacement

6 Data compiled from financial statements of JIL available in public domain

of signage boards; rainwater harvesting; illumination of ramps, and solar-light-based illumination at underpasses; and construction of permanent facility at 107 km.

A few of the above projects were mandated under the concession agreement or directed by YEIDA but many of these were simply done to enhance safety, value, and sustainability.

The safety record of the Yamuna Expressway during JIL's insolvency improved significantly with the number of accidents and fatalities coming down each year. This was achieved by a concerted effort by all stakeholders under the leadership of the IRP and support of the CoC. Table 4 below summarizes the year-wise comparison of traffic and number of accidents on the Yamuna Expressway.[7]

Table 4: Yamuna Expressway: Traffic Vs Accident Data

Years	Total Traffic	Total Accidents	Percentage
2015	16,050,114	919	0.0057
2016	18,577,588	1219	0.0066
2017	20,161,380	763	0.0038
2018	22,145,074	659	0.0030
2019	22,870,940	560	0.0024
2020	21,204,990	509	0.0024
2021	25,768,157	424	0.0016
2022	27,984,862	311	0.0011
2023	29,945,928	411	0.0014
2024	10,375,058	140	0.0013
Total	**215,084,091**	**5,915**	**0.0028**

7 Data compiled from material available in public domain

III

Housing Projects

The residential projects were the toughest task at hand. JIL did not have the cash flow required to continue construction. Not much was left over from the toll collection after meeting the cost of upkeep of the expressway and other costs of keeping JIL afloat. The funds required for the construction were enormous. Just before the insolvency process commenced, a leading independent property consultant appointed by IDBI Bank estimated that the net funding required for completion of real estate projects in Noida (Wishtown and Aman) was Rs 7,262 crore (US$ 874.94 million). This did not include other costs, as explained in Chapter 8. A very ambitious revised schedule of delivery had been submitted to the RERA by the erstwhile management just a month before insolvency commenced. It was impossible to deliver to that schedule unless funds of hundreds of crores was made available.

The IRP tried hard to persuade the CoC to let him raise funds by way of interim finance albeit without success. When companies face financially troubled times, they inevitably find themselves in a situation where their existing lenders and other creditors are looking for a material recovery on their claims as soon as possible. Yet the company itself might be in need of additional borrowings in order to implement a strategy to maximize returns for existing creditors and at least meet the insolvency resolution process costs and provide for regular payments for availing critical input supplies. This assumes greater value when the company has little liquidity but has enough operational capacity to generate revenue and stand on its feet. Funds raised by the debtor company to allow it to continue trading after the commencement of insolvency proceedings and before a plan is prepared and approved are termed as post-commencement finance in insolvency parlance. In the IBC, it is referred to as interim finance.

The IBC allows interim finance to be raised during the resolution process period with the approval of the CoC. To incentivize lenders to extend interim finance, its repayment is assured in priority as insolvency resolution process costs, which gets priority in payment over other debts of the corporate debtor, both in the resolution plan or during settlement of debts in liquidation. However, experience under the IBC shows that convincing potential lenders, pre-existing or new, to fund a business in distress is always a difficult task for an insolvency professional.

Since interim finance could not be arranged, the IRP focused on optimum use of toll collected from the expressway to continue construction to the extent possible. As homebuyers started gaining confidence in the IRP, many started to willingly pay the balance amounts under their instalments when it was demanded from them, particularly those whose units were ready for delivery.

IV

At this stage, the IRP faced another problem. A few members of the CoC were of the opinion that units could be constructed but not transferred to homebuyers as that would amount to making preferential payment to some homebuyers who are also financial creditors. A few also inquired if an asset can be transferred at all given that the moratorium prohibited the debtor from alienating any asset during the insolvency process. The IBBI also appears to be unsure about the legal position on the matter, and so to stay on the side of caution, it advised the IRP to seek clarification from the NCLT.

The author unequivocally advised the IRP that delivering units was part of his duties. One of JIL's main business was to construct and deliver units to its customers. The IRP was duty bound to continue to carry on this business as part of his responsibility to keep JIL as a going concern. Moreover, by delivering units, he would reduce JIL's liabilities because claims filed by homebuyers would also keep reducing. The units were part of inventory and not fixed assets on the balance sheet as they were meant to be sold.

Homebuyers were furious at the suggestion of those who doubted the IRP's powers to deliver the units. The IRP filed an application before the NCLT, but no orders were passed on the application. At no point of time were registrations and transfers between customers stopped as a result of which customers always had the option to sell the units in the secondary market and exit, albeit with a huge loss.

In November 2023, the IBBI floated a discussion paper on real-estate-related proposals in the insolvency process and liquidation. Amongst the many proposals was the proposal to amend regulations to allow execution of registration/sublease deeds with approval of the CoC during the insolvency process. The discussion paper noted that for a business undergoing insolvency process, the IRP/RP needs to ensure continuity, which may involve the acquisition and sale of inventory. However, the real estate sector presented a unique challenge. In some cases, creditors had fulfilled its part of obligation in the contract and the corporate debtor had also constructed the units, but the formal handover remained pending. The courts in their inherent powers permitted the transfer of ownership/registration of the plot, apartment, or building in a few projects during the process.

The proposal stated that keeping in view the larger public good and due consideration to the plight of homebuyers, there is a strong case for allowing transfer of immovable property in appropriate cases if the concerned stakeholders, i.e., creditors have approved the same. This could potentially reduce the disputes at the NCLT as well. Thus, where the allottees have paid the full amount and occupied the units, or possession of a plot, apartment, or building to the allottees has already been handed over to them, the transactions need to be formalized through the transfer of such units during the resolution process with the approval of the CoC. Further, units under technical possession of allotees should not be included in the IBC process by the RP.

Also, it was observed that in a few cases the allottees were interested in taking possession of the units on 'as is where is' basis and would get the remaining development/interiors of their home finished from balance funds which have not been paid by them. The objective in the resolution of the real estate project is a smooth handover of units to the rightful homebuyers. Thus, to expedite the resolution process and avoid delays due to unnecessary hold-ups, allottees can be given the option to take possession of the units on 'as is where is' basis or on payment of the balance amount, if any, after taking into account the funds due and funds required for completing the unit after approval of the CoC.

Once units are handed over, registration/sublease should be done. To facilitate the smooth handover of occupied units or where possession has been transferred to the homebuyers, the IBBI proposed to allow the RP to handover the ownership of a plot, apartment, or building to the allottees through transfer during the resolution process, with the approval of the CoC.

The discussion paper did not result in an amendment apparently on the grounds that such an enabling power of the IRP already existed in the IBC, which had also been recognized by the NCLT in its orders.

V

When the 'going' gets tough, the tough get going. From 9 August 2017 to 7 March 2023, the IRP delivered offer of possession for 8,321 new units to allottees, completed sublease registration of 8,610 units, and handed over 8,930 units.

During the insolvency process, construction was completed and occupancy certificates (OCs) were received for fifty towers (seventeen towers in Kosmos, eight towers in Klassic, four in Kensington Park Apartments, and twenty-two towers in Aman project). Another sixty-two towers were in advanced stage of completion as on 7 March 2023 where some of the units were delivered after approval of the plan. Construction was suspended in eighty-nine towers comprising five projects (Orchard, Garden Isle, Krecent Homes, Kube, and Pebble Court). The cost of construction of these towers was met from the toll collections and payments received from homebuyers. The IRP constantly supervised the quality and standards of construction.

JIL had appointed JAL as the master contractor to construct all the housing units sold by JIL. On the commencement of insolvency, it was decided, with the approval of the CoC, to continue JAL as master contractor, because removing the old and rehiring a new contractor for a company facing insolvency would have been disruptive, and appointing a new contractor challenging. It was decided to continue with JAL as the contractor albeit with adequate safeguards. The IRP appointed Coldwell Banker Richard Ellis (CBRE) initially and Mott Macdonald subsequently as an independent professional agency in order to supervise, monitor, and validate the construction activity on a monthly basis. The running bills by the contractor were certified by the agency before payments were released. This was again a unique solution found to avoid hiccups and build adequate protection for related-party contracts and ensure quality of construction.

Some minor disruptions were caused in construction at times on account of various reasons including shortage of funds. The COVID-19 interrupted the construction twice. On 11 March 2020, the World Health Organisation declared the outbreak of a global pandemic. As cases began to rise in India, Kerala announced a lockdown on 23 March 2020. The Indian government imposed a nationwide lockdown on 25 March 2020. Millions of migrant labourers, including those engaged in construction of JIL's projects, left for their native places. India's second COVID-19 wave was even severe. It hit India from 11 February 2021 onwards, with daily cases reaching nearly triple the first peak on 19 April 2021. The wave started flattening in May but it was a more prolonged, drawn-out process than the first wave. It shook the country hard. Lockdowns, absence of labour, and many other reasons slowed down the work significantly over the two years.

Another cause of slowdown was general prohibition against construction work as ordered by the National Green Tribunal (NGT). New Delhi has been facing severe spells of air pollution over the last decade, causing adverse impacts on the environment, public health, and economy. The concerns related to adverse impacts of increasing levels of pollution have been highlighted by many environmentalists and health practitioners. Various strategies and measures have been implemented by respective authorities to reduce the air pollution levels in Delhi. Since 2017, there have been continuous orders by the Supreme Court and the NGT to stop construction activities every year from October to November to curb air pollution. The real estate sector is directly impacted by the pause in construction activities. As per media reports, the stoppage of construction activities causes up to 3 per cent cost overrun. A fifteen-day stoppage of construction activities leads to project delays of at least three months and also pushes away potential buyers due to postponement and cost escalation.

But patience is a valued virtue for a reason! Despite the many challenges faced while waiting patiently for the insolvency process to come to an end, the IRP acted diligently to keep JIL not just afloat but also sailing ahead. He did more than a reasonable job in delivering thousands of units to homebuyers during the insolvency process period.

18

From the Jaws of a Hungry Tiger

Perseverance is not a long race; it is many short races one after the other.

~ Walter Elliot (1888–1958), Scottish politician

JIL's resolution process was riddled with many intensely contested legal battles, the most contentious among which was the claim over Rs 750 crore deposited by JAL in the Supreme Court in 2017. At first, the Supreme Court refused to refund this amount to JAL and relegated the matter to proceed under the IBC while concluding the hearing in *Chitra Sharma*. Later, in *Jaypee Kensington*, the Supreme Court held that this money belonged to JAL and thwarted NBCC's attempt to stake claim over it and use it for construction of JIL's projects. But the Court permitted JIL to get refund of the amounts advanced to JAL out of Rs 750 crore after reconciliation of accounts and payment of legitimate dues of unadjusted construction advances made by JIL to JAL.

Finally, after a prolonged contest, and favourable order by the NCLT and the NCLAT, the IRP succeeded in recovering sums of Rs 557.77 crore (US$ 67.20 million) and Rs 106.90 crore (US$ 12.88 million) for JIL and homebuyers of JIL, respectively, while the balance amount from Rs 750 crore was released to JAL. This chapter provides an overview of the contest which got JIL Rs 664.67 crore (US$ 80.08 million) back, a task as mighty as extracting a meaty bone from the jaws of a wounded and hungry tiger.

Here's a quick recap: During the hearings in *Chitra Sharma*, JAL had deposited Rs 750 crore in instalments. After the IBC was amended on 6 June 2018 and homebuyers brought under the category of financial creditor, the Supreme Court relegated the insolvency process of JIL to IBC. While doing so, the Court rejected JAL's plea to refund the amount of Rs 750 crore. The homebuyers of JIL who wanted the refund and not the delivery of units sought a pro rata disbursement of this amount. The Court did not accede to this request.

Later, in its resolution plan, as also approved by the NCLT on 3 March 2020, NBCC staked claim over Rs 750 crore for use for the construction of flats. But in *Jaypee Kensington*, the Supreme Court held that the amount of Rs 750 crore, along with accrued interest thereupon, is the property of JAL. The part of the NCLT order of 3 March 2020 that placed this amount in the asset pool of JIL was set aside. The Court held that NBCC could not have prepared the resolution plan under the assumption that this amount was the property of JIL, when it was neither stated so in the orders passed by the Court nor by the IRP in the information memorandum. The Court frowned upon NBCC for staking claim to this amount when the IRP had clearly disclosed in JIL's information memorandum that the money was not JIL's, and its use was subject to the outcome of the decision by the NCLT. The Court directed that JAL was entitled to get its money back.

II

During the hearing of the *Jaypee Kensington* matter, IRP and homebuyers opposed the release of Rs 750 crore to JAL. They contended that as on insolvency commencement date, JAL owed Rs 994 crore (US$ 119.76 million) to JIL and homebuyers, which should get refunded from the amount of Rs 750 crore after adjusting payments for the construction work carried out during the insolvency process period. Out of the amount JAL owed to JIL, a large chunk running into hundreds of crores constituted a mobilization advance given to JAL for construction; the balance was interest-free maintenance deposit collected from homebuyers and kept with JAL. As JAL itself was facing insolvency, it would be impossible to recover this money later.

JAL admitted that it owed various amounts to JIL and its homebuyers and offered to discharge its liability out of Rs 750 crore but disagreed with the IRP on the amount to be refunded. It maintained that the advance for construction had reduced from what was being claimed because of the construction done by JAL, for which bills remained unpaid. The IRP refuted those numbers. Both JIL and JAL suggested to the Supreme Court that the amount to be refunded by JAL could be determined by making a reconciliation of accounts.

After considering the opposition by the IRP and homebuyers for the release of Rs 750 crore to JAL, the Supreme Court decided that although in ordinary circumstances the consequence of finding that the amount was the property of JAL would be that this money got refunded to JAL, the factors relating to the amount owed by JAL to JIL could not be ignored. This was because even as the two are separate corporate entities, JIL is an alter ego of JAL, having been set up as a special purpose vehicle by JAL and substituted as a concessionaire in the concession agreement. The agreements with homebuyers had also been of such a nature where JAL and JIL were both signatories thereto.

Additionally, JIL had extended construction contracts to JAL. Various homebuyers also made payments towards interest-free maintenance deposit to JAL as maintenance agency. Moreover, JAL submitted that balance of Rs 195 crore (as per its calculation)

(US$ 23.49 million), which was to be appropriated for the construction of JIL's project, could be adjusted from Rs 750 crore. However, there was a disagreement between the IRP and JAL on the quantum of amounts to be refunded by JAL. In the given circumstances, the Supreme Court decided that it would serve the interests of all stakeholders if the proposition for reconciliation of accounts got accepted, and after reconciliation, the amount payable by JAL made over to JIL from Rs 750 crore before refunding the remainder to JAL.

The Supreme Court directed the NCLT to nominate an independent accounting expert within seven days of the judgment. The accounting expert so nominated was to carry out the process of reconciliation and submit its report to the NCLT within ten days, the Court further directed. Upon receiving the report from the accounting expert, the NCLT shall pass appropriate orders so that if it is found that any amount is owed to JIL or homebuyers of JIL, the same shall be settled out of the said amount of Rs 750 crore and accrued interest; and remainder thereof shall be returned to JAL in an appropriate account (as petition for insolvency of JAL was pending).

The NCLT would be expected to pass appropriate orders within two weeks of submission of the report by the accounting expert. The Supreme Court made it clear that the process of reconciliation was limited to the determination of only the accounts concerning the amount advanced by JIL to JAL for construction contracts. The process of reconciliation was delinked from the process of approval of the resolution plan.

III

Pursuant to the Supreme Court's directions, the NCLT appointed Grant Thornton (GT; now Grant Thornton Bharat) to carry out the reconciliation task. But due to the restrictions imposed by the

Central and state governments in the light of Covid-19, GT failed to submit the draft report in time. Later, when it did submit a draft report of reconciliation, both the IRP and JAL filed their objections to it. On an application filed by the IRP, the Supreme Court extended the time for the submission of final report by GT to 15 August 2021 and directed the NCLT to consider the objections, if any, and pass appropriate directions as may be permissible in law within two weeks.[8]

In its representation to GT, the IRP sought a refund of Rs 450 crore (US$ 54.22 million) as mobilization advances for construction after the adjustment of running bills of Rs 206.26 crore (US$ 24.85 million) payable to JAL for work carried out under construction contracts. Refund of interest-free maintenance deposit of Rs 380.60 crore (US$ 45.86 million) kept with JAL was also sought out of Rs 750 crore. Another sum of Rs 70.89 crore (US$ 8.54 million) due from Rs 164.29 crore (US$ 19.79 million) given to JAL as advance towards designing, construction and development works was proposed to be adjusted from Rs 750 crore as well.

On the other hand, JAL claimed adjustment of two controversial amounts from a refund of construction advance given by JIL. It sought to offset JIL's alleged liability of Rs 212 crore (US$ 25.54 million) from bank guarantees that JIL's lenders had invoked long before the commencement of insolvency. Moreover, it wanted the adjustment of amounts owed for the construction that was carried in the period prior to commencement of JIL's insolvency process.

The IRP contested the claim of Rs 212 crore on the basis that the Supreme Court had ordered reconciliation of only those amounts that were payable by JAL to JIL. No other amount aside from the construction advance given by JIL had to be reconciled after ascertaining the construction work done by JAL. The amount

8 Order dated 27 July 2021 passed by the Supreme Court in M.A. No.769/2021 in Civil Appeal No. 3395/2020

of Rs 212 crore was towards equity contribution made by JAL and was submitted as part of claims submitted in 2017 which the IRP had already rejected. As it pertained to a period prior to insolvency commencement date, it was in any case, even if found payable, required to be paid as per priorities mentioned in the waterfall mechanism – JAL could not steal a march over creditors standing ahead in queue.

To understand the issue of Rs 212 crore, a brief background on how this amount came to be paid by JAL is necessary: In the year 2012, JIL entered into an agreement with a consortium of lenders led by IDBI Bank for refinancing of the outstanding existing credit of Rs 6,600 crore (US$ 795.18 million), which was availed earlier for the Yamuna Expressway. As per the terms of this agreement, JIL was required to maintain a stipulated fund balance to service its debt or provide bank guarantees for adequate amounts. Meanwhile, JAL was required to execute a promoter support agreement to ensure necessary infusion of funds into JIL to meet its construction obligations so that the project could be completed. The promoter support agreement obligated JAL to provide funds to meet the shortfall in JIL's payment obligations to its lenders and to meet any shortfall in financing the Yamuna Expressway Project by JIL.

JAL furnished five bank guarantees aggregating to Rs 212 crore in favour of IDBI Bank. As JIL could not meet the obligation to its lenders, these bank guarantees were encashed by JIL's lenders in the financial year 2016–17 – well before insolvency proceedings of JIL started on 9 August 2017.

As per the promoter support agreement, the amount of Rs 212 crore was to be treated as infusion of equity or debt. If it was to be treated as debt, it was to be subordinated to the debt of lenders and could only be repaid by JIL after the debt of other lenders had been fully paid. Neither the agreement with the banks nor the promoter support agreement were construction contracts or construction-related agreements. They were agreements between the borrower (JIL), lenders (JIL's lenders), and the borrower's promoter (JAL).

Lenders of JIL invoked bank guarantees for repayment of JIL's debt. In fact, the IRP found that with the agreement of JAL, the amount of Rs 212 crore was treated as promoters' capital contribution in JIL and reflected as equity in books of accounts of JIL for the year 2016–17, as also in the first three quarters of the financial year 2017–18, by both JAL and JIL.

After initiation of JIL's insolvency process on 9 August 2017, no equity could be issued or allotted to JAL by the IRP in lieu of Rs 212 crore. Thus, for the purpose of accounting, the said amount was reclassified as financial liability by JIL in its books of accounts as of 31 March 2018. This was mere accounting treatment and did not have the effect of converting advance against equity into a debt.

Regarding the adjustment of bills of construction from the period prior to insolvency commencement, the IRP objected to their inclusion in the reconciliation exercise by JAL. These bills had already been submitted by JAL as claim pursuant to public announcement made by the IRP. The claims for pre-insolvency period had to be paid in accordance with provisions of the IBC, and it was not permissible to pay it in priority to other creditors' entitlement. JAL could not seek indirectly what it was prohibited to seek directly. JAL, as an operational creditor, had filed a claim in 2017 for Rs 261.73 crore (US$ 31.53 million) of which bills amounting to Rs 48.54 crore (US$ 5.85 million) were construction-related expenses arising prior to commencement of insolvency. Since JIL had a receivable balance of Rs 994 crore (US$ 119.76 million) from JAL as on insolvency commencement date, no liability of JAL was admitted by the IRP.

JAL never challenged the decision of the IRP in the NCLT. This liability being operational debt in nature needed to be dealt with as per the provisions of the IBC. JAL could not, under the garb of reconciliation, seek admission of its claim and preferential payment ahead of other creditors in defiance of the mechanism provided under S. 53 of the IBC, the IRP stated in his objections.

JAL, however, refuted IRP's stance and stated it provided bank guarantees to help JIL avail loan for construction, and therefore, it should be part of reconciliation. The Supreme Court order did not make any distinction between the work carried out by JAL before and after commencement of JIL's insolvency, it insisted.

IV

GT, the accounting expert, submitted the final report on 13 August 2021. It reconciled the various running bills but in the light of the objections raised by the IRP, stopped short of stating if or not these amounts should be adjusted from Rs 750 crore. GT included JAL's claim of Rs 212 crore, stating it was a construction-related payment. At the same time, GT rejected the IRP's claim for adjustment of Rs 70.89 crore (US$ 8.54 million) stating it was a liability that arose from land debt swap with some banks, even though the parties agreed it was to be treated as advance against construction.

A fierce legal battle broke out between JAL and the IRP before the NCLT. Some minor disagreements arising from the final report were mutually resolved by JIL and JAL. The contest was mainly on three issues: adjustment of Rs 212 crore; adjustment of bills for work done prior to insolvency commencement date; and adjustment of Rs 70.89 crore.

The NCLT principal bench of Chief Justice (Retd) Ramalingam Sudhakar and L.N. Gupta decided on all the three issues against the IRP by its order dated 7 March 2023. The NCLT held that there was no bar, under the Supreme Court order in *Jaypee Kensington*, to including in the reconciliation exercise the claim of Rs 212 crore or adjustment of bills for work done prior to the insolvency commencement date. In other words, the NCLT held that Rs 212 crore related to the construction contract. At the same time, the NCLT rejected adjustment of Rs 70.89 crore sought by the IRP maintaining that this amount did not relate to construction.

Even though the NCLT decided the legal issues against the IRP, it opined that because the Supreme Court has held that JIL must be paid the amount found payable to it out of reconciliation first, the decision on legal issues being favourable to JAL was of no consequence to JIL. Differently put, the NCLT held that an amount of Rs 542.62 crore (US$ 65.38 million) was admittedly payable by JAL to JIL, and Rs 106.90 crore (US$12.88 million) payable by JAL to the homebuyers of JIL on account of interest-free maintenance deposit. The NCLT directed JIL to hold the interest-free maintenance deposit in trust on behalf of the homebuyers. Only residual amount was to be refunded to JAL. It directed that Rs 649.52 crore (US$ 78.26 million) be paid to JIL out of Rs 750 crore and the balance be given back to JAL along with the accrued interest on the deposit.

This was a clever order on account of many things. JAL was given a favourable order on objections raised by JIL but not the money; JIL, on the other hand, got an unfavourable order on its objections but got the money it had asked for, except Rs 70.89 crore. The NCLT order smartly fell along the lines of *Jaypee Kensington* which stated that reconciliation of accounts between JAL and JIL was only for crystallizing the amount payable by JAL to JIL, and for the payment of that crystallized amount to be made out of Rs 750 crore and interest accrued thereon. Only the leftover amount from Rs 750 crore was to land in the pocket of JAL as a refund.

It took many hearings before the NCLT could decide the issue of Rs 750 crore as a result of which the decision on application for approval of Suraksha's plan kept getting pushed. Although the Supreme Court had delinked the two issues while directing reconciliation, JAL insisted that the two issues be decided together since Suraksha's plan had assumed that a certain portion of Rs 750 crore would come to JIL and made provisions in its plan based on that assumption. It argued that Suraksha would have to rework its plan if the NCLT's decision was in JAL's favour. The IRP and Suraksha had vehemently opposed this request by JAL.

V

JAL and the IRP challenged the NCLT order before the NCLAT. The IRP confined its challenge to the reasoning given by the NCLT in rejecting his objections. He also challenged the part of the order rejecting the claim of Rs 70.89 crore. But the IRP defended the ultimate direction of the NCLT as being in accordance with the directions of the Supreme Court in *Jaypee Kensington*.

The NCLAT passed interim directions on 16 March 2023 to JAL: pay Rs 265.21 crore (US$ 31.95 million) to JIL, being the amount not disputed by JAL as refundable to JIL, and a further sum of Rs 106.90 crore to JIL to be held in trust on behalf of homebuyers, out of the Rs 750 crore deposited with the registrar of the NCLT. JAL did not object to the interim relief.

In its order dated 28 August 2023, disposing of both the appeals, the NCLAT agreed with the IRP's contentions and rejected the NCLT's findings based on his objections. The NCLAT held that Rs 212 crore could not have been made part of reconciliation as it was not related to construction. Pre-insolvency dues also could not be made part of reconciliation as those were to be treated as per the resolution plan approved by the CoC. It did not, however, disturb the operating principle of the NCLT order with regard to the distribution of amounts to JIL and JAL, by which the IRP was not aggrieved anyway since they were favourable to JIL. On the issue of Rs 70.89 crore, the NCLAT did not agree with the IRP for the purpose of payment, since it was not found to be related to construction advance.

VI

JAL contemplated if it should appeal to the Supreme Court. IMC too debated on the next steps to be taken. Both sides engaged in a dialogue to explore the possibility of closing the issue through mutual agreement. JIL was in need of funds so that the construction could be accelerated. If any appeal were to be filed and then left pending, the registrar of the Allahabad bench of the NCLT was unlikely to release even the undisputed amount without further directions from the Supreme Court. JAL too needed money as it was facing insolvency proceedings and the refund of the balance amount could give it some respite. Suraksha too was in favour of a closure of this matter.

After many negotiations, the IMC, JAL, and Suraksha decided to accept the NCLAT's decision as final and binding. They agreed not to challenge the NCLAT order in the Supreme Court. The IMC insisted that it be paid interest earned from 7 March 2023 on the amount ordered to be released to it by the NCLT. A formal memorandum of undertaking, as approved by the IMC, was executed. Including disbursement under interim order passed by the NCLAT, out of the amount of Rs 750 crore, JIL received a sum of Rs 557.77 crore (US$ 67.20 million) and a separate sum of Rs 106.90 crore (US$ 12.88 million) in trust for homebuyers. At the time when the book went to press, the registrar had yet to release the amount of Rs 15.15 crore (US$ 1.83 million) as interest earned from 7 March 2023 to JIL on payments directed to be made to JIL by the NCLAT.

Recovery of Rs 664.67 crore (US$ 80.08 million) by the IRP was one of the most significant outcomes of JIL's insolvency process. JAL was desperate for every penny due to its precarious financial position and was reeling under tremendous pressure from its own lenders. It was also hurting from many orders carried out since August 2017. It was crucial for JAL to defend the amount with its life and oppose tooth and nail the IRP's stake on any part of Rs 750 crore. But the IRP was relentless in pursuit of his goals, which was to maximize the value of JIL's assets; and this amount was to contribute significantly towards that target.

19

Winning By a Whisker

Haar kar jitney wale ko baazigar kahte hai.

- *Baazigar* (1993)

Taking forward from *Jaypee Kensington*, on the very day the order was passed by the Supreme Court, the IRP requested both NBCC and Suraksha to submit their binding, modified or fresh resolution plan in line with the Court directions. Separately, on 25 March 2021, the IRP filed an application before the NCLT to apprise it of the directions of the Court.

Both the resolution applicants submitted revised resolution plans. The IRP convened the seventeenth meeting of the CoC on 12 April 2021, the first after *Jaypee Kensington*. After deliberating upon the resolution plans, the CoC requested both Suraksha and NBCC to make improvements in their plans. Once again, negotiation of the terms of the resolution plans commenced. The resolution applicants had, in their version, addressed the findings and observations made by the Supreme Court in *Jaypee Kensington*. If resolution applicants were now wiser, the CoC members were even more confident. Every time the revised plans were submitted, detailed deliberation took place not only with the banks but also the homebuyers to address their expectations. Both resolution applicants conducted a series of webinars with the homebuyers where their issues, concerns, and expectations were heard and discussed at length.

The insolvency process that had been going on for over three years had given everyone plenty of insight and experience. There was now greater clarity on law because of the many decisions of the Supreme Court on the IBC. The *Jaypee Kensington* judgment had largely settled the contentious issues within this case. The path was no longer as hazy as it had been at the beginning. Enough time had been spent and many costs incurred. Everyone was exhausted and desperate for closure, most of all the IRP, the author and their teams. Neither could the IRP accept appointment in any other big case nor could the author take up other cases.

Over weeks following the submission of the plans and their review in the CoC meeting, commercial terms were negotiated with both the applicants. The legal advisors discussed legal compliances as per the IBC and *Jaypee Kensington*. The resolution applicants were provided many opportunities to submit their addendum or revised resolution plans to address the issues that cropped up. Meetings of the CoC were held to deliberate on distribution of the estate's proceeds among creditors.

II

In the meantime, the IRP examined both the plans as modified from time to time to ascertain if they were compliant with the IBC as also the findings and observations made by the Supreme Court in *Jaypee Kensington*. The author found the NBCC's resolution plan non-compliant, while the resolution plan submitted by Suraksha met the requirements of the IBC; the IRP was provided a note containing reasons behind such a conclusion and he too was convinced that NBCC's plan did not meet the requirements of the IBC.

The IRP sent his written report on the compliance status of plans to the CoC along with the final plans received from Suraksha and NBCC. In the CoC meeting following this, the issues which made NBCC's plan non-compliant were discussed. It was decided to invite NBCC to the meeting. Its representatives rejected the IRP's objections and insisted that the plan was in conformity with the IBC. After detailed deliberations, the CoC decided to put only Suraksha's plan to vote. Suraksha was elated. It was finally getting a walkover.

The IRP circulated the voting details to the CoC. But, before the voting could begin, NBCC sent an unsolicited addendum to its resolution plan. The addendum, it claimed, addressed the concerns raised by the IRP and made NBCC's plan compliant.

Some members of the CoC objected to the consideration of the unsolicited addendum sent by NBCC just before voting was to start. The others (constituting 33 per cent of the CoC) requested the IRP to convene an urgent meeting of the CoC to discuss if NBCC's plan could be considered. After all, two competing plans would be better than just one. Suraksha strongly protested against consideration of NBCC's belated and unsolicited addendum after a meeting for a vote on the Suraksha plan had been convened.

Taking advantage of the ensuing chaos, Manoj Gaur, the promoter shareholder of JIL, sent a letter along with the settlement proposal under S. 12A of the IBC to the IRP with a copy marked to the CoC members. S. 12A allows the promoter to make a proposal for settlement with its lenders and other creditors at any stage of the process notwithstanding the ineligibility. However, such an application can only be entertained if approved by the CoC with a 90 per cent majority. While the CoC provided an opportunity to Manoj Gaur to present its proposal, it decided not to put it for voting.

A meeting of the CoC was held on 24 May 2021 to discuss the fate of voting and the NBCC addendum. To everyone's disbelief, the NBCC resolution plan still remained non-compliant notwithstanding the addendum. The IRP and the author explained to the members of the CoC and representatives of the NBCC why the plan was still non-compliant, and the CoC lawyers concurred with the author and the IRP's judgement.

NBCC sought an opportunity to submit a revised addendum but also went and complained to the IBBI. The IBBI does not interfere in the processes of cases under the IBC. If any person is aggrieved by any decision taken by an insolvency professional on the matter of compliance of resolution plan, it has to approach the NCLT. And so, the IBBI rightly ignored NBCC's complaint. The IBBI cannot be seen to be acting at the behest of a resolution applicant even if it is a government body.

Suraksha and some CoC members differed on the approach to deal with the unsolicited addendum submitted by NBCC. The first issue to be decided was whether to take on record the addendum already received from NBCC or go ahead with voting on Suraksha's plan. The CoC thought it would be wiser if this decision too was taken by vote. It was also decided that a tie-breaker formula be put for approval of the CoC if both resolution plans receive equal votes – in the case that the CoC decided to give both NBCC and Suraksha another chance to submit a revised addendum. The tie-breaker formula proposed was that the resolution plan having higher score under evaluation matrix be declared successful; or the plan having highest votes (voting share) of assent from class of creditors, i.e., homebuyers and fixed deposit holders combined, be declared successful.

The members of the CoC by a majority of 98.54 per cent votes approved the agenda item proposing that both the resolution applicants be requested to submit revised resolution plan by 4 June 2021 as a final opportunity. By a majority of 90.74 per cent, they also approved the tie-breaker proposing that the resolution plan having highest votes (voting share) of assent from class of creditors be declared successful.

In view of this development, both the resolution applicants were given till 5 p.m., 4 June 2021, to submit their respective resolution plans and reminded that in addition to the plan being compliant with the IBC, it was also supposed to comply with *Jaypee Kensington* passed by the Supreme Court.

NBCC was jubilant with the voting results and Suraksha disappointed. It was expected that Suraksha might challenge the CoC decision in the NCLT or the Supreme Court. However, Suraksha decided to compete based on the merits of its plan. It submitted a revised plan with some improvements. NBCC also submitted a revised plan which was found to be compliant of the IBC.

While placing both the plans before the CoC, the IRP in his report brought to attention that both the resolution applicants sought extinguishment of contingent liability towards additional farmers' compensation by treating it as an operational debt, making the debt payable to YEIDA for this operational debt nil. The IRP stated that it had brought to the attention of the resolution applicants that he had not admitted the claim of Rs 1,689 crore submitted by YEIDA towards additional farmers' compensation as it was a contingent liability; and they were requested to clarify if a claim that was contingent and had not become due and payable as on insolvency commencement date, and thus not admitted, could be extinguished.

To justify the extinguishment, the resolution applicants relied on the provisions of the IBC and various judgments of the Supreme Court mentioned in their resolution plan. Both argued that *Jaypee Kensington* did not prohibit the resolution applicant from providing such extinguishment of an operational debt, made in accordance with the IBC. While it could be stated that extinguishment of debt of an operational creditor could be sought in line with the provisions of the IBC but YEIDA could challenge such extinguishment. The CoC was requested by the IRP to consider the commercial implications of the treatment of farmers' compensation in the resolution plan in line with the directions of the Supreme Court in *Jaypee Kensington*.

In the twenty-fourth meeting of the CoC held on 10 June 2021, the CoC members discussed the addendums to both the plans. The meeting was also attended by the representatives of NBCC and Suraksha. The CoC decided to put both the resolution plans to vote. The e-voting on both the resolution plans was held between 14 June and 23 June.

At the time the plans were put to vote, the CoC comprised 20,590 homebuyers, nine public sector banks, three private banks and financial institutions, and 917 fixed deposit holders, having an admitted claim of Rs 22,619 crore (US$ 2,725 million). The homebuyers were the majority stakeholders in the CoC with 56.62 per cent voting share and an admitted claim of Rs 12,806 crore (US$ 1,543 million).

The resolution plan of Suraksha was approved by 98.66 per cent votes. Only ICICI Bank, with an admitted claim of Rs 394 crore (US$ 36.61 million) and voting share of 1.34 per cent, dissented. NBCC received 98.54 per cent votes, just a fraction less than Suraksha. From a resolution application which had been rejected by the CoC twice previously and was nearly out of fray, this was quite a comeback. NBCC may have lost by a thin margin, but for Suraksha, to have received 98.66 per cent was a big leap forward from the previous round when it had received a mere 2.12 per cent votes.

It was speculated that with such a minor margin of defeat, NBCC would challenge the result on one pretext or the other to initiate a repoll. But NBCC decided to rest the matter. Any litigation at this stage to delay implementation of the plan would not have gone down well with homebuyers. Approval of Suraksha's plan was a call taken by the CoC in its commercial wisdom, and NBCC made a wise decision to let it run its course.

III

From 24 March 2021 (date of the *Jaypee Kensington* verdict) to 23 June 2021 (approval of the resolution plan by the CoC), it had taken double the time than what was granted by the Supreme Court. The delay was both on account of the second wave of the Covid-19 and due to extensive negotiations between resolution applicants, the CoC, and the IRP. Although Covid-19 started receding in the month of May, the recovery to any semblance of normality was a prolonged process. The progress of the process was hampered on account of lockdowns.

The IRP filed an application before the Supreme Court seeking extension of time. On 27 July 2021, the Supreme Court extended the time and condoned the delay of sixty days in the consideration and approval of the resolution plan. The period of insolvency resolution of JIL was therefore extended to 7 July 2021.

IV

In the words of Chinonye J. Chidolue, winning is not always punctual but eventually it comes. The NBCC plan was the preferred choice of the CoC all along, and Suraksha was nowhere close. How Suraksha eventually emerged as an emphatic winner from a point of nearly being a persona non grata requires a standalone case study and perhaps even a thesis. Suffice it to state that while Suraksha deserves full credit for persisting despite repeated rejections, the defeat of the NBCC can also be attributed to it having become complacent.

Banking on its outstanding performance in the second round, the NBCC might have taken approval of its plan by the CoC for granted. NBCC's plan acquired aggressive overhaul but it became rigid in its response to the suggestions made by the IRP and the CoC on the terms of its plan. Any resolution applicant is entitled to make the resolution plan with terms it considers as commercially best and take its own stance on legal matters based on the advice received from experts. But if the resolution applicant does not stay objective in dealing with the suggestions made by the CoC, the result may not be in its interest.

While the NBCC may have increased its number from 97.36 per cent to 98.54 per cent votes, it is Suraksha which emerged as the loud and clear winner, having jumped from a paltry 2.12 per cent to a whopping 98.66 per cent. Led by a surprising turn of events, this leap was high and mighty.

20

Jo Jeeta Wohi Sikandar

The man who moves a mountain begins by carrying away small stones.

~ Confucius

Approval of plan by the CoC is 90 per cent victory for a resolution applicant. The remaining 10 per cent is the jump required over S. 31, the IBC hurdle, which is the approval of the plan by the NCLT. If the resolution plan meets the requirement of the IBC, the NCLT will approve the plan. Of course, if any person has objections against the approval, they would have to be dealt with by the NCLT. Often, approval of an otherwise compliant plan may get dragged on account of time taken in deciding objections. A plan approved by the CoC becomes effective only if sanctioned by the NCLT. Approval of resolution plan by the NCLT makes it binding on the corporate debtor, successful resolution applicant, creditors, shareholders, and guarantors.

On 7 July 2021, the IRP filed an application before the NCLT seeking approval of Suraksha's resolution plan. The Supreme Court had granted forty-five days to the NCLT to consider the plan and approve the application. The NCLT approved Suraksha's Resolution Plan on 7 March 2023. Extension of time was sought from the Supreme Court, which granted further time with request to the NCLT to decide expeditiously.

The time taken by NCLT was mainly on account of an overloaded cause list with the NCLT bench, inadequate strength of members at any given time, and of course, because of lengthy arguments on contentious objections of JAL, YEIDA and ICICI Bank against approval of the plan. Hearing of objections on GT's report on reconciliation of accounts also played a part in the delay.

III

ICICI Bank raised its objection against Suraksha's resolution plan alleging that *Jaypee Kensington* had not been correctly applied by Suraksha and the IRP. It argued that payment of debt to the dissenting financial creditor can be made only in the form of money and not in any another form, while Suraksha was once again offering ICICI Bank land to settle the debt. It also questioned the calculation of value of its debt by the IRP for payment in accordance with S. 53 of the IBC.

It was apparent from the start that the objections raised by ICICI Bank were weak. Perhaps, it was hoping to negotiate for a better deal by making the approval of the plan difficult. Suraksha and the CoC were desperate and any further delay could have broken their patience and compelled them to give in.

Suraksha argued that *Jaypee Kensington* clearly allows for the payment of debt due to the dissenting financial creditor by letting it enforce the security interest. The dissenting financial creditor cannot insist upon payment only in the form of money. The

IBC requires the dissenting financial creditor to be paid ahead of assenting financial creditors (which in JIL's case included the homebuyers). The option of providing upfront cash of Rs 218 crore (US$ 26.27 million), the liquidation value of ICICI Bank's debt, was neither feasible nor viable.

A huge amount of cash was needed to be infused to revive and complete the significant pending construction work in accordance with the resolution plan, in the interest of more than 20,000 families whose hard-earned earnings had been stuck for many years due to delay in completion of the projects. Homebuyers needed to be incentivized by making sufficient provision of funds in the resolution plan for completion of their projects, so that they could finally get their homes. It was against the interest of everyone to make provision for huge cash to satisfy dissenting financial creditors whose number could hypothetically go up to 34 per cent by way of direct cash payment.

The IRP argued that where a dissenting financial creditor holds exclusive security interest in the immovable property, it would be free to enforce such security interest in accordance with the entitlement under the provisions of the IBC. But if security interest is common with other financial creditors who may have assented or dissented, the security allowed to be enforced will have to be identified – if it can be separated from the common security. If separable, it can be carved out with the consent of other security holders and offered to the dissenting financial creditors for enforcement.

Suraksha had identified 1,486 acres of mortgaged land, out of the various security interests, to be available for enforcement by dissenting financial creditors, assuming their number could go up to 34 per cent. It being common security, the dissenting financial creditors could not claim any right to cherry-pick the land. The amount payable to the dissenting financial creditors will be determined in accordance with the IBC; but identification of specific land to be separated from the common pool of security interest will be done by resolution applicant, as it would have to be done keeping in mind various factors, including feasibility and viability of the projects. Neither the IBC nor *Jaypee Kensington* vested any right with the dissenting financial creditors to identify the security interest it should be allowed to enforce from the common pool of security interest in which the assenting creditors or the dissenting financial creditors may hold interest.

The NCLT was informed that ICICI Bank's admitted claim was for an amount of Rs 304.1 crore (US$ 36.64 million). After approval of resolution plan by the CoC, ICICI Bank was the only dissenting financial creditor. The value of ICICI Bank, on the basis of S. 53 of the IBC, as approved by the CoC, amounted to Rs 218 crore. After the plan was approved by the CoC, Suraksha sent a proposal to ICICI Bank identifying 180 acres of land parcels, which could be enforced by it, to which ICICI Bank objected. Suraksha offered 666 acres located in Tappal from which ICICI Bank could identify 180 acres.

Suraksha stated it had proposed a fair and equitable process of identifying the land. It had identified overall parcels required to provide treatment to the dissenting financial creditors. It offered an opportunity to ICICI Bank, but as no consensus could be reached (as claimed by ICICI Bank) in terms of the resolution plan, Suraksha used its discretion to decide which parcel of land would be allowed to be enforced by ICICI Bank. This was done in accordance with the resolution plan approved by the CoC.

ICICI Bank however insisted that it was entitled to receive land for the admitted claim of Rs 304.1 crore, and not reduced amount calculated as per S. 53, as the value of its security interest was greater than Rs 218 crore. IRP invited the attention of NCLT to the decision of the Supreme Court in *Amit Metaliks Limited*, where it had been held that the intent of the legislature was not to give to a dissenting financial creditor right over the assets of the corporate debtor over and above the liquidation value of its debt.

The IRP also clarified that it had calculated liquidation value of JIL and not the amount payable to ICICI Bank; the amount payable to the dissenting financial creditors was calculated by the members of the CoC in the twenty-first CoC meeting held on 20 May 2021. The calculation was approved by the CoC members representing more than 50 per cent voting share. To enable Suraksha to determine how much land was to be made available for enforcement, the CoC had decided to share liquidation value of land with Suraksha after its resolution plan had been approved. Moreover, in its resolution plan, Suraksha provided a shortfall undertaking – in the event there was shortfall in recovery of liquidation value from enforcement of 180 acres of land, Suraksha would make good the shortfall.

The NCLT rejected ICICI Bank's objections. No appeal was filed by ICICI Bank against the NCLT Order.

IV

YEIDA also objected to the approval of the resolution plan on the grounds that Suraksha did not provide contingency for payment of additional farmers' compensation in case the award was turned down by a higher court, as directed by the Supreme Court in *Jaypee Kensington*. Only a payment of Rs 0.10 crore (US$ 0.01 million) was offered towards the other claims submitted by YEIDA, which was not the import of *Jaypee Kensington*, it pleaded. It argued that dues towards additional farmers' compensation and external development charges arose out of the concession agreement. Treatment of any dues arising out of this agreement would require YEIDA's approval. It also opposed payment of only Rs 0.10 crore against admitted claim of YEIDA of Rs 461crore (US$ 55.54 million) towards external development charges.

Notwithstanding *Nand Kishore*, when insolvency proceedings of JIL commenced in August 2017, YEIDA inter alia submitted a claim of Rs 1,689 crore as additional farmers' compensation. The IRP did not admit the claim for additional farmers' compensation as the dispute over its payment was then sub judice before the arbitral tribunal. Later, arbitration proceedings concluded during the insolvency process and were contested by the IRP on behalf of JIL. An arbitral tribunal was constituted which gave an award (November 2019) in JIL's favour.

The arbitral tribunal held that JIL's liability under the concession agreement was to pay the acquisition cost of land and not any additional compensation to the farmers, as demanded by the G.O. Unlike in *Gajraj*, the acquisition of land for the Yamuna Expressway Project was specifically upheld by the Supreme Court in *Nand Kishore*, the tribunal held. The award was challenged by YEIDA before the district judge, Gautam Buddh Nagar, Uttar Pradesh, the appropriate court under the Indian Arbitration and Conciliation Act, 1996.

As stated earlier, in *Jaypee Kensington*, the Supreme Court disapproved NBCC's approach, faulting it for unilaterally deciding that collection of additional farmers' compensation would be made by YEIDA if the need arose; contingency for payment of additional farmers' compensation should have been made in the plan, and the CoC should have considered its commercial implication while reviewing the plan.

Later, as stated, on fresh consideration of the resolution plans resubmitted by NBCC and Suraksha, the CoC approved the plan of Suraksha. In its revised resolution plan, it adopted a novel approach to avoid making payment of additional farmers' compensation, which it argued was on the right side of law. The plan stated that even though the liability of additional farmers' compensation was not payable by JIL on account of the decision of the Supreme Court in *Nand Kishore* and the subsequent award, for the purpose of the resolution plan, Suraksha assumed that if the award was upturned in appeal, payment of additional compensation to farmers would become JIL's liability.

Based on this assumption, it admitted that the liability of additional compensation was that of JIL. It then proceeded to state that additional compensation was an operational debt, and with YEIDA being an operational creditor, the value of debt arising from additional compensation was nil as per the priorities provided in the waterfall mechanism under the IBC; Suraksha thus offered Rs 0.10 crore to YEIDA.

The IRP and the author had apprised the CoC that the Supreme Court had directed it (the CoC) to consider the commercial implication of the contingency of payment of additional farmers' compensation. In other words, it was for the CoC to decide if Suraksha's proposal met the contingency requirement set by the Supreme Court's decision in *Jaypee Kensington*. The issue was discussed at length in the CoC meetings.

Suraksha argued that the Supreme Court had directed that a treatment must be provided in the plan for additional farmers' compensation in the event it becomes payable – such treatment has to be made within the discipline of the IBC, which is what Suraksha had done. Any contrarian view is only a matter of a difference of opinion on the interpretation of *Jaypee Kensington* or provisions of the IBC, which only the Supreme Court decides, and this wasn't a solid ground for faulting Suraksha's resolution plan.

This was how the CoC had come to decide to put the resolution plans of NBCC and Suraksha to simultaneous vote. The resolution plan of Suraksha was approved by the CoC. The NCLT also approved Suraksha's plan by order dated 7 March 2023, holding that the plan's proposal in respect of additional farmers' compensation was compliant of the provisions of the IBC.

The net effect of the approval of Suraksha's plan, if approved, was that the additional farmers' compensation was payable but not in the amount claimed, rather only as determined under S. 53 of the IBC. Its implications would have played out such that the liability of additional farmers' compensation would have fallen on the shoulders of YEIDA, since the farmers would neither have the means to appreciate the nuances of the IBC nor would they accept that they would not receive additional compensation at all.

During the pendency of the matter before the NCLT, on 19 May 2022, in a challenge to the G.O., unconnected to the Yamuna Expressway Project, the Supreme Court decided in *Shakuntala Devi* that the policy decision of the state government to give additional compensation to the farmers was in larger public interest. The decision was taken after considering the material collected by the Chaudhary Committee after due deliberations with all the stakeholders and taking care of the concerns of the allottees as well as the farmers.

The court agreed that the factors which were taken into account by the state government were relevant, rational, and founded on ground realities; it would not be appropriate to question the wisdom of the policy decision, unless it was demonstrated by the aggrieved persons that the said policy had been enacted in an arbitrary, unreasonable, or mala fide manner, or that it offended the provisions of the Constitution of India.

The NCLT did not entertain YEIDA's objections either. Eventually, YEIDA challenged the NCLT order rejecting its objections in NCLAT. The outcome of the challenge is discussed in the later chapters. But, the NCLT, in its order dated 7 March 2023, had not considered the implication of *Shakuntala Education Trust* on YEIDA's claim while rejecting YEIDA's objection to Suraksha's resolution plan presumably because Suraksha had submitted that the decision of *Shakuntala Devi* was not applicable to the facts of JIL.

On the contrary, JIL's case was covered in the decision of the Supreme Court in *Nand Kishore* where the challenge against acquisition of land for the Yamuna Expressway Project was rejected and it had been found that acquisition of land using urgency clause was justified. Suraksha also relied on paragraph 69 of *Shakuntala Education Trust* which stated, 'with respect to the contention of the respondent No.19 – Supertech with regard to initiation of the CIRP, we are not concerned with the said issue in the present proceedings. The law will take its own course…' This implied that the payment of additional compensation by allottees which were undergoing insolvency process would be dealt in accordance with the provision of the IBC.

V

JAL filed a series of objections against the resolution plan and opposed provisions which were included to extinguish its subrogation rights to recover from Suraksha or JIL and the amount recovered from JAL as JIL's guarantor. NCLT rejected its objections.

Minor objections were also filed by a few others. They were also rejected by NCLT while approving Suraksha's resolution plan on 7 March 2023.

VI

With the approval of Suraksha's plan by NCLT on 7 March 2023, JIL's insolvency process formally came to an end albeit after a period of five-and-a-half years. It took 2,037 days – from 9 August 2017 to 7 March 2023 – to complete the process, as against the 270 days provided in the IBC. The litigation challenging the approval of the resolution plan continued beyond this time, taking another one-and-a-half years. No one can be held responsible for this delay, as was observed by the Supreme Court in *Jaiprakash Associates*.

On approval of the resolution plan by the NCLT, the CoC stood dissolved, and the IRP demitted office, both having become *functus officio*. Suraksha's resolution plan provides a mechanism for management, control, and supervision of the affairs of JIL till the resolution plan is finally cleared by the Supreme Court in the event NCLT/NCLAT orders are challenged in appeal by any party. It provides for an IMC to be set up on the date the resolution plan is approved by NCLT. As provided in the resolution plan, the IMC comprising five persons – the IRP, two representatives of Suraksha, one representative of banks, and the authorized representative of homebuyers – was constituted. The decisions in the meetings of the IMC are taken on the basis of majority vote.

Although JIL's insolvency process ended on 7 March 2023, the saga carried on into another year as challenges against the resolution plan's approval first travelled to NCLAT and from there to the Supreme Court.

21
The Hand of Fate

There is no such thing as accident; it is fate misnamed

- Napoleon Bonaparte

While application for the approval of Suraksha's resolution plan was pending before the NCLT, and the appeal before the NCLAT, the Supreme Court decided on four significant questions of law in matters unrelated to JIL's case but which were to have a significant bearing on the distribution of payments under Suraksha's resolution plan:

(i) In *Anand Sonbhadra*[1] (2022), the Supreme Court decided that NOIDA is an operation creditor. Based on this decision, it became certain that YEIDA was operational creditor of JIL;

(ii) In *Rainbow Papers Limited*[2] (2020; Review decided in 2023),

1 *New Okhla Industrial Development Authority v. Anand Sonbhadra*, 2023 1 SCC 724

2 *Sales Tax Officer v. Rainbow Papers Limited*, 2022 SCC Online SC 1162

the Supreme Court held that a government body could become a secured creditor of a corporate debtor by operation of law even if no security interest had been created specifically in its favour. Applying the rationale of *Rainbow Papers Limited,* YEIDA claimed before the NCLT that it had become a secured creditor;

(iii) In *Prabhjit Singh Soni* (2024), the Supreme Court held that Greater Noida Authority was a secured creditor in view of the charge created in its favour on the assets of corporate debtor by operation of the provisions of Ss. 13 and 13A of the Uttar Pradesh Industrial Area Development Act, 1976 (UP Act). Applying the same ratio, YEIDA, a child of the same parent act, could arguably claim to be a secured operational creditor of JIL; and

(iv) In *Shakuntala Education Trust*[3] (2022), the Supreme Court held that the G.O. (Refer Chapter 3) was binding on all allottees and they were required to pay additional farmers' compensations. YEIDA could now argue that the claim of additional farmers' compensation was a secured operational debt, and Rs 0.10 crore offered to it as unsecured operational creditors needed revision.

This changed the dynamics of the situation. It was expected that in its appeal before the NCLAT, YEIDA would stake claim that additional farmers' compensation was a secured debt and the claim of Rs 1,689 crore (US$ 203.49 million) should be paid in full.

3 *Yamuna Expressway Industrial Development Authority v. Shakuntala Education and Welfare Society*, 2022 SCC OnLine SC 655

22

The Deferred Final

In a negotiation, we must find a solution that pleases everyone, because no one accepts that they MUST lose and that the other MUST win ... Both MUST win!

\- Nabil N. Jamal

The saga of JIL's insolvency refused to conclude. The battleground now shifted to the NCLAT. In an unexpected move, the tax department challenged the NCLT order approving Suraksha's plan. It came as a bolt out of the blue because the department had not objected to the IRP's decision on its claim made as far back as in 2018. Nor had it objected to the approval of NBCC's resolution plan in 2020, which provided similar treatment to the department's dues as Suraksha's plan did. The department had not intervened in any of the earlier litigations. It had not even turned up in the NCLT to object to the approval of Suraksha's plan by the NCLT even though Suraksha had sent it a copy of the plan.

As expected, JAL and YEIDA too filed appeals before the NCLAT. Manoj Gaur also challenged the NCLT order.

Some intervening developments added further complexity to the already convoluted set of issues.

II

The thrust of JAL's appeal was that the resolution plan of Suraksha was not in conformity with law due to objections raised by the tax department and YEIDA. Another grievance of JAL and Manoj Gaur was that the NCLT had erred in allowing extinguishment of their subrogation rights. In its resolution plan, Suraksha provided that upon completion of transfer of the beneficial ownership of land parcels to the banks assenting to the plan, their outstanding dues would stand settled, and the banks would not take any action against JIL for recovery of any outstanding dues. Personal and corporate guarantors, other than JIL, would continue to remain liable to the banks for any amounts due to them without any recourse or remedy against JIL. Any right or remedy, including but not limited to the right of subrogation as may be available to corporate or personal guarantors against JIL in the event of exercise of rights by banks, shall stand extinguished.

Simply put, JAL was aggrieved that if JAL ended up paying on behalf of JIL the money the latter had borrowed from banks, JAL should have the right to recover that money from JIL. As Suraksha was to step into the shoes of JIL, Suraksha should have same liability to JAL, they claimed. This is called a subrogation right of a surety under the Indian Contract Act, 1872. JAL and Gaur objected to the term in Suraksha's plan that took away their right of subrogation.

Rejecting their appeal, the NCLAT held that JIL's debt was being discharged as a consequence to the resolution plan under the IBC. The Supreme Court had held in *Lalit Kumar Jain*[1] that approval of resolution plan and finality imparted to it did

1 *Lalit Kumar Jain v. Union of India*, (2021) 9 SCC 321

not operate as a discharge of the guarantor's liability per se. The resolution plan after approval was binding on guarantors. The NCLAT held that the law was well settled and after approval of the resolution plan, the personal guarantors and corporate guarantors have no right of subrogation, especially when right of subrogation was expressly extinguished. Suraksha's plan expressly took away the right of subrogation of the guarantors. The debt against JIL might have extinguished after approval of the plan, but that would not be the consequence for the corporate guarantors and the personal guarantors. The liability of guarantors would be as per the express provisions of the resolution plan approved by the CoC in its commercial wisdom. The NCLAT held that JAL and Manoj Gaur did not have the right of subrogation under the Indian Contract Act.

JAL and Gaur filed appeals before the Supreme Court against the NCLAT decision, which were pending at the time this book was written. The author is refraining from making any comments on the merits of the appeals as the matter is sub judice.

III

Benjamin Franklin had once said that nothing was certain except for death and taxes. The tax department was determined to prove Franklin wrong. Filing of appeal by the tax department had taken everyone aback. Its main grievance was that the IRP should not have rejected the claim as the orders of demand were sub judice and not fully decided. It also stated that Suraksha's resolution plan had made factually incorrect reference to the claim. Both the IMC and Suraksha defended the plan.

The appeal was dismissed by the NCLAT on 26 September 2023 holding that the treatments provided to the claims filed by the department were in accordance with law. As the value of the tax department's debt, being operational debt, was nil, it made no difference even if the orders of assessment were sub judice. But, while dismissing the appeal, the NCLAT made certain observations, which exposed the resolution plan to the risk of a future liability of Rs 33,000 crore.

Neither Suraksha nor any other resolution applicant or JIL itself, which had a much lower value of its assets, would ever be able to pay Rs 33,000 crore. If this liability was to be fastened on JIL, the company was doomed to go into liquidation. No resolution applicant would then be interested in JIL if so enormous an amount was added to JIL's liabilities. And so a fresh wave of uncertainties took over the future of JIL's resolution.

IV

It may be useful to provide a background to the monstrous amount of Rs 33,000 crore and how it came to be.

In September 2017, the tax department filed a claim of Rs 3,334.3 crore (US$ 401.72 million) in response to the public announcement made by the IRP. The genesis of the claim was a decision taken by the department on 31 March 2017, before JIL's insolvency process commenced. It had passed an order stating that the allotment of 6,250 acres of land to JIL by YEIDA was at a price lower than the market value. This, the department concluded, had benefitted JIL to the extent of a revenue subsidy of Rs 100,000 crore (US$ 12,048 million).

As no methodology was prescribed in the concession agreement for appropriation of the revenue subsidy, the department proposed to spread the entire chunk of the 6,250 acres of land over a concession period of thirty-six years on a pro rata basis which comes to 173.61 acres per year. It was further proposed to calculate the value of the revenue subsidy at Rs 40,000 (US$ 482) per square metre as the mean price, taking into consideration the location and state of the land, the localized debilities, etc. Based on this methodology, a tax liability of Rs 33,000 crore (US$ 3,976 million) was fastened on JIL. This amount was to be paid over the term of the concession agreement.

Based on the assessment made, a demand of Rs 2,058 crore (US$ 247.95 million) for the AY 2010–11 was levied on JIL by the tax commissioner. The demand and order of assessment were challenged by JIL before ITAT which decided in JIL's favour on 3 November 2017. As a result, the demand stood reduced to nil. Another demand of Rs 1,276 crore (US$ 153.73 million) was raised on JIL, for the AY 2012–13, which was also challenged by JIL, this time before the tax commissioner, who, however, upheld it. JIL challenged the commissioner's order before the ITAT. The challenge was pending adjudication when the department submitted its claim.

As stated, the department submitted its claim for an aggregate sum of Rs 3,334.30 crore (US$ 401.72 million) with interest for the two demands (one of which had in fact been set aside by the ITAT). An appeal filed by the department against that order was pending before the Allahabad High Court. Notably, the department did not submit a claim of Rs 33,000 crore as crystallized by the commissioner on 31 March 2017. After verifying the record, the IRP recorded the tax liability for the AY 2012–13 as contingent liability of JIL. The claim was not admitted by the IRP who communicated his decision to the department on 29 January 2018.

The tax department did not protest against the IRP's decision in any manner, nor did it challenge his decision in the NCLT. In fact, in its letter dated 26 August 2020, the department stated that apart from the demands already made, an amount of approximately Rs 3,000 crore (US$ 361.45 million) shall be added to JIL's income for the next thirty-five years starting from AY 2013–14 on account of revenue subsidy received by JIL. Despite the moratorium, the department continued to raise demands on JIL during the insolvency process.

In due course, the IRP recorded the history of the assessment of revenue subsidy, together with the orders passed, demands raised, appeals filed, claims submitted, and JIL's contingent liability as in JIL's information memorandum provided to the NBCC and Suraksha Realty. All relevant documents were also made available to them. It is pertinent to mention here that as per S. 30(1) of the IBC, a resolution applicant is required to submit its resolution plan based on the information memorandum of the corporate debtor.

Both NBCC and Suraksha included the tax liability of Rs 33,000 crore, the claim for which was never filed by the tax department, into the total liability of JIL towards the tax department. Both stated in their plans that the liability of Rs 33,000 crore had been assessed and crystallized by the department before the commencement of insolvency.

As per the provisions of the Income Tax Act, 1961, the taxable event occurred during 2007–10, when income in the form of alleged subsidy was received by JIL through transfer of land parcels at subsidized rates. The assessment of this liability was concluded by the commissioner by his order of 31 March 2017. Therefore, while the tax liability was fixed and assessed to a total sum of Rs 33,000 crore prior to JIL's insolvency commencement, only the demand or recovery of the same was decided to be made on JIL on a yearly basis spread over thirty-two years for convenience. As the value of the debt payable to the tax department on Rs 33,000 crore as per the priorities provided under S. 53 of the IBC was nil, Suraksha offered payment of Rs 0.10 crore against the claim.

Although in its appeal the tax department sought rejection of the NCLT order, in its pleading it did not challenge the inclusion of Rs 33,000 crore as a pre-insolvency liability in its plan by Suraksha. However, taking a cue from JAL's appeal, it raised the issue during the arguments. It was argued by the tax department that since no demand for Rs 33,000 crore was made or will be made in over thirty-two years in the future, the liability of Rs 33,000 crore had not become due and payable, and consequently, no claim was required to be filed for this amount, and future liability of Rs. 33,000 crore could not be extinguished by Suraksha.

The tax department's stand was contested by the IMC and Suraksha. Clearly, the liability of Rs 33,000 crore was assessed and crystallized by the department before the insolvency commencement date; only the demand or recovery of the same was decided to be made on a yearly basis. It was the department which had committed an error by not filing the claim for the liability of Rs 33,000 crore as was its obligation under the IBC. A creditor is required to submit all its claims against the corporate debtor even if they have not become due or payable.

Whether a debt is 'due and payable' is relevant only for initiating an application for insolvency under the IBC, which requires that the debtor must be in default of payment of debt of Rs 1 crore (US$ 0.12 million) or more. For in an insolvency resolution process which has already commenced, the creditor is not restricted to filing a claim for an amount which is in 'default' or has become 'due and payable'; the claim for entire liability, irrespective of its date of payment or dispute over it, has to be filed.

It was argued that the IBC is a collective creditor's process; on commencement of insolvency of a defaulting borrower, all creditors are required to submit proof of claim, disclose their security interest held in debtor's assets, and submit claim for the liabilities owed to them, contingent or otherwise, crystallized or not, disputed or admitted, reduced to judgment or not, which are then put in a common bucket. Following which a distribution to creditors is made in accordance with the waterfall mechanism provided in the IBC. If the tax department's stand was accepted, it could lead to a situation where creditors file claim for defaulted amount only and not the entire liability, thus reserving their rights to recover the balance amount after the resolution plan is approved. Insolvency resolution of a debtor cannot be possible in such a situation.

However, the NCLAT did not agree with the IMC or Suraksha. While dismissing the appeal of the tax department on 26 September

2023, the NCLAT observed that the amount of Rs 33,000 crore was not yet due on JIL but will become due only when demands are raised year to year. The NCLAT's finding was unexpected. It also had the potential of changing the commercial terms of Suraksha's resolution plan, probably making it unworkable.

The NCLAT order was challenged by the IMC, Suraksha, and the tax department before the Supreme Court. While the tax department's appeal was dismissed by the Supreme Court outright, the appeals of the IMC and Suraksha were pending decision when this book was written. The author is refraining from making any comment on the merits of the stand taken by the tax department before the Supreme Court as the matter is sub judice.

V

YEIDA, as expected, assailed the NCLT order approving Suraksha's plan in the NCLAT. However, what shocked everyone was its new stance taken that the IRP and the NCLT did not have jurisdiction to adjudicate on YEIDA's claims of external development charges or additional farmers' compensation. It stated that YEIDA's entire claim of Rs 6,111.60 crore (US$ 736.34 million) is payable by JIL as secured debt under the UP Act. That claim, it maintained, fell outside the waterfall mechanism provided in the IBC and should be paid in full as the land leased to JIL was public property, and therefore, public interest was involved. YEIDA also sought payment of enhanced farmers' compensation ordered by some courts during the period when the moratorium was in force.

The IMC refuted YEIDA's contention as being factually incorrect and legally flawed. When YEIDA submitted its claim of Rs 6,111 crore (US$ 736.27 million) in 2017, it was verified by the IRP and admitted to the extent of Rs 461 crore (US$ 55.54 million). The decision was communicated to YEIDA in unequivocal terms via a detailed letter, dated 28 November 2017, which also provided a comprehensive explanation for admission and non-admission of various amounts.

It is pertinent to mention at this juncture that claims submitted by YEIDA fell into three broad categories:

(i) The IRP admitted only Rs 51.4 crore (US$ 6.19 million) out of the claim of Rs 98.1 crore (US$ 11.82 million) towards amount for pending works – work completed by JIL during the insolvency process – which was not disputed by YEIDA.

(ii) The claim of Rs 1,689 crore (US$ 203.49 million) for additional farmers' compensation was not admitted as this matter was sub judice. Later, an arbitration award was also granted in favour of JIL by an arbitral tribunal. The judgment of the Supreme Court in *Shakuntala Education Trust* had not come by then.

(iii) Out of the claim of Rs 4,371.2 crore (US$ 526.65 million) for future works and external development charges, the IRP admitted only Rs 409.6 crore (US$ 49.35 million) – the amount payable by JIL as external development charges for Jagganpur and Mirzapur. It was explained by the IRP that Rs 624.6 crore (US$ 75.25 million) claimed by YEIDA for Jagganpur and Mirzapur appeared to be an error as the balance amount (other than Rs 409.6 crore) was already paid by Axis Bank (Rs 62.05 crore, US$ 7.48 million) and Gaursons Realtech (Rs 36.59 crore, US$ 4.41 million) since the land for which the demand was raised was subleased to them, and Rs 114.21 crore (US$ 13.76 million) was paid by JIL. YEIDA never disputed the IRP's response and explanation. But YEIDA insisted that the entire external development charge of Rs 624.6 crore (US$ 75.25 million) for Jagganpur and Mirzapur was payable by

> JIL and contested the IRP's calculation, unfortunately without having verified thoroughly from its records. In response, the IMC had to file evidence of payment by Axis Bank and Gaursons Realtech after which YEIDA had to file an additional affidavit admitting error on its part and accepting that Axis Bank and Gaursons Realtech had indeed made the payments, as also stated by the IRP in the letter dated 28 November 2017. According to the IMC, the liability of JIL towards the external development charges for Jagganpur and Mirzapur was only Rs 409.6 crore.

The claim of Rs 572.89 crore (US$ 69.02 million) for external development charge for land in Tappal and Agra was not admitted by the IRP because no external development had been done by YEIDA in these areas, nor any demand had ever been raised on JIL (no demand has been raised till the time the book went to press). No such liability existed as on insolvency commencement date of JIL. This too was conveyed to YEIDA through the IRP's letter, and YEIDA never disputed it. Suraksha provided an undertaking in its resolution plan for payment of future external development charge for Tappal and Agra as and when they become due and are demanded. After realizing its mistake, YEIDA in its affidavit admitted that this amount was in respect of future work of external development, and it would go by the IRP's decision and Suraksha's undertaking.

YEIDA also argued that the external development charge payable by JIL is also a secured debt and Suraksha should pay it in full. Suraksha and the IMC refuted that external development was a secured debt. They argued that external development charge was not defined under the UP Act, instead the payment of external development charge arose from a concession agreement – which was not a statutory contract, but a contract by a statutory authority, as held by the Supreme Court in *Jaypee Kensington*.

Undisputedly, YEIDA is an operational creditor making its claim for external development charge as an operational debt. The claim for external development charge is an unsecured operational debt; it does not fall within the ambit of Ss. 13 and 13A of the UP Act. External development charge is neither a payment of consideration of money or instalment thereof for transfer of land, nor is it any other amount on account of transfer of building or site; it is also not rent due to YEIDA from any lease. It is also not a tax or fee. Therefore, distribution of admitted claim for external development charge of Rs 409.6 crore must be made treating it as an unsecured debt. Suraksha had already proposed Rs 0.10 crore against this amount in its resolution plan.

Regarding additional farmers' compensation, the IMC explained to the NCLAT that the claim was not admitted by the IRP as it was under litigation with YEIDA. JIL's stand was that acquisition of land for the Yamuna Expressway Project was done by YEIDA using urgency clause under the Land Acquisition Act, 1984, which had been upheld by the Supreme Court in *Nand Kishore*.[2] The arbitral tribunal had also given an award holding that JIL was not liable to pay additional compensation demanded by the G.O. It was only in 2022 that the Supreme Court upheld the validity of the G.O. in *Shakuntala Education Trust* but stated in paragraph 69 of the judgment, quoted earlier too, that 'with respect to the contention of the respondent No.19 – Supertech with regard to initiation of 218 The Jaypee Infra Insolvency Saga the CIRP, we are not concerned with the said issue in the present proceedings. The law will take its own course...' Therefore, JIL contested the liability of additional farmers' compensation.

The IMC refuted YEIDA's contention that because land leased by YEIDA was public property, its claim from the

2 *Nand Kishore Gupta & Ors. v. State of UP & Ors.*, 2010 10 SCC 282

land should be treated outside the IBC and Article 300A of the Constitution of India cannot apply. The dues of all the creditors of the corporate debtor undergoing insolvency process have to be dealt in accordance with the provisions of the IBC. All creditors are required to submit their claims in prescribed forms to the IRP or the RP, as the case may be, in response to the public announcement. The IBC does not exclude any creditors from submitting a claim. All operational creditors have to submit their claims in Form B if the corporate debtor owes a debt to them. The government and statutory authorities are considered as operational creditors; YEIDA is a statutory authority, and undisputed operation creditor of JIL. In fact, YEIDA submitted its claim in Form B on 23 August 2017 in response to the public announcement made by the IRP.

It was also contended that YEIDA acceded to the IBC's application and jurisdiction of the NCLT by submitting its claim to the IRP; it is estopped under law from raising this plea after six years. After submitting its claim, YEIDA acceded to the jurisdiction under the IBC. At no stage did it question the jurisdiction of the NCLT to adjudicate on its claims. In fact, YEIDA submitted to the NCLT's jurisdiction by calling upon it with its objections to the treatment of its claim by Suraksha in the resolution plan. It was also argued that YEIDA did not challenge before the NCLT the IRP's decision taken as far back as on 28 November 2017 on its claims; it only questioned the treatment of the claim by Suraksha. And the issue of admission of claim cannot be reopened in the current proceedings.

However, instead of contesting YEIDA's claim for additional compensation, Suraksha suddenly took a surprise turn in its position. It offered to pay additional farmers' compensation of Rs 1,216 crore (US$ 146.51 million) out of Rs 1,689 crore (US$ 203.49 million) demanded by YEIDA over and above the amount proposed to other stakeholders under the resolution plan.

It was stated by Suraksha that Rs 143 crore (US$ 17.23 million), pertaining to 744.6 acres of land where homebuyers' projects were situated, had already been paid by NOIDA to farmers, and Rs 330 crore (US$ 39.76 million), pertaining to 1,537.6 acres which were subleased to third parties before commencement of insolvency, cannot be made a liability of the JIL.

Suraksha offered to pay the entire amount of Rs 1,216 crore over a period of four years in five instalments and contended that this was consistent with other financial creditors. It offered full and complete cooperation to assist YEIDA in recovering the additional farmers' compensation from these third parties, and even become facilitator, if required, to collect such amount from third parties; JIL did not have powers like YEIDA and hence, it would be difficult for it to invoke clauses of the UP Act. Suraksha stated that in any event, these amounts, over and above the offer of Rs 1,216 crore (US$ 146.1 million), were not an obligation or liability of JIL because that obligation or liability rested with third-party beneficiaries.

Suraksha also stated that as Rs 143 crore (pertaining to 744.6 acres of land where homebuyers' projects were situated) had already been paid by NOIDA to farmers, Rs 330 crore (pertaining to 1,537.6 acres which had already been subleased to third parties before commencement of JIL's insolvency) cannot be made a liability of JIL.

Suraksha could have defended its resolution plan and the decision of the NCLT as legally correct, but it decided to give up the fight and offered to make payment of additional farmers' compensation of Rs 1,216 crore. The payment was offered to be made over a period of four years – the same time in which the buyers were promised that their homes would get constructed. Suraksha could have offered to make this payment out of the total amount promised by it in Suraksha's plan. However, it decided to pay the amount in addition to and over and above the amounts offered in Suraksha's plan, thus not impacting payments to the banks. Perhaps, Suraksha apprehended that if deduction was made from the banks' kitty, they would go up in challenge claiming that as holders of first charge on the land, their dues had to be paid in priority to YEIDA's dues.

This change in its stance, as informed by Suraksha to the NCLAT, was keeping in mind the interest of the homebuyers and the farmers who had been kept waiting for so long, as also in the interest of early implementation of its plan. It wanted to bring an end to the long and contentious insolvency process and start the construction of the flats so that these could be delivered within the time promised in the plan.

The IMC requested the NCLAT to allow Suraksha to make the payment of additional farmers' compensation within the timelines proposed by Suraksha, without adversely impacting the other payments proposed under the plan, including the construction of units as per the schedule approved by the CoC and the NCLT. It needs to be mentioned that the proposed payment of Rs 1,216 crore (US$ 146.51 million) made up 89 per cent of YEIDA's claim while the banks being paid Rs 7,762 crore (US$ 935.18 million) made up 79 per cent of their debt. Further, the payment to banks was proposed to be made over a period of five to six years under its resolution plan, and units proposed to be delivered to homebuyers within four-and-a-half years.

Moreover, liquidation value of operational creditors had to be paid in priority to other creditors, but there was no provision which required payment to be made upfront. The sum of Rs 1,216 crore (US$ 146.51 million) towards additional farmers' compensation was sought to be paid by Suraksha in addition to the amount proposed under the plan. This made implementation of the resolution plan of paramount importance to all stakeholders, including homebuyers and farmers. The IMC was of the opinion that it would be fair and equitable if this enormous amount of additional farmers' compensation was allowed to be paid over the period proposed so that it did not affect the payment of other liabilities or fulfilment of other commercial obligations under the resolution plan in any manner.

YEIDA rejected the proposal outright and insisted the matter be heard based on merits before the NCLAT. It sought payment of the entire sum of Rs 1,689 crore.

The matter had to be put to rest by the NCLAT.

VI

On 24 May 2024, true to its reputation of churning out quick decisions, the bench of Justice Ashok Bhushan and Barun Mitra decided the issue of both additional farmers' compensation and external development charges.

Additional Farmers' Compensation

As expected, in view of the decisions of the Supreme Court in *Shakuntala Education Trust*, the NCLAT held that the liability of Rs 1,689 crore towards additional farmers' compensation is payable by JIL; the judgment made it clear that farmers whose land was acquired by YEIDA are entitled to additional compensation of 64.7 per cent, which had to be recovered from the lessee/allottees of the land. Therefore, the issue was finally determined by the Supreme Court whose verdict was binding on all concerned. In other words, the NCLAT held that the liability of Rs 1,689 crore was payable by JIL and ought to have been admitted by the IRP.

The NCLAT, however, noted that the IRP did not accept the claim of YEIDA in the year 2018 for additional farmers' compensation on the ground that it was under arbitration, and the judgment of the Supreme Court in *Shakuntala Educational Trust* was delivered only much later on 19 May 2022.

Again, on expected lines, relying on the decision of the Supreme Court in *Prabhjit Singh Soni*, NCLAT further held that the amount of additional compensation payable to the farmers towards additional cost of 64.7 per cent is a secured charge. Like in the facts of *Prabhjit Singh Soni*, where unpaid instalments payable towards premium for the lease was held to be secured charge, similarly, additional farmers' compensation payable to the farmers by JIL was part of the acquisition cost, which as per the provision of the concession agreement, as noted above, was required to be paid by JIL. Being a secured operational creditor, YEIDA was entitled to a different treatment in the resolution plan meted out to other secured creditors, the NCLAT held.

Given all of this, the NCLAT took up for consideration the offer made by Suraksha to pay Rs 1,216 crore (US$ 146.51 million) out of Rs 1,689 crore (US$ 203.49 million) demanded by YEIDA in 100 per cent settlement after deducting the compensation amount of Rs 330 crore (US$ 39.76 million) and Rs143 crore (US$ 17.23 million).

The NCLAT referred to *Jaypee Kensington* where the Supreme Court had held that the resolution applicant of its own could not have decided that end-user would mean sub-lessee and thereby deflect even collection of the amount towards this liability on YEIDA. The amount of Rs 330 crore (US$ 39.76 million) liable to be paid for the land which had been transferred to third party, a liability of JIL, could not be forsaken on the ground that it had subleased to third party. As per the concession agreement, it was the liability of the concessionaire to pay the acquisition cost; deduction of Rs 330 crore from the amount of claim of Rs 1,689 crore cannot be permitted, the NCLAT held.

Similarly, the amount of Rs 143 crore also cannot be deducted from the claim of Rs 1,689 crore. Even if the amount has been paid by NOIDA towards additional farmers' compensation, the same can always be asked to be reimbursed from JIL. The amount proposed in the Suraksha plan, of Rs 1,216 crore, thus, cannot be considered a 100 per cent payment of additional compensation to YEIDA towards additional farmers' compensation.

However, the NCLAT held that YEIDA cannot receive more payment in distribution than what the secured financial creditors are getting under Suraksha's plan approved by the NCLT. Suraksha's plan proposed the payment of 79 per cent of their secured dues to the institutional financial creditors, that is, banks and financial institutions. YEIDA was also entitled for payment of same percentage of amount, which had been offered to other financial creditors, which came to Rs 1,334.31 crore (US$ 160.76 million), the NCLAT decided. Suraksha had already offered to pay Rs 1,216 crore to YEIDA; it should pay Rs 118.31 crore (US$ 14.25 million) more, the NCLAT directed.

The NCLAT rejected YEIDA's request for upfront payment of additional farmers' compensation. Referring to R. 38 of the CIRP Regulations, the NCLAT held that operational creditors were entitled to payment of their dues in priority over financial creditors but payment of priority to operational creditors are not upfront payment of their claims. In the timeline proposed for payment by Suraksha the operational creditors were not in priority. The NCLAT noted that stakeholders, including homebuyers, were waiting for their claims to be considered, and there had been prolonged litigations on different issues. By accepting YEIDA's claim and directing payment of amount equivalent to what has been given to the secured financial creditors justice would be served, paving a way forward for implementation of the resolution plan.

The NCLAT stated that it could have asked Suraksha to move for an addendum to be submitted before the CoC, by including the aforesaid provisions, but it would delay the process. Hence, it had adopted a second course – issuing directions to Suraksha to make payment of 79 per cent of secured claim of YEIDA, amounting to Rs 1,689 crore, within the timeline as indicated in the order, which would make the resolution plan compliant for approval. Such direction would not amount to modification in Suraksha's resolution plan, as it was to make the plan compliant of the IBC provisions. Moreover, the secured financial creditors would not be adversely impacted by the NCLAT's directions as YEIDA was to be paid over and above the amount proposed to be paid to them and other creditors under the plan.

External Development Charges

The NCLAT held that external development charges were not covered by S. 13 in the UP Act. Therefore, the claim of YEIDA towards external development charges was not a secured claim and did not need to be dealt with in the resolution plan as a secured claim. Payment of external development charges in the resolution plan in accordance with the IBC did not amount to tinkering with the concession agreement. It would not require YEIDA's consent. The NCLAT made it clear that payment of Rs 10 lakh (US$ 0.01 million) by Suraksha in the plan towards external development charges was not illegal, and it would not violate any provisions of the IBC.

To obviate the further delay in implementation of the resolution plan and to take care of the interest of stakeholders, including homebuyers, and the claim of additional farmers' compensation, the NCLAT directed Suraksha to make payment to YEIDA of its secured operational debt of Rs 1,689 crore (US$ 203.49 million) in the ratio of 79 per cent, which had been paid to other secured creditors, which amount came to Rs 1,334.31 crore (US$ 160.76 million) as per timeline and ratio indicated in the offer made by Suraksha.

The NCLAT also reminded YEIDA of its assurance made before the Supreme Court, which also reiterated before the NCLAT that it too wanted resolution of JIL. YEIDA also filed appeal against the NCLAT order. As the appeal is pending before the Supreme Court, the author is refraining from making any comment on the subject matter.

VII

When all else failed, fate had stepped in the farmers' favour. This happened not only through *Shakuntala Education Trust*, but also other significant decisions of the apex court after Suraksha's resolution plan was approved by NCLT and during the pendency of YEIDA's appeal in the NCLAT.

Thus ended the decades-long wait of the farmers to be fairly compensated for the land acquired from them. Ironically, in the end, the delay in approval of the resolution plan worked to the advantage of farmers as the decision of the Supreme Court in *Shakuntala Education Trust* and *Prabhjit Singh Soni* turned the law in their favour, paving the way for payment of the compensation. Over and above judicial laws, God often has Her own ways of ironing the creases and delivering justice.

In the end, the insolvency resolution of JIL became a catalyst for the payment of additional compensation of Rs 1,689 crore to the farmers for land acquired from them decades ago for the Yamuna Expressway Project, out of which an amount of Rs 1,334.31 crore would be paid by Suraksha. It was an unexpected outcome of the insolvency process.

Ironically, the term additional farmers' compensation was coined by Justice Ashok Bhushan, who authored the *Gajraj Singh* judgment sitting in Allahabad High Court's full bench. Strange are the ways of fate. Justice Ashok Bhushan became the chairperson of NCLAT after retiring from the Supreme Court and the author of the historic judgment of 24 May 2024 under which farmers would finally be delivered the additional compensation owed to them.

23

The Last Word?

All's well that ends well.

~ William Shakespeare

The NCLAT disposed of the last appeal on 24 May 2024. But, the Jaypee saga was still unfolding and refusing to end as the matter travelled to the Supreme Court where another battle would be fought as the issue of tax assessment and tax department's claim was decided.

On another front, in June 2024, both JAL and JHL were admitted into insolvency by the Allahabad bench of the NCLT, adding yet another twist to the situation. The orders have been challenged before the NCLAT by aggrieved parties. As the matters are sub judice, the author is not making any comment on the facts or merits of these matters, out of proprietary and respect for the NCLAT.

However, much to the surprise of homebuyers, Suraksha decided to implement the resolution plan notwithstanding the pendency of the appeals in the Supreme Court. When this book was being written, steps to implement the plan had started rolling out. Homebuyers were to finally heave a sigh of relief although all eyes are now set on the Supreme Court.

Observing propriety and out of utmost respect for the Supreme Court, the author is not making any comment or remark whatsoever on the subject matter of appeals and proceedings pending before the Supreme Court. Suffice it to state, the Supreme Court will have the last word.

Part II

The Outcomes

24

It's a Deal!

Unlike sport in business the win-win is the best possible score.

~ Rasheed Ogunlaru, *Soul Trader*

The objective of any insolvency procedure is to maximize returns for creditors. The mechanism used to achieve that goal depends on circumstances and the availability of assets. Usually, the greatest returns to creditors are achieved by maintaining the business as a going concern. It is widely accepted that creditors of all classes generally get much better returns from rescues and reconstructions than they do from liquidations. An insolvency practitioner placed in charge of the affairs of the insolvent enterprise must attempt to rescue the business if that provides better returns for the creditors. The IBC takes this rescue approach to corporate insolvency.

The preamble to the IBC mentions that it is a legislation to consolidate and amend the laws relating to reorganization and insolvency resolution of corporate persons, partnership firms, and individuals in a time-bound manner for maximization of value of assets of such persons and to promote entrepreneurship, availability of credit, and balance of interests of all stakeholders (including alteration in the order of priority of the payment of government dues). Simply put, one of the main objective of the IBC is to maximize the value of assets of the corporate debtor.

Despite the long process involved in its insolvency proceedings, JIL will always be celebrated for becoming a classic case of accomplishing maximization of value of assets. This has occurred mainly because of the steps taken by the IRP and the distribution of payments under Suraksha's resolution plan, and the resultant benefits of the successful resolution of JIL's insolvency.

II

Maximization of Value Achieved Through IRP's Efforts

This section lists the maximization of value achieved through the IRP's efforts:

Clawback of 758 Acres

Due to the determined efforts of the IRP, an area of 758 acres of prime real estate was restored to JIL's corpus, adding significantly to the asset value of JIL. As per the IBBI's newsletter,[3] the estimated value of recovery in JIL is 83 per cent of total amount clawed back under IBC at Rs 6,599 crore (US$ 795 million).

As elaborately discussed in Chapter 9, JIL had mortgaged 758 acres of land to its related party JAL without any economic consideration. The mortgage was made when JIL itself was in financial distress. The estimated market value of this land was around Rs 5,000 crore at the time the mortgage was created. Today,

3 *The IBBI Newsletter*, January–March 2024. Last seen on 25 May 2024 at https://ibbi.gov.in/en/publication

it is valued at double the price. Had the mortgage transactions not been set aside by the NCLT at the instance of the IRP, Anuj Jain, JAL's lenders would have sold this to recover their dues from JIL. However, despite the best efforts, 100 acres of land at Tappal could not be retrieved since mortgage of that land had been made prior to the lookback period in the IBC.

Recovery of Advance from JAL

The IRP succeeded in recovering Rs 664.67 crore (US$ 80.08 million) from JAL out of Rs 750 crore (US$ 90.36 million) deposited by it in the Supreme Court. It took a very long and persistent fight in the Court by the IRP to be able to extract this huge sum from JAL. As a result, homebuyers of JIL got back interest-free maintenance deposit of Rs 106.90 crore (US$ 12.88 million) that was kept with JAL. JIL also got back Rs 557.77 crore (US$ 67.20 million) given to JAL as mobilization advance. The contest over this amount was the most acrimonious of all legal battles between JIL and JAL. This was no mean achievement.

The Supreme Court held that this amount of Rs 750 crore belonged to JAL and thwarted the NBCC's attempt to stake claim over it to use it for construction of JIL's projects, but with the IRP's persistence, the Court permitted JIL to get a refund of the sum advanced to JAL out of this amount after reconciliation of accounts. Finally, after a prolonged contest and favourable orders by NCLT and NCLAT, the IRP succeeded in recovering a sum of Rs 557.77 crore and Rs 106.90 crore out of Rs 750 crore for JIL and its homebuyers, whereas the balance amount was released to JAL.

This amount is now available for use by JIL for construction of flats for homebuyers. It is unlikely that this amount would have been recovered in the normal course of business or during JAL's insolvency process, if it continues, given that JIL and its homebuyers are ranked much lower in the waterfall of JAL creditors. Another sum of Rs 15.15 crore, being the interest earned on Rs 557.77

crore from the NCLT order dated 7 March 2023 till its payment, is awaited from the registrar, Allahabad bench, of the NCLT.

Reduction in Liabilities During the CIRP

Maximization of the value of assets of the corporate debtor can occur by increasing its assets or their value, or reducing its liabilities. By ensuring construction of thousands of flats and transferring them to the homebuyers during the insolvency process, the IRP was able to satisfy the corresponding debt of homebuyers, thus reducing the liability of JIL by Rs 3,099 crore (US$ 373.37 million) by executing sublease for 8,610 units.

On JIL's insolvency commencement date, the homebuyer liability stood around Rs 12,300 crore (US$ 1,482 million) which was reduced to nearly Rs 9,200 crore (US$ 1,108 million). This represented 25 per cent reduction in homebuyer liability during the insolvency process. The liability has further reduced as deliveries continue even after the insolvency period ended and JIL was being managed by the IMC. This was unprecedented and sets a very high bar for real estate insolvency cases in the future.

Cash Surplus from Operations

During the entire duration of the insolvency process, JIL remained a going concern. In fact, operations improved under the leadership of the IRP. The toll revenue increased due to increase in toll rates and higher traffic, whereas cost was kept under check with many cost-reduction measures and tighter controls. This resulted in higher cash surplus from toll operations. It is estimated that JIL had a cash surplus of approximately Rs 1,700 crore (US$ 205 million) from the toll operations.

Even after spending Rs 1,400 crore (US$ 169 million) for construction, JIL had a bank balance of Rs 460 crore (US$ 55.42 million) at the time of the completion of insolvency. The money against the JIL–JAL reconciliation was received after the completion of insolvency and added to JIL's bank balance. It may be noted that all payables and expenses are current.

III

Payment Offered by Suraksha under Resolution Plan

This section lists the details of the payments offered by Suraksha to the creditors of JIL under its resolution plan. Suraksha Realty's resolution plan resonated with homebuyers and banks for many reasons, primarily for its attractive terms that served both. In the earlier rounds both preferred the government-backed resolution applicant like NBCC since it provided greater certainty on the implementation of the plan. With its relentless pursuit since 2017, undeterred in the face of delays and prolonged litigations and with constant engagement with homebuyers, Suraksha was able to win their confidence. The banks' votes also showed trust in Suraksha. Eventually, Suraksha edged out NBCC by a thin margin in the voting. The amount of payments and benefits received by creditors against their admitted claims is very substantial. Few cases have resulted in such high returns for creditors.

Homebuyers

The admitted claim of the homebuyers was Rs 12,807.1 crore (US$ 1543.02 million). Of the 20,590 homebuyers of JIL, a staggering 18,767 homebuyers (93 per cent) opted for possession of their houses before the Supreme Court while *Chitra Sharma* was pending, reiterating their preference while submitting their claim in the insolvency process; only 413 homebuyers (1 per cent), who cancelled their units prior to commencement of insolvency, filed claims for refund. A total of 1,410 homebuyers (6 per cent) have already been offered possession of flats. In its plan, Suraksha promised to complete the projects situated in Noida and Mirzapur between six and forty months.

To compensate for the delay suffered by homebuyers in receiving their units, the resolution plan proposes transfer of 150 acres of JIL's land for the benefit of homebuyers. Simply put, Suraksha proposes that it would sell 150 acres of land and use the proceeds for distribution among homebuyers in the ratio of their claims.

The plan also offers a discount of 7 per cent to homebuyers if they buy a new flat in JIL's projects that are under development and a referral incentive of 3 per cent if a homebuyer brings a new customer to buy a flat in an existing project. A discount of 25 per cent is also proposed on the prevailing maintenance charges for a period of two years from the date of possession, upon Suraksha becoming project maintenance agency.

It has been estimated that the completion of projects would require around Rs 6,000 crore (US$ 722.89 million) as against the balance receivables from the homebuyers of around Rs 3,000 crore (US$ 361.50 million). Deployment of 12,000 average daily labour on the project sites has been estimated to complete the projects within committed timelines.

Suraksha has also proposed infusion of a working capital facility of Rs 3,000 crore (US$ 361.45 million). It will utilize toll collection and other cash flow of JIL as well to conduct the construction of such projects and meet the project-related costs for the first three years.

For monitoring the project and transparency in fund utilization, Suraksha has proposed establishment of project-wise monitoring committee comprising representatives of homebuyers, Suraksha, and JIL. It has also provided for opening customer grievance and redressal outlets and developing a mobile application to provide updates on construction, outstanding dues, etc. Project-wise escrow account shall be maintained, as required under the RERA, for collection of payments from all homebuyers.

Suraksha has also proposed to give credit to homebuyers towards early payment discount accrued up till 9 August 2017, the insolvency commencement date of JIL. A corpus of Rs 48 crore (US$ 5.78 million) has been adjusted from the receivables of homebuyers and would be honoured to give fair treatment to such homebuyers. An amount of Rs 15 crore (US$ 1.81 million) accrued towards this discount was not yet adjusted by JIL as on insolvency commencement date. As a goodwill gesture, Suraksha has proposed adjustment/given credit of the accrued amount of Rs 15 crore from the balance receivables as per the respective statement of accounts of the homebuyers.

Suraksha has proposed refund of principal amount of Rs 178 crore (US$ 21.45 million) by homebuyers in the following projects:

Noida projects – *Villa Expanza, Buddh Circuit Studios-II, Nature View Apartments, Aman-III*

Mirzapur projects – *Udaan* and *Boulevard Court*, and

Agra project – *Agra Kensington Park*

Refund of monies will be made in two annual instalments or by offer of allotment of transfer to some other project at market rates, where the homebuyer shall get credit of 20 per cent of the monies paid by them over and above the amount paid, which shall be netted-of in the sale consideration of the new allotments. Homebuyers have the option to continue to hold allotment in these projects, but the completion of the construction will be subject to availability of unencumbered and unfettered possession of the land. Homebuyers who applied for refund prior to commencement of insolvency will be given refund of principal amount of Rs 64 crore (US$ 7.71 million) in two equal annual instalments.

Suraksha decided to deliver units to the 2,000 homebuyers who had not submitted claim and were not part of the CoC, if they were to file their claim any time before the approval of its plan by the NCLT. The resolution plan was approved by the NCLT on 7 March 2023 by which time nearly half of the 2,000 homebuyers submitted their claim.

Fixed Deposit Holders

The admitted claim of fixed deposit holders was Rs 29.3 crore (US$ 3.53 million). Against their claim, Suraksha's plan has proposed full payment in three equal instalments made every six months. In addition, as a gesture of goodwill, an amount of Rs 9.16 crore (US$ 1.1 million) will be paid to fixed deposit holders towards claims submitted subsequent to the finalization of JIL's information memorandum till the date of approval of the resolution plan. As a result, 1,034 fixed deposit holders will also get Rs 9.16 crore (US$ 1.1 million) proportionately.

Payment to Assenting Banks and Financial Institutions

The admitted claim of the consortium comprising IDBI Bank, IIFCL, LIC, SBI, Syndicate Bank, Bank of Maharashtra, ICICI Bank, Union Bank, IFCI, J&K Bank was Rs 9,537.60 crore (US$ 1,150 million); of Axis Bank Limited Rs 218.00 crore (US$ 26.27 million); and of SREI Equipment Finance Limited Rs 27.00 crore (US$ 3.25 million); aggregating to Rs. 9,782.6 crore (US$ 1,178.63 million). Suraksha has offered 2,372 acres of land having fair value of Rs 6,121 crore (US$ 737.47 million) to the assenting financial creditors. Further, payment of Rs 160 crore (US$ 19.28 million) per annum, aggregating to Rs 1,280 crore (US$ 154 million) from the end of the third year up to the end of the tenth year will be made to the assenting financial creditors in accordance with the covenants of the resolution plan.

The transfer of beneficial interest in the land parcels will be made proportionately to banks, which voted in favour of the plan, in a mutually acceptable, suitable structure to facilitate monetization of land parcels into a special purpose vehicle. A sum of Rs 25 crore (US$ 3.01 million) will be set aside for expenses to be incurred for management and monetization of the land parcels of the assenting banks.

In its plan, Suraksha has proposed that the corporate guarantee provided by JAL, and personal guarantees provided by Manoj Gaur to JIL's lenders (banks), will continue to hold and the lenders will have to recover their dues from them as guarantors of JIL's liabilities to banks. The plan further provided that the guarantors would not have any subrogation rights against Suraksha or JIL. As a result, banks will also be able to recover the balance amount from the guarantors.

The total recovery of banks and financial institutions is expected to be around 79 per cent of their admitted claims.

Payment to Dissenting Bank (ICICI)

In its resolution plan, Suraksha proposed payment of its debt to the dissenting financial creditors by allowing them to enforce their security interest. Not knowing how many banks would vote against the plan and become dissenting financial creditors, Suraksha identified 1,486 acres of land out of total immovable property for enforcement by the dissenting financial creditors for the payment of their liquidation value, assuming the dissenting financial creditors to be a maximum of 34 per cent.

Suraksha proposed that it should have the right to identify and earmark specific land at any of the locations, out of the existing security interest on the land, in order to provide specific, exclusive, and distinct security interest for enforcement by each dissenting financial creditor for recovery of its liquidation value. To provide fair and equitable treatment, Suraksha provided that it would invite suggestions from dissenting financial creditors in the exercise of identifying specific, distinct, and exclusive land parcels, but specified that the final decision would be that of Suraksha.

It turned out that ICICI Bank was the only dissenting financial creditor to the resolution plan, having admitted a claim of Rs 304 crore (US$ 36.63 million) with 1.34 per cent voting share. Security interest held by ICICI Bank in JIL's land was, however, not exclusively mortgaged or charged. It was held jointly with the other consortium of banks, and ICICI Bank's interest in it was pari passu. Simply put, ICICI Bank's share in the total security interest held by the consortium of banks was proportionate to the amount of its debt. The security interest was not separable in a sense.

Allowing ICICI Bank to recover its debt by enforcing security interest required innovation and the approval of the assenting creditors who held security interest as a consortium. Suraksha offered 180 acres of land parcels having fair value of Rs 334 crore (US$ 40.24 million) to ICICI Bank which could be enforced.

Other Stakeholders

As there were no outstanding workmen's dues, it did not demand any treatment in resolution plan.

Operational Creditors

In its resolution plan, Suraksha offered only Rs 0.10 crore (US$ 12,000) to YEIDA against the demand of Rs 1,689 crore (US$ 203.49 million) of additional farmers' compensation. However, later, Suraksha offered to pay the amount of Rs 1,216 crore (US$ 146.51 million) over and above the total payments proposed in the resolution plan; the rest, it said, could be collected directly from allottees. However, the NCLAT decided that Suraksha would pay an amount of Rs1,334.31 crore (US$ 160.76 million) to YEIDA against payment of additional farmers' compensation. This led to further maximization of the value of assets of JIL by Rs 1334.31 crore.

Income Tax Demand

Against the tax department's claim of Rs 3,334 crore (US$ 402 million), Suraksha has offered Rs 0.10 crore. Whether any more amount is payable or not will be decided by the Supreme Court.

Jaiprakash Associates Limited

JIL and JAL entered into several related-party agreements, following which JAL had been carrying out development and construction work across Noida, Mirzapur, Jagganpur, Tappal, and Agra. Even though JAL and JIL are two separate corporate entities, JIL is an alter ego of JAL, set up as a special purpose vehicle and substituted as concessionaire in the concession agreement. In its resolution plan, Suraksha has proposed to terminate all the agreements pertaining to development of land parcels, construction, and maintenance contracts or any other contract executed with JAL.

Compared with the other members of the Infamous Twelve, maximization of value is the highest in JIL's case, as is clear from Table 5.

Table 5: JIL's Maximization of Value

Name of Corporate Debtor	Claims of Financial Creditors Dealt Under Resolution			Realization by all Claimants as % of Liquidation Value	Resolution Applicant
	Amount Admitted (Rs)	Amount Realized (Rs)	Realization as % of Claims		
Electrosteel Steel Limited	13175	5320	40.38	183.45	Vedanta Ltd.
Bhushan Steel Limited	56022	35571	63.50	252.88	Bamnipal Steel Ltd.
Monnet Ispat & Energy Ltd	11015	2892	26.26	123.35	Consortium of JSW and AION Investments Pvt. Ltd
Essar Steel India Limited	49473	41018	82.91	266.65	Arcelor Mittal India Pvt. Ltd
Alok Industries Limited	29523	5052	17.11	115.39	Reliance Industries Limited, JM Financial Asset Reconstruction Company Ltd., JMFARC March 2018 Trust
Jyoti Structures Limited	7365	3691	50.12	387.44	Group of HNIs led by Mr Sharad Sanghi

Bhushan Power & Steel Ltd	47158	19350	41.03	209.12	JSW Limited
Amtek Auto Limited	12641	2615	20.68	169.65	Deccan Value Investors L.P. and DVI PE (Mauritius) Ltd
Jaypee Infratech Limited	23083	20363[4]	88.22	114.61	Suraksha Realty Limited and Lakshdeep Investments and Finance Private Limited
Era Infra Engineering Limited	Under CIRP				
Lanco Infratech Limited	Under Liquidation				
ABG Shipyard Limited	Under Liquidation				

IV

Other Beneficial Outcomes

This section looks at the other beneficial outcomes from JIL's successful insolvency process.

4 Note: This does not include the Rs 1,334.31 crore to be paid to YEIDA. The amount of Rs 1,334.31 crore is neither included in claim admitted nor in claim settled. It is over and above this amount.

Access to Land

The Yamuna Expressway covers a total length of 165.537 km – a six-lane (extendable up to eight lanes), an access-controlled, fully concrete, paved expressway connecting Noida and Agra. Most of the land required for the construction of the expressway (approximately 97 per cent) is under the possession of JIL. However, due to delay in handing over of the land, some entry and exit ramps and addition of new cloverleaf junctions are yet to be completed.

Many other parcels of land are not in possession of JIL yet. Nearly 3,672 acres of land is presently under illegal possession of erstwhile landowners for want of 64.7 per cent additional farmers' compensation. This also includes land subleased to third parties in the past. Many farmers have been obstructing access to land as their compensation remains unpaid. Sometimes, farmers' protests for additional compensation adversely affects the expressway operations, resulting in loss of revenue and hardship for the commuters. With payment of additional farmers' compensation offered by Suraksha, JIL is likely to get access to remaining land and further improve toll operations.

End of Widespread Litigation

There are forty-seven separate matters pending in the Allahabad High Court filed by erstwhile landowners in respect of approximately 244 acres of land, challenging acquisition of the land, the adequacy and fairness of compensation, additional farmers' compensation, right of way, ownership, etc. Some of these are filed against the government with JIL being a necessary party. These matters are also likely to come to an end with the resolution of JIL and the long-pending matter of additional farmers' compensation.

The successful conclusion of JIL's insolvency process will bring an end to many longstanding disputes and litigation pending in different forums. It will also bring closure to the petition filed by YEIDA seeking cancellation of arbitration award passed by the arbitral tribunal, which decided that JIL was not liable to pay additional farmers' compensation.

The resolution plan will resolve the subject matter of many cases, bringing all of them to the finish line: the eighty-nine complaints (Rs 627.45 crore, US$ 75.60 million) filed by homebuyers in the National Consumer Disputes Commission in Delhi; seventy-four complaints (Rs 29.01 crore, US$ 3.50 million) in the State Consumer Commission; fifty-nine complaints (Rs 6.14 crore, US$ 0.74 million) in the District Consumer Forum; and twenty-nine cases involving Rs 6.45 crore (US$ 0.78 million) pending in district and other courts. Eleven injunction suits in respect of land involving Rs 1.58 crore (US$ 0.19 million) will also hopefully close as the famers receive their compensation.

Increase in Land Value

The value of the land leased to JIL has increased manifold because of various planned developments in the region. This appreciation in market value of the land is a result of public expenditure made towards construction of the Noida International Airport at Jewar, the linking of the Yamuna Expressway with the Delhi–Mumbai Expressway, and linking of the Noida International Airport with the Dedicated Freight Corridor.

Here's an illustration: in 2011, lands in the district of Gautam Buddh Nagar were procured at the rate of a mere Rs 880 (US$ 10.60) per square metre. In 2024, the lands are being allotted at a substantially higher rate of Rs 25,900 (US$ 312) per square metre, an increase of over 2,800 per cent in market value. While Suraksha will come to benefit from the increase, a part of the benefit will be offset by the cost of the development of projects which have also simultaneously increased multifold.

This increase in land value benefits all the stakeholders of JIL. The value of units for homebuyers who have already received possession of their units has gone up. Those who will receive the completed units going forward will not have to pay any additional cost of construction incurred by Suraksha. It is true they have been waiting for long and their investment has not earned them time value for money, but the resolution plan offers many benefits that will compensate the homebuyers for this delay.

The banks that voted in favour of the resolution plan are receiving land based on valuation made a few years ago. As the price of land has since gone up significantly in the district of Gautam Buddh Nagar, the assenting financial creditors will eventually recover more than what is provided in the resolution plan by selling the land offered to them against payment of their debt. The approval of the plan and payment of farmers' additional compensation will provide a further boost to the land prices. Same benefits would apply to ICICI Bank, the dissenting financial creditor receiving land in lieu of its debt.

Increase in Toll Collection for Construction

The revenue from toll collection on the Yamuna Expressway has also increased steadily over the years. The toll collection rose from Rs 334.18 crore (US$ 40.26 million) in 2020–2021 to Rs 380.03 crore (US$ 45.79 million) in 2021–2022. In the last financial year (2022–2023), the toll collection was Rs 428.91 crore (US$ 51.68 million). With the estimated increase in traffic on the Yamuna Expressway, the revenue from toll collection is likely to increase substantially in the future. Suraksha has provided in its resolution plan that the revenue from the toll will be used exclusively for construction of flats for three years.

According to a techno-economic feasibility report issued by PwC, upon commencement of operations (expected in September 2024), the Noida International Airport at Jewar is expected to serve five million passengers annually.[5] The number of annual passengers is expected to rise to sixteen million by 2029–2030 and to 98 million by 2049–2050. The rise in the number of passengers at the Noida International Airport, Jewar, will lead to a direct increase in traffic on the Yamuna Expressway, causing a cascading and corresponding increase in toll revenues.

Very few insolvency cases under the IBC can boast of this kind of outcome where all stakeholders have received substantial returns.

Toll Expressway Operations

At the commencement of insolvency, construction activity for real estate projects had come to a grinding halt. Toll operations were also suffering because of cash constraints and a lack of focus in management. Insolvency of JIL was a blessing in disguise as moratorium under S. 14 of the IBC helped the IRP to focus on improving operational efficiency for the overall benefit of all stakeholders. Projects halted for lack of funds were restarted with a view to improving efficiency, safety, and sustainability. Specific interventions were made by the IRP and his team with the dual objective of enhancing revenue from toll and non-toll activities and optimizing cost.

Toll expressway operations directly and indirectly employ 1,600 staff and workers. The compensation and benefits to the employees and workers were enhanced during the insolvency

5 Techno-economic Feasibility Study for the Development of Greenfield Airport at Jewar, Uttar Pradesh, by PricewaterhouseCoopers Private Limited & Meinhardt for Yamuna Expressway Industrial Development Authority, April 2018, available at: http://www.nialjewar.com/pdfupload/Noida%20International%20Airport_TEFR.pdf

process, to at least match with the market value and, in a few instances, offer even better than the market value. A lot of emphasis was made on non-financial parameters like training, safety, insurance protection, healthcare benefits, etc.

Real Estate Operations

During the insolvency process, the IRP especially focused on the real estate operations as it was the main bone of contention between JIL and homebuyers. Stalled construction activity was restarted in a phased and calibrated manner. The confidence of employees, homebuyers, contractors, suppliers, and labour force was at an all-time low as all stakeholders had suffered in the period leading up to the insolvency. Unique and innovative solutions were found to instil confidence in suppliers and contractors, assuring them that they will get paid, and in the CoC, assuring them that available money was being judiciously spent to improve the value of the enterprise and keep it as a going concern.

At the peak of the insolvency procedure, average labour deployment increased to 4,000–4,500 on various project sites. Besides the labour force, nearly 418 staff were working on the JIL real estate project.

The regulators, NOIDA and YEIDA, were very sceptical in the initial days as insolvency was relatively new, and to make matters worse, their experience in other real estate cases had not been good. However, as time passed and JIL's progress became evident to all, the regulators came forward to support JIL and its IRP in their endeavour to revive JIL, while safeguarding their own interest. The result was the delivery of flats to homebuyers who had invested their life's savings in the dream of owning their home and had been made to wait for more than ten years to witness the fulfilment of that dream.

This is only the tip of the iceberg; close to 20,000 units are yet to be completed. But the launch pad has been prepared, and hopefully, the momentum achieved during JIL's insolvency will continue and aid Suraksha in achieving its objectives much ahead of the forty months' timeline committed in the resolution plan.

V

An insolvency law is not a mechanism for cleaning up economic trash. It plays a far more important role. It can cause a boost in an economy, thereby fostering growth and helping to resolve or prevent financial and economic crises. Efficient and predictable insolvency framework is key to improving financial inclusion and increasing access to credit, which may lead to reduction in the cost for obtaining credit. Increased access to finance enhances enterprise growth, which in turn leads to preserving employment, growth, and the creation of new jobs.

Every year, billions of dollars in business value, jobs, and capital are lost or sidelined as a result of businesses becoming insolvent and closing their doors. Ineffective debt recovery and weak mechanisms for business exit create a higher cost of capital and heightened perception of risk among investors and financial institutions. Societal considerations also play a key role in establishing a sound insolvency system. Therefore, at a macro level, a robust insolvency law allows allocation of risk in a predictable, equitable, and transparent way, thereby bolstering confidence in the credit system; and at a micro level, it enables maximization of the value assets of the insolvent entity.

VI

The outcome of JIL's insolvency process has been immensely beneficial. It has maximized the value of JIL's assets and increased gains for its stakeholders. The gains achieved from its results go beyond the interested parties. The revival of JIL will provide impetus to the development of the western region of Uttar Pradesh while contributing significantly to the state's economy and also helping a national cause.

Infrastructure is one of the most important accelerators of trade and development in any economy. It is pivotal in propelling progress and setting the stage for possibilities of future development. A country's network of roads plays a critical role in its overall economic growth. It not only helps in improving connectivity across crucial economic zones, but also provides employment, eases access to healthcare, and enhances social inclusion, bringing economic prosperity and better conditions of living for its citizens. Infrastructure development is crucial to achieve the India 2047 vision of a forty-trillion-dollar economy and be reclassified from a developing economy to a developed one.

Uttar Pradesh has made impressive strides in infrastructure in recent years. In the year 2001, the state government decided to undertake systematic development of areas abutting Delhi. A total of 1,187 villages spread over six districts – Gautam Buddh Nagar, Bulandshahr, Aligarh, Hathras, Mathura, and Agra – were entrusted to YEIDA for their development. The vision was to establish a sustainable, efficient, well-connected, and globally recognized region while ensuring high living standards for its citizens. Noida and Greater Noida are the two main upcoming townships under YEIDA. Amongst the many projects envisioned, the Yamuna Expressway Project is extraordinary and perhaps the grandest of all in vision and scale.

The area hosts the Noida International Airport at Jewar, which is being developed as the largest airport in India. The expressway is the lifeline of F1 Track (Buddh International Circuit), a sports city, an international cricket stadium and India's largest film city in the making. With upcoming developments and monumental projects like the Aerotropolis and the Olympic City, this region is moving ahead to become a key economic and commercial hub.

Newspaper reports suggest that YEIDA is developing a semiconductor park on 700 acres of land and bringing in employment opportunities for local and international firms. YEIDA estimates that this project will create about 65,000 jobs in the process and many of these will be fed by the Yamuna Expressway Project. This cluster aims to make India independent enough to manufacture its semiconductors instead of importing them from China or Taiwan.

Western Uttar Pradesh is on a metamorphic journey in terms of development. The Yamuna Expressway Project is the soul of the Master Plan drafted by YEIDA to create the greenfield city with world-class infrastructure and facilities. Development being resumed under the Yamuna Expressway Project is bound to have a huge impact on the economic and industrial growth, not only for Uttar Pradesh but also for the adjoining states of Rajasthan, Madhya Pradesh, and Haryana in the coming years.

VII

One of the main purposes of business rescue is to revitalize a company and sustain its operations so that liquidation can be avoided and jobs safeguarded. JIL had to be rescued not only to save jobs but also for creation of new jobs. The successful outcome of JIL's insolvency is likely to have a profound impact on employment. The toll road provides employment opportunities to about 1,500 local people. And the resumption of stalled projects is expected to generate 12,000–15,000 direct and indirect jobs.

The myriad development activities envisaged under the Yamuna Expressway Project will spur immense economic growth in the region. An increase in demand for goods and services will create a high demand for retail, hospitality, and manufacturing jobs. The development of retail shops, restaurants, and petrol pumps will bring further opportunities for professionals in this sector. Such establishments will call for cashiers, cooks, servers, drivers, security, and attendants, creating more diverse job opportunities.

The expressway touches various tourist destinations such as Mathura, Vrindavan, and Agra, which attract visitors from all around the world. The region has become a hub for hotels and restaurants, creating hospitality job opportunities in these sectors.

As more local and international companies open their industries along the expressway, there will be a surge in job opportunities. Renowned companies like Vivo, LG Electronics, Patanjali, and many more are setting up their manufacturing units, creating lucrative job options for many.

JIL's insolvency has been a dynamic, often volatile, process, but its outcome has been worth all the effort and pain borne by everyone who were part of it. A single metric to measure the outcomes of the process will fail to adequately capture the substantial impact of JIL's insolvency – its noteworthy and lasting effects will manifest over time.

25

A Catalyst for Change

You don't cry over your own story; you change course.

~ Spinoza

When the RBI decided to commence the insolvency process of the Infamous Twelve, IBC was a nascent regime. It was expected to face rough currents created by implementation issues arising in these large cases. JIL's case proved extraordinary in particular. The IBC did not contain solutions to the many difficulties faced in JIL's insolvency process owing to the many unique facets of the enterprise. It is well accepted that substantive and procedural insolvency law does not exist in an institutional vacuum. Its effectiveness relies heavily on the institutions of implementation.

The journey of JIL's insolvency was characterized by numerous unprecedented twists and turns from the very first day, requiring a high level and speed of responsiveness to adapt and surmount the challenges. The government and the IBBI played an active role in promptly addressing the ambiguities in the IBC that were flagged through the duration of the process, with amendments to the law and accompanying regulations that exhibited a consistent and progressive trajectory. Initial amendments in the IBC and the

CIRP Regulations were prompted by the problems faced in JIL's insolvency as more specifically discussed in many chapters of the book. These are summarized here for your ease of reading.

II

It all started within forty-eight hours of the commencement of JIL's insolvency process. On being brought to the notice of the IBBI that no form had been prescribed in the CIRP Regulations (as applicable at that time) for homebuyers to submit their claims, the IBBI promptly amended the CIRP Regulations on 16 August 2017 and inserted R. 9A. Form F was added to provide for creditor other than operational and financial creditor to submit their claim. This speedy intervention by the IBBI helped avert a major crisis and paved the way for homebuyers to submit claims before the expiry of the last date for submission of claims as provided in the public announcement.

III

JIL's insolvency case also influenced the first amendment made in the IBC on 23 November 2017 to insert S. 29A. While JIL's case cannot stake exclusive claim to it, the developments in JIL's case in the preceding months certainly did have a role to play. The government promulgated an ordinance to insert S. 29A in the IBC to provide a criteria for disqualification in the submission of resolution plans in the insolvency process. The objective of the ineligibility criteria is to preclude persons who by their misconduct have contributed to the defaults of the corporate debtor, so that they do not regain control on the corporate debtor at the cost of the creditors during the resolution and the liquidation stage.

S. 29A disqualifies a person whose account is classified as non-performing asset, or who is in management of an account of a corporate debtor which has been classified as non-performing asset, from submitting a resolution plan if more than one year has lapsed from the date of classification. Related parties of such person are also disqualified.

In the first resolution plan[6] approved under the IBC, a related party took over the corporate debtor. The financial creditors took a haircut of about 94 per cent. On another front, during the hearings in *Chitra Sharma* case, JAL was constantly submitting proposals before the Supreme Court to allow it to complete construction. Even after the Supreme Court directed the IRP to prepare and submit an interim resolution plan for the Court's consideration, JAL continued its efforts to persuade the Court to give it a chance.

The government decided it was unacceptable that the promoters, who drove the debtor into the ground, wanted to wrest control of the company through a process under the IBC, while the only outcome of the process was a haircut for financial creditors. It was unacceptable that the IBC would reward unscrupulous persons at the expense of creditors. The IBC made course correction on 23 November 2017 and inserted S. 29A.

JIL's account had been classified as a non-performing asset by Life Insurance Corporation of India on 30 September 2015, and by some of its other lenders on 31 March 2016. As a result, JAL became ineligible to submit resolution plan for JIL.

---

6 *Edelweiss Asset Reconstruction Co. Ltd. v. Synergies Dooray Automotive Ltd. & Ors.*, Company Appeal (AT) (Insolvency) No. 169 of 2017, decided on 14 December 2018. Last seen on 13 August 2024 at: https://ibbi.gov.in/webadmin/pdf/order/2018/Dec/14th%20Dec%202018%20in%20the%20matter%20of%20Edelweiss%20Asset%20Reconstruction%20Company%20Ltd.%20Vs.%20Synergies%20Dooray%20Automotive%20Ltd.%20&%20Ors._2018-12-16%2013:08:49.pdf

This amendment in the IBC was also the springboard of many amendments that followed in quick succession over the next few years.

IV

Classification of real estate allottees as financial creditors by the second amendment in the IBC made on 6 June 2018 was a direct outcome of JIL's insolvency. During the hearings in *Chitra Sharma* case, it became apparent that the IBC could impact the rights of millions of homebuyers across the country, where the entities in which they had invested were to go into insolvency. It was clear that homebuyers deserved participation in the process. The government amended the definition of financial debt in the IBC, consequently making homebuyers financial creditors in the CoC.

Furthermore, the regulation prescribed a notional rate of interest at 8 per cent per annum for the amounts paid by homebuyers for the purpose of voting share. This was done to allow parity between homebuyers and other financial creditors who enjoyed time value of money in the form of interest.

V

The concept of the class of creditors and their representation through authorized representative was also introduced by the second amendment following the issues encountered in JIL's insolvency process. When nearly 900 fixed deposit holders, located all over the country, filed their claims as financial creditor of JIL, it created a peculiar situation. Fixed deposit holders comprised 99.8 per cent of the CoC in number but less than 2 per cent in value of debts. Inviting such a huge number of financial creditors to the meeting of the CoC posed many challenges. There was no provision in the IBC then for representation in the CoC of a class of creditors through a representative.

The IRP moved an application before the NCLT, citing practical problems in convening the CoC meeting with such a huge number of fixed deposit holders, and referring to examples of a class of creditors participating through a representative in many jurisdictions. The IRP requested the NCLT to exempt him from inviting all fixed deposit holders to the CoC meetings and requested for the appointment of an insolvency professional to represent the class of creditors. The NCLT showed tremendous pragmatism and permitted the IRP to convene the first meeting of CoC by dispensing the service of notice to fixed deposit holders and directing their representation in the CoC through two representatives.

This development in Jaypee led to the issue being discussed in the ILC meetings which recommended suitable changes in law. This resulted in the insertion of subsection 6A in S. 21 and S. 25A of the IBC for recognition of a class of creditors and their representation and vote in a meeting by an authorized representative. The IBBI amended[7] the CIRP Regulations to provide that if there are ten or more financial creditors in a class, they shall comprise a class of creditors and require appointment of an authorized representative to represent in the CoC.

---

7 The Insolvency and Bankruptcy Board of India (Insolvency Resolution Process for Corporate Persons) (Second Amendment) Regulations, 2018, No. IBBI/2018-19/GN/REG031 dated 3 July 2018; The Insolvency and Bankruptcy Board of India (Insolvency Resolution Process for Corporate Persons) (Third Amendment) Regulations, 2023, w.e.f. 18 September 2023

VI

An amendment was made in the IBC on 16 August 2019 to provide that the authorized representative shall cast his vote on behalf of all the financial creditors he represents in accordance with the decision taken by a vote of more than 50 per cent of the voting share of the financial creditors he represents. This too was to the credit of JIL's case. When a logjam in voting by homebuyers in a class of creditors stalled decision making in the CoC for a year, the government stepped in to provide a solution by making appropriate changes in law.

It recognized the critical nature of decision making within the CoC, especially when there's a lack of majority due to many homebuyers abstaining from voting. The net effect of the amendment is that the minority in the class of homebuyers is bound by the decision of majority (51 per cent), as explained by the Supreme Court in *Jaypee Kensington*. It took another amendment in the IBC for JIL's insolvency process to finally progress.

VII

The amendment made in the CIRP Regulations on 7 August 2020 to clarify simultaneous voting on more than one plan is also on account of JIL's case. It was the difficulty encountered in JIL's case and the approach followed by the IRP that found acceptance and became instrumental in the amendment to formally include simultaneous voting on two on more plans. The amended regulations provide that the CoC shall evaluate the resolution plans received as per the evaluation matrix; record its deliberations on the feasibility and viability of each resolution plan; and vote on all such resolution plans simultaneously. Later, in *Jaypee Kensington*, the Supreme Court clarified that the decision of the IRP taken was in accordance with law as clarified by the IBBI by amending the CIRP Regulations.

VIII

The position taken by IRP in the press release of 18 August 2017 that no claim of homebuyers will be rejected based on the mere technicality of having been filed in an incorrect form found acceptability with the IBBI. A few months later, the IBBI amended the CIRP Regulations to provide that claims which are not submitted within the deadline stipulated in the public announcement may be filed by the creditor within ninety days from the date of commencement of insolvency.[8]

Later, in *Rainbow Papers*, and *Prabhjit Singh Soni*, the Supreme Court held that a claim cannot be rejected merely on the technicalities that it was filed in wrong form. The NCLAT has also held in many judgments that if the unit allotted to a homebuyer reflects in the records of the corporate debtor, the delay in filing claim is of no consequence.

IX

On 17 August 2018, subsection (5) of S. 16 of the IBC was amended with effect from 6 June 2018 to provide that the term of interim insolvency professional will continue till the RP is appointed. This amendment, although not arising directly from JIL's insolvency process, provided legitimacy to Anuj Jain's appointment through the entire insolvency process of JIL.

---

8 The CIRP Regulations, R. 12(1); The IBBI (Insolvency Resolution Process for Corporate Persons) (Third Amendment) Regulations 2018, w.e.f. 3 July 2018.

X

The loss of time in JIL's insolvency due to the hitches was often to the IBC's gain generally, and of real estate cases which were to face insolvency, particularly. The clarity brought about by the changes made in law benefited the entire insolvency space. The delay in JIL's insolvency process was set off by this immense gain that will be proven in time, as more insolvency cases come about and have this hugely impactful case as a precedent to follow.

It would not be an exaggeration to state that it was JIL's insolvency case which helped shape the IBC into a 'living law'.

26

A Richer Jurisprudence

A chronicle of complications.

~ Justice Dinesh Maheshwari, *Jaypee Kensington* judgment

An economic legislation is typically a skeletal structure. It is judicial pronouncements which provide flesh and blood to it. It takes several years, at times decades, for a major economic law to settle down and for there to be complete clarity, certainty, and predictability about it for stakeholders. The Supreme Court and the NCLAT, which are entrusted with deciding questions of law arising from the IBC, have delivered numerous landmark orders to explain several conceptual problems, settle contentious issues, and resolve grey areas with alacrity.

These orders have imparted clarity to the roles of various stakeholders in the resolution process as to what is permissible and what is not, thereby streamlining the process for future cases. Despite being a relatively nascent regime, the last seven years have seen development of a strong IBC jurisprudence, delineating key legal principles which now form its backbone. However, even as some of these rulings established the key bedrock of the IBC principles, some arguably also diluted the objective of the law.

II

The insolvency process of JIL was fraught with complexities. The stakeholders had to seek intervention of the NCLT/NCLAT and the Supreme Court to answer the questions of law arising from the process. The IBC jurisprudence is now richer from many critical issues decided in JIL's case, arguably at the cost of the delay caused in the resolution. Pertinently, the seeds of many important principles, which were later amplified in other known cases, were sown in *Chitra Sharma*, as early as in August 2018.

Many questions of law were decided which now form the foundation of the IBC jurisprudence: the rights of dissenting financial creditors; the role of financial creditor; the status of the mortgagor of corporate debtor's property; the rights of minority in a class of creditors; the contract in resolution plan; the waterfall mechanism; the value of section 29A of the IBC; the treatment of minority shareholders in resolution plan; the terms of resolution plan (the IBC versus the RERA); the power of the NCLT to modify resolution plan as approved by the CoC; the tests to determine preferential transactions; the scope of exception of ordinary course of business in preferential transactions; the scope of an undervalued transaction; the protection of the insolvency professional in good faith; the treatment of income tax claim, amongst many others. While some of these have been discussed contextually in relevant places in the book, a few are summarized for readers.

Primacy of the IBC Discipline

As early as in August 2018, in *Chitra Sharma*,[1] in a judgment

---

1 *Chitra Sharma & Ors. v. Union of India and Ors,* judgment dated 9 August 2018 (2018) 18 SCC 575 by bench comprising Hon'ble Chief Justice of India Dipak Misra, Hon'ble Justice D.Y. Chandrachud and Hon'ble Justice A.M. Khanwilkar in

authored by Justice D.Y. Chandrachud, presently the Chief Justice of India, the Supreme Court observed that the discipline of the IBC has been enacted to streamline the resolution of corporate insolvencies; the mechanisms laid down in the IBC cannot be supplanted by substituting them with a mechanism under judicial directions. The Court rejected the homebuyers' request to supervise the insolvency process, maintaining that this course of action would not be consistent with the need to ensure complete justice under Article 142 of the Constitution of India, under the regime of law. The Supreme Court noted that the IBC's legislative framework is well-equipped to deal with the concerns of all stakeholders. The decision in *Chitra Sharma* was the first case that paved the way for recognition of the primacy of the IBC, the process, and the institutions under it.

First Clear Signal by the Supreme Court on the Principle of the CoC's Commercial Wisdom

JIL's was also the first case in which the Supreme Court hinted, as early as August 2018, that it would not be appropriate for the Court to assume the task of supervising the work of the CoC. It was held that the Court should not take upon itself the burden of supervising the intricacies of the resolution process outside of the IBC as it will involve the Court in an insuperable burden of evaluating intricate matters of financial expertise on which Parliament has legislated to create specific mechanisms.

A year later, the Supreme Court was to cement this principle of supremacy of the commercial wisdom of the CoC and explain it further in its decision in *K. Sashidhar*.[2] It was in *Chitra Sharma* that

W.P.(C) 744 of 2017, also available at: https://www.sci.gov.in/supremecourt/2017/25878/25878_2017_Judgement_09-Aug-2018.pdf

2 *K. Sashidhar v. Indian Overseas Bank*, (2019) 12 SCC 150.

the Supreme Court first held that the commercial wisdom of CoC is supreme, and the courts are not endowed with the jurisdiction or authority to analyse or evaluate the commercial decisions of the CoC. Subsequently, the view was reaffirmed and further explained in many decisions, including in *Maharashtra Seamless Ltd*,[3] and also in *Jaypee Kensington.*

Recognition of the Rules of Priorities in Distribution of Payment

It was again in *Chitra Sharma* that the Supreme Court first signified the importance of the priority rules in the distribution of payments under the IBC. The Supreme Court rejected the homebuyers' plea that Rs 750 crore deposited by the promoters in Court be distributed to them. The Court decided that allowing such payments would amount to a preferential payment to one class of creditors. Even when the claim of the refund seekers was to be considered with empathy, such request could not be acceded to as it would be manifestly improper and cause injustice to the secured creditors since it would amount to a preferential disbursement to a class of creditors, the Court decided. Once the Court decided to take recourse to the discipline of the IBC, it was necessary that its statutory provisions be followed to facilitate the conclusion of the resolution process, it was held.

First Case of Exercise of Plenary Powers under the Constitution of India to Extend Timelines under the IBC

JIL's was the first case under the IBC in which the Supreme Court exercised its plenary power, under Article 142 of the Constitution

---

3 *Maharashtra Seamless Limited v. Padmanabhan Venkatesh*, (2020) 11 SCC 467

of India, to extend the timelines for completion of the insolvency process. In *Chitra Sharma*, noting the time lost in litigation, from 4 September 2017 (when insolvency was stayed, but later lifted with modification) to 9 August 2018 (date of *Chitra Sharma*'s decision), the Supreme Court ordered recommencement of the insolvency process.

In order to do justice to the interests of all the concerned stakeholders and to prevent JIL from going into liquidation, the Supreme Court directed that the initial period of 180 days be revived with effect from 9 August 2018 (extendable by a further period of ninety days under the provisions of the IBC, if required), and a new CoC be constituted in accordance with the amended provisions of the IBC enforcing the statutory status of homebuyers as financial creditors. The Supreme Court also directed that the IRP would have the option of inviting fresh bids in order to provide a wider field of choice to the CoC.

Later, exercising powers under Article 142 of the Constitution of India, the time was extended again by the Supreme Court in *Jaiprakash Associates* and *Jaypee Kensington*.

Sanctity of Section 29A of the IBC

Another significant decision of the Supreme Court in JIL was to recognize the sanctity of S. 29A inserted in the IBC. It made JIL's promoter ineligible to submit resolution plan. JAL pleaded very hard to let it submit a plan as it was best suited to complete the construction. In *Chitra Sharma*, the Supreme Court rejected the plea of JAL to be allowed to submit resolution plan for JIL. The Supreme Court clarified the position of promoters becoming ineligible to participate in the insolvency process by virtue of the provisions of S. 29A.

The Court also clarified that a prospective resolution applicant should not lack the financial capacity and resources to complete unfinished projects, and if an applicant such as JAL, which was itself on the verge of bankruptcy, was allowed to participate in the process of resolution, it would leave the provisions of the IBC worthless. This view was later reaffirmed by the Supreme Court in *Jaiprakash Associates* and *Jaypee Kensington*.

Payment to Dissenting Financial Creditor

In the approval of a resolution plan by the CoC, there remains an obvious possibility of some financial creditors not voting in favour of the plan. By the very nature of the process, such creditors will not have the voting share of more than 34 per cent and can be described as dissenting financial creditors. The resolution plan is required to carry specific provisions for payment of debts of such dissenting financial creditors, especially in view of the requirements of the second part of S. 30(2)(b) of the IBC.

In the landmark *Jaypee Kensington* judgment, the Supreme Court decided the right to payment of a dissenting financial creditor. The Court held that payment to dissenting financial creditors had to be made in the form of a sum of money and not anything else. If any suggestion was made for payment of debts of dissenting creditors by way of something other than money, and that too in the form of equities in the other corporate entities to be carved out of the corporate debtor, that would not be settling the debts of creditors but would only keep them glued to the corporate debtor or its successor entities. Such a method of payment cannot be a step towards insolvency resolution.

Some members of the CoC may choose to sail with the resolution plan, but the law provides a right to the remainder (who would have not more than 34 per cent of voting share) not to take this voyage but to disembark, while seeking payment of their outstanding dues. However, even this does not guarantee them the time value for money of the entire investment in the corporate debtor; what they get is only the distribution according to the terms of S. 53 of the IBC. Of course, in the scheme of the IBC, the dissenting financial creditors get whatever is due to them in priority over their assenting counterparts. In the given scheme of the statutory provisions, there is no scope for comparing the treatment to be assigned to these two divergent sects of financial creditors.

The Supreme Court, however, hastened to add that in case a dissenting financial creditor was a secured creditor, and a valid security interest created in its favour was already existing, payment could also be satisfied by allowing it to enforce the security interest, to the extent of the value receivable, and in the order of priority available to it. A dissenting financial creditor may also choose to accept any other method of discharge of its payment obligation by the resolution applicant, but such arrangement should be permissible by law and should be made part of the resolution plan.

Right of the Minority in Class to Claim Dissent or Challenge the Resolution Plan

In *Jaypee Kensington*, the Supreme Court decided the rights of the minority members in a class of creditors. In JIL, some homebuyers sought to challenge the resolution plan approved by the CoC, even though the majority in their class had voted in favour of the plan.

The Supreme Court held that the propositions of some of the associations and individual homebuyers to claim themselves as dissenting financial creditors did not stand in conformity with the scheme of the IBC and the manner of voting on a plan of resolution by the CoC. The Court observed that the approval of a resolution plan required a vote of not less than 66 per cent of the voting share of financial creditors; and what is counted for the requisite percentage (66) was the voting share of the financial creditors and not the individual votes of financial creditors. The term 'voting share' has been precisely defined in S. 5(28) of the

IBC to mean the voting rights of a single financial creditor in the CoC, which is based on the proportion of the financial debt owed to such a financial creditor vis-à-vis the financial debt owed by the corporate debtor.

In the scheme of the IBC, the debt owed by the corporate debtor towards allottees of the real estate project is financial debt. But every individual allottee does not become an independent financial creditor of the corporate debtor; if the number of allottees are ten or more they are considered a 'class of creditors' under the IBC. The allottees, like the homebuyers of JIL, do carry the status of financial creditors but they fall in a class collectively; and the voting share of that class is in terms of the financial debt owed to that class as a whole. Even if they are not a homogeneous group, they can vote only to approve the resolution plan or to disapprove the same. Divergence of views may exist within the class but when voting in the CoC, their vote is that of a class.

The Supreme Court held that once a decision is taken, either to reject or to approve a particular plan, by a vote of more than 50 per cent of the voting share of the financial creditors within a class, the minority of those who voted, as also all others within that class, were bound by that decision. There is absolutely no scope for any one person to stand within that class to suggest any dissent as regards the vote over the resolution plan. It is obvious that if this finality and binding force is not provided to the vote cast by the authorized representative in accordance with the majority decision of the class, a resolution plan involving a large number of parties (like an excessively large number of homebuyers herein) may never fructify and the only way out would be liquidation, which is not the prime target of the IBC.

In the larger interest and for common good, the democratic principles of the determinative role of majority opinion have been duly incorporated in the scheme of the IBC, particularly relating to voting on the resolution plan and binding nature of the vote of authorized representative on the entire class of the financial creditors he/she represents. Once the authorized representative has been handed down a particular decision by the requisite majority of voting shares, he shall vote accordingly, and his vote shall bind all the homebuyers of the class he represents. By this provision, majority in a class may 'cram down' on minority within the class.

The Supreme Court was impelled to observe that consideration and voting of the resolution plan was not a process or event where any objection or grievance could be raised even by a person who did not stand in the capacity of a financial creditor. The redressal of his issue, in accordance with law, could happen elsewhere but not in the process of the approval of resolution plan under the IBC. The suggestion by some homebuyers to keep any housing project which is already complete, or nearing completion, out of the purview of the resolution plan was rejected. When approval of the resolution plan is put to vote by the CoC, and its composition is specified by the IBC, there is no such concept of keeping a particular homebuyer out of the CoC, even if the relationship of creditor and debtor subsists between him and the corporate debtor.

The Supreme Court held that after approval of the resolution plan by the CoC, where homebuyers as a class assented to the plan, any individual homebuyer or association in their individual capacity could not maintain any challenge to the resolution plan nor could be treated as carrying a legal grievance.

Modification of Contractual Agreements by Resolution Plan

In *Jaypee Kensington*, the Supreme Court held that the concession agreement executed between YEIDA and JIL was not a statutory contract, but it was a contract by a statutory authority. Noting R. 37 of the CIRP Regulations, the Court held that the terms of agreement could be modified through the resolution plan approved under the IBC, but if the changes proposed had the effect of tinkering with the basic structure of the agreement, approval of statutory authority would be required. Any substantive changes in the agreement could not be deemed to have been approved because of the NCLT's approval of the plan. Any alteration in the essentials of the agreement with a statutory authority would require the NCLT's consent. Such documentation was even otherwise required for avoiding any ambiguity about rights and obligations and also for statutory authority to properly monitor the functioning of SPVs, each of which would stand in its capacity as the concessionaire and would carry the rights and obligations under the agreement.

The rationale of this judgment is that a resolution applicant cannot change the basic structure of an agreement. It also upheld the decision of the NCLT which held that termination of agreement could be in accordance with law.

Simultaneous Voting over Two Resolution Plans by CoC

This was yet another significant decision by the Supreme Court. In JIL's case, on the IRP's insistence, the CoC decided to vote on resolution plans of both NBCC and Suraksha simultaneously. This was opposed by ICICI Bank and Axis Bank. They contended that only one plan could be put to vote. The decision of the IRP was questioned before the Supreme Court on the grounds that there was no provision in the IBC for permitting more than one resolution plan to be put to vote at a time; and under the very scheme of the IBC and its requirements of due consideration, it was necessary that only one plan was considered at one point of time.

In *Jaypee Kensington*, the Supreme Court held that there had not been any prohibition in the scheme of the IBC and the CIRP Regulations that the CoC could not simultaneously consider and vote upon more than one resolution plan at the same time; it had rightly been contended on behalf of the IRP that he was obliged to place both the plans before the CoC when they were found to be conforming with the conditions required by the IBC. The Court also held that it was for the CoC to consider the plans and to vote upon them. Of course, the CoC could have approved only one resolution plan; and that had precisely been done in the case of JIL.

There appeared no flaw or fault in the process adopted by the IRP in the case as regards voting over the resolution plans by the CoC. The Supreme Court noted that moreover, the legislature itself had made the position clear by way of a later amendment with effect from 7 August 2020, by specifically making stipulations for simultaneous voting over more than one resolution plan by the CoC, particularly with amendment of sub-regulation (3) of R. 39 of the CIRP Regulations and insertion of sub-regulations (3A) and (3B) thereto.

R. 39 of the CIRP Regulations Is Clarificatory in Nature

The Supreme Court held that the amendment made in R. 39 of the CIRP Regulations should be visualized as clarificatory in nature; and, in any case, even before amendment, there was no prohibition to putting two or more conforming resolution plans to vote simultaneously. The Court held it was unable to find any fault in simultaneous voting on two plans, and held the objection baseless.

Good Faith Protection of the Insolvency Professional

In its order passed in *Jaypee Kensington*,[4] recognizing the

4 *Anuj Jain, Interim Resolution Professional, Jaypee Infratech Limited v. Yamuna Expressway Industrial Development Authority*, Case no. W.P. (Criminal) No. 0126 of 2021, Order dated 02 March 2021. Last seen on 13 August 2024 at: https://api.sci.gov.in/supremecourt/2020/14741/14741_2020_35_20_26640_Order_02-Mar-2021.pdf

immunity enjoyed by insolvency professionals under S. 233 of IBC, the Supreme Court sent a very emphatic message in favour of protecting insolvency professionals from harassment. On being informed of the high-handedness of the Uttar Pradesh Police in arresting IRP Anuj Jain, the Supreme Court was appalled. The Court expressed anguish that the police official dealing with the case was not familiar with the provision of privilege, in terms of S. 233 of the IBC, of the IRP appointed by the Court. The Court decided to examine this aspect of the matter elaborately at the appropriate time by treating IRP Anuj Jain's application as a substantive writ petition filed under Article 32 of the Constitution of India.

The Supreme Court ordered immediate release of Anuj Jain and ordered the Investigating Officer not to take any coercive action against the IRP. The IO was called upon to explain why appropriate action should not be initiated against him for taking such drastic action against the IRP. He was directed to file a personal affidavit explaining his position within two weeks. Not only did the Court order immediate release of the IRP, it directed the registrar of Supreme Court to personally intimate the office of the concerned judge on telephone to ensure immediate release of Anuj Jain, without imposing any conditions. Later, the IO filed a report in the Supreme Court admitting his mistake and filed a closure report before the magistrate. The magistrate ordered that no criminal case was made out against the IRP and ordered closure of the case.

Role of 'Financial Creditor' Explained

In *Anuj Jain*, another important issue was decided by the Supreme Court. The issue was raised by two banks questioning the decision of the IRP to reject their claims to be recognized as financial creditors of JIL on account of the securities provided by JIL for the facilities they granted to its related party, JAL. The NCLT had upheld the IRP's decision and rejected the applications of the two banks.

The Supreme Court held that JIL had mortgaged its property for creating collateral security with the two banks for the debt of its holding company; however, that does not make JIL a borrower of the two banks. In case of default in payments by JIL, for which security interest has been created by JIL by mortgaging its property in favour of the two banks, the debt amount can be realized from the sale of the mortgaged property but not from JIL. The two banks have not disbursed the debt along with interest against the consideration for the time value of money.

The Court held that mortgage created by JIL cannot be termed as either a guarantee or an indemnity. Mortgage is neither money borrowed against payment of interest nor indemnity or a guarantee, and therefore, the same does not fall within the definition of the financial debt in the IBC. The Court further held that the role of a person having only security interest over the assets of the corporate debtor could easily be contrasted with the role of a financial creditor, because the former should have only the interest of realizing the value of its security (there being no other stakes involved in the corporate debtor's growth or equitable liquidation) while the latter would, apart from looking for safeguards of its own interests, would also simultaneously be interested in rejuvenation, revival, and growth of the corporate debtor.

Thus understood, if a person having only security interest over the assets of the corporate debtor is also included as a financial creditor and thereby allowed to have its say in the insolvency processes contemplated by the IBC, the growth and revival of the corporate debtor may suffer. Such result would defeat the very objective and purpose of the IBC, particularly of the provisions aimed at corporate insolvency resolution.

A person having only security interest over the assets of the corporate debtor (like third-party securities), even if falling within the description of secured creditor by virtue of collateral security extended by the corporate debtor, would nevertheless stand outside the sect of financial creditors. That is, to say, if a corporate debtor has given its property in mortgage to secure debts of a third party, it may lead to a mortgage debt and, therefore, may fall within the definition of 'debt' given in the IBC. However, it would remain a debt alone and cannot become a financial debt. The debts in the form of third-party security – given by the corporate debtor to secure the loans, advances, or facilities obtained by a related party from its lenders – cannot be deemed as a financial debt under the purview of the IBC.

In *Anuj Jain*, the Supreme Court explains in detail the reasons as to why a financial creditor is conferred with a major, rather pivotal, role in the processes contemplated by the IBC. It is the financial creditor who lends finance on a term loan or working capital that enables the corporate debtor to set up and/or operate its business; and it is the financial creditor who has specified repayment schedules with default consequences. The most important feature is that a financial creditor is, from the very beginning, involved in assessing the viability of the corporate debtor, who can indeed engage in restructuring of the loan as well as reorganization of the corporate debtor's business when there is financial stress. Hence, a financial creditor is not only important for no-contest clauses for repayment of dues but also has the unique role of supporting and sustaining the corporate debtor. In short, the financial creditor's stakes are entwined with the well-being of the corporate debtor.

The Court, in the judgment, also explained the meaning and scope of financial debt. It stated that for a debt to become financial debt it ought to be a disbursal against the consideration for time value of money. It may include any of the methods for raising money or incurring liability by the modes prescribed in S. 5(8) of the IBC. In other words, a transaction would fall under the ambit of financial debt only if it carries the essential elements stated in the principal clause or at least has the features which could be traced to the essential elements of the principal clause. In other words, the essential element of disbursal, and that too against the consideration for time value of money, needs to be found in the genesis of any debt before it may be treated as 'financial debt'.

This debt may be of any nature but a part of it is always required to carry, or correspond to, or at least have some traces of disbursal against consideration for the time value of money. Therefore, for a creditor to become financial creditor, there must be a financial debt which is owed to that person. He may be the principal creditor to whom the financial debt is owed, or he may be an assignee in terms of extended meaning of this definition but the requirement of the existence of a debt being owed is not forsaken. Therefore, for a person to be designated as a financial creditor of the corporate debtor, it must be shown that the corporate debtor owes a financial debt to such person.

In other words, the financial creditor, by direct involvement in the functional existence of the corporate debtor, acquires a unique position. A financial creditor, a position akin to that of a guardian, can be entrusted with the task of ensuring the sustenance and growth of the corporate debtor. In the context of insolvency resolution process, this class of stakeholders is entrusted by the legislature with the role of ensuring that the corporate debtor is rejuvenated and gets back to its wheels with reasonable capacity of being able to repay its debts and to attend to its other obligations.

Protecting the rights of all other stakeholders, including other creditors, would naturally accompany the revival of the corporate debtor. Keeping the objectives of the IBC in view, the position and role of a person having only security interest over the assets of the corporate debtor could easily be contrasted with the role of a financial creditor because the former shall have only the interest of realizing the value of its security. Thus understood, it is clear that if the former, i.e., a person having only security interest over the assets of the corporate debtor is also included as a financial creditor and thereby allowed to have its say in the processes contemplated by the IBC, the growth and revival of the corporate debtor may be the casualty. This would defeat the very objective and purpose of the IBC particularly of the provisions aimed at corporate insolvency resolution, the Supreme Court decided.

Tests for Determining a Preferential Transaction under the IBC

In its historical *Anuj Jain* judgment, the Supreme Court decided the import of S. 43 of the IBC. The Court held that a corporate debtor shall be deemed to have given a preference at a relevant time if:

(i) The transaction is of transfer of property or the interest thereof of the corporate debtor, for the benefit of a creditor or surety or guarantor for or on account of an antecedent financial debt or operational debt or other liability;
(ii) Such transfer has the effect of putting such creditor or surety or guarantor in a beneficial position compared to what it would have been in the event of distribution of assets in accordance with S. 53; and
(iii) Preference is given, either during the period of two years preceding the insolvency commencement date when the beneficiary is a related party (other than an employee), or during the period of one year preceding the insolvency commencement date when the beneficiary is an unrelated party.

By way of these statutory provisions, legal fictions are created whereby preference is deemed to have been given; and is deemed to have been given at a relevant time, if the stated requirements are satisfied.

The Court held that although the word 'deemed' is employed for different purposes in different contexts but one of its principal purposes, in essence, is to deem what may or may not be in reality, thereby requiring the subject matter to be treated as if real. Applying the principles to S. 43 of the IBC, it could reasonably be concluded that any transaction that answers the descriptions given in S. 43 is presumed to be a preferential transaction, even though it may not be so in reality. In other words, upon existence of the ingredients stated therein, the legal fiction would come into play; and such transaction entered into by a corporate debtor would be regarded as preferential transaction with the attendant consequences, irrespective of whether the transaction was in fact intended or even anticipated to be so.

The Court also held that in order to find whether a transaction, of transfer of property or an interest thereof of the corporate debtor, falls squarely within the ambit of S. 43 of the IBC, ordinarily, the following questions shall have to be examined in a given case:

(i) Whether such transfer is for the benefit of a creditor or a surety or a guarantor;
(ii) Whether such transfer is for or on account of an antecedent financial debt or operational debt or other liabilities owed by the corporate debtor;
(iii) Whether such transfer has the effect of putting such creditor or surety or guarantor in a beneficial position than it would have been in the event of distribution of assets being made in accordance with Section 53 of the IBC;
(iv) If such transfer had been for the benefit of a related party (other than an employee), whether the same was made during the period of two years preceding the insolvency commencement date; and if such transfer had been for the

benefit of an unrelated party, whether the same was made during the period of one year preceding the insolvency commencement date; and

(v) Whether such transfer is not an excluded transaction in terms of subsection (3) of Section 43.

Scope of ordinary course of business as exception to preferential transaction

The Supreme Court explained what constitutes ordinary course of business as an exception to preferential transaction in *Anuj Jain*. The Court noted that even when the indicting parts of S. 43 as occurring in its subsections (4) and (2) are satisfied and the corporate debtor is deemed to have given preference at a relevant time to a related party or unrelated party, as the case may be, such deemed preference may yet not be an offending preference, if it falls into any or both of the exclusions provided under S. 43, namely, having been entered into during the ordinary course of business of the corporate debtor or transferee or resulting in acquisition of new value for the corporate debtor.

The Court held that in the scheme of avoidance provisions in the IBC, the underlying concept is to disregard and practically annul such transactions which appear, in the course of insolvency resolution or liquidation, to be preferential so as to minimize the potential loss to other stakeholders in the affairs of the corporate debtor, particularly its creditors. What is to be examined for the purpose of S. 43 is the conduct and affairs of the corporate debtor. If the beneficiary of the transaction in question is a related party of the corporate debtor, the period of enquiry is enlarged to two years whereas this period is one year in other cases.

Construction of S. 43 (preferential transactions) has to be made keeping in mind objectives of the IBC

The Supreme Court noted that a feature of vital importance is that whether a transaction that fell in exceptions had to be examined with reference to the dealing and conduct of the corporate debtor; and qua the health and prospects of the corporate debtor. Applying the well-known principles of *noscitur a sociis*, where the questionable meaning of a doubtful word could be derived and understood from its associates and context; and usefully recapping that the scheme of S. 43 of the IBC is essentially of scanning through the affairs of the corporate debtor and to discredit and disregard such transaction by the corporate debtor which tends to give unwarranted benefit to one of its creditor or surety or guarantor over others.

The Court opined that the purport of clause (a) of subsection (3) of S. 43 is also principally directed towards the corporate debtor's dealings. In other words, the whole of conspectus of subsection (3) is that only if any transfer is found to have been made by the corporate debtor, either in the ordinary course of its business or financial affairs or in the process of acquiring any enhancement in its value or worth, that might be considered as having been done without any tinge of favour to any person in preference to others and thus might stand excluded from the purview of being preferential, subject to fulfilment of other requirements of subsection (3) of S. 43.

If the transfer is examined with reference to the ordinary course of business or financial affairs of the transferee alone, it may conveniently get excluded from the rigour of subsection (2) of S. 43, even if not standing within the scope of ordinary course of business or financial affairs of the corporate debtor. Such had never been the scheme of the IBC nor the intent of S. 43 thereof. For the purpose of exception of S. 43, the intent of the legislature is required to be kept in view. If the ordinary course of business or financial affairs of the transferee would itself be decisive for exclusion, almost every transfer made to the transferees like lender-banks/financial institutions would be taken out of the net, which would practically result in frustrating the provision itself. The Court concluded that S. 43 calls for purposive interpretation so as to ensure that the provision operates in sync with the intention of the legislature and achieves the avowed objectives.

The Court held that even when furnishing a security may be one of normal business practices, it would become a part of 'ordinary course of business' of a particular corporate entity only if it falls in place as part of 'the undistinguished common flow of business done'; and is not arising out of 'any special or particular situation'. The Court said that in case of JIL, it had not an iota of doubt that the impugned transactions did not fall within the ordinary course of business of JIL. As noticed, the corporate debtor had been promoted as a special purpose vehicle by JAL for construction and operation of the Yamuna Expressway and for development of the parcels of land along with the expressway and for residential, commercial and other use.

It is difficult to even surmise that the business of JIL, of ensuring execution of the works assigned to its holding company and for execution of housing/building projects, in its ordinary course, had inflated itself to the extent of routinely mortgaging its assets and/or inventories to secure the debts of its holding company. It had also not been the ordinary course of financial affairs of JIL that it would create encumbrances over its properties to secure the debts of its holding company. In other words, the Court held it was clearly of the view that the ordinary course of business or financial affairs of JIL could not be taken to be that of providing mortgages to secure the loans and facilities obtained by its holding company; and that too at the cost of its own financial health. As noticed, JIL was already reeling under debts with its accounts with some of the lenders having been declared NPA;

and it was also under heavy pressure to honour its commitment to homebuyers. In the given circumstances, the Court concluded that the transfers in questions were not made in ordinary course of business or financial affairs of JIL.

Disclosure of preferential transaction in annual reports does not make it a valid transaction

In *Anuj Jain*, the Supreme Court held that disclosure of creation of security interest in the annual reports by the corporate debtor or that none of the creditors expressed dissent were of no effect because such disclosure or want of objection by creditors, by themselves, did not operate as estoppel against anybody nor would take the transaction out of the purview of the legal fiction predicated in S. 43, if it was otherwise of a preference at a relevant time. Similarly, the distinction between 'NPA' and 'wilful default'; the submission that NPA could be regularized; and further the submission that the mortgages were created before the corporate debtor was declared NPA, were hardly of any bearing on the question as to whether the impugned transactions had been in the ordinary course of business or financial affairs of corporate debtor.

Undervalued Transactions

The NCLT held that no economic consideration was received by JIL from JAL in return for mortgage of such valuable land. It rejected the argument of beneficiary banks that it was a case of reciprocity as JAL was supporting JIL in many ways in construction. The NCLT held that, therefore, the transactions were also undervalued under the IBC. In *Anuj Jain*, the Supreme Court concurred with the NCLT that no economic consideration makes the transactions undervalued.

Distinct Features in the Scheme of Companies Act, 2013, and the IBC in Respect of Avoidance Transactions

While deciding JIL's avoidance matter, the Supreme Court noted that there were distinctive features in the scheme of the Companies Act, 2013, and in the IBC, as regards preferences in relation to the corporate personalities. While S. 328 of the Companies Act of 2013 deals with fraudulent preference and S. 329 thereof deals with transfers not in good faith, in the IBC, separate provisions are made as regards the transactions intended at defrauding the creditors[5] as also for fraudulent trading or wrongful trading.[6]

The provisions of the IBC, however, indicate the intention of the legislature that when a transaction falls within the coordinates defined therein, the same shall be deemed to be a preference given at a relevant time and shall not be countenanced. Therefore, intent may not be of a defence or support of any preferential transaction that falls within the ambit of S. 43 of the IBC.

The NCLT Does Not Have Jurisdiction to Modify Resolution Plan Approved by CoC

In *Jaypee Kensington*, the Supreme Court held that the NCLT had no jurisdiction to enter into the commercial aspects of the resolution plan and to interfere with the wisdom of the CoC. If the NCLT was of the view that the resolution plan did not meet with any particular requirement, it ought to send it back to the CoC to consider the proposed modifications, so as to accord an opportunity to the resolution applicant to modify the plan and to the CoC to reconsider and vote upon the same. The NCLT,

5 The IBC, S. 49

6 The IBC, S. 66

of its own, cannot make any modification in the resolution plan, particularly on any commercial aspect thereof.

The suggestions that in carrying out the requisite modifications by the NCLT, the basic structure of the resolution plan is not altered do not merit acceptance, particularly when the terms taken up for modification by the NCLT belong to the thick of commercial aspects of the resolution plan; and any alteration thereof goes to the very root of the financial model propounded by the plan.

Assets of Subsidiary Not Covered by Moratorium

The NBCC in its earlier plan had mentioned that lenders of JHL, a wholly owned subsidiary, could not take legal actions permitted in law to recover their dues, citing the insolvency of JIL and applicability of the moratorium under S. 14 of the IBC. The Supreme Court in *Jaypee Kensington* disagreed with the stand taken by the NBCC and allowed YES Bank to deal with the assets of the subsidiary company in whichever manner permissible by law. This clearly established the principle that assets of a subsidiary company are not covered by the moratorium. The flip side to this is that actions and decisions taken by the IRP with respect to operations in the subsidiary company may not get the protection of good faith under S. 233 of the IBC otherwise available to the IRP.

Treatment of Minority Shareholders

In *Jaypee Kensington*, the Supreme Court considered and decided the rights of minority shareholders in the IBC proceedings. The grievance of the minority shareholders was that the resolution plan did not deal with their interests, and they had not been provided with a fair exit option. It was submitted that non-promoter shareholders invested their hard-earned money in the equity of corporate debtor much before initiation of its insolvency; that they made the investment on the basis of the financial statements filed by the corporate debtor, suggesting that it had adequate and appreciating assets to take care of all the liabilities and interests of the stakeholders. Treatment of minority shareholders was unconscionable, was against the principles of proportionality, and resulted in misappropriation of funds of these shareholders; and these shareholders are being treated in a way so as to enrich the resolution applicant at the cost of stakeholders, they argued.

Although the ultimate decision of what amount to pay may rest with the CoC, the decision should be made by considering the maximum value of the assets of the corporate debtor and after adequately balancing the interests of all stakeholders including operational creditors. The minority shareholders further contended that when the intent of the IBC was to keep the corporate debtor as a going concern, the action of delisting the public shareholding of the corporate debtor totally defeated the objective. It was also submitted that the resolution plan had not been formulated in accordance with the procedure envisaged by the Securities and Exchange Board of India (Delisting of Equity Shares) Regulations, 2009 (SEBI Regulations) which require that an exit opportunity ought to be provided for delisting of shares from the stock exchange. Although minority shareholders were not part of the CoC and did not get the opportunity to attend the meetings of the CoC, they made all efforts to voice their concerns. Thus, the plan failed to maximize the value of assets of the corporate debtor and to protect the interests of all the stakeholders.

The Supreme Court noted that the resolution plan provided an exit option to the existing public shareholders at a price which was higher than the liquidation value; and they were being paid an exit price of Rs 1 crore, which was in contrast to the treatment being accorded to promoter shareholders, whose shareholding was being extinguished and cancelled in its entirety without any consideration. The Court noted that in the scheme of the

IBC, a specific and novel method of insolvency resolution was provided by way of amendment brought on 6 June 2018, when an Explanation was added to S. 30(2)(e) of the IBC providing for deemed approval of shareholders. Therefore, the submissions on behalf of the minority shareholders that their consent was not taken did not deserve consideration.

The Court also noted that in terms of the SEBI Regulations, the procedure provided therein was not applicable for any delisting pursuant to an approved resolution plan under the IBC, if: (a) the resolution plan sets out a specific delisting procedure; or (b) the resolution plan provides an exit option to existing public shareholders at a price which is the higher of the liquidation value (as applied in the order of priority of claims prescribed under S. 53 of the IBC) and the exit price being paid to the promoters. In this regard, the non-promoter shareholders (i.e., the public shareholders) shall be paid an exit price aggregating to Rs 1 crore (US$ 120,000), and pursuant to the same, their shareholding shall be extinguished. The resolution plan provided Rs 1 crore for non-promoter shareholders. The Court held that viewed from any angle, it cannot be said that the resolution plan did not adequately deal with the interests of minority shareholders.

Reasons for Default and Restoration of Value Back to the Insolvent Company

The IBC requires the RP and the CoC to analyse the causes of default and decline in the financial health of the business. In the case of JIL, the Supreme Court consciously tried to restore some value back in the corporate debtor so that it was able to revive for the benefit of 20,000 homebuyers stuck in various projects of JIL. The order of the Supreme Court under S. 43 of the IBC in *Anuj Jain* helped restore 758 acres of prime land valued at Rs 5,000–5,500 crore (US$ 600–660 million), which was otherwise mortgaged with lenders of the promoter. The order of the Supreme Court earlier in *Chitra Sharma* and later in *Jaypee Kensington* had the effect of lifting the corporate veil and ordering the promoter of JIL to deposit Rs 750 crore (US$ 90.36 million) in the Court.

Later, out of this Rs 750 crore deposited by JAL, amounts of Rs 557.77 crore (US$ 67.20 million) and Rs 106.90 crore (US$ 12.88 million) were recovered on behalf of JIL and its homebuyers. This would not have been possible in the normal course of business due to JAL's own precarious financial position. Indirectly, during the entire duration of seven years, the courts and tribunals were mindful of the scale and size of the default and left no stone unturned in ensuring that all decisions were made keeping in mind the best interest of stakeholders. Some such examples include multiple rounds of extension much beyond the stipulated 270 days, decisions in tax department's appeals, YEIDA appeals, *Chitra Sharma*, *Jaypee Kensington*, etc.

The IBC Versus the RERA: Terms of Resolution Plan to Prevail over RERA

The Supreme Court held that if the terms of resolution plan approved by the NCLT are inconsistent with the requirement of the RERA, the terms of resolution plan would prevail. This is because the Supreme Court has held in *Pioneer Urban* that both the RERA and the IBC must be held to coexist but in the event of conflict, the RERA must give way to the IBC.

Registration of Units Allotted to Homebuyers to Continue During the Insolvency Process

Before JIL, it was understood that barring a few exceptions, the IRP and the CoC were not permitted to sell or alienate assets, title in properties and real estate of insolvent company during the insolvency process. In JIL, the IRP was faced with a unique challenge as the business of JIL required construction, registration and delivery of units to allottees. The IRP, in the initial days of insolvency, on the advice of the author, did not suspend registration of units and also issued multiple clarifications and FAQs on the same. Much later, the IRP's stand was reaffirmed by the IBBI and specific clarification was issued confirming the same.

External Development Charge Is Not a Secured Debt

Another important question of law decided by the NCLAT is that claim towards external development charges is not a secured claim within the meaning of the UP Act and does not need to be dealt with in the resolution plan as a secured claim. The NCLAT held that external development charges are neither defined in concession agreement nor in the UP Act. Interpreting the provisions of S. 13 of the UP Act, it held that external development charges are not any consideration of money or instalment or any amount due on account of transfer of any site or building. The payment of external development charges is not covered by any charges towards transfer of land in question. The external development charges are also not payment of any rent due to YEIDA in respect of any lease. There can be no doubt that external development charges are also not a tax or a fee under the UP Act. The expression fee or tax levied under the UP Act must be given meaning. Because for non-payment of any fee or tax levied under the UP Act, imposition of penalty is contemplated. S. 13 of the Act contemplates imposition of penalty to the extent of sum not exceeding the amount that is to be recovered from the transferee or occupier.

This section being a penal provision must be strictly construed. Thus, penalty can be imposed only for any fee or tax levied under the UP Act.

A Claim Has to Be Dealt within the Discipline of the IBC

Another question of law decided by the NCLAT is that distribution of payment as per the IBC does not constitute tinkering with substantive construct of a contract. Such tinkering of commercial terms is permitted by R. 37 of the CIRP Regulations. No creditor can state that its approval is required for such payment under a contract. The claims are to be settled as per the IBC. Alterations of the material terms of the agreement cannot be made without the consent of the YEIDA and such relief could not be given to the resolution applicant.

Insofar as amount to be paid against the claim of creditors, no consent of creditors is required. What is required by creditor is filing of its claim and consideration of his claim in resolution plan. No clause of concession agreement is being tinkered with by the resolution applicant, so as to require consent of YEIDA. The resolution plan deals with the claim of creditors as per the CIRP Regulations. For treatment of claim of YEIDA in insolvency process of JIL and for payment to YEIDA in the resolution plan, consent of YEIDA was not required. Nor was YEIDA's consent required for transfer of leasehold rights of JIL to Suraksha or assenting financial creditors in the resolution plan.

The NCLAT held that the issue of additional compensation payable to the farmers against the acquisition of land had been decided by the Supreme Court in *Shakuntala Education Trust*. Applying the rationale of *Prabhjit Singh Soni*, it is secured debt. The NCLAT did not agree that payment of additional farmers' compensation is a right guaranteed under Article 300A of the

Constitution of India and the said right cannot be taken away by any means. The NCLAT did not agree that payment of just and fair compensation is a constitutional requirement and cannot be extinguished by way of a resolution plan.

At the time the author finished writing this book, YEIDA had filed an appeal against the NCLAT order of 24 May 2024. The Supreme Court may be called upon to interpret the provisions of the UP Act.

Treatment of Income Tax Debt which Provides for Demand to be Raised Annually in Future

At the time of writing of the book, homebuyers eagerly await the Supreme Court decision on appeals of the IMC and those of Suraksha.

27

A Long Walk Home

The phoenix must burn to emerge.

~ Janet Fitch

A distressed asset has a life cycle. Its value gradually declines with time if the distress is not addressed in a timely manner. More the delay, more the erosion in value and less the returns for stakeholders. The IBC provides that insolvency process should be completed within a period of 180 days, with provision for a one-time extension up to ninety days. Another extension of up to sixty days after 270 days is possible only in exceptional circumstances. Time taken in legal proceedings, if any, has to be excluded from the total period of 330 days. A majority of cases under the IBC have breached this deadline set for completion. This delay in completion of insolvency proceedings under the IBC has been a cause for concern.

In the case of JIL, it took 2,037 days from 9 August 2017 (date on which the NCLT passed order of commencement of insolvency) to 7 March 2023 (the date on which the NCLT approved Suraksha's resolution plan) for the completion of the insolvency process. It took another 399 days thereafter for the last of the many appeals filed before the NCLAT to get decided but the time spent in the NCLAT was mainly on account of repeated deferment of hearings sought by YEIDA and Suraksha to enable YEIDA/state government to consider Suraksha's proposal for settlement.

During this period, the matter went to the Supreme Court four times, every time culminating in formidable outcomes as decisions in *Chitra Sharma*; *Jaiprakash Associates*; *Anuj Jain* judgment; and *Jaypee Kensington*. A bunch of appeals were pending before the Supreme Court at the time this book was being written. In addition, the apex court's intervention was sought for extension in timelines fixed by it, and once for release of the IRP, Anuj Jain, after his arrest by the Uttar Pradesh Police. The resolution plan was approved twice by the NCLT: the first time on 3 March 2020, when NBCC's plan was approved which was eventually relegated by the Supreme Court back to CoC; and the second time on 7 March 2023 when Suraksha's plan was approved.

II

Although many factors played a part in this inordinate delay, the duration the insolvency process lasted can be attributed to the following main reasons.

The first and foremost reason was the gaps that became evident in the IBC in its implementation. At the time JIL was sent into insolvency, the IBC was a brand-new law. It introduced many new concepts and principles alien to the Indian market on which neither best practices nor recorded precedents existed. It made a paradigm shift from a debtor-in-possession regime to a creditor-in-control system. Its implementation had yet to fully take off and its effectiveness yet to be tested. It is increasingly being recognized by scholars that in law-making, a gap opens up between law as it is in the books and law in action. History has shown that the law rarely contains all the solutions. Legislative weaknesses get exposed when a law gets implemented and these can only be addressed as we progress. As such, a law is inherently incomplete and its effectiveness relies heavily on the institutions of implementation.

It can be safely said that with many new concepts at play, the IBC was expected to experience rough currents created by implementation issues. What remained to be seen was how the implementation challenges were addressed. India cannot boast of a great track record on implementation of laws. Many international studies have pointed out poor execution of good laws. But in the implementation of the IBC, the government defied its past track record. It did everything to make the IBC robust and its institutions effective. The government stepped in with speed to make multiple legislative interventions, many of them to plug the gaps that surfaced during JIL's complex insolvency process. The IBBI also stepped up to make changes in the CIRP Regulations to address the grey areas.

The changes made in the legislation and regulations, and the reasons that prodded them are discussed in some detail in the book; they are summarized in Chapter 25. Taking note of the various amendments brought about to the IBC and the CIRP Regulations, and the overall circumstances of the case, the Supreme Court observed in *Jaiprakash Associates* that the delay in the completion of JIL's insolvency process was attributable to the mechanisms of the law itself.

The second cause for the delay was the contentious litigation which started in the first few weeks after the commencement of insolvency in August 2017.

The time taken to bring JIL's insolvency process has been disappointing for many, particularly homebuyers. But no one can be blamed for this delay, neither the parties responsible for the cause of litigation nor those who litigated. The insolvency case of JIL was fraught with complexities, and the stakes were high. The law was new, and every individual involved in the case was allowed the right to seek redressal of their grievances in court.

The IBC itself provides three layers of remedies to aggrieved persons: one, approach the NCLT to decide on the issues it feels aggrieved by; two, the person aggrieved from the NCLT order may file a statutory appeal before the NCLAT within thirty days (extendable by fifteen days); and three, assail the NCLAT order before the Supreme Court if it raises a question of law within forty-five days (extendable by fifteen days).

In a society based on rule of law, the right to approach a court is fundamental to a citizen's liberty. In JIL's case, litigation was mostly to seek clarity on the provisions of the IBC, which was provided many times by courts, and sometimes by legislative intervention. No single party could be blamed for the delays that occurred in the process. All were fighting for their legitimate rights. Perhaps some litigation by promoters could be attributed to a zealous person trying to minimize the damage to its own enterprise, and some litigations could be a gamble, or others frivolous, but the decision on these petitions could only be made by the court after considering the petition filed before it. And there were many questions of law that could only be adjudicated by the Supreme Court to put them to rest.

The third reason was a combination of many factors. There were issues not directly related to the resolution of insolvency but their solution was necessary for a meaningful closure of the process. It was critical to effectively close the dispute over payment of additional farmers' compensation. Farmers were not going to allow access to their land for development unless payment was made to them. This would have obstructed the progress of the Yamuna Expressway Project despite closure of JIL's insolvency process. Similarly, it was important to recover from JAL the construction advances and interest-free maintenance deposits given to it. It would have been nearly impossible to recover this money from JAL were it to go into insolvency as the money would have to be paid to JIL in accordance with the priorities under the IBC. As Suraksha would invariably terminate construction contracts with JAL, interest-free maintenance deposit would have to be provided to the new agency appointed for maintenance of projects. If this money would not have been recovered from JAL, homebuyers would have had to give out this amount.

The outbreak of COVID-19 also played a major part in the delays as court hearings were suspended, movements of citizens restricted, and uncertainty loomed large. Construction work was also stopped due to the lockdown and its resumption delayed after lifting of restrictions due to migrant workers taking time to return from their native villages.

There was yet another reason – the transition from a debtor-in-possession system to a creditor-in-control regime. The behaviour of the participants in insolvency proceedings significantly influences the efficiency of the insolvency law. The changes in law do not necessarily lead to a corresponding change in the country's underlying cultural values and political processes. The values and processes may be too firmly embedded. A sophisticated administration procedure requires mature understanding of the rationale behind it.

Indian promoters often value business as an effort of the blood and sweat of their forefathers. They associate family and community prestige with the business. Families are concerned about their personal wealth creation and preservation, the brand of their family names, family reputation and goodwill. Stepping aside for company's shareholders is easy in countries like the UK, where owners perceive themselves as risk-taking investors unlike Indian promoters who have strong emotional involvement in the business. The emotions are linked to the family name, legacy or inheritance. Family businesses are also career avenues for future generations. All this may make it very difficult for the promoter to accept dispossession from the management and assets when insolvency proceedings are commenced under the IBC.

With these reasons constraining the progress of JIL's insolvency process, closure in 270 or 330 days was unattainable. Yet, homebuyers kept hoping, and rightly so, that the process would end soon. They continued to build and maintain pressure on all stakeholders including the NCLT. The delays were immensely frustrating, particularly the time taken in the reconciliation of Rs 750 crore between JIL and JAL. It will, however, be immensely unfair to attribute this delay to the NCLT. Most of the times it was the lawyers who persisted on arguing endlessly.

Although the final outcome of the process has been beneficial to all stakeholders, no one, certainly not homebuyers, will be able to wholly understand or appreciate the reasons for delay in completion of JIL's insolvency. Completion of the process is only a tiny victory for them. The real closure to the case will happen for them only after their homes are delivered.

28

It Takes a Village to Raise a Child

It always seems impossible until it's done.

~ Nelson Mandela

The insolvency process of JIL is amongst the earliest cases that burgeoned under the shadow of a maturing IBC. And although unexpectedly prolonged, in the end, it was a resounding success. In fact, all things considered, the tangible and intangible gains made by the stakeholders, including homebuyers, farmers, and lenders, through the process and towards its end, far outweigh the disappointments caused from the delays and setbacks experienced on the way. The seven-year-long journey was also full of landmark achievements, which were made possible by the efforts of many champions.

Foremost of them is Anuj Jain, IRP of JIL. He withstood many pressures and pulls, from all levels and of many kinds, but stayed true to the cause of the IBC and his profession. That he continued to act as the IRP for seven years, without being confirmed as the RP, even though the IBC expects this transition to take place within thirty days of the start of the insolvency process, is a record in itself. Efforts were made to replace him, but Anuj Jain had his fate written with a special ink. The Supreme Court orders ensured that he remained the IRP for more than the six years that it took for the process to end. At some point, the CoC also accepted him as the RP in the avatar of the IRP. Anuj Jain made the most of this opportunity to perform his duties diligently and to the best of his abilities. He is undoubtedly one of the main heroes of this story. His team members who also deserve a mention include Ram Kumar, Ravi Sethia, Gaurav Khurana, Hitesh Goel, Sahil Aggarwal, Anirudh Agarwal, Tanmay Khandelwal, Ishit Batra, and many more.

Aalok Dave, Suraksha's gifted chief executive officer, is another important party of JIL's multi-starrer insolvency process. He was relentless in the pursuit of marketing his organization's plan to the lenders and homebuyers, never backing down despite the setbacks he faced, including losing to NBCC in the first round. A great negotiator, he showed the flexibility and objectivity that were much required in a case like this. Suraksha owes a lot to him. Hopefully, his superiors will make the best of Aalok's efforts and the efforts of his team members, like Devang Patel and Sagar Bansal, who worked hard alongside him. Aalok made Suraksha the dark horse it became towards the end.

Judgments are commonly identified with the courts that they come from and not necessarily by their authors. Out of propriety, I am refraining from naming the judges whose many judgments made a remarkable contribution in the shaping of the IBC's jurisprudence, and in the process allowed JIL's insolvency case to get a deserving closure. The role of the Supreme Court of India in protecting the liberty of Anuj Jain, as a citizen of the country, and recognizing the immunity enjoyed by the IRP under the IBC, is historic. For this, Tushar Mehta, the Solicitor General of India, also deserves to be thankfully acknowledged. He intervened and forthwith advised higher authorities in the state government to take steps to close the case without any delay as no case was made against Anuj Jain and the IMC.

True to his reputation, the NCLAT chairperson, Justice Ashok Bhushan, a former judge of the Supreme Court, was quick to dispose of appeals against the NCLT orders. The principal bench headed by former Chief Justice Sudhakar Ramalingam which heard the applications for approval of Suraksha's plan and reconciliation of accounts on many successive days, sometimes sitting until 7 p.m. to meet the deadline set by the Supreme Court, deserves to be applauded. Also deserving acknowledgement are members of the Insolvency Law Committee, officials of the Ministry of Corporate Affairs, and the Insolvency and Bankruptcy Board of India. They were amongst the key problem solvers. The response to the implementation of the IBC by the government and the IBBI, as explained in the book, has helped redeem the image of India being good at making laws but poor at their implementation.

JIL's CoC, with members carrying divergent interests often pulling the discussions and decisions in different directions, also demonstrated tremendous maturity in the face of all challenges.

Insolvency professionals Kuldeep Verma and Anju Agarwal, the authorized representatives appointed by the classes of homebuyers and fixed deposit holders respectively, performed their tasks diligently. With nearly 20,000 homebuyers to represent, Kuldeep Verma, an Ernst & Young product, had an arduous task to perform, and he stayed true to his duty. After the approval of Suraksha's resolution plan by the NCLT, Verma continued to represent homebuyers in the interim monitoring committee constituted to oversee the affairs of JIL till the plan was implemented by Suraksha, which only shows the confidence homebuyers repose in him.

Sanjay Bhatt, managing partner of Kesar Dass, the law firm from where I retired in 2023, played a rock-solid role as a key member of the IRP's legal team. Over time, my colleagues Abhishek Anand (now a busy independent lawyer), Niharika Sharma (a bright and budding lawyer), Ruchi Goel, Sarthak Agarwal and Nidhi Yadav contributed significantly with their assistance. Uday Khare, the partner of Cyril Amarchand Mangaldas, led the team of lawyers advising JIL's committee of creditors, and his colleague, Biswajit Dubey, stood for the lenders in courts when needed. They both made remarkable contributions, until the lenders assigned their debts to the National Asset Reconstruction Company Limited. The differences in approach or understanding of the IBC, many of them deep-rooted, were handled as gracefully and politely as possible, not once allowing them to come in the way of the common goals that both the IRP and the CoC were pursuing. Misha, the partner with Shardul Amarchand Mangaldas, who contested us in courts, was ever dignified in her opposition.

Most of all, it is the homebuyers who are real heroes of *The Jaypee Infra Insolvency Saga*. They demonstrated incredible resilience and perseverance. But for their determination, stubbornness, and devotion, it would not have been possible to achieve the outcomes which we eventually did. The insolvency process of JIL has been full of stress for homebuyers whose hard-earned money was put into the projects. They displayed immense organization and put up a brave flight. I truly hope and pray they reap the benefits of the resolution plan's implementation, and Suraksha keeps its promise to deliver homes to thousands of homebuyers. Completion of the insolvency process is only a tiny victory for them. The real closure will happen for them only after their homes are delivered.

This book is a documentation of the most extraordinary efforts of a community of stakeholders that shaped one of the most interesting insolvency cases in India's history. Without them there would be no story, no book. It is these people who worked together as a community and scripted the success of JIL's insolvency process, delivering on the faith of the government and the RBI which had pushed JIL into insolvency in the early days of the IBC.

Author's Note

How did you go bankrupt? Two ways. Gradually, then suddenly.

~ Ernest Hemingway, *The Sun Also Rises*

Failures are not unusual in a dynamic market economy. There are a number of reasons why a company might become insolvent. It is usually when insolvency has already occurred that it becomes clearer what its causes were.

This book is not an inquiry into the causes of JIL's distress. Suffice it to state that it was JIL's own doing. It made many reckless and irresponsible decisions, particularly payments of thousands of crores to JAL as interest-free mobilization advance for construction and towards maintenance deposit even for units that had not yet been sold. Hundreds of acres of land were swapped with lenders of JAL to settle JAL's debt. JIL mortgaged hundreds of acres of land to various public and private sector banks to secure JAL's debt without any economic consideration. Many such decisions were taken at a time when JIL was itself in dire need of funds and faced severe liquidity crunch to complete the construction of projects. While it was unable to fulfil its own obligations to deliver flats to homebuyers or honour its payment obligations to banks and deposit holders, it was benefitting JAL – these are not my conclusions but matters of court record.

JIL's is arguably the most complex case to undergo corporate insolvency resolution process under the IBC. It is unlikely that any other insolvency case will have to undergo the maze of complications and uncertainties as JIL did. The insolvency process took a much longer time than one would expect. Compared with the 270 days provided in the IBC, the foremost criticism of JIL's insolvency process can be of the time taken to close the case. The more the time taken, the higher the costs incurred. Judged by the number of days taken and the financial costs, the criticism might appear fair to some. For the 20,000 homebuyers of JIL, the long turbulent process would have been exasperating and no number of arguments can justify the delay. They were surely entitled to a much quicker outcome.

A student of law and economics, however, looks at insolvency reform from a much deeper perspective. The seven years involved unstoppable litigation, with multiple rounds to the Supreme Court. When evaluated thoroughly, it can be concluded that the successful outcome of JIL's insolvency process is not only historic but also immensely beneficial to all the stakeholders, and has, in the end, emphatically offset the cost of delay and process, tangibly and intangibly. That is not to suggest that costs can be disregarded or that there were no shortcomings. But if weighed carefully, the scale would tilt in favour of the benefits. Any independent and objective assessment by an insolvency scholar would reinforce this assessment.

Success is not just measured by quantifying results or comparing performance. It is also about understanding the impact and value of your work as well as identifying areas of improvement and growth. Additionally, measuring success on these standards can be rewarding for your team and help keep them motivated. By doing so, you can ensure accountability and that your actions are aligned with your purpose and mission; you can learn of your successes and failures, how to adapt and innovate in response to changes and challenges, and how to inspire and engage your team and stakeholders.

The book undertakes an innate analysis of JIL's corporate insolvency resolution process to underscore the direct and indirect outcomes of the process, sunny or dark. Yet, it is not a scientific or a cost-versus-benefit study. It is merely a sanguine and scholarly inquiry, much like many of my other works.

In the dark clouds, there is a silver lining to be found. The pristine insolvency system offered Anuj Jain and me a tremendous opportunity to innovate, experiment, and create many best practices. Taking risks was inevitable, and we ensured we stayed on the side of caution in moderation. The process was filled with many challenges and difficulties, but there were lessons to be learnt from every trial. We stayed optimist, confident and objective, focussing only on the outcomes. We never allowed ourselves to run out of steam despite the incredibly strenuous and demanding processes. Yes, we may have dropped a catch or two but none that may have changed the result.

Never again, I think, should a case be conducted under full public scrutiny as was JIL's insolvency. JIL's case will remain unprecedented in many ways. To quote Dr M.S. Sahoo, 'This will go down as the most significant insolvency proceeding in the annals of history. Given its uniqueness and several lessons on the way, this will be the most interesting case study for insolvency courses.'

Looking back, it was satisfying to see foresights on the IBC made in my book, *Corporate Insolvency, Law and Practice* (2017), come true during the IBC's span of seven years in which JIL's process will always occupy a distinct place. I had ended my book with three comments:

> Firstly … no economic law can remain static for this long and must adapt to the changing times. The Indian insolvency law, long neglected, has taken a leap, no less than a leap of faith, to make up for the lost time. It will now have to continue to maintain pace with the developments

in the business world, in and outside India. Insolvency law and its rules and regulations will need constant evaluation. The policy-makers and the regulator will need to be on their toes, stay abreast of market developments and be willing to adopt changes, with objectivity and without stubbornness. It is crucial that the IBC and its regulations stay relevant at any given point in time in future.

A law is inherently incomplete. History has shown that reforms rarely contain all the solutions needed to resolve all the problems in a legal system. In law-making, a gap opens up between law as in the books and law in action. Insolvency law in particular is extremely fertile; it has acquired richness, depth and maturity with every transaction. No legislation is free of the reforms it will have to undergo in the future. These reforms can be ex-post in nature, i.e., the reforms that follow an incident.

The government and the IBBI addressed the legislative weaknesses as the law progressed, never hesitant of making changes even if they happened in quick succession. The IBC was amended eight times and regulations multiple times in the last seven years.

Secondly, some observations made in the book may sound as criticism. They should be taken as suggestions for improvement and not a critique of the good work that has gone into the shaping of the legislation and regulations. Having been involved in insolvency reforms for nearly two decades, the author has nothing but the best interest of the country at heart while making suggestions.

Many suggestions made in my book (2017) have found their place in the policy, legislation or regulation today and others will too as we mature as an insolvency system. The only disappointment is the obviously shrinking confidence of the government in insolvency professionals and shrinking their role in the insolvency and liquidation processes. Much of that is insolvency professionals' own doing. When the market fails to self-regulate itself, the regulator is bound to step in and tighten the noose.

> Thirdly, in the business world, rear-view mirror is always clear than the windshield. But the past should serve as a rudder to guide us, not as an anchor to drag us down. As the quote in the opening pages of the book states, 'Remembering a past experience can be a catalyst that may temporarily eclipse a normally sunny demeanour. Let us look at the new light rising in the horizon and have faith.' As Rabindranath Tagore said, 'Faith is the bird that feels the light and sings when the dawn in still dark.' Let us accept the law with its flaws and work together for its success.

This is exactly what we did.

JIL's insolvency process demonstrated the force of composure, maturity, grit, and resilience. Yet, this book is not aimed at glorifying the work of IRP Anuj Jain or that of the author or any of the other parties involved. It is only to tell, and to do so dispassionately, the tale of the most fascinating insolvency case India has ever seen.

In the success of JIL's insolvency case also lies the triumph of the IBC itself and the story of the evolution of a robust insolvency law that is of India's own making. Based on global best practices, the IBC is largely an Indian production with many indigenous features and characteristics. Although inspired from the UK's insolvency regime, it is not a transplant of its administration system. What the IBC has achieved in seven years is unprecedented; in no other jurisdiction has such crucial outcomes come from a nascent law. The IBC story is not just about a vigorous law, it is about putting together an entire ecosystem of institutions and stakeholders.

In 2016, the IBC was enacted as a proactive, incentive-compliant, market-led, and time-bound law. Many new institutions for implementation of this law were introduced, such as the NCLT, the NCLAT, and the IBBI. A full-fledged insolvency industry was brought up from scratch in a matter of no time. There is no parallel precedence in any other part of the world of a wholesome and large insolvency industry being in place and fully functional in such a short time. A slew of service providers – insolvency professionals, insolvency professionals' agencies, insolvency professional entities, valuers, and information utilities – have been introduced.

In the year 2022, the Insolvency Law Academy was established as an institute of excellence in insolvency. Its body of work includes studies, best practices documents and papers based on cutting-edge research.[1] In less than two years, Insolvency Law Academy has earned recognition as the fifth pillar of the Indian insolvency ecosystem, after the NCLT, the IBBI, the insolvency profession, and the information utilities.

The rapid development that the new insolvency regime in India has seen reminds me of the remarks of the British historian E.P. Thompson that India is not an important country, but perhaps the most important country for the future of the world. Here is a country that submits to no one's condescension. The country's insolvency system is set to complement India's surge ahead as a leader in the twenty-first century.

1 See, www.insolvencylawacademy.com

Index

Y

Acknowledgements

It may sound terribly immodest, but this book was written in thirty-one days, on my MacBook Air, using every possible minute between court hearings and meetings on weekdays, by sacrificing leisure time on weekends, and impinging on precious family time after office hours. In this one month, conversations with my wife Asha involved only nodding or shaking my head, as my eyes stayed glued to the screen and fingers typed relentlessly, and as my memory pulled out the words for JIL's insolvency memoir.

In the research for the book, I was helped by Vaidehi Gulati, senior research associate at Insolvency Law Academy, and Siya Batra, an intern.

The book has been meticulously reviewed by Anuj Jain to spot any mistakes I may have made. Yet, any mistakes in the book are mine, and only mine.

I thank my publisher, Om Books International, and Shantanu Ray Chaudhuri, its Editor-in-Chief, for his painstaking efforts in editing the book on very short notice and little time in hand given his immense commitments.

Readers, particularly, scholars of insolvency may find the writing style used in the book perplexing. It comes across as a mix of a textbook and a novel. This is intentional so as to make it readable for scholars, students, homebuyers, financial and legal experts, journalist and readers alike.